REVENANT

MELANIE TEM

A Dell Book

*For my friends
David Burgess and Roberta Robertson,
who have not been afraid
of my grief
or of my healing.*

*And for Steve,
who knows where Revenant is.*

Published by
Dell Publishing
a division of
Bantam Doubleday Dell Publishing Group, Inc.
1540 Broadway
New York, New York 10036

ISBN: 0-440-21503-X

Printed in the United States of America

Published simultaneously in Canada

September 1994

10 9 8 7 6 5 4 3 2 1

OPM

Jason Bock

WELCOME TO

ABYSS

The Abyss line of cutting-edge psychological horror is committed to publishing the best, most innovative works of dark fiction available. ABYSS is horror unlike anything you've ever read before. It's not about haunted houses or evil children or ancient Indian burial grounds. We've all read those books, and we all know their plots by heart.

ABYSS is for the seeker of truth, no matter how disturbing or twisted it may be. It's about people, and the darkness we all carry within us. ABYSS is the new horror from the dark frontier. And in that place, where we come face-to-face with terror, what we find is ourselves.

"Thank you for introducing me to the remarkable line of novels currently being issued under Dell's Abyss imprint. I have given a great many blurbs over the last twelve years or so, but this one marks two firsts: first *unsolicited* blurb (*I* called *you*) and the first time I have blurbed a whole *line* of books. In terms of quality, production, and plain old story-telling reliability (that's the bottom line, isn't it?), Dell's new line is amazingly satisfying . . . a rare and wonderful bargain for readers. I hope to be looking into the Abyss for a long time to come."

—Stephen King

PLEASE TURN THE PAGE FOR MORE EXTRAORDINARY ACCLAIM . . .

1

The name of this place is Revenant. Few will ask the name. Few will have thought of it as an actual site, with a particular geography, a sense of place, and boundaries, entrances, and exits, until they find themselves here. Find or lose themselves.

Revenant is a ghost town. No one lives here anymore but me. Many people come. Most of them stay here, but they do not live.

Revenant is laid out along four streets: Rattlesnake Avenue and Silver Alley north to south, Pine and Aspen Streets west to east. At the intersection of Rattlesnake and Pine is a good-sized rectangle of intact asphalt, a human-made amalgam no less a part of the natural environment than rock made by volcanic activity, sedimentation, or metamorphosis. For much of the length of Rattlesnake, Pine, and Aspen, and intermittently along Silver, the thoroughfares are only darker worn trails across the bright red sandstone and speckled gray granite, bare spots and patches of newer growth through fescue and bearded wheatgrass. At the edges of town, the streets have disappeared altogether, though whatever underground alterations have occurred because of them may well still exist in the substrata.

Visible or not, these four streets and their numerous diminishing arteries still carry considerable traffic. People come here, ghosts to the ghost town and their mourners, to tread the paths that others like them have trodden before, and also to forge their own. I myself traverse the streets and byways endlessly, every day and night, afternoon and morning, dawn and twilight, laying down my footprints even when they seem to be leaving no impression, taking away bits of the place on my shoes. I crisscross the meadows, scale cliffs and mountainsides, climb along and across the creek which is sometimes swollen with white water and sometimes hardly there.

Parts of twenty-eight buildings remain as of today, where once there were more than two hundred and once, of course, there were none. Tomorrow there may be twenty-three, or forty. Not precisely ruins, these are structures radically or subtly altered by the elements, by the passage of time, by the stories they shelter. Most are clustered along the axes of the four main streets, although a few straggle down along the creekbank and higher up into the hills. Mostly gray, with the occasional startling swatch of black or brown, they look as if they have been burned, water-leeched, wind-blasted, pocked by insect and grub; in fact, all of that happens to them, and more.

The General Store is nearly intact, having been restored numerous times. Naturally, though, it has changed over the years to accommodate the changing needs of its customers. It is still open for business. I trade there.

The jail hunkers on a rise overlooking the spot in the creek where a pretty little waterfall forms when there's enough rain or snow runoff. The gapping bars on its single tiny window would not prevent an escape anymore, though they have been thoroughly webbed by spiders and ivy.

Half-walls and foundations, alterations in the color and

texture and lay of the land show where houses used to be. Spans of roof and walls meeting snugly to make corners show where houses still are. A steeple, a pew, an altar mark each of the four corners of town. South, across the creek where an amusement park once welcomed droves of summer visitors from Denver, Laramie, even Chicago, there are archways, walkways, fanciful bridges become even more fanciful now that they lead to nowhere.

Mourning cycles. When it subsides and I can bear being alone, I sleep in these houses, one after another. In these churches, when the pain gathers and rises again as it always does and always will, I worship and pray, despair and give thanks. When the pain is at its peak, I fling myself off the bridges to nowhere and tear myself open for the others to come.

The Revenant Valley is high in the Colorado Rockies, near the Continental Divide. Air is thin up here. Thin to the lungs and brain, causing nausea, fainting, hallucinations. Thin to the senses, so that people see vividly, hear without the usual distortion, feel without intermediary. The alpine meadows are green brushed with white, yellow, indigo, chartreuse, or they are golden brown lightly glazed with the gray of seed pods and plumes, or they are brilliant with snow. Rough tree trunks can hurt living flesh; smooth bark peels off like souls. Mountain ranges are green-treed and red-rocked up close, vivid blue in the middle distance, lavender and misty far away.

Grief echoes against canyon walls, making the chasm seem both narrower and wider than it was before. In fact, narrowing and widening it: setting off avalanches, rending rock. A series of variations, the echo is never identical to the original sound. Grief's echoes undulate along the valley and from peak to peak above it, and they remind of its source, remind, remind, until they become echoes of themselves, become echoes.

It is often quiet here, but never still. Something is always moving, some animal or bird, some aspen leaf or spruce branch, water in the creek or particles of soil filtering downslope, the ascent and descent of those who are drawn here to me. I am constantly moving, a spiral, a gyre. I cannot stay still.

I have lived here a long time. I have no reason to believe I will not live here forever. By now I am both ghost and mourner. It is my grief which populates this town, which fills this mountain valley and will never be satisfied. My pain, forever uneased, which walks and crawls the streets, flies through the thin, clear air to nest in high places, furnishes buildings and razes them, collapses roofs and seals them over, chars the earth where a cookstove once stood and mounds it where there was an altar and furrows it to record the trace of fence or ditch or interior wall.

Grief has long ago become my life. The cycles of it are my seasons. This place is my home, and tending it my life's work.

In Revenant the difference between form and function is obscured. Everything is in the service of keeping my grief alive; I must not lose it. Walls here are broken down randomly or, randomly, still stand, predictable patterns interrupted. Windows and doors lead nowhere that matters, let in light, frame air. Sills and thresholds shift into ledges, walls into cliffs, floors into slopes, steps and sidewalks into canyons. Mountain mahogany grows like a chair in a rubbled corner. Clouds could be curtains. The shaft of an abandoned silver mine could be an artery no longer drawing anything from any heart.

Supplying my heart, though. Sustaining my pulse.

At its peaks, the power of my grief draws ghosts and

their mourners to Revenant from everywhere and by all means. The tangle of pathways is wide at the upper rim of the Revenant Valley and then spirals downward more and more tightly. Revenant goes both very high and very deep.

Sun spirals along this valley. Fog spins, pulling in sorrow from all over with a violent and ponderous force that I set and keep in motion. Rain comes in torrents or in gentle showers, each drop collecting layers as it falls through the charged atmosphere, each layered drop spinning. Snow falls hard as hail, hail soft as snowflakes spinning perpetually inward.

If my lost ones were restored to me today, I would not receive them. I would not know or claim them. Pure, without referent, it is the grieving itself which nourishes me now and tells me who I am.

Sometimes I take the form of a woman so old as to be ageless. I wander and keen. I screech at windows when the night wind blows, or when there is no wind. Eternally, stubbornly, I mourn my lost children, the parents who orphaned me, my lost lover. Then I am called simply Dona, the title without a given name.

Sometimes these mountains are my broken heart, red and gray strata visible in the lifted cliffs and known to extend under the town, under the peaks, roots down to the molten core.

Sometimes I am fog in the valley, or glaciers that move imperceptibly but make profound changes in the landscape, change what grows there and what is buried.

But even myth does not come near to telling the story of my grief. Even legend does not contain the meaning of my loss. Even metaphor, simile, symbol do not express my pain.

I gather others: The widower. The orphan. The mothers whose children were killed, the mother whose child was never born. The wife whose husband is no longer her husband; the father whose son is no longer his son; the lover whose beloved never was what he imagined her to be.

I wait for them in Revenant. In the hollows of the churches and the jail. In the streets that have held footprints and wheel ruts for centuries. In the cobwebbed corners of the dance hall and General Store.

I have no need to hear their stories. I am not interested in whom they have lost or how, only that they have. But they tell, obsessively, and those who stay in Revenant with me never believe that they have told their stories all the way through.

Call me Mother Grief. I am the wellspring and nurturer, source of the sorrow of the world.

Others come, ghosts and mourners. Human life being what it is, the supply of both is unending. Again and again I have called them to me, when the mysterious rhythm brings the anguish round again, as though my loss had happened yesterday, as though it had happened at the beginning of time. This exacerbation is the worst in years; I really cannot bear it alone. I must surround myself with others whose paltry pain has become all time and all space to them.

Again and again, when the cycle of my grief demands it, I welcome them, and I bitterly resent their intrusion. Their pain is nothing compared to mine. Their sorrow is not nearly so beautiful or profound. Their grief is not holy. No one has lost what I have lost. No one hurts like me. Nobody knows my trouble.

The nearly unbelievable centrifugal force of mourning, whirling outward, threatens to fling fragments of the mourner off the face of the earth. But I stay, because each time I come round again I draw others in to me. The nearly unimaginable centripetal force of mourning, whirling inward, threatens to crush the mourner at the core. But I withstand it, I expand in the face of it, because my grief consumes the grief of others, and I am never satisfied for long. Grief has become an end in itself, the only reason for existence that means anything and will not die, and I am intensely gratified, though not for long, each time it is renewed.

Avidly I watch them come up my valley now, a panoramic view. Like mist swirling around the peaks, gray and lavender and silver blue. Like the movements of the earth, rotation and revolution, the uplifting of more mountains around valleys that were already there.

This time promises to take me higher and lower than I have gone in a long time, wider and deeper. I can hardly wait.

Here they come.

2

The child at the next table had a blue-and-white stuffed panda bear bigger than he was. Patrick stared at it, remembering the giant blue-and-white panda he'd bought for his little sister Juliet the year she turned eight. Remembered the pleasure of choosing it just for her from among the cute stuffed pigs, cats, monkeys, and other pandas brown, gray, black, black-and-white. Remembered the look on her face when she opened the package. A few years later, she was gone.

Today was Danny's twenty-first birthday, and Hannelore was busy with last-minute preparations for a very special celebration. She'd puzzled over what gifts to buy, what kind of cake to order, whom to invite to the party. For a son on the brink of adulthood, everything had to be perfect.

"Hannelore, you're destroying yourself. Giving up your own life won't bring them back."

That was Phil. She tried to ignore him. Especially she tried to ignore her own sometime suspicion that, if she wasn't very vigilant, she could go on with her life, too. It had now been fourteen years.

The more years passed, incredibly, since the death of her children, the more deliberately and desperately she had to work to keep them from becoming part of her past instead of her present. Memories did fade, almost minute by minute, no matter what she did to keep them vivid. Past time did accumulate, although it outraged her that time should pass at all, and the more time went by the less sure she was that she was truly remembering the brush of Debbie's baby-fine hair across her cheek and the *whoo whoo chugga chugga chugga* of Danny playing train in the bathtub, or whether her bereft imagination had invented and embellished these things and then called them memories.

Again this time, she crossed Phil off the party guest list, the children's own father. She didn't even ask him to sign the card. The shoebox under her bed was full of cards for both Danny and Debbie—fourteen years' worth of birthday cards, Halloween cards, Easter cards, Valentines—with only her signature on them, but every other time she'd asked him to sign them, too, and he'd refused. In the beginning, on the primary-colored ones with teddy bears and cute ghosts and bunnies, she'd printed: I LOVE YOU! FROM MOMMY!'' As the cards became more sophisticated, staying age-appropriate—"Happy Easter to a Wonderful Son," "To a Dear Daughter on Valentine's Day"—she'd inscribed loving little messages of her own, taking care to get just the right wording. This year, Danny's card spoke of how proud she was of the man he'd become, and she had already begun looking for the perfect card for Debbie's twentieth birthday on September 7th.

Looking through the cards in that shoebox, one would think that the father of these children didn't love them anymore, didn't think about them at all. But it would be obvious to anyone how much their mother would always love them, more than life itself.

"Hannelore, this is *insane*!" her mother pronounced every chance she got. But Sophie Levinson—who, admittedly, had survived the camps—did not know what it meant to have lost *Danny* and *Debbie* specifically, in a matter of seconds on a wintry afternoon when the baby-sitter misjudged the speed of the oncoming train.

The babysitter had died, too. Her name was Cheryl Lisbaum, and she had been nineteen years old. Hannelore sometimes mourned her, too, though she hadn't known her well—hadn't known her well enough, apparently, to trust her with her children. More often, as the years passed, she was relieved that Cheryl had died, because she would have wished her dead. Once at the beginning Cheryl's mother had called her, but Hannelore had refused to come to the phone. They didn't share anything. Cheryl's mother hadn't lost Danny and Debbie.

Maybe she'd invite Cheryl's mother to the birthday party this year. Cheryl would be—she had to figure it out—thirty-three years old now. It was a magnanimous thought. But almost immediately the idea of sharing such a personal and private occasion with a stranger with whom she had nothing in common made Hannelore a little sick to her stomach, and she put it out of her mind.

So she and Debbie would be the only guests for Danny's twenty-first birthday party. An intimate celebration, if not an especially exuberant one. And Debbie would come, Hannelore knew. Debbie and Danny always came to these things. Hannelore and her dead children were very close.

Debbie was here already, in fact. Setting the pretty table in the sunroom, worrying suddenly that it was *too* pretty and not masculine enough, Hannelore caught sight of her daughter out of the corner of her eye. A bit distractedly, she called, "Hello, honey."

Hannelore stepped back, considered the table, and decided that it did look nice. Yellow tablecloth, pale yellow napkins with darker yellow geometric designs around the borders, plates and cups to match. Yellow was

Danny's favorite color; she didn't know how she knew that, but she did.

His presents were in a cheery pile at his place, a smaller stack than when he was eight, nine, ten, because presents for older kids, she'd discovered, tended to become increasingly both smaller and more expensive. This year his main present was the brand new car parked in the garage. She'd wrapped the key in a ring box and couldn't wait till he opened it. She was also a bit nervous that the car wouldn't be to Danny's taste; at twenty-one, kids were independent and unfathomable.

Suddenly she was thinking of all the things that Danny at twenty-one would not do, because he was dead, and despair threatened to burst through. But there was still so much to do to get ready for the party that she was able, without much effort, to put her mind back on that.

Debbie asked, "Anything I can do to help?" and her mother marveled proudly at what a grown-up young lady she was.

"You can sit and talk to me," said Hannelore, who hated having anyone else in her kitchen, "while I make the garlic bread." She'd fixed lasagna, because Danny had requested it. Any leftovers she and Phil could have for dinner tonight, if Phil was home for dinner. She didn't mind having the same thing twice in one day, and she'd made a big panful. Her appetite was prodigious. She never could seem to get full no matter how much she ate, and she kept gaining weight while still feeling insubstantial.

Debbie did follow her into the kitchen. Hannelore couldn't quite see her yet, beyond a certain silvery shimmer, and her daughter's kiss on her temple was so soft that it might have been—but was *not*—only a movement of the air or a strand of her own hair stirring. But Debbie's presence was always unmistakable. "Where's the birthday boy?" Hannelore asked gaily.

"Not coming," Debbie said in her ear.

Hannelore turned as quickly as her bulk would allow and frantically scanned the room for any sign of her errant son. "Not *coming*? But it's his *birthday*!"

"He wants you to come to where he is."

"I don't *know* where he is!" Hannelore was nearly wailing. "Where is he?"

"I'm supposed to take you there."

It surprised Hannelore that Debbie was willing to do anything her brother asked her to do. When they were little they'd squabbled incessantly—"Mom, he's *lookin'* at me!" "Daddy, tell her to quit breathing my air!"—and since they'd died they'd kept it up, sibling rivalry so intense it persisted beyond the grave.

If Danny got new socks, Debbie had to have new socks, too, whether she needed them or not. If Hannelore poured more Cheerios into Debbie's bowl than Danny's—or if he imagined she did—he'd dump his out on the table and refuse to eat any. They shoved each other aside, pulled hair, and punched and tripped, always on the verge of really hurting each other and not infrequently succeeding—Debbie had fallen down the side steps at least twice; Danny's fingers had been shut in both the car door and the back door of the house, once severely enough to require a trip to the emergency room.

They'd been evenly matched. Danny was older, bigger, stronger, more experienced, while Debbie was cleverer and, from an early age, much more verbal. Hannelore always knew that many of the terrible things they did and said to each other escaped her notice.

Their bickering had kept her constantly on edge. Worried that it meant they didn't feel loved enough, she'd unceasingly looked for ways to prove to them that they were. Her mother shook her head, wrung her hands, tsked. Phil said they would grow out of it. Of course, they didn't.

"But—but the party." Hannelore gestured helplessly toward the table, the food, gifts, decorations, card, cake, which now looked forlorn instead of festive.

There was a grip on her upper arm, strong and insistent young fingers pressing into the sagging flesh. "Ma, give it up. We all know this stuff's not real. Believe me, Danny doesn't give a shit anymore about lasagna. Or about new cars, either."

Hannelore sucked in her breath, offended by her daughter's coarse language and worried by the fact that Debbie knew about the car. "Debbie, did you tell him? The car was to be a surprise."

"Oh, Ma, get a life!"

Through tears Hannelore tried to stare at her daughter and couldn't quite find her. She turned back to the counter, resolutely resumed spreading garlic butter on the thick slices of crusty French bread. Her feelings were hurt. More, she was afraid.

The bread was jerked out of her hand and tossed onto the cutting board. A thin trail of melted butter crossed the clear, hard plastic. The oven was shut off; she saw the knob turn and heard the click. The stack of packages on the table was tumbled and scattered, and Hannelore watched unhappily as the yellow bow was pulled loose from the small package, the silver paper ripped off, the box opened, and the car keys taken out.

Debbie dangled the keys in the air for a minute; Hannelore could see the outline of her fingers and outstretched arm. Then the girl came across the room, seemingly without steps, and gave the keys to her. Hannelore didn't want to take them, but she did; it was gratifying that her children had grown up enough to take charge of their own lives and even of hers, that she didn't have to make every single decision for all of them anymore.

"Let's go, Ma," Debbie said.

"Your father—"

"Daddy's fine. He doesn't need to know about this. Let's go."

Debbie was already through the door. Hannelore rushed after her, terrified of losing her and of never being able to find Danny on her own. As she opened the door and turned to close it again behind her, already out of breath, she took one last look at the disheveled party arrangements and wasted a thought on what Phil would think when he came home and found them there and her gone. If he came home tonight.

It wasn't right for Hannelore to be the one driving Danny's new car for the first time. What she'd planned was to leave it in the garage for a while, and every morning after Phil left for work she'd go out there and admire it, show it off to her son, run her hand over its smooth red surfaces. Maybe she'd sit in it and play the radio, letting his spirit guide her fingers until she settled on a station he liked.

The hard thing about Danny was that he'd always pretend he liked something whether he really did or not, because he didn't want to hurt anybody's feelings. So you had to be really attuned to his secret inner self, as Hannelore was, in order to tell what he truly felt about things. After a few weeks if he hadn't claimed it—she didn't know exactly how he would do that, but she would know when he did—she'd have to admit that she'd made another mistake. Grown children turned into such strangers, no matter how close their parents tried to remain to them. Then she'd make up some excuse to Phil about why she didn't want the car after all, and since he thought she was crazy anyway he probably wouldn't even question it. He'd be vexed with her, but no more so than usual, and he'd just trade the car back in or something.

But Debbie insisted that her mother drive the car. She always had been a headstrong child, and for all of her nearly twenty years—certainly for all of the last fourteen —Hannelore had found it impossible to deny her anything. By the time she was three years old, neither of her parents had been able to do much with her—you'd tell her to do something and she'd say "no" and mean it, not just because she was exercising a toddler's newfound power but with the sophisticated determination of someone who already understood her own autonomy. You'd tell her "no" and she'd say "yes" back emphatically, and do whatever she wanted to do. You'd stand her in the corner and she wouldn't stay there. You'd swat her bottom and she'd hit you back.

"Willful," was how her grandmother Sophie had characterized her, with a dismissive wave of the hand. Danny, on the other hand, had always been "too sweet, not enough backbone, too much a schlemiel."

Hannelore's brother's boys had always been the perfect grandchildren: smart, respectful, ambitious. "You'd better do something about *that* one," Sophie had repeatedly warned her daughter, whether it was willful Debbie or no-backbone Danny she was talking about.

But when they'd died, both willfulness and sweetness had transformed into qualities of angels, and the surviving grandchildren forevermore were held to that impossible standard. It made Hannelore secretly proud to hear her brother's boys unfavorably compared to her own children, most often subtly but sometimes flat-out: "if Danny had lived he'd never have talked to his own grandmother that way." "If Debbie had lived she'd be on the honor roll *every* time."

"Ma," Debbie said, with impatience so characteristic that it made her mother's heart faint, "let's *go.*"

Hannelore took a deep breath, inserted the key in the ignition, and started her son's new car. Very cautiously, she backed it out of the garage.

From the back seat—the same spot, Hannelore imagined, where she'd been strapped in for safety at the moment the train slammed into the babysitter's car and killed them all on impact—Debbie snapped, "Get yourself together here, Ma, if you want me to take you to your precious son. We got a fucking drive ahead of us."

Hannelore flinched, both in offense at her daughter's foul language and in pain because of the memories it evoked. Just before she died, Debbie had discovered profanity, though not yet its specific purpose; that very morning, Hannelore had overheard her crooning to her stuffed animals, when she was supposed to be getting ready for school, "Fuck, shit, piss, poop, dummy." Keeping a straight face only with difficulty, Hannelore had ignored the verbiage and urged the little girl to get dressed, then hastened to make a note of the incident for Debbie's scrapbook, fondly anticipating how cute it would be when Debbie was grown up.

One of the first things she'd done after the children died was to put their scrapbooks away. Planned as a loving record of their growing-up years, the books had already been bulging with ticket stubs, school reports, birthday party invitations—only good things, only happy memories. Which, it had seemed at first, had now been cruelly cut off. Hannelore remembered weeping wildly to Phil, whose tears had been quieter, "Not only have I lost my children, I've lost my memories of my children, too, because they hurt so much!"

But when she'd realized, out of the desperate depths of her grief, that she could go on creating memories, she'd unpacked the scrapbooks and set to work again.

A trip to the Grand Canyon that Phil had said they could take that next summer was lovingly documented as though they had, with postcards and tour brochures that Hannelore sent away for. Danny's temper tantrum, because he didn't want to get off his burro at the bottom or the top of the Canyon, and Debbie's temper tantrum, because they weren't going fast enough, could have happened if they'd actually taken the trip, and once Hannelore had recorded these things in the scrapbooks it was easy for her to believe that they were true.

Danny would have played the flute; he'd already been showing some interest in music, and Hannelore loved the flute, though she'd never been very good on it herself. She typed up a program for a school concert he'd have been in in the fifth grade, with his name prominent: DANIEL P. AMBROSE, FLAUTIST. Once it was pasted into the scrapbook it became a memory as real as any other, along with the trilling, sweet notes of the flute (with only a few endearing mistakes), the look of rapture on her son's face, the applause of the crowd (some of whom obviously thought it odd for a boy to play flute, which only made Hannelore prouder of him, though she sensed Phil's uneasiness).

For Debbie's first-place awards in spelling bees and gymnastics events, her doting mother bought a spool of blue satin ribbon and gilt edging at a trophy shop. She wrote a touching little note from Debbie to Phil, dated Father's Day 1989 when Debbie would have been thirteen and, no doubt, impossible; when she was writing, "I'm sorry I gave you such a hard time, Daddy. You're the best father in the whole entire world," her hand was guided by the hand of a headstrong young girl.

Every party she'd given for them these past fourteen years, every trip to the zoo, every cute saying and precocious behavior and amusing incident she could come up with was lovingly recorded, and the scrapbooks bulged. Already she was considering what mementos to save from this day, her son's twenty-first birthday—had, in fact, bought party napkins and saved the car dealer's advertising flyer with Danny's scrapbook in mind. But this day was turning out rather differently than she'd planned.

"What's the problem *now*?" Debbie demanded.

Obediently, Hannelore pulled out of the alley and into the street. She was shaking, and her heart was pounding so hard and fast that it made her dizzy; she didn't think she could drive like this.

She took several deep breaths. Forcing oxygen past the mere surface of her lungs was unaccustomed and painful, but did seem to calm her down. She dried her eyes with the back of her wrist.

She tried to settle herself into the driver's seat. Her stomach and breasts pressed uncomfortably against the steering wheel, and she was a little nonplussed by this irrefutable evidence of how much weight she'd put on. Her feet barely reached the pedals—as though someone taller, like Danny, had driven the car before her—but there was no room for her to adjust the seat forward.

She made it to the end of the block without incident. While they waited at the stop sign, Debbie was complaining, "I don't believe the jerk actually gave me *directions*. Like he's the only one who knows anything." There was the impatient rustling of paper, as though, after all, she did have to check what her brother had written down. Hannelore smiled to herself, making sure to keep her back turned to the spot where she thought her daughter was. "We always have to do what *Danny* says. He always was your little pet, and he still is."

It wasn't the first time Debbie had said something like that, but still Hannelore was appalled. "Debbie, that's not true," she protested, as she had so many times before.

"I mean, look. You throw him this party, you buy him this fancy car, and you know he's not going to be here."

Hannelore winced. "I'm just trying everything I know to keep him alive. To keep both of you alive. I'm your mother and that's my job."

"Ma, he's *dead,* for Chrissake."

"So are you," Hannelore said as gently as she could, "and I've already started planning your party."

"So what's my present?"

"I'm not telling," Hannelore said slyly, as though she knew, which she didn't.

"Oh, fuck it," Debbie snarled, and Hannelore took one hand off the wheel to press it to her heart. "Just drive. Turn west, toward the mountains. That's left."

In the rearview mirror Hannelore caught the first real glimpse of her daughter she'd had in fourteen years. The reddish brown hair that never would stay combed, still hanging in her eyes. Hannelore's hand twitched with the urge to brush it back the way she'd always done. Debbie had hated that.

"Ma, will you watch what you're doing? You just missed the highway." Debbie's voice was thick with contempt. Hannelore was afraid, as she'd always been afraid, that she couldn't do what her children wanted her to do. But she managed to get the car turned around and headed back toward the ramp from the opposite direction, and then they were on their way toward the mountains.

"Where are we going?" she asked, not much caring,

really, as long as she was with her children, was able to
please them, was able to make them stay with her at
least for a little while.

"Oh, Danny's found this *place*," came the elaborately
cynical reply from the back seat. At six years old, Debbie
had already had that tone down pat. "He says there you'll
either see what you're doing to us and cut it out, or
you'll croak yourself."

Chilled, Hannelore took both hands off the wheel to
rub her arms, then jerked them back when the car
swerved. "What am I doing to you? I love you and your
brother more than life itself."

"I *told* him you'd never get it. You're nothing but a
bereaved mother. I bet when people ask you about yourself that's all you can think to tell them, right? 'I had two
children and they died.' "

"People don't—I never see anybody." Hannelore defended herself.

"You don't have a clue what we're talking about, do
you? Danny says it's worth a shot, it's the only chance
we've got. And we *always* do what Danny says, don't
we, Ma?"

"I—I don't—"

"Danny always makes things sound simple, and half
the time he doesn't know shit." Debbie paused, then
added grudgingly, "Half the time he does, though. Drives
me crazy."

"Debbie, please—"

"Fuck, just drive, okay?" Then Debbie wouldn't say
anything more for a long time. She was so quiet, in fact,
that Hannelore was afraid she'd left in exasperation.
When she strained to peer in a corner of the rearview
mirror, which hadn't been adjusted for someone as short
as she was, she didn't see anybody in the back seat.

She was on the westbound interstate now, though,

and that's where her children had directed her to go, so she must be doing something right. She just kept going. The high-tech automobile handled so well that she barely had to think about changing lanes for it to make its way subtly right or left. The constantly reconfiguring dashboard lights—pinpoints, starbursts, grids, bars, and rectangles of various hues—obviously were intended to convey information, but she didn't know what most of their messages meant and apparently didn't need to, because the car seemed to adjust itself.

She'd thought the sky was blue and the sunshine bright through the windows of her house in town, but the farther up into the mountains she drove the bluer the sky became, the brighter the sunshine, until she almost couldn't bear it. Where the highway had been cut down through the mountainside, the dirt was striped red. The river whose bed the highway shared sparkled bright white, bright blue and brown.

They'd left the city and entered the foothills quickly. Hannelore had forgotten how easy it was to leave one world and enter another. Ruefully, she observed to herself that she, of all people, should have known.

When the children were small the family had taken day trips almost every Sunday of good weather, which was almost every Sunday, to a pretty little mountain park whose name, if it had one, they'd never known. Even Phil had gone. Those were happy times, happy memories, which the children's deaths would have stolen from Hannelore, too, if she hadn't done something about it.

Even at two and four and six years old, Debbie had been a daredevil. Even at seven, Danny had tried, with limited success, to look after her, which took the form of bossing her around and instigated many of their fights. One Sunday she'd wandered off and been missing for more than an hour, and Danny'd been the one to find her happily drawing pictures in the mud too near the edge of the stream and just as happily watching the water fill up her drawings and wash them away. Hannelore remembered the terror of that hour, the relief so intense it made her nauseated when Danny came out of the woods yelling, "Dad! Mom! I found her!" and dragging his furious little sister behind him, who'd been shrieking, "You let me go, Danny Ambrose, or I'm telling!"

There. That turnoff was, she thought, the road to the nameless little park. Or there, another one just like it at a slightly different angle to the highway. It frightened her that she didn't know for sure: yet another piece of her life with her children lost to her. She could not lose it. So she decided: the road just ahead, going down through pine trees instead of up, going away from the roadside stream instead of parallel to it, was the one they'd taken all those long-ago Sunday afternoons, and must be where her son was waiting for her and where her daughter was taking her. Heart in her mouth, Hannelore prepared herself to slow the car and make the sharp right-hand turn.

But Debbie said nothing, and they went past the turnoff. Anxiety growing, Hannelore tried to shift position, but her thick body fit too snugly behind the wheel for her to move very much.

Somewhere up here was where Danny had gone to his first overnight camp the summer before he died. His mother had remembered again and again, to solidify the image in her memory as if in amber, and had memorized every detail of the single photograph she had, staring at it and cataloguing the cast of the light, the interplay of colors, the background and foreground and middle ground, and then looking away and closing her eyes and testing herself to see if she could remember: a small boy carrying a large sleeping bag with a pillow and a bulging duffel bag beside him, grinning at the camera, with Phil in the car behind him waiting to drive him to camp. By now, she couldn't be sure whether what she remembered so clearly was the photograph itself or the incident it had been meant to record.

Danny had been gone two nights and three days, and hadn't been in the least homesick. Hannelore did remember being a little taken aback by how easily her son went away from her.

Here was the place. She hadn't gone to take him or to pick him up because Debbie'd had the measles, but she wanted to know where the place was that her little boy had happily spent three days and two nights away from her just before he died. So she decided: here was the place. This pretty little meadow overlooking a bend in the stream. Tents were pitched there now, khaki and tan, and children were playing. Danny had played there, at that very spot. Danny had slept there. She knew he had.

"Don't slow down!" Debbie complained. "I want to get there and get this over with. I got other things to do."

Debbie started to sing then. Hannelore caught her breath and had to take a hand off the wheel to brush sudden tears out of her eyes just as the road banked in a startling hairpin turn. She remembered that song. She'd forgotten about it until this very moment, which made her feel terrible—made her feel as if the ground she walked on, the air she breathed, the road she was traveling up and deep into the mountains, were pocked under their surfaces with gaping, sucking holes. She could *not* forget anything. She had already lost too much to bear.

It was a Brownie song. Debbie had been a Brownie for only a few months and hadn't much liked it—too boring, too sedentary—but she'd learned all the songs. Hannelore reminded herself again, and was gratified by the stab of guilty pain, that she'd not remembered the

Brownie songs until this moment, when her daughter sang one of them from the back seat:

> *Make new friends*
> *But keep the old*
> *One is silver*
> *And the other gold.*

It was a round. Hannelore had sung it herself when she was a Brownie and a Girl Scout; she'd enjoyed scouting. When Debbie was little, when she was alive, she hadn't understood about rounds, so when her mother would start the second part of it it threw her off and she'd irritably object: "Mom, no! That's not right!"

In the rearview mirror Hannelore caught her almost-grown daughter's eye. Debbie grinned at her, and Hannelore was almost overcome by gratitude and joy. As Debbie started "One is silver" she took up with "Make new friends." This time it worked, and the two of them sang it over and over as they wound up the mountain road, crossing over the creek and then back over it again. It was such a companionable thing to be doing. Hannelore was so happy.

"Stop," Debbie commanded.

Hannelore stopped singing, bewildered.

"Ma, get with it, will you? I said stop!"

Awkwardly, Hannelore pulled over to the side of the highway and stopped the car. A motorcyclist roared past them but there was no other traffic. An old woman was walking by the side of the road, but she didn't look up.

"We have to walk from here," Debbie told her, and Hannelore could tell from the angle and tone of her voice that she was already out of the car. "Leave it to my brother to make things difficult."

Filled with trepidation, Hannelore managed to extricate herself from the car to stand on the graveled berm. She was already short of breath. "I don't think I can walk very far—" she started to protest, but Debbie interrupted with an impatient "Come *on*" from some distance down the steep incline that dropped off from the very edge of the highway. Terrified of falling or losing her way or collapsing from the unaccustomed exertion, Hannelore was far more terrified of being left once and for all by her children, so she did her best to follow Debbie's lead.

The guardrail seemed like an impossible obstacle, and Hannelore was close to tears. It wasn't fair, after everything she'd done for them, that her children should make her do this, too. Grunting unhappily, she put both hands on the dirty gray metal and managed to get one leg over. There she stood, panting from exertion, straddling the guardrail with her stomach pressed uncomfortably against it and her rump up in the air, hoping somebody would come along to rescue her, hoping nobody would come along to see her in such a ridiculous position.

"Honey," she pleaded, but Debbie just stood there, lithe and energetic and laughing at her.

With great effort, Hannelore heaved her left leg over the guardrail. Momentum threw her off-balance, but she caught herself on a branch of an evergreen tree that grew at the edge of the road. It swayed and she stumbled two or three steps forward, and then she was beside her daughter, triumphant in this latest sacrifice which was more proof of her maternal dedication.

They went down into a meadow shaped like a bowl—not a very pretty place, Hannelore thought, full of rough brown grass. Debbie went too fast, and Hannelore had to take quick short steps that made her ankles ache and jarred her head. Then they went up the other side of the bowl, the slope so steep that she had to grab clumps of weeds and roots to pull herself along; leaning over like that hurt both her back and her stomach. The sun was too hot. She was going to get a sunburn; she hadn't been out of the house in so long. Now she didn't really see her daughter, but there was definitely movement ahead of her and a strong sense of tugging, demanding impatience, just like Debbie. She followed it up to the top of the slope, because she was afraid she'd lose her children forever if she didn't. Right in front of her was another slope—a cliff, really—but she didn't want to think about that.

"Ma," said Danny.

There he was. It was good to see him. Backlit by the too-bright sky, he didn't have features, but of course she'd have known her own child anywhere, especially on his twenty-first birthday. She managed to find breath to say, "Happy birthday, son."

"Thank you," he answered, gracious as always.

"Okay, okay, let's cut the crap," came Debbie's sharper voice. "Come on, bro, let's *do* it."

Danny took a deep breath and said "Ma" again, as if he had something important to talk to her about, but all of a sudden Hannelore's right foot went out from under her and she was falling.

Down the side of the cliff with nothing to slow her fall, her hands clutched at rocks and branches and were cut and bruised but couldn't hold on. Her own bulk made her fall faster and harder, and her knee, shoulder, temple were scraped. Her head hit something hard, smashed through something scratchy, and then colors were swirling in and out of each other like frayed ribbons —red bleeding into rust into gold and green and blue and violet. Her head and heart twisted in despair.

Then she came to rest.

Her children were with her. Debbie stood over her,

broad-shouldered and broad-hipped like Hannelore herself, arms folded sternly. Danny crouched beside her, finer-boned and sweeter-eyed, ready to help. "Are you okay, Ma? Are you hurt?" He was wearing a nice yellow shirt.

Hannelore tried to sit up and couldn't. Danny helped her, strong young arm solid behind her back. There was a rip in the knee of her sweatpants with blood around it, and she'd lost a shoe. Her head pounded. Her body hurt.

She looked around and saw that this was not a place she'd ever been before, was not the valley of the mountain stream the highway had been following or any of the spots she'd glimpsed from along the road. She was in a valley whose walls went high and were splotched like a patchwork quilt. She saw buildings, parts of buildings, remnants of streets, sections of an old wooden sidewalk tipped every which way like scattered combs.

"Where are we?" she asked her children.

"This is Revenant," Danny said.

"It's a ghost town," Debbie said with a sharp laugh. "Get it? A *ghost* town?"

"Let's get you cleaned up and then we'll tell you all about it," Danny said gently. Debbie guffawed, and he said to her, "Help me, Deb."

The two of them, one on each side, lifted their mother to her feet. Though her body hurt and she was scared, Hannelore reveled in the undeniable and inescapable *presence* of her children and in the enormously gratifying detail of them. As hard as she'd worked at imagining them over the years, as growing children and then as teenagers and now as young adults, she'd never even thought of: the stubble on Danny's cheeks that looked like marks from a lead pencil and felt rough as an emery board against her maternal palm, or the distressing odor of cigarette smoke on Debbie's breath, or the pressure of their hands at her elbows and her son's arm partway around her waist, or the swath of their three shadows mingled across the grass. She saw that, after all, she'd failed them: she'd never been up to imagining them as real as they'd turned out to be. As they led her down into town, Hannelore was ashamed.

3

The smell of citrus through a brown paper bag. Years ago, Warren used to buy grapefruit every time he went to the store. Elinor never did like grapefruit. She'd be mad before he'd ever set the sacks down on the kitchen counter for her to unpack. "I'm the one who's shopping," he'd say, half mad himself. "I'll get what I think is best." That Warren was gone. The Warren she lived with now couldn't make a decision if his life depended on it, and she'd never let him go to a grocery store by himself. No telling what he'd bring home.

 The baby was crying.

Annie woke up.

She sat up and turned on the light. The baby was still crying.

This was some dream. Annie got herself untangled from the bedclothes and crawled to the edge of the bed. The pile of clothes on the floor could have been a bassinet. The cries seemed to be coming from inside it.

She sprawled on her stomach and hung over the side of the bed and rummaged through the pile. Damp towels, Mom's turtleneck that she'd borrowed weeks ago, school clothes waiting since last spring to be washed or ironed, Laurel's underwear that kept getting mixed up with hers even though Laurel's had Looney Tunes on them. No baby.

She wondered how many times she'd do this same

stupid thing before she finally figured out that the baby wasn't there.

But the baby was crying.

The baby was calling her.

The baby wanted her to do something.

Annie collapsed and let her arms dangle off the mattress until they prickled. The bed lamp was glarey from underneath like this, and she shut her eyes. There wasn't anything she could do for the baby now. The only two things she'd ever done for it were conceive it and keep it from being born where it wasn't wanted.

She was really tired of this. She wished she'd just accept it, one way or the other. Either she'd been right to have the abortion or she'd been wrong. Either the baby was gone—had never existed, really—or it was going to haunt her for the rest of her life. One way or the other.

Having an abortion had been the right decision. Annie believed that. She was only fifteen. She wasn't ready to be a mother. She couldn't take care of a baby; she couldn't even take care of herself. Besides, she had plans: she was going to college and major in foreign languages and be a translator for international businesses, maybe, or a diplomat. She didn't know if she'd ever get married and have children. This might have been her only chance to have a baby. But she couldn't. She had her whole life ahead of her.

The baby's life was over.

It depended on when life started. If you thought that life didn't start until somebody was actually born, then the baby's life hadn't ever started. If you thought that life started at the moment of conception, then the baby's life had lasted almost three months.

The baby would have been born right about now. A summer baby. Maybe today, at this very moment, it would have been two days old, or ten minutes, or maybe she'd be in labor right now.

But the baby wasn't any age at all. It was stupid to keep figuring out in different ways how old it was, because it wasn't any age at all. It was gone. Dead. It didn't have a name, either. If it was a boy it would have been named Sebastian, and Bianca Charice if it was a girl.

Annie got up and went down the hall to the bathroom, trying to wake up enough to stop the dreams but not enough to keep her from going back to sleep. There was a trick to it, which she hadn't mastered. Most nights, she wasn't getting much sleep.

Standing in front of the mirror, she looked herself in the eye and reminded herself sternly that there never *had* been a baby, really. All there'd been was a collection of cells and blood and stuff from her own body.

And from Sean's, but that was hard to imagine.

Before she could stop herself, she was bending closer to the mirror and wondering if the baby would have had thin eyebrows like hers. Or if Sean would have passed something along. Annie thought Sean had had really nice reddish hair, and it would have been nice if the baby had got that. But she wasn't exactly sure what color Sean's hair was, which was embarrassing but not surprising; she'd only known him a couple of weeks, seeing him every morning for maybe twenty minutes when he walked her to school, and after she'd slept with him those two times his car had mysteriously gotten fixed and he didn't walk that way to his work anymore. Funny thing.

Still staring into the mirror with her nose almost touching the glass, Annie reached awkwardly behind her and turned off the light. She stood there in the dark for a couple of minutes, except it wasn't really dark because of the hall light and the streetlight. There were still shapes in the mirror, washed-out colors and straggly movement.

She hadn't killed the baby. What she'd had was an abortion. A procedure. It had been the sensible thing to do, the best thing for the baby, too. You didn't have the right to bring a child into this world if you couldn't take care of it. If you didn't want it. She didn't see how girls could carry a baby in their bodies for nine months and give birth to it and then give it away to somebody else. She knew she could never do that. So she really hadn't had a choice.

The baby cried.

Annie wanted the baby.

She didn't search in the bathroom for it. She'd never be dumb enough or crazy enough to do that. She knew perfectly well it wasn't really there. She left the bathroom and went back down the hall toward her room.

In the hallway, the cry came again. Annie paused outside Ryan's room, thinking maybe he was talking in his sleep; he did that sometimes, and was proud of it when they teased him in the morning. He did move around and mumble something about trains, but that wasn't what she'd heard. She stopped outside Laurel's room, too, and her mom and dad's, but all of them were still asleep and quiet.

The baby *cried.* Annie covered her ears. The baby kept crying. It wanted something from her. It wanted her to follow it and find it and do something.

"I can't," she whispered. "Leave me alone." She went back to bed, put her earphones on, and fell asleep again listening to love songs that made her feel both bad and good, made her think of Sean only because love had totally nothing to do with him.

In the morning her mother, passing behind her at the

breakfast table, touched her hair and said gently, "Another rough night, honey?"

Annie didn't mind Mom saying just that much, but she *really* didn't want to talk about this. They already had talked about it and talked about it till there was nothing else to say. "Whatever," she answered. She sounded snotty, even to herself, and she didn't exactly mean to, but she did *not* want to talk about the abortion or Sean or her bad dreams or any of it.

Laurel and Ryan were fighting over the syrup, so Mom took it off the table and they both complained. Mom just ignored them. Annie didn't think that was right. When she was their age it used to make her furious, and she remembered yelling louder on purpose just to see what it would take to get Mom's attention.

When she was a mother, she would never ignore her kids.

If she was ever a mother. If she hadn't lost her chance.

"Maybe you'll be able to relax at Paula's, catch up on your sleep," Mom said carefully. Whenever she talked to Annie these days, it was careful, as if Annie might break or go crazy or something. She might, too.

"I'm not going," Annie announced, surprising herself.

Mom flipped another pancake and Annie saw her take a deep breath. She'd had that spatula with the flowered ceramic handle since Annie was Laurel's age. "The ticket is nonrefundable, Annie. And Paula's really looking forward to having you. Your flight leaves at eight o'clock tomorrow morning. I think it's too late to change your mind."

"I don't want to go." She didn't even know if that was true.

Mom wouldn't quit. "You've always been close to your sister."

"Does she know?"

Annie couldn't bring herself to say either "abortion" or "baby," and she hated herself for being such a wimp —if you could *do* it you ought to be able to *say* it. But she didn't want Ryan and Laurel to hear. You'd think they weren't paying attention or they were too little to understand something, and then they'd say something out of the blue at the dinner table or the teacher would send a note home that they'd been talking about it in class, or you'd catch them playing some dumb game. The last thing she needed was them playing "abortion."

"Does she know what happened?" was the best she could do.

"Yes," Mom told her.

Annie'd expected that. Her parents were forever saying, "We don't keep secrets in this family."

That wasn't totally true. Annie didn't think you could live in the world if you knew everything there was to know about everybody else, or if they knew everything about you. Sean had been a secret from beginning to end. The baby had been nothing but a secret. More so now than when it had been alive.

She wasn't upset that they'd told Paula, and if they hadn't she'd probably have thought they were ashamed or something. The baby was nothing to be ashamed of, but she could see how they might be ashamed of *her*.

"Colorado isn't going to be any better than Michigan," she said, scowling and trying to make it sound like Mom was the stupidest person in the world for thinking it would be. "It won't change anything."

Mom reached over her shoulder and set the blue plate with two pancakes on it in front of her. "Mountains, sunshine, maybe just the change of scenery," she said hopefully. "Paula says it's beautiful there." She rested her hand on Annie's head for a minute, and Annie thought sure they were both going to cry.

But Ryan spilled his juice. Laurel announced at the top of her lungs that she didn't *like* pancakes anymore. Dad came rushing through the kitchen, knotting his tie, grabbed the coffee Mom always had ready for him in the styrofoam travel cup, kissed them all good-bye, and left for work.

All this distracted Mom, and for the moment she didn't say anything more to Annie about Paula's. She would, though. Mom never let anything go. Annie ate both pancakes; there were strawberries in them, and for a little while she was comforted.

The day stretched long ahead of her. When she was little she used to just *die* waiting for school to be out for the summer, and then two or three weeks into vacation she'd be bored already and by the end of July, tops, she'd be secretly anxious for school to start again. Now she didn't even have that first part. She was bored from Day One. Ryan and Laurel had day camp, Mom and Dad had work, and she didn't have anything to do.

There were things she could do. She could clean her room, for instance. She could unload and load the dishwasher. She could call somebody and go to the pool when it opened. She could go to the pool herself, work on her tan, see who was there. She could study for her driving test; it was embarrassing to be almost sixteen and not even have her learner's permit yet.

But she couldn't get herself motivated to do any of that stuff. After breakfast, after everybody was out of the house, she just went back up to her room. She lay on her bed with her earphones on and tried to go back to sleep. Sometimes sleeping made the time go faster. Sometimes it didn't, if she dreamed, but she was tired all the time and it was worth a try.

The baby wouldn't let her sleep.

It kept calling her. It didn't say her name, and it didn't call her "Mama" because it had been too little when it died, but it called her. It said something that she couldn't quite catch but that she knew was its own special name for her.

She turned up the tape. She knew the baby was inside her head; she wasn't dumb or crazy, and she knew she was imagining this. The baby wasn't real. The baby had been real, inside her whole body and not just her head. The baby had been alive, and now it was dead.

Annie found her photo album. She'd started working on it right after she got pregnant, even before she went to the doctor and found out for sure, and she kept it up even after the procedure, which sometimes she thought was kind of sick. At least once a day she looked through it.

Without turning the radio off, she took off the earphones. Right now the baby wasn't calling. It scared her every time that happened; to think she might not ever hear it again, might never feel it inside her anywhere again, it might really be totally gone. She sat cross-legged on the floor and opened the album to the first page.

Baby pictures. All kinds of babies. Since she didn't know what her baby might have looked like, any of these pictures could have been her baby. Well, not *any*. Sean had been white, she thought, and so was she, so chances were the baby wouldn't have looked like this adorable little black kid or this beautiful Hispanic baby girl with all the thick black hair. But it might have looked like this one, with the red topknot, or like this one with the incredibly fat cheeks. They were all so *cute*. Annie ran her fingertips over the glossy magazine pages that were curling around the edges. Her eyes filled with welcome tears.

She turned pages. Here was a baby with the biggest blue eyes. Sean had had brown eyes and so did she, but she'd heard that all babies had blue eyes at first. Was that just white babies, she wondered, or did Indian and black and Asian babies have blue eyes, too? The baby in the picture had a frizz of hair almost the same color as hers —kind of a red-brown; Mom called it chestnut—and tiny little fingers, tiny toes. Annie was really crying now.

Here was one of her own baby pictures that she'd taken very carefully out of an old family album. Mom and Dad didn't know she had it. Probably they'd have said yes if she'd asked, but she didn't want to ask. She would put it back when she was done with it. She didn't know when that would be.

She stared at it through her tears, quickly wiped off wet spots where tears fell on it. She tried to imagine herself that small, tried to imagine herself dead before she even got to be born. Could almost do it.

Here was a picture of a really old lady. Annie had no idea how that got in here. The old lady had on like a hood so you couldn't see her face very well. Annie wondered what she'd been thinking when she'd cut out that picture and pasted it in there. She thought about ripping it out now, but that would leave an ugly mark on the page and a page with nothing on it, so she didn't.

Here was a picture she'd cut out of a book about where babies come from that was on the living room shelf for anybody to look at whenever they felt like it, no big deal. A two-month-old fetus. This was what her baby had actually looked like inside her just before it died.

"No longer an embryo, now a fetus," the book said. More than an inch long. Almost unconsciously, Annie measured about an inch with her fingertips. Everything present that will be in the full-term baby: a heart, beating; a human face with eyes half closed; feet that can kick; hands that can grip gently. Huge heart-shaped head with a distinct cleft down the middle, and everything soft watery pink.

Sobbing now, Annie raised her head and saw her baby.

Right there, floating in the air the way it had floated in her womb. Eyes half open so she knew it could see her. Smudges where its ears were so she knew it could hear; the first sound a fetus hears is its mother's heartbeat. Mouth O'd and calling, calling her with its special name for her. Little arms curled up against its chest; little legs curled up; little heart—Annie could plainly see and hear and feel her baby's heartbeat, which of course wasn't beating anymore.

The baby kept itself just out of her reach, like a game where she was supposed to chase it. Gently, not to scare it, Annie edged forward and held out her arms, opened her hands. She wanted to call it to come to her, but she'd never given it a name.

The baby kept backing off until it faded into the rectangle of pale sunlight from her window. The last thing Annie saw of it was its brain, under the thin pink layer of scalp stretched over the open place on the top of its skull like the paper seal across the top of a bottle of pills.

Then the baby disappeared again. It hadn't really been there in the first place. Annie knew that. But somehow she understood now—and it made her feel creepy and happy at the same time—that she hadn't really lost it yet, either, that it would keep coming back. Even if it was just in her head.

She did go to Paula's the next day. Now that she knew the baby would stay with her wherever she went, there was no reason not to go. In fact, she had the weird feeling that the baby actually wanted her to go to Colorado.

Mom and Dad and Ryan and Laurel all took her to the

airport. The twins were more interested in fighting with each other over who got to stand where to watch the planes, even though windows stretched along one whole wall and they could have both watched the planes without ever having to admit each other existed. Mom and Dad hugged her, and Dad took her face in his hands but he didn't say anything. She knew he hoped Paula would help her get over the baby. She would never get over the baby. Even if she had other kids someday, this would be her first. Not firstborn, but first loved.

All the way to Denver there was a rainbow in her window. When she was leaning back as far as the seat would go, with both the seatbelt and the earphones on, the rainbow was a clear arc with seven bands of color that she kept naming in her mind, using the trick they'd been taught in seventh grade: ROY G BIV, red orange yellow green blue indigo violet; red orange yellow green blue indigo violet; red orange yellow—

In order to really see out the window she had to lean forward awkwardly. She wondered why they would arrange the windows like that. Now they were flying right under the rainbow's arch. Annie was thrilled. It must be some sort of sign.

It wasn't until they were coming in for landing at Stapleton that she realized, with an unpleasant little shock to the pit of her stomach, that this wasn't a real rainbow that had somehow traveled across the country with them, and they weren't flying under it after all. The light was in the glass, something about how light was trapped and broken up between the two thick panes, and not in the sky. Annie felt stupid and cheated, and a lot more hopeless than if she'd never seen a fake sign of hope in the first place.

But as she waited to deplane, standing up at her seat with her neck crooked under the overhead compartment, another thought came to her. What was "real" about a rainbow anyway? Who said that light broken up into colors in an airplane window wasn't as much a sign of hope as light broken up in the sky?

So she was feeling happy and excited, as if she had a neat secret—kind of the way she'd felt the first few days she'd been pregnant—when she got off the plane and saw Paula waiting for her at the gate. Paula had already seen her and was waving and calling her name. That embarrassed Annie a little, but then they were hugging and Annie was so glad to see her sister that she didn't care.

Paula held her at arm's length and cried, "You look *great*! Your hair looks *cool* that way!" Annie knew that wasn't true. *Paula* looked great, in short white shorts and a pale blue midriff top and high laced sandals. Paula looked like a model. Annie's hair just sort of hung there, boring brown, while Paula's, which was basically the same color, bounced and shone and waved just right over her forehead. Annie had bitten her nails off to the quick, some of them below the quick so that she'd had to put Band-Aids around the fingers. Paula's nails were perfect pink ovals.

They went to the baggage claim to get her suitcases. Paula kept her arm around Annie's waist the whole time they were waiting by the carousel for the baggage to come through on the conveyor belt, and she didn't stop talking about how much fun they were going to have this summer and how gorgeous the mountains were, flatlanders just had no idea, and all the people she wanted Annie to meet—"there are some *really* cool dudes around here, must be the pure mountain air, wait'll you see."

Annie thought it didn't all quite ring true; the slang was a little off and Paula seemed overly cheerful, overly friendly. But then she hadn't seen her sister in a long time. In a way she was glad she didn't have to say much, but in another way she felt weird. *I just had an abortion,* she wanted to say out loud but would never. *I killed my baby, and now it's haunting me. What do I care about cool dudes and gorgeous mountains?* Maybe Paula was afraid of what she'd say if she ever got a word in. Annie was a little afraid of that herself.

She was waiting at the curb with her suitcases and boxes piled around her while her sister went to get the car out of the parking lot, feeling self-conscious even though nobody really looked at her, wrinkling her nose at how dry the air was and thinking how every airport looked and smelled like every other airport, when the baby came to her again. Like all the other little kids in the crowd who laughed and yelled and cried, in play or because they got hurt or because they wanted some-body's attention, the baby called to her in its own voice. When some kid yelled, "Mom!" Annie didn't turn her head because it wasn't her baby calling her because her baby was dead, hadn't ever lived, and because anyway it didn't call her Mom. It had its own special wordless name for her. She heard it calling her, clearly, over the honking of the taxis and the loudspeaker announcement, repeated over and over, about "will be ticketed and towed away."

Then she saw it, just barely out of reach. It was curled up in the fetal position on top of her garment bag. The open top of its head was to her, even though she had the definite impression that it was staring right at her with its half closed muddy blue eyes. The umbilical cord was still attached, still pinkish and full, not shriveled up.

This was getting ridiculous. She must be losing her mind. One time she'd watched a TV movie where some girl had gone crazy because she'd done something in her

past she was ashamed of—killed her mother or something; Annie couldn't remember. Annie hadn't known
she was ashamed of what'd she done. The procedure
had been too easy, in fact; she'd been prepared for lots
more pain and trauma. But she was definitely losing her
mind, seeing things that couldn't possibly be there. It
was like being high or something. Annie had been high
on weed a few times and didn't like it much. This was
worse, and better. Higher.

Annie took a step toward the baby, crouched and held
out her hands. She'd thought she could reach it easily,
but it was still just out of her reach. That's because it
wasn't really there.

Paula pulled up in a bright red pickup, and the baby
vanished. Annie straightened and shoved her hands into
the pockets of her cutoffs. Paula got out and came
around to where Annie was standing. Annie couldn't
completely stop shaking, and she winced when her sister put a hand on her shoulder. "You okay, kid?"

"Sure." Annie took a breath and steeled herself, then
grabbed the handle of the garment bag. There was nothing curled up on it, of course, and the only reason the
vinyl handle was warm was because it had been out in
the sun. An old lady was watching her from the other
side of a crowd of people waiting for taxis. Probably
thought she was nuts. "Cool truck," she said.

Paula looked at her hard for a minute, just the way
Mom did, then nodded and started loading Annie's stuff
into the bed of the truck. Annie swung the garment bag
up and over the tailgate as Paula said, "Ever since I was
your age just learning to drive I've wanted a little red
truck. Now I've got one. *Really* cool, huh?"

Annie remembered that. Paula had gone on and on
about the little red truck she wanted, till she about drove

the rest of the family crazy. Annie laughed. Paula laughed, too.

They drove on a highway away from the airport. A small town girl, Annie had imagined that a city was a city was a city, but Denver didn't look much like what she'd seen of either Detroit or Chicago. It wasn't so dark and dense. The yards and medians were more brown than green. It had this incredibly blue sky, with a faint yellow-brown fuzz along the horizon that Paula said with great disgust was pollution but Annie thought was actually kind of pretty. The mountains were *right there* ahead of them, blue and green and red. Annie hadn't expected the red. She had never seen mountains before. "Can we go to the mountains sometime?" she asked.

Her sister reached over and patted her knee. "I *live* in the mountains, kid. Wait'll you see."

"Oh," said Annie, feeling dumb. "I knew that. With Brad, right?"

"Not anymore."

"Since when?"

"Month or so ago."

"Mom didn't tell me."

"Mom and Dad don't know. They'd just worry about me living alone. They liked Brad. At the time, I was glad. Now I wish they didn't like him so much."

"So what happened?"

"Oh, the truth is, it never was all that serious. He's nice enough, and he's terrific in bed, but I'm nowhere near ready to settle down."

"Oh," Annie said, hoping she sounded as if she understood.

"So," said Paula, "tell me about this guy Sean."

For a split second, Annie didn't know who Sean was. Then, feeling ambushed, she said, "Just some guy. He was nice enough, and he was terrific in bed, but it was never serious." It sounded dumb when she said it, like a little kid trying to play grown-up, and it sounded sarcastic, which she hadn't meant at all.

Paula said, "He was older, right?"

"Thirty-four." She braced herself for Paula's reaction. Mom and Dad had freaked out more about Sean's age than anything else. But Paula just nodded and kept her eyes on the road. Annie admired how her sister drove, how she seemed to know what she was doing when she changed lanes and took corners and kept right up with a semi whose tires were almost as tall as the bed of her truck. Annie remembered, as if it had been a long time ago, how she herself couldn't *wait* to drive. Now, compared to being pregnant and having the abortion and everything, it didn't seem very important. She would turn sixteen in Colorado. Mom had said something about maybe Paula could teach her to drive. Annie didn't much care whether she did or not. But she liked watching Paula behind the wheel.

Annie ventured, "The first time I—the first time we did it was his birthday."

Paula glanced at her. "How sweet. Why am I not surprised. And he was lonely, and you were his birthday present. Right?" Annie blushed and looked down. Traffic got heavier, and for a few minutes Paula didn't say anything, which was just as well. Then, as they moved along an open stretch of highway where striped cliffs came right to the edge of the road, she asked, more gently, "Did he even know you were pregnant?"

Annie shook her head. "Mom and Dad threw such a fit about how old he was that I wasn't even seeing him anymore by the time I found out. Anyway, he wasn't from around there." The truth was, he must have left town, because she hadn't even been able to find him to tell him she couldn't see him anymore, let alone to tell him she was pregnant.

"That's what I told Mom," Paula said. "I told her he probably didn't know."

There was a silence. Annie thought they'd come through the main part of the city now, and this must be at least the beginning of the mountains. The foothills. Despite herself, there was something exciting about the unfamiliar word.

The road had gotten narrower, and it curved sharply one way and then the other. Hairpin turns, Paula called them, but since Annie had never seen a hairpin—she doubted Paula had, either—the analogy was lost on her. She was appalled that there weren't always guardrails where the cliff dropped straight off. Shelf roads, Paula called them, laughing at her nervousness, calling her a flatlander, but Annie saw how Paula kept glancing over at the edge of the pavement, which was awfully close to where the tires went.

The highway followed a streambed; the stream was on the left side of the car most of the way, sometimes smooth and sometimes with lots of rapids. On the right were sheer cliffs of red-striped and gray rock. In some places the stripes were broken and tilted where the rocks must have been lifted up and then set down again. Across the stream were tall hillsides coated with very dark green pines. Trails and roads were like parts in a head of hair, and sometimes there were houses impossibly high up. The strip of brilliant blue sky overhead got narrower and narrower as the road cut deeper through the mountainside. Annie's ears were plugged.

All of a sudden Paula pulled off the road. It reminded Annie of one of the few times she'd actually gone out with Sean; he'd pulled off the road, and it had been exciting to make love like that, right out in the open where somebody might come by and see. Nobody had, and thinking back on it now made her feel weird, but at the time it had been fun. It had not been rape no matter what her dad said.

"Scenic overlook," Paula was saying. "I could hardly wait to show you this. I go by this place every time I go up or down the mountain, and it still takes my breath away."

Annie got out of the truck when Paula did and followed her to the brink of an incredibly steep slope. Here, at least, there was a guardrail, and Annie held on to it with both hands while she looked over. The first thing she saw was the baby, floating through the trees, going away from her and, somehow, looking back with its massive head over its tiny shoulder to tell her to follow it.

Annie was getting seriously freaked. If she told anybody she was seeing things nobody else saw, they'd lock her up somewhere for sure. Even Paula.

But she was definitely seeing the baby.

"Isn't it just absolutely *gorgeous*?" Paula breathed, and for just a second Annie thought she was talking about the baby. Because the baby *was* gorgeous. Was worth stopping to look at. Was worth following.

Except that it couldn't really be there.

But Paula was talking about the scenery, and it was beautiful, Annie had to admit as soon as the baby disappeared and she could turn her attention to anything else. Red and dark brown soil, red and gray and glittery and golden brown rocks, dark green pine trees and some other kind of trees with bright white bark and bright yellow-green leaves that were heart-shaped and fluttered in a breeze she didn't even feel. Way down below—like lace, like a braid of baby-fine hair—was a waterfall, thin and long down a cliff she couldn't see for the trees.

The baby was out there somewhere, down there somewhere, in the midst of all that beauty.

No, it was *not.*

Annie was having trouble breathing. Paula was looking at her. "Annie, what's wrong?"

Annie managed to shake her head. "Nothing. I—"

"You look terrible."

"It's just—the baby—"

"Oh, sweetie." Paula put her arms around her, and Annie let herself be held. When she raised her head to look out over the scenic view again, she thought at first that was the baby there, crawling across the sky with the umbilical cord trailing behind it, but that was a bird with long wings and long legs. Or there, making a scared little sighing sound, but that was the mountain stream. The truth was, there was no sign of the baby anymore. It was completely gone.

She buried her face in her sister's shoulder and cried. Paula stroked her hair and crooned to her things that were supposed to make her feel better and didn't because they weren't true: "Everything's going to be all right" and "You've got to put this behind you and get on with your life" and "There are plenty of other fish in the sea." And: "You know it wasn't ever really a baby. Maybe if you didn't think of it as a baby?"

That made Annie know that Paula couldn't be trusted. She really was alone in this. There wasn't anybody she could talk to. She and the baby would have to work things out, which was a crazy thing to be thinking but which made sense, calmed her down, and was true.

Paula's house was on a little street in a little town that couldn't stretch very far on either side of the highway or the stream because the walls of the valley hemmed it in. Behind the town on one side of the road was a treeless cliff, mostly red and brown with a couple of mustard yellow places that Paula said were played-out silver mines. "Ugly, aren't they?" But Annie, who was seeing the cliff and the town and the mines for the first time, regarded them as part of the spectacular scenery.

Paula's house was really small. It had a steep roof, and one whole wall was windows that let in—*invited* in—trees, cliffs, sky. You couldn't go anywhere in the house to get away from the outside. Even the bathroom had a skylight that took up practically the entire ceiling.

Annie was ill at ease the minute she set foot in her sister's house, and that disappointed her; she'd come here to relax. Houses were supposed to enclose and shelter you, to keep you safe, like wombs. This house was too open and too cold. Its protection seemed flimsy and tenuous. The two tiny bedrooms upstairs, one of which was to be hers for the summer, didn't even have four complete walls; one whole side of them was an open balcony. Annie wondered if she'd be able to sleep at all.

The first few days and nights Annie was at Paula's, the baby didn't come. She'd thought sure it would, and she'd thought sure she'd never be able to sleep in her sister's weird house, so she kept being disappointed when she woke up and it was morning.

Sunlight through pine trees looked so cool and silvery yellow, compared to the hot yellow-gold stuff she was used to, that it almost didn't seem like the same thing. It came in through all the windows. Birds sang, and there was a squirrel as loud as a jackhammer right outside her room; she could hear it, but she could only see part of its bushy tail because it always kept a tree trunk between it and her.

She'd try to remember what she'd dreamed and whether there'd been any waking visions. They said everybody dreamed every night. Well, she didn't, and the baby wasn't coming at all. She was sleeping straight through the night. She was catching up on her rest, just like everybody said. Annie was getting less and less upset, and more and more depressed.

Every morning she woke up late to the sounds of Paula puttering around. At first Annie was never sure where her sister was exactly, because without walls sounds traveled every which way in this house. She heard dishes clinking, too, or firewood being stacked; most mornings she smelled coffee.

Sooner or later she'd get up and get dressed. It felt weird getting dressed and undressed in front of all those windows, even with curtains closed across the bottom half, even though the second floor was way up in the trees and there probably wasn't anybody around to be looking in anyway. Annie put on as much as she could under her nightgown and made sure her T-shirt was right-side-out and ready to slip on over her head the minute she pulled her nightgown off.

For just a flash, she remembered what it was like getting dressed and undressed while she was pregnant. Flinching when clothes brushed her nipples. Running her hands over her stomach to see if she was getting fat yet, if anything showed. She didn't want to remember that, but she stood still for a minute, half dressed in front of all those windows, and did. She hadn't been pregnant for very long; you'd have thought it was a lifetime.

Bitterly, she thought: it *was* a lifetime. The baby's. My being pregnant that short time was the baby's entire lifetime.

Paula was in the kitchen area—there weren't any separate rooms downstairs—with her bare feet up on the table, a blue mug of light brown coffee in one hand, and a book open on her thighs. Sunshine made cool pools on her skin, her hair, her pink shirt.

"Hey, little sister," she said, but she didn't look up

from her book right away. Annie used to hate it when she was little and Paula would be right there in the same room with her, maybe babysitting, and she'd completely ignore her for some book, or she'd say, "Leave me *alone*! I'm *reading*!" A little insulted like that now, Annie waited while her sister finished the paragraph or chapter or whatever. Finally, Paula sighed in satisfaction, shut the book over a tasseled bookmark, and stretched. "So, did you sleep okay?"

"Straight through the night," Annie told her.

"Any dreams?"

Annie stiffened and turned away. Obviously their parents had told Paula that she'd been having dreams about the baby, which was how she'd explained it to them but wasn't exactly true.

"You know," Paula said, carefully not looking at her, "I personally don't see anything wrong with dreams. I think they show that your mind is working on something, trying to find a way for you to live with something."

"They're not exactly dreams," Annie said cautiously.

Paula was paying such close attention now and listening so seriously that it made Annie nervous. "What do you mean?"

"More like—visions," Annie said, not quite having the nerve to say "visitations."

After a minute Paula asked again, "What do you mean, Annie?"

But Annie didn't know what else to say. She said, "I don't know, I don't *know*," and went upstairs and shut herself in the bathroom for a long time. When she came back down, Paula was making French toast for breakfast.

Those first few days they didn't really do much. They went for long walks in the woods, sometimes on roads or trails and sometimes not. Paula told her names of birds and animals and flowers and rocks and stuff, and interesting facts about them, such as that there was a certain kind of pine cone that only burst open and spread its seeds if there'd been a really hot fire to clear away enough of the ground cover that the seedlings could grow, and that the hole in that dead tree was probably an owl's burrow. Annie was impressed that she knew so much (although she could have been making it all up for all Annie knew). But she didn't try very hard to remember much of it. This wasn't school.

They drove in Paula's truck way up above timberline, over the Continental Divide. Annie had heard about the Continental Divide. They drove down into Denver for pizza and a movie. They played cards. Annie watched TV while Paula read, but the reception was lousy.

Mom called every day. Annie would tell her what they'd done that day and try to sound up but not too up. She ran out of things to say pretty fast and then there were these long, awkward silences. When Paula got on the phone she'd say things like, "I'm fine, Mom. Annie's fine. We're both just fine," and the two sisters would exchange knowing, exasperated looks: *mothers.* Annie suspected that Paula would be telling Mom more if she weren't there, but the house was too small and too open for her to get out of earshot, even if she wanted to, which sometimes she did.

The second Monday after Annie got there, Paula had to go back to work. She complained a lot, and said about a hundred times that she couldn't come home for lunch but there was stuff in the refrigerator for sandwiches and she'd be home by about six if the traffic wasn't too bad up the mountain. Annie kept saying, "Okay. O*kay.*" Finally Paula hugged her and hurried out to the truck. She came back in swearing because she couldn't find her keys. After a frantic search Annie found them under the couch.

Then Annie was alone in the house for the first time. She waited a while for the baby to come, but it didn't.

She read all of Paula's magazines, even the articles on Iraq and keeping a household budget and heart disease. She took a couple of quizzes to see how insecure and how passionate she was. She made herself a peanut butter and jelly sandwich but then she wasn't hungry so she didn't eat much of it. She watched *Oprah,* which had bill collectors on and the people they were trying to collect money from. She washed her hair and just let it dry, so it frizzed and drooped and she didn't much care. It was barely afternoon.

She decided to go for a walk. The minute she set foot outside Paula's house, she was sure she was going to get lost, and there wouldn't be anybody to ask directions from. She almost turned around then and went back up the steps. But that was silly. All she had to do was pay attention to which way she turned, and watch for landmarks—the cabin with the red roof, the big pine tree just off the road that had been struck by lightning.

She turned right out of Paula's driveway, walked past the first intersecting road to the second one, turned left at the cabin with the red roof (but she'd already counted three of them), turned off the road onto a trail where the giant downed tree lay, and was definitely lost.

From the position of the sun, she thought it was probably not all that long till dark, although she didn't have a lot of experience reading the position of the sun. The sun was like silver sliding down through the trees, pouring down, and the trees were almost black with silvery auras. Where the sun came through, the air was warm; where it didn't, the air was cool. Annie could tell with her eyes shut where was sun and where was shadow. A lot of good that did.

Annie wasn't particularly afraid, just really alert. This was the first time since the baby that she'd paid attention to anything else. It was hard to do, and she felt disloyal, but she had to. This could be a matter of life and death.

All of a sudden she found herself going uphill, at enough of an angle that the muscles in the tops of her thighs ached some. Going uphill didn't seem right, so she turned around and went back down, but that didn't seem right, either, and the slope wasn't anywhere near as steep as the one going up had been. There really wasn't much of a path. She stumbled, slipped, grabbed on to a branch that broke and scratched her arm. Way up in the tree a bird squawked, and Annie had the impression that it would be big and black. She squinted up and saw it, big but not black, kind of silvery against the bright sky and the black tree. It wasn't a bird. It was the baby.

Floating like a balloon among the feathery branches, moving not like a bird at all but like a balloon on a long string. Silvery sun and sky behind it so she shouldn't have been able to make out its face, but she could because she was its mother. Face down, it was staring right at her.

Annie shuddered. She'd been so worried about being lost, so determined to find a way out, that for a few minutes she actually hadn't been thinking about the baby. Seeing it now was a shock, and she didn't want it to be. She wanted it to be the most natural thing in the world.

Okay, okay, she thought, addressing the baby which didn't exist anywhere outside her mind anymore, but that was something, that was enough. *I give up. So what do you want?* She did her best to stare up at it, but the glare made her eyes water and sting.

The baby started to fall.

Annie gasped and held out her arms to catch it. But it didn't fall that far. It stopped just out of her reach and hovered there. She could smell it now. It smelled of blood and baby powder and disinfectant.

Its face was a triangle. Its eyes were slits. Its nose wasn't much more than a little bump with two holes in it. It looked weird. And because Annie hadn't let it live, it never would look right.

The baby hovered there for a minute or two, as if it wanted its mother to get a good look at it. Then it took off like a Frisbee through the trees.

Annie went after it. She had no idea what this thing really was that she was chasing, and if anybody saw her they'd think she was completely insane, but she was not going to let it just fly away when she could do something about it. She couldn't keep up, so every once in a while the baby stopped and waited for her. It never let itself get out of her sight. It would half turn corners, leaving part of itself showing—its little bent-up knee, its bulging forehead, its bottom—until she got almost to it, and then it would zoom off again. Obviously, it was leading her somewhere.

Back to Paula's, she assumed at first. The baby was like her guardian angel, come to protect her and show her the way. That made her feel horrible. She didn't deserve it. The baby ought to hate her. But she followed it gratefully, almost blindly, for some reason trusting it to know more than she did and to take care of her.

They kept going for a long time and they were moving pretty fast, so Annie started wondering how far they'd traveled. She was sure she hadn't come this far from Paula's, and they were definitely climbing. The woods were getting thinner. The trees and bushes were getting shorter and more crooked. The air was cooler; she shivered in her shorts and T-shirt. This was a place she'd never been before, and the baby was still soaring ahead of her, calling her by its own special, secret name for her.

Now Annie thought maybe the baby wanted to hurt her. Wanted to suck her out of herself, like an abortion. Wanted to take her somewhere and leave her there to die alone. And that seemed perfectly right to Annie.

Then they were at and over the ridge of a steep slope, which was rocky at the top and covered with grasses and thin bushes and then pine trees as the baby took her down into the deep valley without a pause or a second thought. Colors swirled up to meet and then engulf her, red spinning into gold then turning into blue and green and violet. The swishing sound of grasses in the wind spun into birds singing, twisted into the rushing of her own blood in her veins and in her baby's veins.

Then Annie saw that there was a whole little town down there, strung out along the valley floor, houses with broken walls, stores with their signs still up but faded so you couldn't read them, roads and fences. A ghost town.

The baby spoke to her. *Great,* she thought. *Now I'm hearing things, too.* Then she made herself shut up and listen. The baby spoke to her. Not with words, exactly, because it had never gotten old enough to have words, but Annie was its mother and she understood it perfectly. "Welcome," it said to her, from where it was curled up in the jagged foundation of what might have been a church. Annie felt a sharp, painful tug at her navel, and she was reeled toward the baby. "Welcome to Revenant."

4

The sound of running water. The sound of a waterfall over a series of ledges made of rock harder than the streambed in which they were embedded. The sound of water dashing against its banks and hissing up into the air. Tom heard the sound of water everywhere, and he never stopped thinking about the day Emily died.

 Patrick crouched on the mountainside and gazed down at the apartment building where Juliet lived. He had been there for a long time—days, weeks—and his attention never wandered. From the day she was born, it never had.

Gazed along and across the red-earth roads with the striated sides where they'd been cut through the mountainside, whose bright strata and others too subtle to be detected by the naked eye had been lifted and folded and broken and re-formed over the millennia, whose every rock had altered its composition under the focus of heat and gravity and upward pressure. He had read that the same red-rock formation he saw here, sometimes called the Devil's Backbone, extended a hundred miles north, a hundred miles south, and a hundred miles down beneath the surface of the earth. The idea of such obsessive geologic connectedness was more than a little unnerving.

Sent his gaze among pines and spruces—separate trees, not dense like the woods back East, dark green, tall and straight-trunked as bristles on a brush (brush her hair, child-fine and silky around his fingers, have her brush his hair, for years she wasn't strong enough to get the bristles through his thick curls to his scalp and then one night he suddenly felt their scratch, harder and harder, and she wouldn't stop until he reached back and caught her child's wrists. When he saw her face he knew he'd lost her, she wasn't in love with him anymore although she'd pledged herself to him forever. She was twelve.)

Stared among aspens with bark like white tissue paper and heart-shaped green-gold leaves whose long stems made them flutter in the slightest movement of air, their undersides paler and veined as a child's hidden skin, no shame in seeing them. (He'd given her a heart-shaped locket. He wondered if she still had it, if she'd put his picture in it as he'd intended but hadn't wanted to suggest, or someone else's. He remembered how his heart had fluttered in his chest when he'd bought it for her, a grown-up locket for a beautiful little girl, and when he'd given it to her, shyly, and when her face had lit up at the sight of it. Then, he had still been able to please her.

And she him. His penis pulsed but did not rise, and he thought for a moment—in panic, in relief—that her power over him had at last diminished. But he dared not allow that to be true.

For a long time she'd kept the locket at his place so nobody would know, part of their sweet secret, and he'd looked at it more than she had, kissed it, stroked it, reverently fastened it around her neck before he made love to her. Then one day it was missing, and Juliet had said she never wanted to see him again.)

Sent his adoring, desperate gaze under the cerulean sky and the pale brown haze that furred the city like the down on Juliet's arms and the small of her back when she was seven years old.

Directed his gaze and his urgent thoughts down into the bevy of dun-colored apartment buildings, found her building and her apartment without any trouble of any kind. That first evening, exhausted from days on the road and terrified of being seen (though he still found it almost impossible to believe that Juliet hated him; he'd still wake up more mornings than not aglow from the love they shared), he'd skulked among the buildings until he'd found the right door. Since then, he could go directly to it in his mind. Of course he would know where she lived.

There was a time when she'd have known he was there, too. Would have sensed him following her, watching her, needing her, without his having to say so. But he *would* say so, more easily than to any other woman. He would say he loved her, and nobody would ever love her as much as he did, and what they were doing wasn't wrong because they loved each other but she mustn't tell because nobody would believe her and anyway she liked it, too, didn't she? Didn't she sometimes start it? Kiss him first? Put her little hand on his butt? And if anybody did believe her, he would go to jail because most people were too crass, too plebeian to understand the kind of beautiful, holy love that could be between a brother and sister.

Juliet didn't understand "crass" and "plebeian" but she did understand "secret." She understood "jail," too. Her brown eyes would get even bigger, and full of tears. She wouldn't want her big brother who loved her to go to jail, would she, and it would be her fault? No. Shaking her head. Tiny hands stroking his cheeks the way no grown woman's ever had or ever would. Do you love me? I love you, Pat.

But she'd betrayed him. That thought caused Patrick such acute pain that he hardly dared think about it and could not stop himself. The world was not to be trusted. Even his lovely little Juliet was not to be trusted. She hadn't remained a child, willing and able to take the imprint of his imagination. She'd learned to block the bathroom keyhole with toilet paper so that he was left wholly to imagine her there, her pale thin limbs, her pussy beginning to grow hair that spoiled the smooth purity of it, the swelling mounds of her bottom, her flat chest contouring into breasts that disappointed and frightened Patrick profoundly but that also had given him brief dizzy hope: maybe through his little sister Juliet he could, after all, learn to love a woman. Be loved.

But she left him, as did they all. She grew up, and she wouldn't let him see her even partly undressed, and when he passed her in the yard and rested his hand (secretly, beautifully, respectfully, as he'd done so many times before) on her small hip, she jerked away. She wouldn't come to his apartment to visit him anymore, even with their mother. She said to him once, in the hallway of their mother's house when Patrick wasn't even sure they were alone, "Leave me alone. I don't want to do this anymore, Pat. It's sick." Hurt as he was, Patrick had also been proud of her, in a proprietary way because he liked to think he'd had something to do with how strong and mature she turned out to be.

Then she'd told.

She'd told their mother. Their mother had decided not to believe what Juliet said. She wanted so desperately not to take sides in her children's disputes. She begged her son and her daughter not to have any harsh words, please, we're a family. She did not dare think of her son as a child molester (and she wouldn't have known the word pedophile, because she would do almost anything to avoid things that were hard or unpleasant. Juliet. Juliet, honey, don't. You're tearing the family apart. You and Patrick are all I've got since your daddy left us).

Patrick had been outraged that she hadn't believed every word his little sister said. Juliet didn't lie.

He'd also been terrified to imagine what would happen to him if their mother or anyone else did believe her, did take her seriously. He knew that he would not survive prison. He would not be able to tolerate the loss of his freedom, and he was not tough. He had read and seen movies about what other prisoners did to child molesters, which is what they would believe him to be. He loathed crowds and the prolonged company of other men under the best of circumstances. He was well-educated, thoughtful, interested in philosophy and theology and appreciative of cultural things; he and Juliet used to lie blissfully in his bed listening to classical music, and he liked to think he'd been responsible for broadening her cultural horizons. Their mother had never shown any interest in music of any kind, or art or literature either, and Juliet's artistic and spiritual development would have been woefully lacking if not for his influences.

It broke his heart that Juliet didn't love him anymore. He had had so much more to teach her, and she him. Sometimes, more and more often as the barren years went by, he thought he would not be able to survive her loss.

She was twenty years old now, a grown woman with a life of her own.

He could not think of her that way. He couldn't hold her in his mind the way she was now. That wasn't real, somehow. He himself had turned thirty-six this year. That didn't seem entirely real, either.

Juliet as she had been, *his* Juliet, was real. Tiny. An elfin child, frightened and lonely after her daddy left. Her father had sexually abused her; Patrick had suspected that long before she'd confessed, and it made him want to kill the man for not revering her. When Patrick touched her, kissed her, made love to her, the acts were holy; when he climaxed, both he and she were transformed.

Juliet as she had been. Four years old the first time and already knowing what to do, already inviting him to love her in just that way. Flirtatious and coy, watching him, eager to please. "You want me to do like with my daddy?"

Blood had rushed to his head when she said that, a wild passion and hope he'd never allowed himself to experience before and was afraid of now because it would be so easy to misinterpret what she meant. Outrage, too, that any father would molest his child. He'd held his breath and nodded at her, smiled at her. "Yes, sweetheart, yes."

She'd contorted her pale little face and hesitated, then laid both hands on his penis, which was already hard for her. He'd had to help her with his zipper, and that first touch of her little hands on his scrotum was still the most beautiful thing that had ever happened to him.

Patrick thought about it now, and his penis rose painfully. Watching the apartment building where the grown Juliet lived, he unzipped his pants and masturbated to the much clearer image of Juliet the child, whom he had loved and lost.

He hadn't seen or heard from her since she'd run away from home when she was sixteen. He understood why she'd run away; there wasn't much going on in the little Appalachian town they'd both grown up in, and their mother was getting more and more foolish. It had taken him the better part of four years to track her down, following clues she doubtless hadn't even known she was leaving.

Unless she'd left them on purpose. He'd wondered about that. Maybe she'd wanted to be found. Maybe she'd wanted him to find her. Maybe she still loved him after all.

When she was a child they used to play games like that, sweet sexy games that only the two of them knew about, the secrecy intensifying the excitement for both of them. Patrick knew her, knew what she was thinking and feeling sometimes better than she did.

She'd hide from him in his apartment. It was a small place and he'd always find her easily, curled up in a fetal position behind the couch with her thumb in her mouth and her eyes wide, or crouched in the bathtub on her sharp knees, often crying, but that was just part of the game. His Juliet had no reason to be afraid of him, and anyway she'd wanted this as much as he did.

When he found her, he'd undress her, put her over his knee, and spank her. Not hard enough to really hurt, the way their mother did when she was punishing her (at those times Patrick had to restrain himself from hurting the woman who was hurting Juliet), just enough to turn the smooth white flesh of her bottom pink.

Then, at just the perfect exquisite moment, he would turn her over so that she was arched backward across his lap, and he'd spread her child's thighs with his two hands. Sometimes she would pretend to resist, but it wasn't hard to overpower her. He would gaze for a while, for as long as he could stand the gathering pleasure, at her delicate labia, at her clitoris small as a seed, at the smooth opening of her vaginal canal no bigger around than a pink crayon, and he would be nearly overcome, every time, by his good fortune. Sometimes he would kiss; she would squirm under him, so he knew

she liked that. Gradually he would insert his fingers—
one, two, eventually all four.

If he and Juliet were synchronized in the magical way
of true lovers, they would cry out at the same instant.
Then it was perfect. Their spirits as well as their bodies
had been joined. Patrick had never experienced that
kind of union with anyone else, before Juliet or since.

That was why he couldn't believe it when later she'd
insisted that he'd *forced* her to do things she'd never
wanted to do. That he'd hurt her. That it was wrong.
That she'd been just a vulnerable child and he'd taken
advantage of her. That he made her sick, he made her
hate him and hate herself. The adolescent who'd said
such cruel things to him and who'd looked at him with
such pity and revulsion was not the Juliet he had loved,
the Juliet who had loved him. The child Juliet was the
great love and the great loss of his life; it was she, really,
whom he had followed across the country, and she
whom he yearned and waited for now.

A train went by in the distance. Patrick didn't see it,
but he heard its whistle and the rhythmic clatter of its
wheels on the tracks. Trains were practically an arche-
type by now, a symbol so basic that the listener didn't
even have to think about its referent, about what was
actually creating the sound, in order to feel restless and
lonely. A plane crossed the sky, the buzz of it lagging
behind its blue and silver visual trajectory. Patrick's left
foot had fallen asleep; he stretched his leg, rubbed his
instep. He was getting hungry, but he'd wait awhile before he went down into Boulder for lunch.

There was movement around Juliet's apartment building, a bright flutter. Patrick caught his breath. He leaned
forward, got up on his knees, and peered. A lone figure.
Wearing yellow; he could make out no other details. The
figure had emerged from one of the eight look-alike

doors on the flat back of the building and was now crossing the parking lot, heading toward the road that wound up the mountainside. It could be Juliet, coming right to him.

Heart racing, Patrick tried to sit absolutely still and to focus all his mental energy on summoning her: *come to me, my sweet little sister, my lover, my child. I love you. I am nothing without you.* The words were his mantra.

The figure was gone. Patrick blinked, stood up, walked out of the trees to stare down at the road and the plateau where the apartment house stood. Juliet had vanished, again.

Staggering and breathless from the renewed pain of loss, Patrick desperately remembered:

How soft her skin had been, how clear and pure, before she'd started using makeup, before she'd started shaving her legs and under her arms. How soft her baby skin had been. Patrick clenched his fists.

How soft her hair had been, like water across his cupped palms, until she'd ruined it by cutting, perming, moussing it. Their mother had allowed her to dye her hair red when she was only twelve years old. Patrick had studied psychology fairly seriously in college; he knew how damaging something like that could be to a developing child, and it made him livid.

How small and damp her mouth had been, a permanent moue, how delicate her teeth and tongue. The first few times he'd guided her head down and positioned his penis, then had had to hold her head in place so she wouldn't stop too soon, although it certainly had never taken very long.

Patrick squirmed. He leaned back against a tree trunk and bent his knees to make a valley of his lap. Carefully he withdrew his engorged penis from his pants and began to slide his slightly clenched fist up and down the shaft, letting the loose skin fold over the head and then stretching it taut, squeezing just hard enough and then loosening and then squeezing again. He didn't need to close his eyes; the image of the little girl Juliet was always with him, and he had only to summon it into the foreground.

The first few times she'd gagged and struggled. Patrick didn't like to think about that; it was only because it was something new and she didn't quite know what to do. Patrick had tried his best to go slow. By the time she was eight she'd been quite accomplished, and then he could tell she was enjoying it herself. Often she'd initiate it without being asked.

Patrick climaxed now, weakly. Release and disappointment flooded through him at the same time, and tears for Juliet sprang to his eyes. In the mountain air, the semen on his belly quickly became cold and stiff.

For her eighth birthday he'd bought her an enormous blue-and-white panda, bigger than she was. She'd been thrilled, and she'd told him coyly that it reminded her of him; she'd named it Patty. But she hadn't taken care of it very well; in a matter of days its eyes were gouged out and there was a long ugly rip across its abdomen. Juliet had cried.

Since she'd left him, Patrick's orgasms were never complete; he was never quite spent. He could see her now: heart-shaped face like a pale aspen leaf between his legs, big brown tear-shiny eyes on his face over the mound of his erection so she could be sure she was doing what she was supposed to do. She loved him. She wanted to please him, and she did.

He could see her. He could feel her. He could taste her on his lips and tongue, her bittersweet childish sweat, the oil in her hair when she hadn't washed it often enough. Her fragrance was even more vivid than the other sensations—the odors of baby powder and sex and fear, the undefinable personal odor of Juliet that nobody else in the world possessed and that she hadn't lost when she grew up no matter how she tried to camouflage and corrupt it with perfume and distance. He heard her, humming tunelessly in her nervous way, saying his name and saying she loved him.

But Patrick had always believed in facing the truth, and the truth was she was not here. He was utterly alone. And something was trapped inside him like a genie in a bottle, some fundamental essence of him that had lain dormant before Juliet came into his life and that could never again be released without her. There was constant, unrelieved pain, constant pressure. Patrick knew he could not bear it much longer.

His fly still open and a hand protecting his crotch, Patrick went back to the gravel road where his truck was parked. There he cleaned himself up as best he could with the Baby Wipes he kept in the glove compartment for this purpose. Then he adjusted and fastened his clothes, combed his hair and beard in the rearview mirror, and drove down the hill into town.

On the way, he checked his notebook. McDonald's today. He made sure not to go to the same place very often, and certainly not two days in a row, in case somebody would notice him and think his presence suspicious. In the sixteen days since he'd tracked Juliet here, he'd eaten twice at Arby's and twice at IHOP, but otherwise he hadn't repeated himself. There were enough restaurants in the phone book to last him another couple of weeks. He considered again, and rejected again, the safer but lonelier possibility of packing his lunch.

He wasn't exactly hungry. He couldn't really think of anything he *wanted* to eat. Nothing had tasted good in years. For a while their mother had worked evening shift and he'd regularly babysat Juliet, which had been the most satisfying time of his life. He was twenty-five and she had turned nine that year, a gaminlike child with huge eyes and a smile she would use fully only after she'd looked at him for approval. He'd fixed macaroni and cheese or tomato soup practically every night, because they were just about the only things she would eat, and then only if he made them. He'd bathed her, washed her hair. He'd almost quit smoking, because she begged him to and because, even before the official warnings about secondhand smoke had started coming out, Patrick had known it wasn't good for her. They'd made love every evening before dinner, sometimes more than once.

He would never love anyone the way he'd loved Juliet. He would never love Juliet herself the way he'd loved her then. His Juliet, his adored little sister, his child-lover, the love of his life, was lost to him forever. There was a grim satisfaction in the pain that thought brought him, and he thought it again and again, deliberately, by now a rosary that gave meaning and order to his suffering.

Since the idyll had ended, since Juliet had informed him with preadolescent gawkiness that she didn't want to love him *that way* anymore, Patrick hadn't found much pleasure in anything, eating included. Since she'd run away he'd hardly been able to eat at all—missing her, mourning her loss, worrying obsessively that she would tell somebody about him who wouldn't understand. He'd lost a good twenty-five pounds; he was smoking two packs a day and putting away a six-pack of beer every night, all because of her. Since he'd found her here, though, he'd learned from experience that if he didn't eat lunch he'd lose his concentration during the afternoon, and he couldn't afford to let that happen.

There was a fair amount of traffic, which surprised him and made him uneasy. He felt conspicuous and clumsy, as though it was only a matter of time before he made some foolish driving error and the Boulder police pulled him over. He turned his signal off and on twice to make sure it was working.

Patrick turned into the lot, parked, and sat in his truck for a few minutes, concentrating on taking the deep, even breaths that would calm him down. Before he went into the restaurant he stopped by the playground, put his foot up on the stone bench, and leaned his crossed arms on his knee to stare at the mountains until his vision cleared. The playground was full of children, charming little girls and boys. Patrick noted them, observed them, but they held little interest and almost no attraction for him. He was not a pedophile. He had, pure and simple, loved Juliet. Pure and simple.

For all his precautions, he still had to stop in the men's room to collect himself before he entered the crowded restaurant itself. No one else was in there, so he stood in front of the mirror with his hands braced on the sink and wept openly. It amazed and gratified him to discover how profoundly, after all these years, he still mourned Juliet.

Two little boys came in, handsome and rowdy. Hastily Patrick doused his face with cold water, dried it on an abrasive paper towel, and left the room.

He had to stand in a long line. The girl ahead of him had shoulder-length limp hair like Juliet's. But she was maybe fifteen or sixteen, and when she turned and scanned the restaurant her gaze didn't light on him.

Ahead of the teenage girl was a couple in their thirties, holding hands and laughing together. Patrick frowned. Most couples his age seemed either so harassed or so indifferent to each other that it was easy for him to keep from envying their relationships. He tried not to look at these two, but they were directly in his line of vision as he advanced toward the counter—the slightly overweight woman whose just-graying hair separated unattractively over her collar in back, the balding man. Carrying their white bags of food and talking animatedly to each other, the man jostled Patrick and the woman said for him, "Oh, sorry." Patrick's surge of acute, nauseating loneliness was ameliorated by the answering image of the little girl Juliet in his arms, Juliet small and quiet and compliant under him, Juliet eager to do anything to make him happy because he was her big brother and she had to and because she loved him.

Ahead of the couple was a very old woman. Thinking it odd that an old person would be in a fast-food restaurant, he watched her for a minute or two. She didn't seem to be ordering anything. Patrick was on the verge of impatience because she was holding up the line when he realized she wasn't actually in the line; she was just standing there. Old people made him profoundly uncomfortable, and he looked away.

The girl behind the counter flirted with him. It took him a beat or two to realize what she was doing. As soon as he did, he felt himself reddening and could barely stammer out his order. The girl tapped her long silver nails impatiently on the counter, and the look on her face turned from perkiness to disdain. She rang up the purchase and didn't bother to say how much he owed, just waited for him to read the numbers displayed on the back of the cash register, as though she didn't want to speak to him any more than she had to. She laid his change on the counter, not wanting to touch him; when he retrieved it, he saw with a small triumph that she'd given him a dollar too much. She dropped his order haphazardly on the tray and gave the tray a single sharp push toward him, having decided he was a complete fool, and immediately turned her flirtatious attention to whoever was behind him in line.

Patrick's shame and fury were not new. Women had always treated him like that, even Juliet once she'd started growing up. But when she was a child, her love for him had been a thing of inordinate beauty, and that was the way he liked to think of her.

He carried his tray to a back booth, forcing himself to hold his head high. He slid into the seat whose back was to the room, so that he didn't have to see many people. Only the woman at the next table: unwillingly, he noted that she was mildly pretty, haughty, and self-absorbed. He turned his head enough that he had to look at only a triangle of her red-shirted shoulder and the side of her short sandy hair. That was the best he could do.

While he was taking his cheeseburger, fries, and chocolate shake off the tray, he remembered—without warning and against his will—the last girl he'd dated. He'd turned thirty in her company. Several years older than he, she'd kept insisting that thirty was no big deal, and she'd suggested that maybe his impotence would ease once his birthday was past. It hadn't. Patrick had known it wouldn't, because it was her fault in the first place, just as it had been the fault of all the other women with whom he'd had the same trouble. None of them had understood him. She'd finally left him, saying—gently, her gentleness a further affront—that she was too young to be celibate. Her hair had been short and sandy. She'd had a bright red shirt.

Someone had left today's *Boulder Daily Camera* on the seat. Patrick smoothed it out on the table, extracted a handful of fries from the bag, and scanned the headlines. The banner announced a story about a water-rights dispute involving the Colorado River, which didn't interest him. There were several items of local interest that he hadn't been here long enough to appreciate. He started to flip past those, then went back and read them through. If he had to stay here awhile, he might have to find a job and a place to live. He had enough money for another week at the motel, with meals in fast food places and doughnut shops, and then he would have to make some decisions.

He finished a story about a mountain lion sighted in a couple of yards that backed up to the foothills, and skimmed a piece about a new homeopathic clinic opening on the Hill. On the top of page three was a wire-service story about an Iowa couple who'd left their four-year-old alone while they went to a party because they couldn't afford a babysitter. The apartment had caught fire and the child had died; no one had even been able to locate the parents until the next afternoon. By the time Patrick found the continuation of the story on page eight, he was trembling with outrage. He simply could not fathom how people could mistreat children.

"Pat?"

Juliet's voice.

It was Juliet's voice. The sweet, sad, unbelievably sexy voice of Juliet when she was seven years old.

Patrick held himself very still.

"Pat?"

She wasn't there, of course. The child who could have spoken his name like that didn't exist anywhere anymore except in his mind.

And every time Patrick was forced to confront that truth again, his heart broke again, as if for the first time, or the last.

Fighting back tears and the nearly omnipresent lump in his throat, he finished as much of his lunch as he could stomach. He left the tray and his scattered trash for somebody else to pick up, an act of defiance which brought him a small spurt of satisfaction.

He'd forgotten how hot it was outside, how dry and bright. Out of the humidified, air-conditioned, and fluorescent-lit restaurant, he lost his breath for a few seconds and could hardly see. Now he was anxious to get back to his post, afraid he would miss a sighting after all this time, effort, and risk.

Nonetheless, he had to take time for a cigarette in order to keep his nerves under some semblance of control. He thought of Juliet whenever he lit up, thought of her guiltily *(I'm sorry, Juliet, I'm sorry, I never meant to hurt you, you're the most important thing in the world to me)* or defiantly *(It's your fault, Juliet, you're the one who ruined everything, you betrayed my trust)* or wistfully *(God I miss you you were my reason for living please come back to me)*. The year she was five, when they'd just been discovering the full potential of their relationship, she'd written a letter to Santa which, translated, had said she wanted just one thing for Christmas: "for my big brother Pat to stop smoking and drinking." Their mother had thought that was so cute that she'd pasted the letter into Juliet's scrapbook.

Colorado shade was clearly demarcated from sun, with none of the blending and blurring of the moisture-laden atmosphere he was accustomed to back East. Out here you could tell with your eyes closed when you had crossed the line from sunlight into shadow. Patrick leaned against the shaded side of the truck and smoked a cigarette as quickly as he could while still extracting from it some calm and relief. Regarding the foothills that curved around the southwestern corner of the city, he tried again and still failed to see anything in their form to justify the name Flatirons.

"Pat?" said Juliet behind him. He felt the tentative caress of her hand at his back pocket. His breath caught.

He put his hand back and caught hers—tiny, delicate, fragile—as he had done so many times before, and as he'd thought he'd never do again, never again. Her fingers curled around his; he felt the contours of her palm and the rough edges of her bitten nails.

Then he turned and saw her at her most precious, her most needy, her most open and vulnerable to him. Seven years old, the perfect age, innocent but able to be taught, able to be both coerced and cajoled subtly and with style, sometimes startling in the things she could teach him. Thin and pale, small for her age. Brown hair straggly to her shoulders (their mother had cropped it short the next year because Juliet couldn't or wouldn't keep the tangles brushed out, and Patrick had never forgiven her for that desecration; he'd have brushed her hair every morning if they'd asked him). Brown eyes wide and anxious, darting, always on the lookout for signs that she was pleasing him or that she was not, the white skin around her eyes always stretched and creased with worry and the thick eyebrows pursed.

Following his instincts, which had served him well in the past, he crouched and picked her up. As usual, he marveled at how light and how substantial she was. The flats of his hands rested in the warm cups of her still-smooth, still-lovely armpits. The tender insides of his forearms pressed against the sides of her ribcage where there was as yet no swelling of breasts to mar the clean, straight lines.

Then her little legs spread to clasp his torso, and her little arms circled his neck, reminding him how strong she was for such a thin and frightened person. He supported her weight with a hand under the curves of her bottom. Through the thin pink cloth of her sundress he felt no evidence that she was wearing panties, and he longed to slide his hand under there. He dared not do it here, though he knew she wanted him to.

His desire for her sprang awake, nearly overcoming him before he caught and held it by sheer effort of will. He could take her to his motel room, he supposed, but that was both sordid and risky.

Juliet had an apartment. Perhaps, he thought, she would invite him there.

Juliet was twenty years old. Had told him to go to hell. Had told him, snickering bitterly, to go fuck himself. The sweet little sister who'd been willing—eager—to do anything to please him was gone forever, as good as dead. Patrick realized he did not know who this was, this child he held in his arms who, though she was so much like his Juliet, must, after all, be a stranger.

He tried to extricate himself from her, but she wouldn't let him go. He tried to put her down, but she wouldn't lower her feet. Heart racing in alarm, he glanced around, indignant that her parents would let her out of their sight where she could wander into the company of strangers who might not wish her well. He pulled at one leg and then the other, one hand and then the other. They refastened themselves on him faster than he could pry them loose.

The child piped, just exactly as Juliet had learned to do, "I love you, Patrick. I belong to you. I'll never love another man but you."

Almost involuntarily he pressed her to him. "I love you, too," he whispered. Then, their old game, "But someday you'll grow up and you'll meet a handsome young man and he'll steal you away from me."

She was shaking her head before he finished and whispering the response he'd taught her: "No, no, Pat, I'm yours forever."

"Juliet," he breathed. When she accepted his use of the name, he felt emboldened to add, "I've missed you."

"I know," she said, leaning back in his arms to smile at him so that he had to move his hand up rapidly and brace it against her back to keep her from tipping over backward. Then, in a rush that took his breath away, she snuggled against him and buried her face in his neck. "I missed you, too."

Standing there in the sharp shadow of his truck, holding as tightly as he could this little girl who meant everything to him and who could not possibly be here, Patrick was suffused with love for her. The emotion was so ferocious that it unnerved, even frightened him. It also made him feel alive again for the first time since that apocalyptic moment when Juliet had looked at him with sudden grown-up contempt, as though he were some kind of pervert and not the big brother who adored her more than anything in the world.

During the heady years when they were so close, Patrick had frequently—not to say obsessively—amused, reassured, and aroused himself by trying to imagine what people thought when they saw him and Juliet together. Any passerby would assume they were no more than brother and sister, and would be impressed by the older brother's attentiveness. Or, more likely, the observer would think she was his daughter, and would note with approval how comfortable and affectionate they were with each other. Patrick had always been meticulously careful, and Juliet had modeled her behavior after his in public as well as in private, so he'd been certain it would never occur to anyone that they were lovers.

Playing with perspective again, he imagined how he and Juliet would look to others at this very moment. It would never occur to anyone that the child he held in his arms was a ghost.

"Wanna see something?" she whispered in his ear. His heart skittered at the sweet familiarity of the query. She used to bring school papers to show him, Brownie badges. He shivered again at the caress of her fingertips, her breath, her tongue.

"Sure," he always agreed. Too often their harried mother hadn't made time for Juliet. Patrick always had time, because nothing in his life was as important or as interesting as she was. "Show me."

She wriggled to get down. He was afraid to let her go, but he didn't want a struggle. People might be watching. In fact, he was sure that old lady standing in the weeds at the edge of the parking lot was watching. Just standing there, watching. So he set Juliet carefully on her feet and kept a firm grip on her hand. She tugged at him. "This way."

"What?"

"You gotta come over here."

"Where are we going?"

"You'll see. It's a secret." She giggled. Juliet knew about secrets.

She led him across the parking lot behind McDonald's, across a gravel apron and through a shallow weedy ravine, toward the foothills. "I've got my truck," he said, a little taken aback by her determination. "If it's very far."

She tossed her head. Her hand in his was sweaty. He could feel the tender flesh, the tender bones. "It's okay, we can walk," she told him.

"I don't think this is a good idea," Patrick began. They were walking quickly now over the roughening terrain, and he'd never known Juliet to be so forceful. He was actually having trouble keeping up with her. "Who are you?" But she didn't answer, and he didn't press.

They crossed a narrow field of dry golden grass that

made his ankles itch through his socks. Pine trees knee-high to him, waist-high to her were scattered around them now. In a few steps the trees had become taller and thicker, a stand, a forest up a steep long incline, but still not dense and most of them skinny, straight lodgepole pines whose branches didn't start much below twenty feet off the ground. Occasionally there was a single aspen or a small grove of them, with fine fluttery leaves that shouldn't have been capable of casting much shade.

(They had liked to play hide-and-seek in the thick hardwood forest behind the house they had both grown up in. Juliet would run away from him, crying and shrieking as if she were afraid of him, which of course she wasn't. As if she wanted to escape from him, which was all part of the sweet game. But one day he really could not find her. He had searched for some time; he remembered the rapid patterns of sun and shade on the forest floor, the coolness, the terror that something bad had happened to her and so something bad would happen to him. Finally, in the heat of the afternoon, he had gone home, sickened by the anticipation of calling the police, rehearsing what he would tell them, aroused by the proximity of such danger. But Juliet had been in her bed with the blankets pulled over her head. The spanking he had given her that time had been protracted and sensuous and well deserved, alternately smoothing and swatting the smooth skin of her little bottom and legs. Their lovemaking was rendered sweeter and more passionate by his fear and anger and relief. Juliet had sobbed the whole time, her tears on his penis and in the crook of his shoulder as he held her in place.)

He felt the child's hand twist in his. Before he could tighten his grip or quicken his pace, Juliet had pulled free and run on ahead. Almost at once he lost sight of her.

.

The prospect of losing her again was more than Patrick could bear. He couldn't catch his breath for the pain and pressure in his chest, then uselessly gulped the thin air in a sob. Over the years he had wept prodigiously for Juliet, sitting alone in his apartment night after night with only the vapid television and his vapid fretting mother and an ever-increasing volume of beer for company, or over his lunch hour when he was alone in the shop and could lock himself in the back room and prostrate himself on the concrete floor. Gradually, to his horror, the tears had diminished, until he'd come reluctantly to believe that he was done.

But it had required only this apparition of her as she'd once been—brought on, he could see now, by the single distant sighting of her as she was now, after all this time —to plumb the depths of his sorrow again and loose fresh tears. Patrick wept now without any attempt to stop or to hide.

Clumsily he made his way through the crowding woods. The path was seldom where he first placed his feet. Roots and runners bulging the surface of the ground seemed to lift him upward.

Through the distortions brought on by his grieving (the literal physical anguish of a heart only metaphorically broken, the panic of being unable to breathe when in fact he was inhaling and exhaling without much interruption, the sensation that his heart was in his throat, in his temples, about to explode out of his body when it was simply beating hard and fast), Patrick was astounded by the range and complexity of the human imagination. He had not merely seen Juliet, though the visual hallucination had been minutely detailed—the color of her hair in light and shadow, the shape of her upper arm inside the short sleeve of her blue shirt and of her bare forearm, wrist, hand, fingers. The vision had engaged all his senses.

He had heard her voice, and the inhalation and exhalation of her small breath, and the beating of her heart that he'd once listened to for an entire afternoon, making her lie still, thinking how like a castanet it was, how like the iambic meter of a wordless poem.

He had smelled her little-girl sweat, the bittersweet mixture he'd so loved of fear and desire and simple dirty socks. He had tasted in his own mouth hers, and he had touched her (*touched* her; for some reason, this was the sense most difficult to deny), had pressed her against his chest and drawn his lips across the downy side of her head and supported the weight of her thighs along his forearm.

He stumbled. His eyes were blurred with tears, and his body seemed blurred, too, disconnected and beyond his control. He was lost, and he was alone.

He stopped. Vaguely, he thought to lower himself into that thicket, or to squat inside the cupped and twisted trunks of this tree. Thought to stay here and, finally, die.

"Pat?"

Patrick sobbed. He sank onto the rocky, needle-cushioned ground, drew up his knees and bent his head between them, protected his head with crossed arms.

"Pat?"

Hands brushed his exposed neck. He'd taught her to give massages; by the time she'd left him, her hands had grown too large and too strong. Hands slid under his collar, made feathery circles on the soft flesh under his ears.

"Hey, Pat, wanna see?"

Against his will, feeling both foolish and guilty, Patrick mumbled, "Leave me alone."

There was a sharp gasp, a telling little pause. Then

Juliet pleaded in a quavering voice, "Are you mad at me? Don't you love me anymore?"

"Oh, God," Patrick moaned. "I love you."

Hands tugged at his shirt. Lips brushed his cheek above the line of his beard. He slitted his swollen eyes against the sunlight and turned his head sideways on the scaffold made by his knees.

She was standing naked before him. He swore she was standing there in the fringed light. He'd thought he would never see her again, would certainly never see her like this again.

He saw her now: the web of her ribcage, the tips like eyes of her brown nipples unspoiled by swelling, the pale pure V of her pubic skin. He reached for her, trying to convince himself that she wasn't really there, and the instant his fingers closed around her upper arm (more roughly than he'd intended *I'm sorry, Juliet, I never meant to hurt you, please don't leave me),* his gaze broadened and focused until he saw that she was standing on the brink of a cliff. Behind her a valley opened vertiginously, gashing the surface of the earth. Her small heels slanted backward over the rim, and her little toes curled with holding on.

She flinched at first when he touched her. She'd done that before, as if she'd forgotten who he was, and it broke his heart. Then, as usual, she steadied herself and came right to him. When she crouched close in front of him, in that extraordinarily limber manner of hers, he saw clearly the pink valley between her thighs, and his head spun as if he were about to fall or fly.

"Come with me," the little girl begged. "I wanna *show* you something. Come *on.*" She rested her hand, knuckles down, in the sensitive crease of his palm, and wrapped his fingers snugly around her hand. Lifting her eyes (wide, brown, frightened, and knowing) to his face, she guided his hand to her legs, to her vulva, to her small smooth vagina and inside. Her tiny clitoris was wet as a kernel of corn.

He must, then, have fallen or flown, because abruptly he was no longer in contact with the ground. He was suspended in some sort of viscous medium, then in mid-air, then moving in a direction and at a speed he couldn't judge, propelled somehow by the child lover he'd pledged to follow to the ends of the earth.

The valley swelled and swirled around him, red swelling into gold and then swirling into blue and green and violet. The valley (a gash of deep loneliness, twisting deeper) yawned at his feet, closed over his head. Juliet pulled him into it. Buildings took shape around him, the outlines and pieces of buildings, and then the odors and movements of a host of other people, and, just at the edge of his perception, a primordial tug and howl.

5

The overtone came pure and high, the unsung tone above a perfectly balanced and matched chord. Corinne held her breath with everyone else in the chorus. But the overtone sounded to her like Maura's voice, her dead daughter's clarion tenor. She knew better. She knew nobody was singing it. Lord knows, she better than anybody knew Maura was dead. But it sounded like Maura.

The kitchen floor was dirty again. Elinor had scrubbed it just yesterday on her hands and knees.

It was the dog, Warren's dog. Elinor sighed. A lot of things were more trouble than they were worth. She sipped her coffee, kept an ear cocked for sounds of Warren waking up, and took stock of her upcoming day.

Katie would be here at eight o'clock and they'd head up to the cabin. That meant she had to get Warren up by six-thirty, get him his breakfast, get him dressed. She had them both packed, except for last-minute items like toothbrushes and Warren's medicine. She hoped she didn't forget Warren's medicine.

Elinor got up and got the notebook from the counter by the phone, where she'd been crossing things off a long list all week. The man had come yesterday and fixed the wash machine. Last Saturday—was it Saturday? She concentrated and determined it had been Friday. Friday

—the machine had leaked all over the laundry room floor and spoiled her whole day. Warren had insisted he could fix it, no sense throwing away good money. There was a time when he could have fixed it, too; he'd always been handy. A year ago, even, he could have fixed it.

He always had been handy, and she'd depended on him to be, so when he said somewhat testily that he could fix the washer she'd wanted to believe him. That was something Elinor had appreciated about being married for forty-three years to Warren Dietrich. Well, they wouldn't make it to fifty. That was just the way things were.

"I don't know what I'd do without you, Elinor," he said every five minutes, his voice shaking. The older he got the more he mumbled, and Elinor had trouble hearing him sometimes. But she could tell from the look on his face what he was saying when he said something like that. For years she'd have given anything for him to say things like that to her. Now it was some stranger talking.

She'd take his old face between her hands and kiss him, tell him she loved him. But at the same time she'd be thinking: *this isn't my husband. This isn't the man I married. I want my Warren back.*

Thinking she heard a voice, she listened carefully, then got up stiffly and went to the bedroom door. It wasn't Warren. He was still asleep in bed, the familiar humps of his hip and shoulder. Used to be, he'd look strong and self-sufficient even when he was asleep. Now he looked like a child.

Looking at him there, Elinor felt the mixture of tenderness and irritation that she almost always felt toward Warren these days—sometimes more tenderness, so sweet and sad that she wanted to cry but didn't; sometimes irritation so sharp that she wanted to holler at him that he better come to his senses, which she sometimes did. Her feelings toward Warren were as strange to her as he was.

He was still asleep. She'd have a few minutes more, maybe, of peace and quiet. Wistfully, she thought of all the years when she'd had time by herself every day while Warren was at work and Katie was at school. Times she could count on, so she could really relax, not these few minutes sneaked away from him, always on guard, always resentful even when he didn't actually intrude.

She couldn't stop fuming about the wash machine. Every day for a week she'd reminded Warren about it at breakfast, and he acted as if he'd never heard of a wash machine before, let alone a leak in it. Every day she'd reminded him again at their midday meal. They didn't eat three full meals anymore; when you got older you didn't need so much food. Elinor fixed a nice meal about two o'clock in the afternoon, and then just before bedtime she'd slice some fruit or put jelly on slices of her home-made bread.

Warren used to never say anything about her cooking unless there was something wrong with it. The first time she'd tried to make mashed potatoes, not a month after they were married, she'd put too much milk in too fast so they turned out watery and lumpy, and he'd said they weren't fit for a dog. A new bride, Elinor had let him see her cry. She teased him about it now, forty-three years later, and told the story to make Katie laugh, but it still hurt her feelings to think about it.

Now Warren raved about everything she fixed, from cheese sandwiches to cornflakes with sliced bananas to his favorite strawberry-rhubarb pie. She was pretty sure he couldn't tell one from another most of the time, so his compliments didn't mean much.

She'd reminded him and reminded him about the

wash machine, trying her best to be patient. Every time, he'd looked confused and vaguely guilty, as if he'd completely forgotten about the leak and only knew that he'd made a mistake again, disappointed her again, made her cross. That made her feel bad, and that made her even more cross, and she knew he didn't understand.

He'd fix it, he'd said every time. But he didn't. Monday afternoon she'd been doing dishes at the sink and all of a sudden she'd missed him. She'd gone looking for him all over the house and had finally found him wandering around the backyard, crying, hunting for whatever it was he was supposed to fix. Appalled, embarrassed, Elinor had led him back inside, settled him into his chair, peeled him a nice orange, and called Sears.

Seventy-three dollars and eighty-two cents, and he hadn't been there an hour. Elinor scowled, thinking of it. But she'd had to have the wash machine in order to wash clothes for the trip to the cabin, so now that was done.

She looked again at the little spiral notebook, running her finger down the list. She was so afraid of forgetting things, like Warren; she didn't know how they'd manage if they *both* got senile. The list was a good deal longer than usual because of all the things she had to do to get ready to go up to the cabin. *Call Sears to fix wash machine*—at least that was checked off. She wished she could check it off again. *Take dog to neighbors. Clean house. Turn heat down. Cancel newspaper.*

Briefly Elinor covered her eyes with her hand. She'd forgotten to cancel the paper. Maybe she could still do it before they left. Katie was always late. She squinted at the clock. It was too early to call now. She hoped she wouldn't forget. With her red pen she made a box around the item on the list. *Cancel newspaper.*

She'd been trying to pack for a week. Katie said she shouldn't pack until the day before, but Elinor couldn't stand to wait till the last minute like that. Warren kept taking things out of the suitcase and putting them somewhere where it took her a long time to find them—six pairs of his socks in the box where they kept important papers, the cosmetic bag with the neat travel-sized bottles of shampoo and lotion and denture cleaner in the freezer on the back porch. She like to never found the cosmetic bag. He always swore he hadn't touched anything, didn't know a thing about it. It made her so mad. Katie said he couldn't help it. One shirt of his, the short-sleeved blue knit she'd been saving just for this trip, was still missing.

It was too much. She didn't know how much longer she'd be able to hold up. Too much responsibility. Too many details to keep track of. Too many decisions to make all on her own. If she put the checkbook in front of Warren and showed him where to sign he could still write his name, but that was about all. She didn't like to bother Katie; Katie had enough on her mind. But Elinor didn't know how much longer she could hold up. It was all too much. She longed for a quiet, peaceful day, without anything to get done, and wondered if they'd ever have one of those again. Well, at least she wouldn't have to fuss with going to the cabin any more after this year. That was a relief. A little bitterly, she wondered if she would even miss it.

Thinking she heard a noise from the bedroom, she looked up and tried to listen hard. Her hearing wasn't what it used to be, she admitted, but the idea of wearing a hearing aid embarrassed her, no matter what Katie said.

She didn't hear anything else from the bedroom and was tempted to ignore the whole thing, but she knew she better not. Sighing heavily, bracing herself on the table, she got up, then paused and defiantly took a minute to finish the last of her coffee. Another *hot* cup would have been nice.

Peering, she didn't see him in the rumpled bed or anywhere else in the room. She took a step forward and still didn't see him. The shades were drawn, so the bright morning sunshine was brownish and dim. She turned on the light. Her heart was beating hard and she put her hand over it. Her breath hurt. The doctor said that tests showed that sometime in the past she'd had what he called a silent heart attack. Well, she hadn't. A person in their right mind would know if they'd had a heart attack. But ever since he'd told her that she got nervous when she noticed the beating of her heart.

Warren wasn't there.

Fury and fear made Elinor clutch the door frame with both hands. "Warren!" She checked the closet, hoping she wouldn't find him there because that would *really* mean his mind was gone. He wasn't in there.

She leaned across the bed, her back catching the way it did every morning when she tucked in the blankets, and patted it none too gently with the flats of her hands. Maybe she'd missed him still sleeping there. Maybe he'd had a stroke, maybe he was dead. She might well wake up some morning and find him dead in bed beside her.

"Warren!"

Rocky came running down the hallway and into the room. His big flat paws slid on the tile and his tail was wagging so hard that he lost his balance and tipped into Elinor's ankles. Katie had got him for her dad because, she said, people with Alzheimer's sometimes relate well to animals. Warren did like him. Of course, it was Elinor who had to clean up after him.

Slowly pulling herself up straight, Elinor chucked him under his freckled chin and said, "Rocky, where's Warren?" He licked her hand and wiggled all over so hard he almost knocked her down, but he no more knew where Warren was than she did.

This was the third dog Warren had named Rocky. The first one, a beautiful and high-strung Irish setter, hadn't been with them very long: a stray when he showed up on their doorstep, he'd simply run away again. The second one, a big golden retriever, had, if you listened to Warren, been the smartest, most wonderful, most affectionate dog in history.

Elinor indulged herself in a moment of bittersweet memory: Walking with Warren of an early morning in the woods with the second Rocky racing around them in wide circles. Warren the crotchety man whose gentleness you had to know to look for, not laid open like now.

Then she thought of that golden Rocky dying, and of that Warren being gone now, too, and she indulged herself in a moment of terrible sorrow which she stopped sternly before it could go too far.

No sense in that. She had to find Warren.

For a split second she was imagining what it would be like if she never did find him, or if he wandered out into the street and got hit by a car and died instantly with no suffering and no fear because he was too confused to even know what was happening to him. If he just never came back. If he disappeared in some way that wouldn't be her fault.

But the fear and guilt and anticipated loneliness were too much for her. She hurried through the house toward the back door with Rocky playing at her heels.

There was dust on the windowsill of the sunroom, which she wiped off hastily with the flat of her hand before anybody could see. She'd been through this room like a dose of salts just Saturday. It was so hard to keep up. Yesterday's newspaper was stacked on Warren's chair. At least this time he hadn't left it scattered all over the floor. Frowning, she picked up all its sections and folded them under her arm. With her other hand she smoothed the wrinkled cover on the seat of his chair. Under the chair was a juice glass. Elinor was horrified. Rocky nosed at it, tipped it onto its side. Elinor bent quickly, groaning a little, and snatched the glass up before anything could dribble onto the carpet, although it looked empty. She'd told him and told him about leaving things around.

Warren wasn't in the sunroom.

"Warren!"

He wasn't in the backyard. The grass needed mowed. Warren couldn't mow anymore because of his back. Sometimes he insisted that he did all the yard work around here, always had, and that made her mad. She mowed on Fridays.

He wasn't in the garage.

Elinor was starting to panic. She stood in the cool gloom and considered the steep steps up to the storage loft. It actually was possible that he'd climbed up there.

The nice young man from the moving company—she didn't remember his name, which worried her—had found a shell in the old shotgun Warren used to use for hunting rabbits until Katie, no more than four years old, had got so upset at the sight of her daddy holding the bloody, floppy-eared carcasses up by their long hind legs. He'd given up hunting altogether then, hadn't touched the shotgun since, but for some reason had kept it around. The mover had held up the shell between his thumb and forefinger and scolded her—the gun shouldn't have been left lying around loaded all these years, somebody could have got hurt, it could have gone off in the van and killed him or his helper. Obviously he didn't know a thing about guns, because Warren said it was loaded, yes, but it wasn't cocked so it was perfectly safe.

Katie had carried the unloaded shotgun up the steps to the garage loft and shoved it into the darkness under the eaves as far back as she could. Warren didn't know it was up there. Elinor hadn't seen what Katie had done with the shell. As if they couldn't take care of things. As if they hadn't lived together just fine, doing things the same way, for forty-three almost forty-four years. As if they hadn't raised Katie herself, who hadn't always been an easy child if truth be told. As if they hadn't worked hard and saved money and Warren hadn't invested so that now in their old age they wouldn't have to worry, they wouldn't be a burden and now they were a burden anyway because of Warren. But he didn't worry. Elinor worried.

On her way out of the garage, Elinor straightened the broom, rake, shovel, hoe, and snow shovel leaning in the corner by the door. She picked up a bit of cardboard off the floor, swept her hand across Warren's workbench—which he never used anymore—to get rid of dust. She hadn't brought her keys, but Warren said if vandals wanted in they could get in whether your door was locked or not, so she just pulled it carefully shut behind her. She went out the gate into the cool dawn alley and deposited the newspaper and the scrap of cardboard into the trash can, snugly resetting the lid. Trash day wasn't till Wednesday.

She stepped out into the alley, taking care to adjust her balance to the uneven surface, and peered as far up and down it as she could. Warren wasn't anywhere to be seen. She didn't want to call for him out here. For one thing, she might not be able to hear him if he did answer, his voice was so low and he would not speak up. And, besides, she didn't want the neighbors to know there was anything wrong at their house. "Warren," she whispered.

She found herself thinking, almost frantically: Warren was a decent man, a good provider, and she'd been absolutely sure of him when it came to other women. He'd never been what you would call easy to live with, but he had been dependable.

He'd always been moody. He'd get cross all of a sudden and you wouldn't know why. She used to go out behind the garage and cry with her apron over her head, he'd make her so mad.

Now, he wasn't moody like that anymore. She'd learned to cope with his moods and they'd been doing fine, and now he'd *changed.* Now she couldn't count on him for much of anything anymore. He wandered off, and he did foolish things that she could hardly stand to think about, let alone understand. He'd take it into his head not to eat certain things that had always been his favorites, as if she were trying to poison him. Sometimes he'd insist that this wasn't their house, and then other times he'd talk as if he'd lived here since he was a little boy.

This was not the Warren Dietrich she'd married. This was not the Warren Dietrich who'd been her husband for forty-three almost forty-four years. Whether he was doing it on purpose or not (Katie said he wasn't), whether he could help it or not (Katie said he couldn't), it was more and more like living with a stranger.

Last night he'd made a pass at her in bed. She'd thought they were past that. She'd accustomed herself to being past that, since he hadn't shown any interest along those lines for years. The abrupt, fresh memory of last night in bed made her blush and glance furtively around as if somehow the neighbors might know.

Old as he was—old as *she* was, for heaven's sake—last

night he'd reached for her long after she'd thought he was asleep and she'd been lost in the mental exercise she did every night: forcing herself to remember the names of people she used to know, as a way of keeping her memory strong. She'd come up with Bob Morganthal, who'd worked at the store with Warren, and Margaret Voorhies from church, but she couldn't for the life of her think of the man's name at the garage where Warren used to take the car when there was something he couldn't fix himself. Warren couldn't fix a thing anymore, she had to do it herself or hire somebody to do it, which just galled her.

She'd been lying there rigid, struggling to think of that mechanic's name—she could just see his face—when she'd felt Warren tugging at her from behind. His back must have hurt him because he winced and grunted, and he couldn't reach as far or tug as much as she knew he wanted to.

Thinking he just wanted to cuddle and there was no harm in that—sometimes she still liked that, too—Elinor had helped him by scooting herself back into the curve of his body. Into his arms. Old arms, and frail now, but familiar. It would have been nice to just fall asleep like that.

But no. He'd started saying things. Half under his breath, so she didn't catch all of it, which probably was just as well but it made her want to *scream* when he mumbled like that. "You're a wonderful woman, Elinor. I don't know what I'd do without you. You're so strong and kind, and you're so *beautiful*."

Not everything he'd said had even made sense, but that part had, and she resented it. Time was when she'd longed for him to say things like that to her, to look at her adoringly the way he did now. Not a few of those crying sessions out behind the garage with her apron over her head had been because he wouldn't say nice things to her, he hardly ever even said he loved her. But it was too late now, and his mind wasn't right. This wasn't Warren.

He kept it up. "You changed my life. You straightened me out. I was nothing but a bum when I met you."

"Oh, Warren, for heaven's sake, you were not a bum." She was not going to have him change their past, too.

"I didn't have direction in my life. I didn't have— You gave me something to live for."

"Once you told Katie that you'd never wanted to get married," she heard herself say, and right away wished she hadn't. She felt him stiffen. It was too dark to see him, but she knew he had that look of horrified embarrassment he always got these days when she informed him that he'd said or done something mean or childish or nonsensical. He'd insist he didn't remember, but Elinor knew that was nothing but an excuse.

"I—I never— Who?"

"Katie," Elinor'd said caustically. "Your *daughter*. Remember her?" But at the moment he didn't, or for some reason he was pretending he didn't, and so, to distract him and herself, Elinor had hastily changed the subject. "Remember how we met on the porch of that boardinghouse in Philadelphia? On Pine Street." She was gratified that the name came to her so easily.

As usual, the strategy had worked. It bothered Elinor how easy he was to trick now. Used to be, nothing got past Warren. "You were the most beautiful—I couldn't resist you. I—"

"Well, it certainly did take you long enough to notice." She'd teased him about this countless times during their marriage, but lately it had become sharper, not so much playing anymore. "Mae told me you were planning to leave."

"But you didn't let me." He'd hugged her, as best he could.

"You proposed on that front porch the night before you were going to leave."

"You changed my life. You—"

"Not altogether for the better, you used to tell me sometimes."

He'd caught his breath and stiffened again. Then he'd started touching her and kissing her in a way that could only mean one thing. Elinor couldn't believe it. She hadn't done anything back or said anything, and eventually he'd forgotten what he wanted, or, old as he was, he just couldn't do it. Elinor had been relieved, but she was also mad. Shouldn't start things you can't finish.

Thoroughly disgusted, Elinor had got out of bed to go to the bathroom and discovered that Rocky had made a mess by the door. By the time she'd cleaned it up and put the dog out—even though, of course, he didn't have to go out *now*—and waited and then let him back in and got back into bed herself, Warren had been asleep.

Warren used to get cross with her because she could always sleep, no matter what. He'd be up pacing or sitting tense in his chair with the radio on, worrying about the problem with the car or waiting for Katie to get home, and she'd be sound asleep. He used to accuse her of not caring. That wasn't true. It was just that she could worry a lot better after a good night's sleep. Lately she was the one who almost never slept the whole night through, and Warren slept like a baby.

Now she made her way down the alley, past people's garages and trash cans. It embarrassed her to be here, as if she were spying on things she wasn't supposed to see, and as soon as she could she turned off onto the street that curved behind their house and led down to the lake. She and Warren walked down to the lake every morning.

Maybe that was where he'd gone. It scared her to think about him being by the water alone, and then she resented being scared all the time because of him.

In some of the houses people were just waking up. None of them had problems like this. None of them had senile husbands they had to go looking for all over the neighborhood. Once a light came on in a window just as she passed under it, startling her, making her feel alone and out in the cold.

At the big, pretty house in the middle of the block, a girl about Katie's age in a blue housecoat was out setting her sprinkler. A lady a lot older than Elinor, the girl's mother or maybe even her grandmother, was watching through the big front window. Elinor had always admired the house and especially the immaculate lawn; she pointed it out to Warren every time they walked by, and every time he behaved as though she'd never mentioned it before. Their house and their yard could look like that, if Warren would just do it. He used to take pride. People used to comment that their little place looked like a garden spot. Now he didn't care about anything for longer than a minute or two. He'd mow maybe one strip in the backyard, and then he'd wander off to sit in one of the lawn chairs without even any pillow, or to dig in the flower bed where there weren't any flowers because she hadn't had time to set any out this year and he wouldn't. Laziness, was all it was. Just because you got old didn't mean you had to get lazy.

Elinor prepared a polite smile and a "Good morning" that wouldn't let on to the girl that anything was the matter. She didn't want to have to have to stop and visit with her, but you couldn't be rude. But when the girl didn't even look up, Elinor was miffed. She just kept walking, and her smile lasted for no good reason until the end of the block.

There he was.

Elinor sidestepped, thinking to hide behind a protruding juniper so he wouldn't see her until she was ready for him to. She stared at him, trying to see him the way others might see him, the way she would see him if she didn't know him. She *didn't* know him, so it wasn't hard to do:

A small, frail, bent old man sitting on the curb. A little fear on his face but mostly just dullness, just blankness. Wearing striped pajama bottoms, a red sweatshirt, and backless maroon houseslippers, no underwear, and no socks.

To look at him, you'd think he had nobody to take care of him. You'd certainly never guess at the man he'd been—dapper, grim, and so intelligent. This old man sitting on the curb could have been any kind of man when he was younger and his mind was right, could have been Warren Dietrich or anybody else.

Sitting on the low curb like a child, or like an elf out of a fairy tale—really, like nothing so much as a lost and senile old man—he had his knees drawn up almost to his chin. The thin pajamas had pulled up to expose his thin ankles, and the sweatshirt had ridden up in back so you could tell he wasn't wearing any underwear.

Elinor was terribly embarrassed by his shins and by the small of his back. He'd always been so modest, and such a nice dresser. So dignified. Every week for years she'd had six white shirts, lightly starched, to press for him, and if there was so much as one tiny wrinkle she'd have to sprinkle the shirt again and start all over because Warren was so particular about his appearance. She hadn't minded; she'd liked that about him.

Elinor was enraged. How dare he go out of the house looking like this? She still washed and ironed and mended his clothes, just as she'd always done; she doubted he could thread a needle if he had to do it himself, or separate dark clothes from white, and that wasn't just since his mind had started to go, either. Now, though, she laid his clothes out for him, and sometimes she had to help him get into them on mornings when he acted as if he'd never seen a zipper or a sleeve before. Sometimes she had to argue with him—stomp her feet, shout, stand in the bedroom door—to make him wear what she said and wear it right, not backwards or buttoned up wrong. Fine how-do-you-do, having to dress a grown man. And now here he was, out in public where the world could see, looking like a man nobody loved.

He raised his head and looked right at her. She'd been caught. She started to go toward him.

But apparently he didn't see her. Or if he did, he didn't recognize her. Stiffly, he crossed his arms on the square tops of his knees and laid his cheek on his arms. He might be crying. He might have fallen asleep. He might just be sitting in the morning sun not worrying about a thing.

Elinor considered going to him and taking him in her arms. She considered stooping in front of him, out of his reach, and politely offering, "May I help you, sir?" At first he'd think she was his wife, but quickly he'd be persuaded that his mind wasn't working right again and she was a stranger, cautiously offering help. She considered just turning around and leaving him there. Somebody would come along. Let somebody else take care of him.

Instead of any of those things, Elinor said his name and walked purposefully over to him. When she got right up to him he lifted his head a little, though not all the way as she'd expected him to. She saw that he hadn't been crying or sleeping. His eyes—still a nice pretty brown, but distant and blank, the left one filmed by a cataract—scanned across her face without pausing.

"Warren?" she scolded. "What do you think you're *doing?"*

His eyes focused and for a minute he *was* looking at her. Then he braced his hands on the curb and straightened his legs, trying to push himself to his feet. But he didn't get up. He just sat there in that peculiar position and smiled. She saw that he'd bothered to put his teeth in, and for some reason *that* made her mad, too. "Good morning," he said to her pleasantly. "I believe I'm lost."

Elinor sighed and held out her hand. "Come on, Warren, let's go home."

He looked surprised and shook his head. "Ah, no, I'm waiting here for my wife. She knows right where to find me. She's a wonderful woman. She'll give me hell if I'm not here when she comes back."

Elinor didn't know what to say. She was shaking, and she was noticing her heartbeat. Finally, feeling ridiculous, she told Warren, "I am your wife. You know that. Now you stop this, and let's go home and have breakfast."

Again he shook his head. Still very polite, even dignified, he explained reasonably, "I am Warren Dietrich. My wife is Elinor Dietrich. She is a wonderful woman."

"I am Elinor Dietrich!" Her voice rose and she lowered it immediately, thinking of the neighbors.

Then Warren did struggle to his feet, but he pulled back from her helping hands. Wanting more than anything to get him out of there, to get him home and all dressed and settled in his chair in front of the television with his cereal and juice so she could keep an eye on him and things would be back to normal and they could forget this whole thing had ever happened, Elinor had half turned in the direction of home when Warren said, "I don't know you."

Whirling to face him again, she stamped her foot on

the pavement, clenched her fists, and hissed, "You *stop* this, Warren! You do so know me!" Turning so fast had made her dizzy. For a second she thought she was going to faint, and then what would he do?

"I don't know you. I don't trust you. I don't give a damn about you."

She took a quick few steps toward him. Her head had stopped spinning. She grabbed his hand and did her best to gentle her voice. Katie kept telling her it didn't do any good to lose her patience, he couldn't help it, but Elinor wasn't so sure. "Warren, dear, I am your wife Elinor."

He threw her hand off. Just as she'd suspected: he'd just been putting on that weak-as-a-kitten routine. He started down the street at quite a clip, away from her and away from their home, then paused to fling back at her, "I don't care a damn about anybody in the world but my daughter Katie, and you don't even know her."

"Of course I know her!" Elinor was indignant. "I'm her mother!"

His head was shaking harder and harder. Somewhat nastily, Elinor wondered if he even remembered by now what he was saying no to. His fists were raised. He'd never made the slightest move to hit her. Her sister Twyla had stayed with Ralph for more than fifty years, and everybody knew he hit her. She didn't die of that, though; she died of cancer.

Elinor got herself ready. She would *not* stay for one minute with a man who hit her. No second chance for him.

But *he* was afraid of *her*. "Stay away from me!" he was shouting at her, although really it wasn't much of a shout because his voice had gotten so thin and breathy. "Get away from me! I don't trust you! I don't know you! Leave me alone!"

"Warren—"

And then, to get away from her, he almost ran down the street. Elinor was amazed and angered by how fast he could go when he wanted to. He wanted her to believe that it was hard for him just to walk from his chair to the bathroom. He shuffled, and he had to hold on to the door frame, and if she didn't watch him he might turn the wrong way and start to go down the basement steps instead, and it took him such a long time. But now he was practically jogging toward the lake, and he seemed to know exactly where he was going.

Helplessly, Elinor stood on the sidewalk right in front of her neighbors' house while her husband of forty-three years ran away from her for all the world to see. She bent and studiously retied one shoe, pretending that was why she'd stopped here. When she straightened, she had to shade her eyes with her hand in order to see Warren. He was still heading for the lake, which now was glinting in the sun.

By now she'd have had to yell after him, and she wasn't about to do that. Fine, let him go. There were tears in her eyes as she turned her back on him and made her way back to her house, but she didn't let them fall.

The neighbor on the corner was already out weeding the garden, so early. She was younger than Warren and Elinor but still a senior citizen, probably sixty-five or so. Sometimes she brought them carrots and onions from her garden. Warren couldn't eat onions anymore; they gave him diarrhea.

Now the neighbor's back was bent over her weeds, so Elinor probably could have passed without being noticed. She didn't want to talk to her, but she couldn't be rude, and she didn't want to act as if anything was wrong. So she stopped, took a deep breath to steady herself, and called, "Your garden sure is looking nice!"

The woman turned on her knees in the dirt and shaded her eyes with a gloved hand, then waved. "The weeds grow a lot better than the vegetables! And how are you this fine morning, Elinor?"

"Just fine, thank you. And you?"

"Oh, I can't complain. And where's that handsome husband of yours?"

She was just trying to be friendly, but Elinor was offended. "Oh, he decided to go for a longer walk so I said I'd go back to the house and have breakfast ready when he got home."

"By himself?"

The woman's surprise and concern—and disapproval?—were so obvious that Elinor had to wonder what she knew. She smiled and waved, pretending she hadn't heard, even though that was embarrassing, too, and started to move away. "I'd better go get the coffee on. Warren likes his coffee in the morning. Nice talking to you."

"Elinor, if you ever need any help, I'm right here," the neighbor called after her, but it was easy now for Elinor to pretend she didn't hear. She enjoyed having friendly little conversations with bank tellers and grocery store clerks and she'd tell them to Katie word-for-word, but there was no need to tell other people your personal business or to listen to theirs.

In the weeds at the edge of the alley behind her house was a child's ball. When Elinor bent to examine it, her back caught and she grunted. Then hastily—still bent, the striped ball in one hand and a clump of weeds in the other—she looked around to make sure nobody had heard. Thankfully, the gardener must have been out of earshot, and nobody else came rushing to her aid, either. The twinge passed in its own time, and then she was able to straighten up without any trouble.

She'd seen and heard the children playing on the block, but she'd never exchanged two words with them or their parents. She carried the ball to the back fence next door and dropped it over carefully, letting it slide to the ground rather than tossing it, hoping she wasn't calling attention to herself. She dropped the clump of weeds into the Dumpster and brushed the dirt off her hands.

As she came in through the back gate, she noticed that the tree had littered its dusty seed pods all over the patio again, and grass around the edges of the flagstone path was too tall. She would sweep the patio. The least Warren could do was trim the grass.

Inside the house, Rocky was yipping wildly and jumping on the screen. Elinor let herself in and told him to *settle down*. When she'd rushed out after Warren, she'd forgotten to barricade Rocky in the kitchen, where he couldn't do much harm except drag the trash out from under the kitchen sink. Probably he'd spent the whole time she was gone racing from one window to another, frantic for her to come back.

Once she'd satisfied herself that he hadn't torn the screen or scratched the paint, Elinor bent stiffly to pat him. His yipping had turned to ecstatic whining, and he was beside himself with joy, his pug-nosed freckled face animated and, at some times in his whirling, all four splayed feet off the ground. When she scratched his ears he did his best to stay still. When she slid her hand along his feathery side, he instantly rolled onto his back so she could rub his stomach. His head lolled back, his eyes half closed, and his feet wriggled in the air.

"What am I going to do?" Elinor said aloud, and Rocky, thinking she was talking to him, turned his head so he could lick her hand.

Every once in a while Warren said they shouldn't have taken the dog. Whoever it was who'd given it to them should have known a dog would be too much for them. It was more trouble than it was worth. But then he'd sit for hours with Rocky right on his feet, and he'd pet him and talk to him and while she worked in the kitchen or knitted in the evening both of them would sit there and stare at her until she thought she would lose her mind.

The dog certainly was extra work, no doubt about it. All of it hers. Bathing him and cleaning up after him and seeing to it that he had food and water. Warren left it all up to her. Acted as if he didn't remember, but Elinor wasn't so sure. She'd always had to do a lot of the work for the dogs he'd spent so much time training and playing with when he was younger, too.

Before she closed and locked the back door, she peered around the yard and down the streets and alley as far as she could see without going outside again looking for him. She was not going to chase him all over the neighborhood. Just the thought of it made her flush and move away from the door in a hurry. There was no sign of Warren.

Something in the act of looking out a door for him in early morning light, something in the mix of anger and fear and shame and love she was feeling, reminded her of something, of some other time and place, and all of a sudden Elinor was flooded with memory. She fumbled for a chair, lowered herself into it, and closed her eyes.

For a few years, they'd been friends with Norma and Ed Humphrey. Not long, really—they'd never had what you'd call old friends. Katie had been seven, eight, nine, and Ed and Norma, married late, hadn't had children yet. Once they'd had their first baby—Kimberly, or something like that, Kimberly Ann; Elinor remembered Norma saying how she wanted her daughter's name to sound like flowing water—they hadn't called much anymore, and Elinor, who kept meticulous mental note of such things, was not about to call when it wasn't her turn. So the friendship had just petered out, if that's what it had been in the first place—Elinor wasn't sure she'd ever really had a friend other than Warren, and now *he* was petering out, too. She hadn't seen or heard from or even thought about the Humphreys for a long time.

Now she remembered all in a rush of nearly wordless impressions:

Black glossy ponds like a string of flat glass beads on the property Ed and Norma insisted on calling "the farm," even though it wasn't.

Huge black dogs—in her memory the impression was of a whole sloppy pack of them, but she knew there'd actually been no more than two or three. Before Norma did the dishes she'd let the dogs lick off the plates. On the drive home through glossy black country nights with Katie curled up asleep under an afghan in the back seat and the radio turned to the classical music Elinor had never really liked but hadn't said so because to Warren it was the only proper kind of music, Elinor would go on about how disgusting it was to let dogs lick the plates like that, what a terrible housekeeper Norma was, no wonder she'd been past thirty when she finally got married, and then to Ed Humphrey who was no prize himself.

Almost every time they were together Ed and Warren had argued about bomb shelters. All during the time they'd known him, Ed had been building a bomb shelter somewhere on his "farm," he never would tell them exactly where, and stocking up on supplies. There was no doubt in his mind that there would be a nuclear war; the question was only when. Elinor hadn't liked Katie to hear that. Ed said if anybody tried to break into his shelter after the bomb fell he'd shoot them; he practiced with a shotgun in his woods. What if it was a family?

Warren would demand. Women and children? Suppose they were starving or sick, needed help? Didn't matter. Ed vowed he'd never let strangers jeopardize his family's survival. Warren, who didn't have a bomb shelter but who did have a family, would argue heatedly that the only hope for the human race was if we all worked together and took care of each other. He'd tell the story that Katie loved, about the bones scientists had found of a crippled caveman whom somebody must have taken care of because even with one leg a lot shorter than the other he'd lived to be old; the first evidence of human compassion. Warren would insist: I'd let them in. We have to let each other in.

In the kitchen, talking to Norma endlessly about babies, her stomach turning as she tried not to watch the dogs lick the plates, Elinor never had taken the men's talk about bomb shelters and nuclear war very seriously. But she'd been so proud of her husband. So proud.

The doorbell was ringing. Elinor jumped, wondered uneasily how long it had been ringing. Her hearing wasn't what it used to be. Sometimes the phone would ring and she wouldn't hear it and Warren would just sit in his chair with that blank look on his face as though he didn't know what the noise was. Drove Katie crazy when she was trying to call them. Katie got miffed with *her* because she wouldn't get a hearing aid, instead of blaming Warren.

Rocky was going crazy, leaping at the door and yapping an alarm. Elinor raised her voice to him but it didn't do any good. Katie said it was a good thing he barked when somebody came to the door, for protection. Elinor swatted him with the rolled-up newspaper she always kept handy, and he stopped barking and sat down on his haunches, growling. Elinor said, "Good boy."

She smoothed her hair, wished she'd put on lipstick,

was glad she'd gotten dressed right away instead of sitting around in her robe for a while the way she used to like to do. Holding Rocky by the collar, she reached up and opened the door with the other hand.

There stood Warren. Relief and anger made Elinor's eyes burn. Behind him was a tall girl about Katie's age, in a business suit. Elinor thought again about her dirty kitchen floor.

The minute he saw her, Warren burst into tears. "I was *lost*!" he wailed, and shakily held out his arms to her like a child come home. Elinor was mortified. A grown man.

For a second she didn't know what to do. She tried telling herself that this wasn't her husband. She smiled apologetically at the woman and said, "Oh, how nice of you. Please come in. Would you like a cup of coffee?" She did wish she'd mopped the floor again this morning, first thing. Rocky, still growling but also wagging his tail now, twisted in her grasp.

"You're okay now, sir," the woman was telling Warren. She had his elbow and was helping him over the threshold. Elinor knew he could do it himself if he just kept his mind on what he was doing; he didn't need a stranger helping him like that. To Elinor she said huffily, "I found him sitting on the curb in front of my house, four blocks away. I was just on my way to work."

"You hear that, Warren?" Elinor scolded at once, almost eagerly. "You made this lady late for her work." Still sniffing, Warren nodded, but Elinor could tell he didn't know what she was talking about. The girl was frowning and shaking her head. Elinor rushed on. "Let me put the dog out so we can visit. He gets *so* excited! Warren, for heaven's sake, why don't you offer your guest a seat."

Glad to escape for a minute or two, but nervous about

having somebody she didn't know in her house (she'd been after Warren for weeks to straighten that picture for her, and there were dog footprints all over the kitchen floor), she took Rocky outside and put him on his chain. He whined and set his feet so she had to drag him, and he looked up at her as if she'd broken his heart. Between the two of them, Warren and Rocky, she was about to lose her mind.

Hurrying back inside, she noticed that Warren had left one slipper in the hall by the bathroom door. Just left it there for her to pick up. He was so lazy anymore. She'd always been able to say that Warren wasn't like other men, he would pick up after himself. Not now.

Elinor didn't think the woman could see the slipper from where she was standing, but she couldn't shake the dreadful thought that she might have. It would have been better if he'd left both slippers out; just the one looked so pitiful, so old-man senile. She made a hasty detour to retrieve it and put it in the bedroom closet, on his side where it belonged. The whole time, she worried about what in the world he'd done with the other one. Last week he'd put his dentures in the china cabinet and she like to never found them.

Warren hadn't sat down. She'd told him to sit down. Neither had the girl. Warren was still standing by the front door. He hadn't bothered to shut it, and the sunshine made a white rectangle in the dark wall so that everything was blurry. Silhouetted like that, Warren was bent like an old-fashioned bobby pin, elbows and knees crooked as if he'd been about to do something and had forgotten what it was. He did that all the time.

The girl was leaning over the kitchen table, writing something. Elinor's heart sank when she saw that her coffee cup was still there. The girl looked up and said, obviously put out, "I'm your neighbor."

She was talking in a loud voice and pronouncing her words very carefully. It always bothered Elinor to think that people could tell she was a little hard-of-hearing. That was why she wouldn't wear a hearing aid.

The woman said her name, which Elinor had to admit she didn't quite catch. "Here's my card. I've written my home phone number on the back. Can you see that, Mrs. Dietrich?"

Elinor accepted the card, hesitated, turned it over. In her day, no women and not very many men had had business cards. The phone number on the back was big and black. Of course she could see it. There was nothing wrong with her eyes.

"Please don't hesitate to call me if there's anything I can do," the girl was saying. "After all, we are neighbors."

Elinor would, of course, never dream of bothering her, wouldn't even bother Katie unless she absolutely had to. Of all things, would never call a number on a business card. But it wouldn't do to say so. She smiled politely and said, "Thank you. That's very kind of you." She squinted at the much smaller italicized printing on the front of the card that anybody would have trouble reading and she couldn't quite make out the name there. Not wanting to make a mistake, she didn't try to say the woman's name, although it would have been a lot more polite. She just said again, "That's very nice of you. But my daughter does live nearby. By the way, where are my manners, my name is Elinor Dietrich and this is my husband Warren."

The girl nodded and smiled at Warren, who was staring blankly at Elinor the way he did that like to drove her crazy. The girl was looking at him fondly, as if they were friends. As if, because she'd helped him, now she thought she had some kind of special interest in him, some kind of claim. Elinor didn't like that. "Oh, yes," the woman gushed. "Mr. Dietrich and I had quite a nice little chat, didn't we, Mr. Dietrich? He was able to tell me his name and to spell it for me, so then we could look up your address in the phone book. He doesn't have any ID with him, did you know that?"

As if that was *her* fault. Elinor hoped it didn't show that she was insulted. She'd told him and told him to keep his wallet on him whenever he left the house. She'd *told* him not to leave the house without her. And she didn't for one minute believe that he couldn't remember his own address. Why, they'd lived here a good thirty-five years. She didn't understand why he'd be pretending like this, but she did not believe he really could not remember the place where he'd lived for most of their married life. Lived with *her*.

After the girl left—promising to drop by and visit them every once in a while, which Elinor did *not* want her to do—Elinor just went about her business and left Warren standing there. Except that she couldn't completely ignore him, she had to keep an eye on him or he'd do some other fool thing that would call attention to them or make more work for her.

She went back to the kitchen, put the kettle on for coffee, got the cereal out, poured the juice. "You work too hard," Warren said from right behind her, and she jumped and almost backed into him and spilled the milk out of the bowls.

She wasn't working hard *now*. All she was doing was getting breakfast. All those years when she *had* worked too hard—raised a child, kept house, pressed his six starched white shirts every Saturday—he hadn't bothered to say anything then. "Sit down and eat your breakfast," she told him wearily, with a pang of tenderness and regret that she did not want to be feeling.

He looked as if he didn't know what "breakfast" was. That blank look on his face absolutely infuriated her, like when he was too lazy to put his teeth in and the bottom half of his face sank. He stood there, nervously rubbing his fingertips together, sucking his teeth, shifting his weight from one foot to the other.

"Sit *down*!" she snapped and, like a sad, scolded child, he did. In the wrong chair, not in his chair, but that was just to aggravate her and she wasn't going to give him the satisfaction of letting him know that it did.

"Elinor?" he asked in a worried voice. "Is something—? Have I—?"

She put her hands on her hips and glared at him. Over the years she'd learned how to stand up for herself. "How dare you say those awful things to me, Warren Dietrich? Who do you think you are, talking to me like that?"

He tried to stare at her, but his gaze couldn't quite find her face. On purpose, she didn't make it any easier for him, didn't move closer or into better light. "I didn't—" he started to say.

Elinor could be merciless. Sometimes you had to be. "You said you didn't know who I was. You said I wasn't your *wife*, Warren, after all these years. You said you didn't care a damn about me, and you didn't trust me. You said you didn't care a damn about anybody in the world except Katie."

"Katie?" he asked, vaguely, not exactly like asking a question about Katie but more like repeating a word he didn't recognize. "I don't—I—"

This man who had wanted to be a poet when he was young, who used to write long, elegant letters to the editor about the Vietnam War and Communism and prayer in schools—things Elinor never had cared much about, but she'd been proud of the letters, proud of the words—this man who used to think he won all their arguments just because he was smarter than she was and knew more big words and it never dawned on him that most of the time she just went ahead and did what she wanted to do anyway—now more often than not he couldn't find the right word. He'd come up to a word in a sentence he was trying to say—a simple word: "banana" or "tired"—and not be able to say it. Every day he lost more words, more ideas, more knowledge. He couldn't remember the names of everyday things: clock, newspaper, dog, wife. He couldn't understand anymore how things worked. He couldn't figure out what one thing had to do with another thing—what the sound of ringing had to do with answering the phone, what eating properly had to do with keeping his health, what his daughter Katie had to do with him.

"You're the most wonderful woman in the world," he said clearly. "I don't know what I'd do without you."

Elinor looked at Warren across the sunny morning room, and he was a stranger. This was not the man she'd spent over half her life learning to live with. This was not the man she'd planned on growing old with. That Warren was as good as dead. This one was a stranger in her house and in her heart.

And, she admitted unwillingly, he wasn't doing these things to annoy her or embarrass her or hurt her. The old Warren might have. The old Warren had always been quick to take offense and to strike back, and often he'd sulked for days at a time. She'd learned when to ignore him and when to humor him to bring him out of it, and she'd passed that skill on to her daughter, who didn't want it. The old Warren had said to her half a dozen times over the years that he never should have gotten married, he'd never wanted to get married in the first place but she'd trapped him into it, and that was when

Elinor would hide out behind the garage with her apron over her head rather than let him have the satisfaction of seeing her cry.

She stared at this stranger, this frail and befuddled Warren, and she didn't *want* him here. "I—I love you, Elinor," he managed to tell her. "I'm sorry. I—"

She didn't wait for him to find whatever word he was looking for this time, and she didn't supply it for him. Without a word she took his breakfast to him where he was sitting in the wrong chair. He looked up at her pleadingly, but she paid him no attention.

Then she went out back to get Rocky, who was yipping like crazy. She shouldn't leave Warren alone but she did, left him sitting there with his bowl of cornflakes tilting in his lap as if he didn't know what to do with it, and his spoon in his left hand (he was right-handed), obviously a foreign object, sticking straight up in the air.

Rocky wrapped his chain around her ankles and almost knocked her down. She yelled at him because it scared her. What would she do, what would become of Warren, if she fell out here and broke a hip? How long would it be before he finally figured out that something was wrong?

Finally she managed to untangle herself and unhook Rocky's chain. The little dog raced around and around the yard, making Elinor chuckle in spite of herself, so obviously delighted to be free that Elinor felt guilty for chaining him in the first place. Then he came and flung himself at her feet.

She sank onto one of the patio chairs and gingerly leaned back. A whole flock of birds was chirping in the big tree; she was pleased, vindicated, that she could hear them. There was no sound from her house, and no lights were on. It might as well be empty.

Elinor allowed herself to sit there for a few minutes in the gathering morning, petting Rocky and remembering:

Warren looking dapper in his pale gray suit and pale blue shirt, lightly starched. Both the suit and the shirt had needed careful pressing.

Warren coming in for lunch smelling of garden dirt and man's sweat. She'd liked that smell. She'd told him to go wash his hands.

Warren wanting to do things in bed that even now she couldn't think about. When she'd refused, he'd sulked, and Katie—no more than five or six years old—had asked, as she'd often asked, "What's wrong with Daddy? Is Daddy mad at me?" Elinor had answered, as usual, "I don't know," although that time she did know very well.

Elinor roused herself. Rocky was nuzzling her hand. Warren, or the old man who passed for Warren, was in the house by himself. She didn't have her watch on so she didn't know how long she'd been out here, but the sky was noticeably lighter and there was more activity in the neighborhood—kids on their way to school, adults going to work. It didn't bother Elinor in the slightest not to be part of such things anymore.

She got up stiffly and took a minute to critically survey the yard, garage, patio, sidewalk, back of the house. The grass needed mowing. Warren's "job"—she snorted to think of it—had been to hold the lawn mower cord up out of her way. Instead he'd all of a sudden taken it into his head to unplug it. Said *he* did the yard work, he'd always done the yard work. She didn't know what she was doing. Who the hell did she think she was, anyway, taking over his job?

Then said this was *his* house, *he* owned this house, and he didn't want her here anymore.

Then said he didn't live here, they didn't live here, this wasn't their house. Elinor, Elinor, what happened to their house? Where had she put him? That wasn't a lawn mower, lawn mowers didn't have electrical cords, did she think he was a fool?

He wasn't going to let her touch that thing. He tugged on the cord and, to her amazement, was strong enough to pull it partway out of the machine.

He was going home. She couldn't keep him here. His wife would be worried about him. He was going home.

Elinor had argued with him a long time that day, more and more heatedly. She'd blocked his way so he couldn't leave, thinking for a minute that he was going to hit her, but he didn't. When he'd dropped the cord, forgotten all about it, she couldn't fix it, of course, and she'd be too embarrassed to hire anyone else, they'd just have to buy a new mower, waste the money. She'd sputtered, cursed, even cried in frustration, and finally she'd *made* him come to his senses and behave.

Katie said she shouldn't do that. Both Katie and the doctor said that arguing with somebody with Alzheimer's would only make things worse. But Elinor was not going to let him get away with treating her like that. A woman had to stand up for herself.

Now she noticed two places where the fence was sagging back toward the alley side of the yard. She'd tell Warren to fix it.

The patio was a mess. She'd swept it just yesterday afternoon. She'd have to get after it again today, couldn't let it stay this way. She sighed. So much to do. So many things to keep in her head.

Rocky had run ahead of her and was sitting expectantly by the door, wriggling all over and looking back over his shoulder. It was time for his breakfast, and Elinor was a little hungry herself. She never got very hungry anymore, and oftentimes she'd just as soon not eat, but you had to eat right to keep up your strength. She kept telling Warren that, but most times he hardly ate a thing. Inside the house, the phone was ringing, she thought, and Warren wasn't answering it. She reached for the doorknob.

The door wouldn't open.

It must be stuck. She tugged. Rocky gave a series of little jumps toward her hand, thinking she was playing. She scolded him and tugged again. There must be something wrong with the mechanism. Something *else* it was Warren's job to fix, but she knew full-well he wouldn't.

Increasingly irritated, having to go to the bathroom now and definitely hearing the phone, Elinor rattled the knob, and realized with a sinking heart that the door was locked.

For a minute, she couldn't bring herself to believe it.

Then she saw Warren through the sunroom window, clutching the key ring in both hands. Obviously, at the moment, he knew what keys were. He was staring at her with a look of utter terror and fury on his face, as if she were a stranger trying to break into his house.

Elinor rapped sharply on the pane, even though she already had his attention. She gestured and mouthed for him to open the door *this minute*. He took one last panic-stricken look at her and backed away. Helpless to stop him, helpless even to communicate with him, Elinor watched as he turned around—swaying; she thought he would fall, and then what would he do? what would she do?—and hobbled into the living room, where she couldn't see him anymore.

Now she couldn't hear the phone, and she wondered if the person had given up or if Warren had answered it. Sometimes he would say, "Hello?" and just stand there, not knowing what to say next, until she went over and snatched the receiver out of his hand.

Not wanting to make a scene, she said but did not shout his name. "War-*ren*."

Then she made her way as fast as she could, which wasn't very fast, around the end of the house, through the gate that she had to be careful to shut because sometimes the latch slipped and she didn't know how to fix it. She guessed she could learn, but that was Warren's job.

She stooped to pick up an empty potato chip bag that had blown into their yard, muttering to herself about inconsiderate young people, where were their manners, didn't their parents teach them any respect for other people's property? She noted again how ragged the hedge was looking and vowed she'd say something to Warren about it, again. But the last time he'd gone out to trim it, she'd watched through the window over the sink how gingerly he'd handled the clippers and, afraid he'd hurt himself or do something awful to the hedge, she'd finally stormed out and taken them away from him.

At the time, it hadn't crossed her mind that he might use them as a weapon and do something to her. Now, she had to wonder.

The front door was locked, too.

Frantic with frustration, Elinor stamped her foot. There was a painful lump in her throat. She tried the doorknob again and knocked on the door. It was *locked*.

Katie would be here to pick them up and Elinor didn't have them ready. She took a step or two sideways and peered in the living room window through the narrow gap between the drapes. That looked sloppy; drapes should always be drawn with a bit of an overlap so that no streak of light showed through. Elinor wondered how she could have missed something like that.

She could just see Warren. He'd sat himself down, in the right chair this time, but he didn't look as if he belonged there. He looked as if he'd forgotten how to sit in

a rocking chair altogether. His shoulders were kind of
hunched up and his hands were limp in his lap, and he
was staring at the floor. He wasn't looking back at her.
She knew he knew she was there, even though she was
trying not to be obvious to anybody else, trying not to
make a fuss about having to stand on tiptoe and peek in
her own front window at her own husband, who had
locked her out.

She rapped once sharply on the glass. He didn't look
up. As far as she could tell, he didn't have the keys. In
despair, Elinor wondered what he could have done with
them.

She was swept with a hatred for him that made her
weak and dizzy. She *hated* him, this stranger in her
home, this interloper. He might as well be a robber come
to steal her heirlooms, or an arsonist intent on burning
the house to the ground. She didn't know this man, and
she didn't want to know him, and she didn't want him
here.

Warren had left her, was what it came down to. She'd
thought she was long past having to worry about that,
and now she had to handle everything by herself because Warren, damn him, had left her as surely as if he'd
run off with another woman.

Holding on to the shutter to keep her balance while
she tried to step out of the flower bed onto the grass
without getting too much mud on her shoes, Elinor
missed him, *missed* her husband, in a rapid succession
of images:

Her husband, working long summer hours in the garden and so pleased whenever somebody called his place
a garden spot. In particular, Elinor remembered peach
and lavender gladiolas, and blueberries.

Her husband, meticulously planning for their future
with ledgers and portfolios, sudden phone calls to stock-

brokers and long sessions at their kitchen table with financial planners. Elinor had kept the books and papers in order, but she'd never even tried to understand all the transactions. He didn't want them to have to worry about money, he'd always said. If something should happen to him, he didn't want her to worry.

Her husband, who'd always been so intelligent, who could have gone to college if he hadn't graduated from high school in the middle of the Depression, who'd always wanted so much to go to college that he was still talking about it while Katie was growing up. He used to love to "discuss" things—the economy, the space program, nuclear war, the drug problem—that Elinor had no real opinion about and didn't care to, which was fine with him because "discussing" meant she let him carry on and she nodded and said, "Uh huh" and "Oh, I see" just often enough to make him think she was paying attention, while really her mind was on more important things, like making Katie's prom dress, or starting a letter to her sister in her head. Over the years they'd passed many a pleasant evening in each other's company that way.

Now, she went out of her way to find things in the paper or on the news that might interest Warren. "Did you hear what the President said about taxes?" she'd say, trying to sound indignant. Or, "They've discovered another planet out beyond Pluto, did you see that?" and only recently had she learned what Pluto was.

He wouldn't discuss anything anymore. His face never lit up. The other day she'd overheard him say to Katie, "You know, your mother's mind has actually improved since she's gotten older. Mine has gotten—worse, but hers has actually improved," and Elinor had thought her heart would break.

Trembling now with helpless anger, standing there in

broad daylight on her own front stoop, Elinor didn't know what she was going to do.

"Mom?"

Elinor half turned and, too late, shielded her eyes against the glare of the sun on the pavement. Katie was hurrying up the walk and Rocky, yapping, ran to meet her, couldn't stop, shot past her before he got himself turned around and shot past her again in the opposite direction. Elinor almost chuckled. She had the distinct impression that her daughter was putting on weight, and was somewhat calmed by the everyday irritation of the thought.

Katie was talking fast and too loud; the neighbors would hear. "I tried to call you to tell you I was on my way, but there wasn't any answer. You have *got* to get a hearing aid, Mom. Are you ready? Where's Dad? What are you doing out here?"

"Your father says he doesn't care a damn about me," Elinor informed her huffily, and then, to her horror, burst into tears.

Katie stared at her for a second or two, then came and put her arms around her. Elinor held herself rigid and struggled for control. "He *said* that?" Katie demanded.

"He said he didn't know who I was, and he didn't trust me, and the only person he cared a damn about was his daughter Katie." *You always were your daddy's girl,* Elinor thought fiercely. She didn't say it out loud, but she did pull away.

"Oh, Mom, I'm sorry."

Elinor shushed her. "Keep your voice down."

Katie glanced around and said, in a voice only a little quieter, "What do you care who hears? He's sick. He has Alzheimer's disease. It's nothing to be ashamed of."

Elinor took off her glasses and wiped her eyes. She

took a deep breath so she could say clearly, "Now he's locked me out of the house."

Katie smiled a little and held up her key ring. "We'll fix him. I have my key to your house right here."

She unlocked the front door without any fuss and politely stood back to let her mother go in first. Afraid of what she'd find, Elinor didn't want to go in. But she did, and there was nothing unusual at all. Warren was sitting in his chair awkwardly, as if he didn't know what a chair was, or sitting. His half-empty cereal bowl was barely balanced on his craggy knees, and he held his spoon straight up like a lollipop; she could see the milk drooling down his wrist and could tell from the look on his face that he didn't like it but he didn't know what to do about it.

With obvious effort, he brought his gaze around to focus on Elinor. She knew when he found her and when, a split second later, he recognized her, because his fretful face folded into a childish grin and he asked, "Could I have—" He couldn't think of the word. She knew he wanted orange juice, but she would not say it for him. She clenched her fists, so furious that she didn't dare say anything to him in front of Katie. If they'd been alone, she'd have happily given him a piece of her mind.

Katie put a hand on her shoulder. "Mom, why don't you finish packing, and I'll get Daddy's juice for him? Then he can get ready."

Elinor didn't want her daughter doing things for her that she was perfectly capable of doing for herself, and she didn't like Katie's attitude that came with it—watchful, too bright.

But she was more than glad not to have anything more to do with Warren right now. She stalked into the bedroom, pretending she didn't hear him when he said part of her name.

There was a strong, sharp odor in the room. Her nostrils flared and her eyes stung, and a bad taste lodged at the back of her tongue. Urine. She turned on the light and searched quickly, gingerly, for his soaked clothes. It wouldn't be the first time he'd left soaked pajamas or shorts on the floor for her to take care of.

Then she realized with a sinking heart that the odor was coming from the open suitcase on the bed. Right away she knew what he'd done. He'd gone to the bathroom *in the suitcase.* Her socks and underwear, neatly folded in one corner, were saturated, and the suitcase itself reeked.

In a rage now, Elinor slammed the bag shut, latched it, and lugged it into the laundry room, where she sorted the colors from the whites and started a load. Then she stormed back into the living room to inform her daughter what he'd done, and that now they couldn't leave until the laundry was done.

Interrupting her, Warren got up out of his chair with Katie's help and started coming toward her. "Elinor," he croaked, and the look on his face was appalled. "Elinor, I —She says—I'm *sorry.*"

In all the years they'd been together, he'd never once apologized to her, until the last few months. Now there was something every day, sometimes a dozen times a day, that he was sorry for. She didn't want him to be sorry. She just wanted him to *stop.*

It wasn't hard to stay out of his reach. Katie said, "Mom," reproachfully, but Elinor just talked over her, told her in no uncertain terms what her father had done this time. Then she turned her back on both of them, putting herself out of earshot, and made herself another cup of instant coffee that she didn't really want.

Thanks to Warren, it was after noon before they finally got out of there.

Warren sat up front with Katie. Elinor resented having to ride in back, but she was glad to be behind him where he couldn't stare at her all the time. He couldn't figure out how to use his seatbelt. He fumbled, muttering, his neck bent thin and old under his gray fedora. Elinor tried not to watch as Katie leaned across the seat to help her father.

You could tell from behind that there was something wrong with him. His posture was slack. His shoulders were thin and sharp. His head in the hat like the hats he'd always worn looked too big for his neck, and never once turned to one side or the other to look at anything they passed.

Elinor didn't try to talk. She wouldn't be able to hear what Katie or Warren said back anyway, and she was put out with them both. She sat back and watched the city thin out as they entered the foothills, watched the foothills sharpen and deepen into mountains, and remembered against her will how Warren used to look in a car.

He had loved to drive. She never had, and he'd never completely trusted her behind the wheel, so almost always he'd been the driver. She'd sit beside him in the passenger seat, crocheting or singing with Katie when Katie was little, or fretting about getting everything settled once they reached their destination. At least once every trip he'd get mad because he'd miss a turn and she hadn't told him it was coming up—not that he'd asked her to—but mostly she could just ride and feel that she was in good hands.

Now she had to drive wherever they went. Which wasn't very many places or very far—to the grocery store, to the bank. The last couple of times he'd tried to drive he couldn't even get the keys in the ignition. Elinor didn't like driving. It wasn't her job. Traffic got worse every day.

She sat in the corner of the back seat directly behind Warren, in what she hoped would be his blind spot if he took it into his head that he wanted to see her. She let herself relax a little. If Warren did something foolish now, Katie could just handle it for once, see for herself what kind of man her father had turned into.

The undecipherable sounds of Katie trying to carry on a conversation with Warren in the front seat irritated her. The classical music on the radio, which Katie probably had on to appeal to the old folks, just made Elinor nervous. For a while, she kept going over and over the preparations for the trip: Had she packed the aspirin for when Warren got one of his headaches? Yes. Had she brought both warm and cool clothes for both of them, because you couldn't predict the weather in the mountains? Yes, and probably this year he wouldn't complain that she'd brought the wrong shirts; probably this year he wouldn't even notice if he was too warm or too cold. Had she given the next-door neighbor instructions for taking care of Rocky? Yes, and she would still worry. Had she made arrangements for the paper to be stopped? Her heart sank. No, she hadn't. She was getting as bad as Warren. The thought made her sick to her stomach. She frowned and told herself it didn't matter about the paper, they were only going to be gone a week. But she kept thinking about the neighbors watching the papers pile up and saying they didn't know how much longer the little old Dietrich couple would be able to take care of themselves.

Gradually, though, Elinor drifted into memories of other trips to the cabin. They'd gone every autumn without fail because that was the best time of year in the high country, and many years they'd gone spring and summer, too. Warren, especially, had loved the cabin. At some ages Katie had enjoyed it, too; at others, she'd pronounced it boring, and she'd stopped going once she got out of high school. Elinor had regarded it as mostly more work, more things to worry about—another set of cupboards to organize, another bathroom to clean, the paper to stop and start again. She'd always been relieved when cabin season was over, though one year Warren had actually talked her into going up in the *winter*.

But now, knowing that this would probably be their last time, Elinor was sad. And mad at Warren for taking something else away from her. And awash in memories that proved how much she would miss coming up here and how it was Warren's fault.

They stopped in Idaho Springs for Warren to go to the bathroom. Unless she hadn't heard it, he hadn't said he had to go, and Elinor resented it a little that Katie had noticed something about him that she hadn't.

She didn't have to go. She'd stay in the car. Katie took Warren into the men's room at the service station. Neither one of them seemed embarrassed. Elinor was embarrassed and couldn't watch, turned her head against the seat and dozed off.

They were gone a long time. The sun through the windows was hot. She needed to stretch her legs. Sudden pressure in her bladder warned her that she'd better not wait much longer to find a restroom herself. She was worried about Warren and about whether Katie could take care of him right.

A little stiffly, she got out of the car into the crisp, thin air. For long moments she puzzled over whether to lock the car doors, getting more and more irritated with her daughter for not telling her. Finally she reasoned that since Katie had taken her purse she must have her keys, and she went around the car and carefully locked all four doors.

She paused to gaze at the mountainside across the

highway, deep green with patches of brilliant gold under the brilliant blue sky, and to mourn that she would most likely never see such a sight again. Then she turned and hurried across the gravel parking lot toward the side of the yellow building where the RESTROOMS sign hung. The soles of her tennis shoes rolled and crunched on the gravel, and her eyes squinted against the glare.

There was Warren, walking briskly toward her, alone. Katie must have gone to the restroom herself, or gone in to pay for gas. Bright sunshine on the white gravel made him no more than a silhouette, gray in the middle and rainbowed around the edges. But it was his dignified walk, the erect way he'd always held himself, the square angles of his shoulders, and the way he always looked just over her head although he wasn't that much taller than she was.

Of course she knew him. They'd been married for forty-three years. Through it all, she'd never doubted his love, or her own.

"Warren," she said, and was close to tears. She felt the way she used to feel sometimes when he'd come home from the afternoon shift and she'd still be ironing or canning. Glad to see him. Tired. A little nervous because she'd been alone. A little sad because she'd been missing him. Refreshed by the time to herself. And so glad he was home.

He said her name, and his voice was the way it had been before the Alzheimer's—controlled, sure of itself, cool. He said, "Come with me."

At first she thought he'd forgotten they were in Idaho Springs on their way to the cabin, and she was fiercely disappointed, as though he'd come home after a long absence and then right away left again.

But then he said, "No, not with him. With *me*."

"Mom?"

A hand came onto her arm at the same instant that she heard the word. Elinor jumped and turned, almost falling as the gravel slid under her soles. She had the distinct impression, as she often did, that things had been being said long before she'd heard them (that was so *rude*), and she was not going to keep asking her own daughter to repeat things. She glared at Katie, close-up, and then at Warren on Katie's arm, shuffling and bewildered.

"Mom, is something wrong?"

"No, why?" Elinor risked a glance back over her shoulder. The other Warren wasn't there. Resolutely, she did not allow herself to think about what would happen if they *both* got senile. She shook off her daughter's hand. "For heaven's sake, Katie," she snapped. "I just have to go to the ladies' room, that's all," and then she trudged across the parking lot by herself, resolutely not thinking about what it might mean that she was seeing and hearing ghosts.

The highway took them past Dumont and Berthoud Falls, little mountain towns Elinor had noticed every trip off to the side of the road. They'd never had much to do with her. Now she found herself thinking that nobody in those towns had a husband with Alzheimer's who didn't even know them after forty-three years of marriage. Sternly, she made herself stop thinking that.

The mountainside behind Dumont was so breathtakingly lovely that Katie pulled off the road. "Look, Daddy," she urged. "Look at that hillside. Right there. Isn't it *beautiful*? The dark green pines and the golden aspen and the bright blue sky and the silver waterfalls? *Look,* Daddy." Finally she had to put her fingertips under his chin and turn his head herself to get him to look in the right direction. His face did light up; Elinor saw it, too. But as soon as Katie took her hand away, his head swung randomly and he lost the view again.

Warren had taught both of them to notice the physical beauty in the world. Elinor remembered him kneeling beside Katie to show her the soft black inside of a red tulip. Pulling her to a stop on a Philadelphia sidewalk to smell the fragrance of lilacs that seemed headier at twilight than at any other time. Gazing for hours on end through his small red telescope at the stars and the moon, which Elinor—even when he'd half crouched close behind her and put both arms around her to adjust the eyepiece for her and the white moon with its black-and-gray craters had suddenly swum into view—had privately thought you could see perfectly well with what he disparagingly called "the naked eye."

"Let's *go*," Elinor ordered her daughter. "At this rate it'll be next week before we get there." She made her way back to the car by herself and, grimly impatient, waited while they came, much more slowly.

"Sit up front with me, Mom," Katie invited. "So we can talk." Startled, Elinor hesitated. It always made her nervous when Katie wanted to talk. Katie said to her father, "You don't mind, do you, Daddy?" and he shook his head, but of course he didn't have the vaguest idea what he was being asked.

If she'd refused to sit up front, it would have required an explanation and Elinor wasn't up to it. So she buckled herself into the passenger seat while Katie got Warren settled in the back seat. Now she thought of all sorts of things she could have said: she wanted to take a nap. Warren got carsick if he didn't ride in front. But it was too late. Katie fastened her father's seatbelt, patted his knee, and got in behind the steering wheel.

"It's nice to be traveling this road again," Katie said with a happy sigh. "Lots of good memories up here."

"Be the last time," Elinor declared.

Katie glanced at her. "Why do you say that?"

Elinor snorted and jerked her head toward the back seat. "Why, with him the way he is?"

"Daddy can still enjoy things. In fact, I think he enjoys things more than he used to. He's not so—defended." There was a pause. When Elinor didn't say anything, Katie went on. Obviously she'd been saving this up, waiting for a time she could say it. Elinor didn't like that. She didn't see any point in talking about unpleasant things. "He's also a lot more loving. Have you noticed that? All my life I've never heard him say he loved you or me, and now it's as if he can't say it enough."

"That isn't love." Elinor didn't *want* to be talking about this, and she resented her daughter for trapping her into it. "That isn't even *him*."

"Sure, it is. It's who he is now."

Elinor lowered her voice until, as far as she could tell, it was almost a whisper. "It's not the man I married. It's not the man I want."

Katie nodded. She checked the rearview mirror. From the back seat Elinor heard Warren snore. "I know it's hard. You two have been married for over forty years—"

"Forty-three," Elinor snapped.

"—and now you've lost the man you knew as your husband. He's changed. He's changed so much it's almost as if he died."

Worse, Elinor thought. *If he died, you could be done with it.* She shivered and wrapped her sweater around herself, thankful that she had made it bulky and oversized. She didn't say anything. There wasn't anything to say. Deliberately she set her mind to planning the supper they'd have tonight, their first night in the cabin. She'd brought chicken salad for sandwiches. When Warren would eat anything, he'd usually eat chicken salad.

Katie was silent, too, and Elinor hoped she would drop the subject now. They went around the switchback that always, after all these years, made Elinor nervous, and then the road narrowed and climbed steeply. "Do you want to put him in a nursing home?" Katie asked. Quietly, gently, but it was a sneak attack, and Elinor heard.

She was insulted. "Katharyn Dietrich, he's your *father*."

"He's also your husband. That doesn't mean you have to sacrifice your life for him. You seem so tense and unhappy. And so angry all the time."

"I'm fine." She thought she heard Warren stirring. She turned around in her seat as far as the belt would let her, but he was sitting in the blind spot directly behind her and she couldn't see him. It hurt her neck to turn like that.

"The thing is, Mom," Katie said, "the man who's here now is Warren Dietrich as much as the other man was. And I think you're missing an opportunity to know and love this one because you won't let go of the one who's gone."

That made no sense at all to Elinor. She was saved from having to say anything by Warren himself, who said carefully, "*I'm* Warren Dietrich. That much I know."

Katie chuckled and said loudly, "That's right, Daddy. You are. And there's nobody in the whole world like you." Elinor turned her head to the window and watched as the pine woods closed in.

They stopped again in Frazier—"Icebox of the Nation" until the town had sold the nickname to Great Falls, Montana, but it was still cold—and ate lunch at the Kentucky Fried Chicken. Elinor thought they should have packed a picnic lunch and waited till they got to the cabin to eat it; no sense wasting money and time. But Katie insisted, reminding Elinor—as if she'd forget a thing like that—how fond Warren was of Colonel San-

ders, how they'd teased him about it because it had been
so out of character. For as long as Katie could remember,
they'd stopped for lunch at the Frazier KFC on every trip
to and from the cabin.

This time, of course, he had no idea where they were.
Elinor just hoped he didn't make a scene.

Katie and her father stood in line while Elinor found a
table, which didn't take much doing because there was
hardly anybody else in the place. Head high, she looked
around, ready to meet anyone's gaze and smile her polite
smile so they wouldn't think something was wrong with
her, but the bald man in the opposite corner didn't look
up from his newspaper, the old woman silhouetted by
the windows looked to be just kind of staring off into
space, and the three teenagers in the back booth were
leaning close to each other and having an animated conversation that Elinor didn't care to hear. They were
laughing loudly; maybe they were laughing at Warren.

Floor-to-ceiling windows on three sides of the restaurant gave a spectacular wraparound view of the mountains. Elinor couldn't imagine why you'd want a view in a
fast-food place. It was cold in here because of all the
glass. You could actually see that the air was thinner up
here—not just clearer, but visibly thinner; Warren had
pointed that out to her more times than she could count,
and now she couldn't get it out of her mind.

She chose a booth that looked more or less clean.
Before she sat down, she wiped the seat off with a napkin, then wiped the table off; she didn't know what to
do with the handful of crumbs she'd collected, finally
walked self-consciously across the room to deposit them
in the trash can by the door. She saw that Katie was
ordering. She saw Warren's blank face and sagging shoulders and twitching fingertips.

When she'd settled herself into the booth, she looked

up and saw Warren sitting across from her, sipping a vanilla milk shake. Elinor remembered how Katie, then eleven or twelve, had pestered him until he'd tried one, and he'd loved vanilla shakes ever since. It wasn't like him to have such a fondness for food. He'd never have *said* he liked vanilla shakes but he ordered one every time.

"Notice how the air even *looks* thinner up here?" he said.

Elinor squinted at him. It had been a long time since he'd spoken like that. "Yes," she experimented. "And what causes that, again?"

An old ploy. He would be pleased to explain the same things to her over and over and, if she didn't pay too close attention in the first place, she could stand it. This time, though, she was paying attention, not so much to what he said as how.

Clearly, with the old intelligence, he said, "The gravitational pull of the earth decreases as you get further away from the core. So there aren't as many molecules of atmosphere per cubic foot." Or something like that. She didn't know what it meant and didn't much care, but Warren acted as though he knew.

Wanting desperately to keep him like this, Elinor struggled for just the right thing to say. "It sure is pretty up here," was the best she could come up with.

He was frowning slightly. Even in the glare from all the windows that made his features fuzzy, she recognized that expression, although it had been a while since she'd seen it. "We'll go to a valley I've discovered where it's even more beautiful," he said, as usual not asking but informing.

She bristled. "What are you talking about now? We're going to the cabin."

"Here's the food." Katie's too-cheery voice startled

Elinor. She jumped and looked over her shoulder. For a moment she couldn't see for the glare, and she was afraid she hadn't really heard her daughter. Then she made out the styrofoam plate Katie had set in front of her with chicken nuggets, mashed potatoes, and cole-slaw on it, and Katie bustling with plates and napkins and plasticware on a paper-covered tray, and Warren standing beside Katie, staring blankly at a point in the middle distance where there was nothing to stare at, and rubbing his fingertips together.

Katie raised her voice and started to repeat, "Mom, here's your—" and Elinor cut her off, "Yes, yes, I *heard* you." When she repositioned herself to let them into the booth, she had to admit that nobody had been sitting opposite her, nobody had been talking to her.

Warren—slack-jawed again, anxious, sucking his teeth —finally managed to make Katie understand that he didn't drink those things anymore (he meant milkshakes) because they clogged his throat. He tried to get started again describing the phlegm that collected in his throat, but, thankfully, he couldn't organize enough words. He just frowned and pushed his milkshake away, almost spilling it before Katie caught it.

Elinor sighed and tried to catch her daughter's eye so the two of them could exchange a knowing glance, but Katie was watching her father and not her. The girl looked disappointed, the way she'd often looked, even as a grown woman, when she'd tried to please her father and it hadn't worked. Warren had always been a hard man to please, especially if he knew you were trying to.

But now he looked up, reached across the table, and patted Katie's hand. Katie smiled at him. "Thank you for getting it for me," he said softly. Elinor couldn't believe it, and she shuddered at how strange it was. Hastily, for something to do, she picked up the milkshake and tasted

it, didn't like it, and made a face and set it down again.
Katie didn't notice.

Warren made almost no sense at all during the entire
meal. He didn't seem to know who Katie was, although
he was pleasant and polite to her; he kept asking her
questions out of the blue, such as where had she grown
up and what was Paul Carroll doing these days. Paul Carroll was a boyhood friend; even Elinor hadn't known
him. Meaning to defend her daughter, Elinor scolded,
"Warren, for heaven's sake, she wasn't even *born* when
you knew Paul Carroll. How could she be?" But Katie
shook her head and put her finger to her lips, as if *Elinor*
had done something wrong, and Warren just looked confused.

While Katie was fussing with her father to get him out
of the restaurant, across the parking lot, and into the car,
Elinor went on ahead of them and just got in the back.
She tried not to watch as Katie got him settled in the
front seat. She just wanted to get through this.

As they drove past the first of the three lakes, Warren
spoke up. "What's the name of that? I don't believe I've
ever seen that before." He sounded like a man holding a
normal polite conversation, not one who had lost his
mind.

Elinor was going to answer sharply, at least insist that
he say the word "lake," but Katie spoke up first. "That's
Diamond Lake, Daddy. You always did like the lakes.
We're just a few miles from our cabin now. The turnoff's
right up here."

They took the turnoff that led away from the string of
lakes, then turned left onto the narrower road that went
right into the woods. The development of cabins up here
was really quite extensive, but they were far enough
apart and built to blend with the scenery so it didn't feel
like a development at all. It was a lovely place. When

Katie pulled up to their green-and-brown cabin, nestled among tall pines, Elinor's eyes stung.

The cabin smelled stale when Katie opened the door and ushered them in. It wasn't a pleasant odor—it made Elinor wrinkle her nose and itch to get at it with ammonia and furniture polish—but in a funny way it was welcoming.

Warren just stood there, smiling uncertainly. As recently as last year, he'd bustled around as much as she had to get the place in order—cut and stocked firewood, patrolled for evidence of mouse and squirrel damage, methodically opened windows to air the place out, and then methodically closed them all again. "This is a nice place," he said vaguely now. "Do you—have you owned it long?"

Katie and Elinor started to answer him at the same time; Katie's gentle, reasonable reply won out over Elinor's sharp one. Abruptly, Elinor couldn't stand it anymore. If she stayed around him one second longer she was going to shake some sense into him or scream something mean or, worse, she was going to cry. "I'm going for a walk," she announced, and turned to go back up the steep steps.

Katie turned her attention from her father long enough to raise her eyebrows and ask, "Mom?"

"I just need some air."

Katie said, "*Mom,*" again, more insistently. But Elinor had no intention of being stopped and Katie, busy with her father, didn't really try.

When she was away from here, she remembered it as beautiful, but the memories were nothing compared to the reality of it. Now, as always, she was astonished, breathless, and uneasy in the company of so much beauty. Every year this place seemed, impossibly, more beautiful and more difficult—the air purer and sweeter and harder to fill her lungs with, the sky bluer and more glaring, the calling of birds and chittering of squirrels and rasping of cicadas and creaking of high pine boughs more wonderful and harder to interpret so that she couldn't be sure whether she was in danger at any given moment.

She turned left outside the cabin and walked along the paved road. She and Warren used to walk here three or four or five times a day, sometimes with Katie running like a puppy ahead of them, sometimes with Katie walking with them, sometimes by themselves. Trying not to think about Warren, she couldn't stop thinking about him, and finally she just gave herself up to the memories, hoping that would satisfy them and they'd leave her alone for a while:

Two or three times a week, Warren used to stop at the grocery store on his way home from work. Kroger's or Loblaw's, whichever had the best sales. Never an imposing man, he'd been, with his arms full of brown paper bags, somebody she could absolutely count on, a partner in the complicated business of running a household. He hadn't always bought what she'd had on the list; sometimes he'd deliberately left things off because he decided they didn't need them, or he'd spot something she hadn't thought of and she'd find a surprise when she unpacked the bags. He bought grapefruit a lot, and she never did like grapefruit. The sharp citrus odor would seep through the brown paper bags, and she'd be mad before he'd even set the groceries down on the counter. "I'm the one doing the shopping," he'd tell her flatly, "and I have to eat the food," and she'd feel displaced and intruded on, but also taken care of. She'd use every item he brought home, whether she'd planned on it or not, and work around the things he didn't get.

And:

In the spring and early summer of 1942, Elinor and
Warren had sat on the dusty front porch of Mae's Boardinghouse on Pine Street in Philadelphia and—gradually,
because she didn't give up—got to know each other.
She'd lived in the city several years by then, working as a
secretary for an insurance company, and she hadn't
found the right man yet; when she encountered Warren
Dietrich across Mae's big supper table she'd decided
right away that he would be the one. He wasn't planning
to stay, he told her right away; he was just passing
through. But evening after evening long after the other
boarders had gone inside, Warren and Elinor would sit in
rocking chairs on the porch and talk. He didn't talk much
or easily; she'd had to pull it out of him. Around ten
o'clock Mae would bustle out in her long white apron
and tsk at them about the lateness of the hour and shoo
Elinor, laughing and triumphant, inside the house. Elinor
remembered him vividly from those evenings when her
life had just started to be intertwined with his, how she
could have extricated herself if she'd known what was
coming but doubted that she would have anyway: not a
young man, really; already balding; always neatly dressed
even though he didn't have much money and, worse,
didn't have a wife to see to him; with an air about him of
self-confidence and unhappiness that had made her set
her cap for him right away, never mind Mae's motherly
warning that Warren Dietrich wasn't the marrying kind,
and then had been amazed herself when one afternoon
he'd suggested they take in a show.

And:

Warren on his back in the driveway fixing the car.
Building the living room fireplace, carefully placing the
flat rocks with attention to both their shape and their
relative shades of brown or gray, carefully smoothing the
mortar between them. Planting and watering and weed-

ing and harvesting his garden year after year until one spring he just didn't do it, just lost interest no matter how many times she reminded him—corn, tomatoes, yellow wax beans.

And:

They'd seen a good deal of the country when they retired. Warren had been an interesting traveling companion. Yellowstone, they visited, and the Grand Canyon, the Everglades, Penn's Caves. For nine seasons they took classes through Elderhostel, and Warren was always the best student in the class. He never said much, but when he did, people paid attention, even the teachers. It used to make her proud.

Elinor was lost.

She stopped and looked around. She didn't know where she was.

She couldn't believe it. She didn't want to believe it, because it was too much like Warren with his blank eyes and pointlessly fluttering hands. But she was definitely lost.

Frantically she looked for clues. She couldn't see much of the sky, and what she could see was featureless. This grove of aspens and pine trees looked like any other; in fact, there weren't really groves, just trees and more trees. She took a few hesitant steps along a path and then realized that it wasn't a path at all, just a slightly smoother place among rocks and roots that faded away under her feet. She had no idea which way the cabin was, or any cabin. She couldn't hear any voices or cars, couldn't smell woodsmoke.

No doubt about it, she was lost.

And she was weary.

Carefully, old bones creaking and old muscles aching, she lowered herself to sit on a not-very-stable log and lean against a rough tree trunk. She sat there for a minute or two, shaking. Then she bent her brittle old face toward her lap, bunched up her sweater around her ears as if it were an apron, and gave in to tears.

This was not the way things were supposed to be. She was going to be seventy-six years old in October. This was not the way life ought to be.

That Warren—who sometimes hated her and didn't know who she was and sometimes stared at her unblinking like a puppy—that man was not the husband she wanted to grow old with and die with.

It wasn't fair.

Elinor hadn't cried in years. Now she sat on a fallen log somewhere in the mountains, an old woman cheated by life, and cried with her face hidden in her sweater, as if somebody would see or hear. As if anybody would care.

Probably she didn't actually cry for very long. The human mind and body can't sustain active mourning for long unbroken stretches. They require periodic respite, to renew strength and concentration, to renew the sorrow itself.

But it seemed like a long time, because when Elinor lifted her head the shadows were long, the sky was dim, and the quality of the air had changed. Night can fall quickly in the wooded high country, alpine warmth and light fading with the minutest rotation of the earth. Now Elinor found herself shivering in a blue-green twilight, the high horizon swabbed with pale peach. The tall pines began to sway and rustle in a wind she didn't yet feel down below.

Maybe she'd freeze to death. The tears on her cheeks had already chilled, and she had had poor circulation in her hands and feet for years. Maybe she'd just die of exposure out here by herself. That didn't seem like such a bad idea.

Arms came around her.

She was hugged back against someone whose body heat was as intense as if she were crawling into bed beside sleeping Warren on a cold winter night, her side of the sheets icy but his body heat radiating for all the world as if he had an electric blanket on, so that in just a few minutes everything was warmed but her feet. The temptation to press her ice-cold toes into the crooks of his knees was sometimes more than she could resist.

A head bent beside hers. Breath came against her neck.

She recognized his faint sweet odor. She recognized the particular warmth and solidity of him before she opened her eyes and smoothed her dress and lifted her head and saw that it was Warren.

He looked different, but just a little. Not exactly younger, but like himself before the Alzheimer's started —which, she reminded herself, hadn't been all that long ago. His face was firmer. His mouth didn't drool. He stood up straight. His eyes looked right at her the way they used to, didn't glance away to be looking at things that were not in *this* world.

This was not the man her husband had turned into, that Katie kept saying she had to accept. She did *not* have to accept that. Warren was better. Warren had come back to her. She'd been afraid she'd lost him forever. But maybe now she hadn't.

In the hard times, he'd been such a comfort. Without trying to be, she was sure; without even knowing he was. Since his mind started to go, she'd been alone. She longed not to be alone anymore. She yearned for him to comfort her in this hardest of times, when she was losing him.

She pressed herself against him and was warmed.

Then she came to her senses and pulled away. "Warren Roy Dietrich, what in the *world* are you doing here?"

"Looking for you," he informed her, a little sternly, as if she'd done something foolish, which she supposed she had.

"Well, you found me. Now we're both lost. That's a fine how-do-you-do. Katie will be worried to death—"

He interrupted her in his no-nonsense tone of voice that she hadn't heard in so long. "I'm not lost. You're lost. I've come to take you with me."

"Oh, and do you know the way back to the cabin, Warren?" she asked with more than a little sarcasm, but what she was thinking was: *He's better.* "For heaven's sake, what are you talking about?"

He got easily to his feet, not stiff or dizzy at all. And not confused, either; he knew exactly what he was doing. She peered at him in the dimming peach-and-blue dusk as he took her elbows and helped her to her feet. He was quite a bit steadier and stronger than she was.

He's cured, she let herself think again. *Warren's back.*

"We're going for a little walk," he told her.

It crossed her mind to object, to say she didn't want to or *she* had work to do even if *some* people didn't, the way she'd often done over the years even when she'd wanted to do something he suggested, just so he wouldn't get on his high horse and start thinking he could boss her around. But this time, she just held on to his arm, which was thin and wiry in her grasp but strong and not at all shaky, and she went with him.

Warren went ahead over a tree that had been struck by lightning. It bothered Elinor to look at the black gash with its edges of charred, softened wood, so she didn't. Warren turned and reached back to help her over, and all of a sudden she was insulted. Slapping his hand away, she almost lost her balance. He reached for her again and she pushed him away again.

She stood on one side of the log and he stood on the other. Both of them had always been stubborn. She put her hands on her hips. She spoke quietly, in case anybody was listening, but she was so mad she was spitting. "You've got a lot of nerve, Warren Roy Dietrich."

"Elinor," he said warningly, and drew himself up. That meant he was not going to discuss this, no matter how much of a hissy she threw.

After forty-three years of marriage, she knew a lost cause when she saw one. But also, after forty-three years of marriage, she was not going to be pushed around. She folded her arms, wincing at the stiffness in her shoulders, and snapped, " 'Elinor,' what?"

"I want you to come with me."

Elinor lost all patience. "Warren, is this another one of your silly ideas? Like the time you insisted you could control how fast the water came out of the faucet by which chair you sat in at the kitchen table? Or the time last month when you got mad at me because I wouldn't take you to see your mother out in the garage?" She felt a little mean bringing up those things, but, really, she had had enough. She finished with, "Just who do you think you are?"

"I have made an interesting discovery," Warren informed her evenly. "I want you to share it." He hadn't taken his eyes off her.

"I'm not going off on some wild-goose chase," Elinor fumed. "I'm tired, and Katie will be worried to death. We have to get back to the cabin before it gets completely dark." Having said that, she noticed how dark it already was. The sky was a purple-blue like taffeta, and there were all sorts of animal, bird, insect, and no telling what-all sounds that she hadn't heard before.

"We will go to the valley first," Warren said.

Elinor prepared to do battle over the principle of the thing. Warren put one foot up on the felled tree, as if taking a step toward her. She was pleased to notice how shiny his shoe was, and her next thought was that she would never get the ash and dirt out of his pantleg. But then she had to admit that he was being careful, holding the crisp gray fabric between thumb and forefinger, pulling it up out of harm's way and in the process showing his black sock and his pale ankle.

That was something she'd seen him do thousands of times. That one gesture told her better than anything that whatever had been wrong with him was cured now and the real Warren was back. She was mad and hurt that he'd left her in the first place, and so glad that he had come back.

He said, "It's time to go now."

She made one last feeble attempt to resist him, to assert herself. "*I'm* going back to the cabin. Katie will be worried to death. Which way is the cabin, Warren, do you know?"

He took hold of her elbow. He'd always been a small man, but when he was young he'd lifted weights and then after he'd retired he'd taken some exercise every day, even if it was just walking up and down steps, so he was strong. He was also determined. He was hurting her arm. Sternly, he informed her, "This is important for our future, Elinor. Do you understand?"

Of course she didn't understand. But, abruptly, she was tired of arguing with him, and anyway she didn't know how to get back to the cabin by herself. So she gave in and did what he said.

First she had to step over the log. It was bent up from both ends like a child doing a backbend, so most of it was higher than her knees, and there wasn't much to hold on to. Warren was already on the other side of it, erect and watchful, frowning in that way of his that made her think he was impatient with her although he always denied it. This time, when she wanted him to, he didn't reach out a hand to help her. They'd never been much for showing affection in public.

She bent down and tried to hold on to the log itself. It swayed and bobbed. She tried to steady herself on one foot while she lifted the other one up and over. It took her several tries to get her knee high enough. Then the first spot where she set down her foot wasn't as firm as she'd thought it would be, so she had to start over.

But she made it, finally, and slowly straightened up to catch her breath and look for Warren again. He was already ahead of her, hard to see in the dark woods, but beckoning impatiently.

Elinor would have said there wasn't any path. But if Warren could find one, so could she. She followed him, stumbling over roots and rocks, hanging on to each tree as long as she could before she had to let it go and find another one. The trunks and branches got smaller, lower to the ground, and more twisted. The ground was sloping up slightly. Before long she was feeling the strain in her thighs, back, and chest. The air was getting thinner and colder, too, and Elinor had trouble breathing enough into her lungs.

She kept losing Warren and then finding him again, or thinking she found him. He seemed to be making his way steadily through the woods, and he expected her to keep up with him. The strain of focusing her eyes over and over again on him was giving her a headache. It also meant she couldn't really watch where she set her feet or hands.

She was afraid. She didn't like to be afraid. She asked herself sternly if there was really anything to be afraid of and decided that of course there was, plenty. Wild animals; she didn't know what kind, but there must be wild animals in these mountains. Storms and avalanches. Falling and breaking a hip. Getting lost and nobody ever rescuing her, including Warren. Being alone for the rest of her life, however long that was. Losing Warren again.

From up ahead Warren announced, "Here we are." At least she thought that was what he said. For a minute she thought somebody else said something, too, but she didn't see anybody and if they were talking to her they could just speak up. She herself didn't see anything she hadn't already been looking at: big blue-black sky, tangled rocks and bushes and just a few trees now, Warren flickering just out of arm's reach, turned partly away from her and looking out and down. She took a few quick, careless steps toward him, holding out both hands like a sleepwalker.

Then all of a sudden there was nothing but air ahead of her—no woods and no sky, really; no solid ground. "Oh, my!" she gasped, and stopped.

She squinted through mist and twilight and realized that they must be standing on the edge of a cliff. She had that funny feeling that heights gave her, low in her stomach, an unnerving mixture of fear and nausea and an excitement that was almost, though it embarrassed her to admit it, sexual.

Before she had time to figure out anything else, Warren had started down the cliff. "Warren," she protested, but she was going after him.

There wasn't any lip or edge, nothing to step over; all she had to do was stretch one leg out as far as it would go and put her foot down. Then she was descending, faster than she wanted to, skidding on loose dirt, trying to steady herself but not being able to get hold of anything. She was bruised and scratched. Her old muscles and bones were getting twisted and bumped. She was afraid. She was also mad. Who did he think he was?

The valley was filled with fog. The fog glowed as if it were lit by moonlight, except that the light seemed to be coming from underneath instead of above. There were blurry colors—red winding into gold and then spinning out into blue and green and violet. It was like being swaddled in a faded quilt, or an afghan crocheted out of variegated yarn.

Then—just like that and not because of anything she did—she stopped going down. She was on one knee. Her other leg was straight out in front of her. Her dress was torn and bunched up indecently around her thighs; when she tried to pull it down, everything hurt. She could feel that both hands were bleeding, and something was wrong with her left shoulder. She was covered with dirt, leaves, twigs, and that strange fog. Warren was looking down at her, and behind him—through him—she saw broken outlines of buildings and half-buildings along the valley floor.

Warren said again, "Here we are." He held out his hands. Elinor took them, and he helped her to her feet. She didn't think she'd broken anything, but she was pretty shook up; at her age, once you broke a hip or something you were done for. He put his arm around her waist and she let herself slump against him as they stood together looking at the ghost town.

6

Baby pictures. All kinds of babies. Since Annie didn't know what her baby might have looked like, any picture of any baby made her think of hers. An adorable little black kid with lots of bows on lots of braids. A beautiful Hispanic baby girl with lots of thick black hair and pierced ears. A white baby with a red topknot and incredibly fat cheeks. They were all so cute. Annie ran her fingertips over the glossy magazine pages that were curling around the edges, and her eyes filled with welcome tears.

 "What spectacular country this is," Tom's father observed. He sat in the driver's seat, in command as always, erect and relaxed. When they'd set out this afternoon, Tom had thought dimly that he ought to be the one to drive—his father was, after all, nearly eighty years old—and as darkness had gathered and they'd entered the foothills of the Rockies, he'd managed to say so, haltingly. But he knew he could not drive, and it was his father who apparently knew where they were going.

He couldn't drive. He couldn't work. He couldn't listen to music or read or engage in conversation with anybody about anything, because Emily was dead.

He'd watched her die. He'd seen her trapped under the canoe, and he'd not been able to get to her, though he'd tried. Was still trying. His wife had died and he had not, three hundred eighty-eight days now of life that ought to have been hers. He could not keep this up.

His father glanced over at him and said gently, "We should be there by midday tomorrow. There is a lodge not far from here where we can stay the night, if memory serves. The transportation networks have changed, of course, since I made my own journey here, and the fabric of the terrain has been altered, but I recognize the area and will recognize the place itself, I am sure, the valley and the town. Or it will recognize me." He did not laugh.

Thomas Krieg, Sr. was slight, like Tom himself. Silver hair to his light brown. Pale gray or pale blue suits, white shirts, always a tie, to Tom's blue jeans and workshirts, which had become bedraggled and stained since Emily died because he couldn't hold in his head all the details required to wash, dry, mend them. His father had a distinctive manner: elegant without being in the least aloof, simultaneously dignified and warm, self-possessed and self-assured but not at all self-centered. he spoke with a formality and precision of expression that might have been expected to render his words haughty or cold, but people loved to hear him speak, publicly when he delivered professional papers or statements to the press, and privately, across a dim table or walking in a mountain park. His long hands on the wheel, his gaze calmly taking in the highway and the scenery and Tom, his knees in their creased linen trousers and his feet in their shiny black shoes, the words and diction he employed to speak of things that were important to him, of which there were many—the design of a park or a garden, Emily, Emily's death—all had an idiosyncratic grace.

Emily had adored him, and he her. Tom shifted his body under the weight of her name in his mind, and realized dully that he'd been staring at and beyond his father, understanding that his father was there and the mountains and the car was transporting him somewhere, but having neither the desire nor the ability to interpret anything in relation to himself. Having no self.

Emily would have loved it here, he thought before he could protect himself. There was no point in vocalizing such a thing, though, and he knew he wouldn't be able to organize the anguish into anything like usable syllables. He did manage to comment, "God's country," without intending irony. Without intending anything.

His father declared, at once and emphatically, "All country is God's country, son."

They had passed around Denver at twilight and had kept heading westward, lately through Glenwood Canyon, across the Continental Divide. Tom had never been much west of Chicago, or very far east, either, which was somewhat disconcerting. He did not regard himself as provincial, but perhaps he was. His father had traveled around the world and now, clearly, had a destination and a purpose, was taking him somewhere.

From several states distant, via the popular press and professional networks, the landscape architecture firm of Thomas L. Krieg, Sr. and Thomas L. Krieg, Jr. had kept apprised of the Glenwood project from the time state officials had started putting feelers out to transportation engineers, geologists, landscape designers, public relations experts about the need to improve Highway 40 through what was always referred to as "scenic Glenwood Canyon." Then environmentalists and local residents got wind of it, and battle was joined.

Environmental Impact Statements were prepared, approved, and protested. Injunctions were requested, granted, overturned. There were organized protests and petitions to the governor; letters to various editors from both sides; press conferences, carefully packaged stories in the media, much-hyped investigative reports.

Thomas Krieg, Sr., had been especially fascinated by the entire process. At more than a few staff meetings, in numerous memos clipped to articles about the Glenwood project, he'd remarked to his colleagues, which included his son and daughter-in-law, "This project will be a public demonstration of the commitment of our profession and allied professions to maintaining and supporting harmony with other components of the natural world while we develop our own nature. It is nothing less than a test of the technological, moral, and spiritual evolution of our species."

Tom, thoroughly a pragmatist and a secularist, had been bemused. Emily had shushed his mild mockery.

Thomas had made arrangements with Denver colleagues, as other people might arrange to see the Super Bowl or a solar eclipse. A few days before the Glenwood project was scheduled to open, he'd flown west, and was in the first caravan of vehicles to traverse the new highway on the morning its ribbon was cut. From Glenwood Springs, at the upper end of the canyon, he'd made an exuberant phone call back to the firm. He'd happened to speak to Emily, and pronounced the completed project "marvelous, a triumph and a vindication, a true alliance of form and function." As it turned out, he was not alone in his praise; some of the staunchest critics of the project in progress expressed surprised approval when it was done, and the canyon remained majestic. More than being unobtrusive, the highway was part of the natural beauty, no less, say, than a beaver dam or the nest of a bird.

At the time, Tom had been preoccupied with a complex low-income housing development that wasn't going well, and with his complex and demanding new marriage, which was going very well indeed. He'd kept himself informed about the Glenwood project at a cursory professional level, but he hadn't taken much of an interest.

Now, of course, he didn't take an interest in anything, and he was offended that his father did. Emily was dead. He had seen her die. He had heard and felt, been doused by, the instrument of her death. The sound of running water. The sound of water splashing over a cliff to make a wild fall. The sound of water dashing against its banks, swirling in sinkholes, hissing up into the air. Tom heard the sound of water everywhere and never stopped thinking about the day, the moment Emily died, and he could not bear to think about it.

Emily had been dead for thirteen months, nearly thirteen months, and Tom still could not fathom the meaning of the phrase *Emily is dead.* The juxtaposition of those words was horrific and endless. He couldn't bear to think *Emily is dead,* and he couldn't stop thinking it, and he dared not let himself think anything else.

He must have made a noise, because his father glanced over at him in the blurry mountain twilight and asked, as he'd asked so many times in the last thirteen months, "Are you all right, son?"

Tom took a ragged breath and managed to say with some force what he'd said every time his father had asked that question. "No, I'm not all right, Dad. I'll never be all right again."

There was a pause while his father negotiated a hairpin turn and an unhelmeted bicyclist speeding downhill without lights. Then Thomas declared, "Tom, I am concerned about you. It has been more than a year now since Emily died."

A shudder rushed through Tom at the sound of his wife's name and the word "died" spoken aloud by someone else. He heard the sound of running water, heard her cry out (did she cry his name?), saw her go down. He cried out himself and was amazed and gratified, dimly, by his own lack of self-control.

"I understand grief," Thomas persisted gently. "I have lost people, too, whom I loved beyond reckoning."

"You didn't—lose—Emily," Tom gasped.

"Yes, actually, I did. But more to the point, if you recall the story, I very nearly lost my life when I was about your age, as you are on the verge of losing yours; I very nearly sacrificed it, as you are doing now."

Tom said nothing. He was consumed with pain, and with outrage that his father would talk to him this way. The cavity of his torso might have been filled with fire. He felt his heart beating and wished it would not, for each beat, each diastolic and systolic pair, hurt sharply. The pain in his gut seared.

"It is no tribute to Emily," Thomas went on, "to mourn like this forever. The honor to her is to find a way to live again."

There was something Tom needed to say. He gripped the armrest, tried to fill his lungs with air past the enormous obstruction in his throat, and pushed out, "I—won't—let—her—go."

The silence from his father was as deliberate then as the old man's words had been. Tom felt himself in good hands, and instantly rejected any suggestion of safety or peace, for that was a massive delusion, given that Emily was dead.

As the highway gracefully bore them higher, the canyon walls on either side darkened and deepened. The rising rushing noise of Coal Creek through the open car windows chafed Tom's nerves. His ears were plugged from the relentless change in altitude, and his head ached. His head had ached since the day Emily died. At times he'd thought, almost wistfully, that he might have a brain tumor. Almost every day, sometimes half a dozen times a day, he thought he was having a heart attack. But his brain and his heart, for no good reason, kept functioning.

Sinking back into his seat, he purposefully began again the process of reliving Emily's death: events leading up to it, the moment itself, its aftermath. He did this countless times every day and night and was terrified, sickened, whenever a detail seemed lost or blurred. He dared not lose anything more.

There was no order or sequence, though, no progression or perspective to his memories. They appeared to him as if frozen in layered amber, or flew at him like sharp bits of torn paper in the crazed gales of his grief:

Emily trudging ahead of him, carrying the front end of the canoe. He'd been concentrating on keeping his footing, not dropping the canoe, on the heat and general physical discomfort. Canoeing, like every other physical activity they'd engaged in, had been Emily's idea, not his. Then he hadn't even realized he'd been noticing her.

But now what came to him were specific impressions of her, apparently gathered then and stored for just this torturous use: The tanned and sinewed backs of her legs below ragged bleached cutoffs. Gold-brown tendrils of hair forever escaping her blue headband to wander down the back of her gold-brown neck.

The peacefulness of floating on flat water between close banks. Warm sun. The exhilaration of rapids, white noise and brilliant light and cold water in his face, thrilling motion and his own mind and muscles controlling it, guiding it. The gleam of Emily's strong muscles through the rainbow spray. Her laughter. The shaft of the oar, wet and smooth and solid in his right hand, his left hand cupped over the nub on the end. Moments when the canoe was airborne, moments when it crashed, the surface of the rushing water hard but parting, a metamorphic substance like everything else in the world.

Then the canoe capsized.

At first it was part of the fun. Emily whooped. His heart leaped exactly as if this were an adventure. But then came the acute, primal apprehension of mortal danger.

There was loud pain in his right temple where he must have struck a rock, and grainy pain in his lungs. The two sensations were so different that there should have been differentiating words for them, and for the pain to come.

His nose and mouth broke the surface of the water and he could breathe again, and for a few seconds he knew nothing but that he could breathe again, dizzying relief. His feet connected with solid ground, allowing him to stand up and keep his balance, even make some forward progress across the current.

Then terror exploded when he saw—could not believe his eyes—understood, *believed* that Emily was trapped under the canoe, which, overturned, was wedged under the ridge of rock that created the rapids and falls.

The instant he comprehended what had happened, he dived in. *The* instant, but it was too late, he should have understood sooner. He managed to grasp her hair, her arm, but his grip would not hold. He had to come up for air. He gasped, could not force enough oxygen into his straining lungs but could not wait for more, thrashed back underwater to his wife and this time with hardly any effort pulled her free.

He carried, tugged, pushed her to the surface, to the shore. A few other people were on the riverbank by then and Tom let them take her from him. He shouldn't have done that. He shouldn't have let her go then, because he never got her back.

They laid her on the shady ground. Her face was blotched and contorted so nearly beyond recognition that Tom half believed then, half believed still, that it wasn't really Emily. They bent over her, pressed their mouths to hers, pressed her chest. River water came up. Tom was vomiting up river water and bile, and trying desperately to get to Emily. It was too late. Emily had died. He lost consciousness, but not for long enough.

"There it is," his father announced. Tom tried not to know or care what he was talking about. But he knew they were at the lodge, and he cared because, as always since Emily's death, he was exhausted. His body ached from sitting in the car so long, his head throbbed from the altitude, his mind and heart rattled wearily from the effrontery of going somewhere without Emily, of living this day when she was dead.

His father turned left off the highway onto a dirt road that climbed a dark mountainside. "Just as I remember it."

Memories like rocks pummeling his temples, like white water in the exquisitely sensitive pockets of his lungs:

Emily, rapt and motionless, watching a killdeer in a field outside Iowa City. Rain spotting the shoulders of her dark denim shirt and downing her skin. He should have noticed her more.

Emily's arms around him from behind, her palms flat and warm against his chest, her forehead warm between his shoulder blades. Her body heat.

Emily arguing with a client. You'd never realize she was arguing if you didn't know her. Her voice would drop in both pitch and volume. Her gray eyes would take on a pewter luster which the uninitiated mistook for warmth. Tom used to reflect in somewhat nervous amusement that the client had no idea what she was up against, while Emily landed major accounts and was able to use her considerable design skills; a few of her projects had been truly stunning, his own favorite being the garden that juxtaposed the American romantic tradition of borderlessness with Japanese formality. The client, who had thought he wanted a cozy English dooryard garden, had been delighted.

Emily's foot floating in the river. Her cold toes marbling his palm.

"A bit dearer than I remember, of course," his father commented as he got back into the driver's seat. "But they do have vacancies."

Their room on the second floor of the small rectangular building was reached by metal steps up to a metal balcony on which their footsteps were unbearably loud. It was a small denlike room with paneled walls, curtains and bedspread of an orange-and-brown open-weave material like burlap, and stylized prints of mountain flora on the walls. It wasn't until his father said, "Put your bag down, son, and let's see if the restaurant is still serving dinner," that Tom realized he'd been staring at the prints and compulsively listing the plants over and over in his head: wild aster, mountain mahogany, Indian paintbrush, yucca, columbine, wild aster, columbine, columbine.

He laid his duffel bag on the bed farther from the window—not out of any choice; he dreaded and avoided choices—but because his father seemed to have chosen the other one. The effort of swinging the bag up and then lowering it was nearly too much for him, the motion nearly too complex.

His father was waiting by the open door, room key in his hand. Tom dared not have a room key; since Emily's death he'd lost two sets of car keys, his wallet with over two hundred dollars in it, and countless documents, letters, site plans, notes. "Are you hungry?" Thomas inquired. Tom didn't know whether he was hungry or not, and didn't know what he answered.

He couldn't bear to be with anyone. He also couldn't bear to be left alone. As far as he knew Emily had never been in this lodge, but the room, like every other space he encountered, was so defined by her absence that there was hardly any place for him. Tom stood where he was, unable and unwilling to move, until he was forced to flinch away from his father's firm touch at the small of his back.

They ate a light, late dinner. The only other diners were an old lady eating alone at a table in the farthest corner and a gay couple in earnest, hand-holding conversation on the other side of the restaurant. More than once, Thomas glanced their way, averted his eyes, glanced their way again. He was obviously put off by them, although he would never have said so.

It took Tom a long time to decide what to order. He kept losing track of what he'd read about each item on the menu, and he couldn't imagine how anything would taste. The persistently patient waiter came back three times. Thomas had long since finished his cocktail and more than his half of the crusty dinner rolls from the napkin-covered basket by the time Tom finally chose the clam chowder, today's house special. He thought he'd probably be able to swallow most of it if there weren't any substantial solid chunks.

Often, though, he couldn't eat more than a bite or two, and certainly he couldn't cook for himself—couldn't keep in his head the sequence of steps required to make a sandwich or open a can of soup, couldn't trust himself to have turned a burner on or off. And he couldn't shop: the arrangement of items on the shelves didn't make sense; he couldn't always figure out how he was expected to pay; the fluorescent lights and the gaudy colors of the things for sale and the hubbub of conversation and the Muzak and the cavorting children and the odors of fresh-baked bread and of fresh peaches were too much.

He'd lost a considerable amount of weight. He hadn't weighed himself and couldn't look in a mirror, hadn't seen what he looked like since he was, surely, grief personified. But his clothes hung loose now, and his watch band slipped down over his hand.

"Before I was married to your mother," Thomas said without prelude, "I was married to another lovely woman named Cecelia."

Not having realized that he'd been staring vacantly at the white cloth placemat whose pattern was so subtle that it might have been blank, Tom now looked up. He'd always known that his father had been widowed; there'd been no family secret, no dramatic confessional scene. He'd known her name without remembering having been told. Countless times he'd seen her photograph among the other family pictures on the stairwell wall, a face of no particular distinction.

He'd never thought much about his father's long-ago loss, and it hadn't entered his mind at all since his own. Even now, the two events did not truly seem related. His father had lost a stranger named Cecelia. He'd lost Emily.

What pierced the fog of his mourning now and caught his unwilling attention was, first, his father's unmistakable air of having begun something. A story. A presentation. A lecture. Then with a dim shock he saw tears streaming down the old man's elegantly lined cheeks. Reacting sluggishly, as had become his habit, Tom had the half-formed thought that he ought to look discreetly away to give his father time to compose himself.

The old man wiped the tears away with his white linen monogrammed handkerchief—TLK, Tom's initials, too, but Tom had never carried a handkerchief in his life —but made no attempt to conceal them. The waiter set his filet mignon in front of him, warned about the hot plate, and raised his eyebrows worriedly at Tom while inquiring whether they needed anything else. As if Tom would know. Thomas lifted his flushed face and smiled benignly at the fluttering young man. "No, thank you. You are most kind." The waiter dropped a presumptuous hand on his shoulder, over his head caught Tom's eye in an obvious signal that they, the young ones, must take care of this pitiable old man, and went away.

Thomas turned his attention to the preparation of his steak and his baked potato for consumption. Tom took a shallow spoonful of chowder, raised it shakily toward his mouth, and let it fall back into the bowl.

"The hospital notified me at work that Cecelia had been taken ill," Thomas continued. "I was out on site. By the time my secretary located me and I was able to get to the hospital, she was unconscious. By nightfall she was dead. Viral meningitis."

Tom was distressed to hear himself murmur, "You never had a chance to say good-bye."

"That is not so." Thomas leaned forward to make his point. His dark blue eyes were purposefully fixed on his son. "I have said good-bye in countless ways. Cecelia insisted on it. It was in my own heart and mind that farewells were required, and Cecelia herself gave me instruction."

Tom managed to echo, "Cecelia?" but couldn't think how to arrange any more syllables to ask what he wanted to ask. He did not, in fact, want very much to ask anything.

"She took me to Revenant," his father said, "where I will take you tomorrow."

Tom didn't understand and didn't much care to. He looked down to see that he was taking chowder onto his spoon again, and then wasn't sure what to do next. So he just sat there with the bowl of the spoon and part of the handle submerged in the viscous yellow-gray liquid.

Eventually, he was able to rouse himself sufficiently to insert the spoon into his mouth. The small amount of chowder that had not drooled back into the bowl made a film on the smooth curved surface which created synecdochical reflections—the tip of the nose for the whole face, a flicker of a tear for sorrow itself. The chowder coagulated at the back of his throat. Tom put the spoon down and waited without much preference for the soup either to dissolve or to choke him.

His father's story, which seemed but surely was not disjointed and disconnected, continued somewhere around him. Tom couldn't imagine what the point of it might be. He was sure there was one. He was also sure that he was supposed to have some reaction to it, that it was intended to have some impact on him, which, of course, it would not. Nothing did, except the ongoing fact that Emily had died. There was nothing to do, then, but to feign listening for as long as possible and without interruption to mourn Emily.

Emily was dead.

Emily was dead.

"After Cecelia died, my life simply disintegrated. There was no explosion or any other discrete moment of self-destruction. I believe, in fact, that my friends and colleagues considered me to be remarkably stoic and well-adjusted. I went to work every day and was involved with some rather significant projects. I came home every day to an empty house, a house without Cecelia. I ate and slept, bathed, went to the barber, attended to the details of civilized daily life. After a fashion.

"This continued for some months. I bore the first Christmas without her, the first anniversary of our wedding without her, the first spring, summer, autumn.

"On the first anniversary of Cecelia's death, which is October 24, I finally succumbed to the devastating realization that I would be compelled to spend the rest of my life without her. And with that realization, I very nearly ceased to exist.

"In fact, I did my best to do so. I moved out of the fine house we had built, which had been Cecelia's pride and joy, leaving the doors unlocked and tossing the keys into the hedge. I took a room in a questionable single-room-occupancy hotel downtown. Questionable, I say, but actually I blended in quite splendidly, and no one ever inquired as to how a refined and well-educated gentleman such as myself had come to be in such straits. There were, in point of fact, others like me, and I never asked them their stories either. I wish now that I had.

"From the mailbox in the dingy lobby of my hotel—which smelled, as I recall, of all manner of human excretion—I mailed a postcard to the firm informing my partners that I was taking an extended leave of absence. I gave no details as to where I was and what I was doing, and quite deliberately I left no instructions or information regarding my work in progress. To this day, I know only from anecdote and observation how those projects progressed.

"I stopped bathing, shaving, reading; for all intents and purposes I stopped thinking. I drank far more than I ate. I slept only in fits and starts, trying to train myself not to dream. I gave myself entirely over to grieving. In a shockingly brief period of time I became, quite thoroughly, a derelict."

"Why?" Tom whispered, although he knew.

"Cecelia had claimed my life."

Tom swallowed. "She was—dead."

"I could not let her go. I refused to let her go."

"Why didn't you just—commit suicide?"

"A direct act of self-destruction would have required focused energy and forethought, of which I was incapable. It was easier, and it seemed more fitting, to surrender to the outside forces of alcohol, the elements, the perils of street life. To succumb without resistance to the ravages of fate, since fate had taken from me the one thing that had given my life meaning, form, and function."

Tom nodded. The apparition of his father—successful, self-assured, at peace with himself and the world—in such a desperate, dissolute state had cruelly caught his attention.

"And then," said Thomas, openly weeping again, "Cecelia came to me."

Tom waited.

"It was a bitterly cold night. I had exhausted my resources and was no longer able to afford even a questionable hotel room, so I had quite literally been living on the streets. On that particular night, I was huddled in an alley behind the old Denver Dry, wrapped somewhat haphazardly in newspapers and ineffectually backed into a shallow doorway as cursory protection from the wind and snow. Freezing to death had come to seem a satisfying end to my misery, allowing as it reputedly did the numbing of all senses past use or recall, including the ultimate numbing of pain.

"I was not intoxicated. I clearly recall having declined the offer of a fellow twilight denizen to share his bottle. But I may well have been hallucinating. Or perhaps—and in truth this is the theory to which I give most credence

—the extremity of my physical and psychic conditions had brought me into contact with levels of perception that are commonly obscured from us.

"Whatever the explanation, Cecelia appeared. She did not suddenly materialize. Her appearance to me was quite as though she had been in attendance all along, simply beyond the capacity of my senses to apprehend, until now, when they were sufficiently pliant and open to receive her.

"She crouched beside me. I could see the clouds of her breath in the frigid air. Her hands were warm where they cupped my freezing face. Her voice was clear and precise, precisely familiar. Cecelia always had a remarkably pleasing voice, for both singing and speaking.

"She spoke my name. I had, of course, longed to hear her speak my name—*one more time,* I would entreat, but that was a ruse, for had I been granted that wish I would instantly have begged for *one more* and *one more time again.* She said, urgently, 'Thomas, my love, you must come with me.' "

The old man stopped speaking. At first, he appeared lost in reverie, staring off into the middle distance. Tom wondered whether he was seeing and hearing, touching, the lost Cecelia now. Then Thomas roused himself enough to finish his main course. Discreetly, he wiped his mouth and white moustache with his white napkin, refolded the napkin neatly beside his plate, and sat back.

"She took me then to a true ghost town, high in the Rocky Mountains, and there I—in the company of scores of other mourners haunted by their lost loved ones whom they would not allow to rest in peace—there I engaged in an apocryphal battle between the forces of life and the forces of death, which were arrayed rather differently from what one would expect."

Tom, who had been unable to consume any more

chowder, gripped his water glass in a futile attempt to stanch the shaking of his hands, and took a small sip. The tepid water made his throat constrict and his stomach churn. "Emily," he said, and her name sent a cold shudder through him, "has never come to me. No dreams. No visions. No messages. She just *left*, completely."

His father nodded. "I have been waiting for her to summon you the way Cecelia summoned me."

"You're talking about ghosts. Don't tell me you believe in ghosts, Dad." Tom felt a ludicrous buzz of hope. The strength of his father's personality, the clarity of his vision, had always strongly impacted Tom's definition of both found and built reality, and he was absurdly eager to have the older man tell him what was real now, too, if it offered the slightest possibility that he hadn't lost Emily after all, that he didn't have to let her go.

His father tipped his head again, the start of another nod, which became instead a thoughtful inclination, a gesture of profound and unprotested agnosticism. "I have long since given up trying to identify what happened to me. There are a myriad plausible explanations—symbol, hallucination, wish-fulfillment. Ghost is, clearly, one of them. What I know is that, in one form or another, Cecelia made it possible for me to let her go."

Tom caught his breath. "No."

As though he hadn't spoken—and perhaps he hadn't; his thoughts these days were often quite as articulate and audible to him as his spoken words—his father went on. "I had thought that perhaps our respective experiences of this life-changing event, thus far so eerily similar, would continue along parallel paths, and that you would be given the same kind of epiphany I received. Apparently that is not to be the case. But I feel you are in significant danger, and as your father I dare not wait any longer. So I have taken the roles of messenger and ferryman upon myself, which is why I have told you my tale of loss and redemption, and why tomorrow I shall deliver you to Revenant."

"I won't—" Tom began, and lost his train of thought. He glanced distractedly around the restaurant. There were now several other tables of diners, including a party too near them with three boisterous children. He and Emily had talked vaguely of having children someday. Voice breaking, he said, "I don't want—" but stopped, because there was so much he did not want to do.

With an expression of such tenderness that Tom had to look away, his father said, "I understand, son. This will be an act of supreme courage for both of us."

Tom got to his feet and shoved his chair back, in a burst of rage that made dishes clatter, made him grab the edge of the table to stop himself from knocking it over with a swipe of his hand. He meant to keep his voice down; it seemed to him that he might be either shouting or whispering. "In the morning we're going back to Denver," he declared. "This is insane."

His father had risen, too, a fluid motion in response to his own abrupt and hard-edged one. Father and son almost exactly the same height, the same build, the same stance, faced each other, and blue eyes met blue eyes.

Thomas spoke, also obviously attempting to keep his voice down although it carried from years of purposeful development. "Tom, I believe Revenant to be your only chance of survival. The risk of going there is great, but the risk of not going is far greater. I know of no other way to help you reclaim your life."

"My life is shit!" Tom hissed. "I have no life!" He wadded up his napkin and, in a ridiculous act of childish defiance, stuffed it into the nearly full bowl of now cool and gelatinous chowder. Taking care not to stumble or to careen into things—but stumbling and careening anyway; snagging his foot on the leg of an empty chair; misjudging the width of the door so that his knuckles glanced painfully off the frame—he strode out of the restaurant. His father, who could have followed him, did not.

As the cool night air struck and then enveloped him, so did grief for Emily, and he gasped, lightly pummeling his chest with both fists. Gasped for her. The pain choked him. His extremities stung.

Standing in edgeless space, Tom visualized his grief for Emily as a ziggurat. A mountain he had designed and constructed. A high place which gave order and meaning to everything else within the wall. All roads led to it, provided sight lines to it, and ended at its base. Its shadow fell over everything, informed everything.

Grief was the central organizing principle of his consciousness now; without grief, everything would be random, everything would collapse. Oddly recalling a phrase from a grad school course in the theory and history of landscape architecture, *access from the ground to the heavens,* Tom thought that this sacred, built mountain of his, this grief, provided access to hell.

He managed to make his way around the downslope end of the lodge, following a narrow, ill-lit sidewalk to the side of the building that flatly faced the mountainside. Although the room numbers didn't seem to him to be sequential, didn't seem in any sense predictable or usable, he knew that they were, and, proceeding on this theory, he was able to find the room.

But he didn't have a key. He searched his pockets, confusedly searched again. He didn't remember ever having had one, but it was quite possible that he had. Most likely he'd lost it.

Unable to come up with anything else to do because

he was unable to position any particular thought in relation to any other, Tom just stood there in the open dark air. He didn't lean against a post. He didn't sit down on a step. He didn't put his hands in his pockets or cross his arms or shift his weight one way or another. If he could have removed the soles of his feet from contact with the ground, he would have. He waited for his father to come and let him in, and while he waited he thought of nothing but Emily, Emily. When his father came, Tom was, for a long instant, startled and afraid.

In the morning he awoke appalled by having slept so soundly, untroubled by dreams; he didn't think he'd stirred all night. Consciousness was an enclosed courtyard, *space* made *place* by a boundary; Tom reentered it through the corridor of Emily's absence. By the time he got there—by the time he was sitting up, fully awake, on the edge of the bed in a new day without her—he was panting and sweating from the exertion.

"Good morning," said his father. It took Tom a moment to locate and then to identify him. Fully and dapperly attired, Thomas sat in the chair in the opposite corner of the small room, legs smartly crossed, reading an issue of *Places* that Tom thought, utterly without interest, he hadn't seen yet.

He mumbled, "Good morning," and thought to stand up. Tried to stand up, but his knees didn't flex or extend in anything approximating the necessary pattern. He braced himself on the headboard and pushed, did get to his feet this time but then didn't at all know what to do next and next, and so stood there, bent uselessly because that motion was supposed to be part of a relay and wasn't, stayed that way for a period of time he couldn't have measured.

Often since Emily's death he'd found himself sitting or

standing or lying or crouching in one position for a while, his brain unable or unwilling to send any message to his body other than "Emily. Emily is dead." His brain was not even transmitting danger signals, although it recognized that the organism was in mortal danger; neither "fight" nor "flight" would do any good.

Eventually, Tom made his way to the bathroom and shut the door. For perhaps two or three minutes he stood in there, head bowed. Then he used the toilet. Then he turned on the faucet and filled his cupped palms with increasingly cold water. He thought he'd planned to splash the water onto his face and hair, but it dribbled out between his fingers while he was staring at the reflection in the mirror, and he couldn't think how to get it back.

Meanwhile, his father had called room service. Tom was able to eat a little, a few pulpy sections of grapefruit and half a slice of hard toast. He tasted none of it, could have identified none of it five minutes later. He drank three cups of black coffee one after the other and was jittery, his nerves pointlessly too near the surface of his skin, which should have been shielding them and was not.

Thomas, however, had always enjoyed breakfast, and subscribed to the nutritional wisdom that it was the most important meal of the day. Dimly, Tom wondered whether his father had eaten hearty breakfasts after Cecelia had died, while he was living in the seedy hotel, in shelters, and on the street. But he didn't want to take that much of an interest in someone else's story, and so he nudged it easily back out of his consciousness. This soon after Emily's death, the old man ate steadily and made no attempt to conceal his enjoyment, although his manners, of course, were both impeccable and unobtrusive. The pedestrian act of consumption, of self-nourishment, was made to look stylish.

Tom had been sitting back in his chair for some time, mourning Emily, when Thomas intruded. "I did not complete my story last evening. I have saved for today the tale of what happened to me during and after my sojourn in Revenant, how I came to be who and what I am today."

Tom heard himself say, "No," before he even partially knew what he was denying or protesting.

His father stood up and, alarmingly, came to him. Tom couldn't retreat far enough from the paternal hand on his shoulder, the long fingers caressing his cheek, the stentorian voice lowered to address him with frightening gentleness and intimacy. "Tom, I understand that you cannot hear any detailed narrative. But you must hear its theme, if you will, its central plot thrust: I was haunted and nearly destroyed by Cecelia because I would not release her. Some of our group never left the valley, were, in fact, destroyed by their great losses, as we had all believed we would be. Revenant would have kept us all there if it could. But some of us were freed as we freed our beloved ghosts, And it was because of Revenant, and ultimately because of Cecelia herself, that I was to live to meet your mother, and to father you and your sister, and to have the truly rich and splendid life I have today."

Tom, of course, said nothing. It didn't matter to him what his father said or did, what happened anywhere in the world. He dared have no self-interest of any kind, did his best to silence any instinct for self-preservation. It couldn't matter. Emily was dead. After a while his father shook his head and let him go.

All that morning they traveled an increasingly geomorphic highway that rose sharply, dipped sharply, curved sharply with the lay of the land. Pine and aspen stands gave way to elfin timber, which then faded into the coarse and sparse flora of alpine tundra. Snow glittered on the peaks and in the perpetually shadowed north-facing hollows. The highway became a dirt road; Tom did not note the transition, but now the rental car was whining and bumping along a rougher and narrower pathway, and his father observed, "We will not be able to drive much farther." There was a curious, faint comfort in traveling with this resolute man, the distant hope that he would make all decisions and determine what was real. Beyond that, Tom didn't care where they were going.

Soon thereafter, Thomas stopped the car and both men got out, Tom reluctantly, but his father opened the door so that there was nothing to lean against, no barrier between him and the cool open outside. The old man's hand, when Tom took it just long enough to propel and steady himself to his feet, was trembling, and his father's grip tightened before Tom withdrew his hand in muted alarm.

They walked across a high meadow, forded a small shallow white-laced stream, and negotiated a boulder field that sloped upward, upward. Tom was short of breath and dizzy. *Emily,* he thought, and yearned for her. *Emily.*

"Tommy."

Through tears he saw her and, though he was sure he couldn't keep his balance or direction, he went toward her. There she was, hair auburn in the sun, blue-and-white striped shirt, voice like wind in the trees, like wind over scoured rock. Someone else was standing behind her, and then was not. His father had stayed behind. He was alone with Emily.

"Tommy. I've been waiting for you."

Her hand closed over his and he was drawn forward, up and then startlingly down, red gold blue brown gray green, the built environment of Revenant designed to take him in.

7

Yellow blanket. Gabriel saw a baby in a yellow blanket and he wanted his mother.

 He couldn't stand to look at the kid, so he looked out somewhere over his head. Which was easy enough, since Will was a helluva lot shorter than he was these days, either flat on his back in bed or confined to that damn wheelchair. Before the accident he'd been two inches taller, and only sixteen, still a couple of years to grow. "Taller than your old man," Bill had challenged, proudly, feinting, punching him in the arm. "Think you're hot shit, don't you, kid, taller than your old man." No more.

"Dad," said Will in that breathy, girlish voice that made Bill want to puke. That one word, that "Dad," was all he could get out without having to gasp for air, so that he always sounded winded or upset.

"What?"

"I'm—getting married."

"Oh, for Chrissake." Bill slammed his paper down across his lap and forced himself to look at the boy to see if he was making some kind of sick joke. Not that you could tell. Supposedly the accident hadn't affected his face or his brain, but that was just doctor bullshit and Bill knew better.

The truth was, Will was as good as dead. For maybe

the millionth time since the accident, Bill wished his son had just kept it simple and just *died.*

"Thanks—a lot—Dad. I—appreciate—your support."

For a second Bill thought maybe the kid had read his mind. But then he realized Will was still on this getting married business. "So who's the lucky lady?" He made no effort to hide the sarcasm—tried, in fact, to be as obvious about it as possible. Didn't do Will any favors to act like things made sense when they didn't.

Will stared at him without saying anything. You never could tell if he'd heard you or not, or if he knew what the fuck was going on.

Bill was just about to give up and go back to his paper when Will said, "Stacey."

Bill knew who she was. Cute little brunette, one of the girls from the nursing service that came in and did the stuff the kid couldn't do for himself. Which was everything. Actually, Bill had entertained lecherous thoughts about her himself.

Trying to imagine Stacey and his cripple son *together* gave him the creeps. How could a girl want to marry somebody she had to clean shit off of? How could she fuck somebody who couldn't fucking move?

Will looked at him then. A good-looking kid, if you forgot the fact that he couldn't move. Anything. Square face like Bill's own, dirty blond hair like Bill's but down to the middle of his back, Brenda's eyes so blue they were almost purple and still sharp, still dancing. Since the accident, Bill had gone out of his way to avoid meeting either his wife's or his son's eyes, and now he looked away as fast as he could and said, "Why?"

Will blinked. Taking a breath after every other word, sounding unsure of himself even when maybe he wasn't although Bill couldn't imagine how he could ever be any-

thing *but* unsure of himself again, Will said, "What do—
you mean—why? We—love—each other."

If there was one thing Bill had learned in life, it was
that you had to sound like you knew what you were
doing whether you did or not. He snorted.

"I—know—that's hard—for you to—believe," Will
said, "but—we do."

"Would she 'love' you if you didn't get three hundred
dollars a month from the government free and clear?"
Bill snapped his newspaper out flat and turned the page.
He didn't need this. He'd had a hard day. National on his
ass, and he hadn't had decent sales figures in weeks.

"She—might." The kid's voice had practically no expression anymore and neither did his face, so it was hard
to tell what he really meant when he said something.
Brenda swore she could understand him, but Bill didn't
believe it. She was his mother, after all, and mothers
would say anything. "Some—people—do, you know,"
Will said.

Bill kept his mouth shut, which wasn't easy. The idea
of some reasonably sexy girl wanting to marry a geek,
especially his own son, enraged him. He turned to the
market report and studied it.

After a while Will left the room, propelling his wheelchair with his mouth. Sip and puff, they called it. Bill
tried not to hear it, tried not to think about it.

But he couldn't help hearing the unnatural noises the
kid made going into his room—the annoying whir of the
wheelchair, the clumsy opening and then shutting of the
bedroom door. Just getting the fucking doors in this
house wide enough for the wheelchair had set Bill back
over six grand, not to mention the ramps and the
replumbing and now Brenda was on him to get some
kind of an adapted computer system. Hell, *he* didn't even
have a computer at work to tell him how many cars he

hadn't sold. Will ought to be in an institution where they knew how to take care of him, and where normal people wouldn't have to look at him except maybe for a few hours on Sundays. Life was hard enough.

His only son. His heir. William Eric Cleary, Jr. Bill snorted at the concept, which used to make him so proud, like maybe there was one thing in his life he'd done right. Now it made his skin crawl.

Will had been wild, wilder than his old man had ever had the balls to be, and Bill had admired that. Kept telling Brenda to quit fussing, quit coddling the boy, he was just sowing his wild oats before some girl got her claws in him and his oats all got domesticated, which would happen soon enough. Screwed around in school. Drank a lot, probably some dope. Girls, lots of girls. A string of DUIs; in fact, he'd been driving without a license the night he rolled the Jeep, which was the fourth time Bill knew of he'd totaled a vehicle drunk. Bill had replaced them all off the lot.

Will would have done a lot more with his life than be a car salesman, but he'd never acted like he thought he was better than his old man. Now he wouldn't be doing shit, his life was ruined, and *now* he acted like Bill was the scum of the earth. Bill was not going to put up with it.

He finished his beer, dropped the can with the others on the floor around his chair, and went to the kitchen for another one. These days it was harder and harder to keep a buzz on.

Brenda was just now fixing dinner. Stew, it looked like. Bill was sick to death of stews and soups and other stuff the kid could swallow. Anyway, it would be a while before he got anything to eat, because she'd feed the kid first, spoonful by painstaking spoonful. It drove Bill nuts. Will chewed and swallowed so slowly that you'd swear his jaw and throat weren't moving at all, and then you'd swear he was going to choke. At least Brenda'd stopped suggesting that Bill feed him, and stopped doing it herself right at the dinner table. Talk about ruining a man's appetite.

Used to be, father and son weren't home for meals about half the time. Brenda used to complain. Baseball, football, action movies—they had a lot in common. Nothing in common anymore—how could you have anything in common with a crip?

After she fed him, she'd put him to bed. Christ, he was just like a damn baby—had to go to bed early, had to have his mommy tuck him in, had to have her brush his *teeth,* for God's sake. Sometimes Will wondered what the kid thought all those hours in bed. Theoretically, the accident hadn't damaged his mind,

Probably these days he thought about Stacey. Bill thought about her himself for a minute. Pretty little thing. But the thought of Stacey with somebody whose dick didn't even work, who wasn't even a man, so turned him off that it was easy to put her out of his mind.

But thinking of her made him think of Kathy. Now *Kathy* was a different story. He could tell he was already getting bored with her, but thinking about her still gave him a hard-on, and he grinned.

Brenda was humming, the picture of domestic tranquility. Bill could not understand how she could be happy, how she could be fucking *content,* when they'd lost their only child. She said he had to adjust, but he didn't. Adjusting was like what had happened to them didn't matter, wasn't important.

He'd lost the young athlete on the field, better than he'd ever been, shortstop in warm months and tight end in cool, and Bill hadn't missed a single game or more

than a handful of practices since Will had played Little
League and Peewee Football.

He'd never bought the sentimental bullshit that sports
were metaphors for life. He'd just liked being able to
cheer his son for simple, clear-cut achievements and give
him hell for fuck-ups that were anything but subtle. Will
would have played varsity team ball this year. Bill still
went to every game, cheered and swore at other people's kids.

He'd bought two season tickets for the Rockies' first
season. He didn't know why two. He and Will had talked
for years about major league baseball coming to Denver,
and Brenda kept saying he could still take him, the sta-
dium was wheelchair-accessible. But the idea turned
Bill's stomach. What would you say to people you knew
—customers, say, or guys from the lot? What if the kid's
pee bag broke? Would you have to pour the beer down
his throat or what? Would he yell the way he talked?
"Low—and—outside—ump! What—are ya—blind?"

He'd also lost the good-looking heartthrob who'd cut
a swath through young womanhood like Bill only
dreamed of doing. Will's prowess with girls had started
young. He'd been about twelve when Brenda'd found
rubbers in his jeans pocket. Dutifully Bill had talked to
him, made sure he didn't think they were water balloons. Proud and uneasy, the old stud teaching his young
challenger everything he knew—well, maybe keeping
back a few secrets the kid could find out on his own just
like every other man did. Nowhere near ready to just get
out of the way, Bill had had his first affair long about
then, Kelly or Kerry her name had been. A cute little girl
hot to trot who, he'd found out later, had actually been
interested in Will.

That wouldn't happen again. The doctor had told
them Will would never have sex "in the usual way," and

Bill had wanted to grab him by the throat and demand to know what the fuck other ways there were. But he didn't.

Bill was staring at his wife from behind, thinking that she used to be fairly attractive. Now she was more and more on the dumpy side, and she didn't get her hair colored or permed often enough. These days she hardly wore makeup at all. Her clothes were either too tight from all the weight she'd put on, or they looked sloppy. Hell, if she didn't care enough to keep herself up for him, Bill couldn't be blamed for going elsewhere.

Squatting in front of the open refrigerator door, he noted that he had only one can of beer left after this. Good. Not that he needed an excuse, but he'd say he was just going out for a six-pack, which would be the truth, just not the whole truth, and he'd call Kathy from the car phone. With any luck, he'd be in and out of her tight little pussy and back home in time for dinner, and he could keep both Kathy and Brenda happy. Actually, he didn't much care if they were happy or not, except for the hassle it would save him. He did not need more hassle.

"Oh, Bill, did Will tell you his news?" Brenda came to him as he straightened up, her blue eyes shining like she'd just won Publishers Clearing House, and put her arms around his neck. He didn't have much room to get away from her; he took the one available step back, which pinned him against the refrigerator. He didn't have any choice but to return her hug, but he did it as briefly as he thought he could get away with, trying not to come into contact with the little roll of fat around her waist but not able to avoid it completely. Up this close, he also couldn't help seeing the gray in her hair. "Yeah," he said.

"Isn't it *wonderful*? Our son's in college, and he's getting married."

"Yeah, terrific." He dropped his arms from around her, but she didn't take the hint and he had to stand there awhile longer while she nuzzled and kissed him. She wasn't wearing perfume. Faint but definite, he could smell her body odor.

She was still going on. Bill wished she'd just shut up. "After he got hurt, we both thought his life was over, didn't we? Remember? But he's going to have a normal life after all."

This was more than Bill could take. "Jesus Christ, Brenda, give me a break. He is *not* going to have a normal life."

Now she pulled away from him, which was a relief. "I don't understand you, Bill," she whispered fiercely. "Since he got hurt you act like he isn't even your son, like you're ashamed of him and you don't love him at all anymore."

"Will is as good as dead," he told her. He'd told her that before. He made no effort to keep his voice down. He didn't care if the kid heard. Probably it would be a good thing if he did. And Brenda was lying when she said she didn't understand. "*My* son is gone."

She was shaking her head violently. There were crow's feet around her eyes and at the corners of her mouth. He could not believe he was *married* to this woman, the mother of the son he had lost. "Your son is right here," she insisted, "and you're missing him."

"He's not himself. He hasn't been himself since the accident."

"Then who is he? He's not who he used to be, but he is himself. *This* is himself. You're so obsessed with the son you lost in the accident that you're depriving yourself of the son you have right now, who's a pretty wonderful young man in his own right. He needs you, Bill. And you need him."

"Well, I don't have whatever it is he *needs,*" Bill declared, curling his lip snidely, ignoring the second part of what she'd said because it was pure and utter bullshit. "It's asking too much."

Brenda had taken his face in her hands before he could think fast enough to dodge. He could hardly stand to look at her, let alone touch her like that. He could hardly stand the smell of her, or the sound her breath made in and out of her nostrils. She was the mother of the perfect son Bill had lost, and the mother of the cripple in the next room that he was expected to love and take care of for the rest of his life. It was asking too much.

Bill knew his rage against his wife was a dangerous and powerful thing, and he longed to just let it loose. To punch her fat face. To push her down on the floor for not keeping Will safe, for not keeping him safe from losing Will. To kick her in the gut for getting over losing their son and going on with her life. But he restrained himself from doing anything more than slapping her hands away.

Brenda was yelling. "What happened to Will was a terrible thing! What happened to *us* was a terrible thing! But enough already, Bill! Our lives didn't end there!"

"Go fuck yourself!" Bill yelled back.

Brenda started to say something else, but from behind her Will broke in. Bill thought he might have been trying to say something for some time, but they'd been talking over him. That gave Bill a certain satisfaction. "It's—all right—Ma. I—don't need—him."

Brenda rushed to him. Freed, Bill grabbed the last beer out of the refrigerator and started out of the house.

"Wait," Will said.

It was such a weak, pansy voice that it would have been easy to pretend he hadn't heard it. Bill didn't know why he stopped.

"You're not—upset—about what—happened—to me," Will said. Bill couldn't tell for sure because of the flat, expressionless tone, but it seemed to him the kid was accusing him of something. Accusing *him*. "You're —pissed off—because of—what happened—to you."

"I wish to hell it *had* happened to me," Bill heard himself say. There was a silence.

Then Will said, "Dad. Look—at me."

Trapped, Bill let his gaze slide across the kid before he focused on some point on the opposite wall. It was the best he could do. Even at that, he saw the monster wheelchair and the body in it, stick legs and shoulders and arms with practically no meat or muscle on the bones. He couldn't help but see it. Brenda had dressed the kid in a muscle shirt. They could at least have the decency to cover him up.

"I'm—happy," Will said.

Bill couldn't think of anything to say except, "Bullshit."

"I'm—happy," Will said again. There wasn't any real change in the way his voice sounded, but somehow Bill had the distinct impression that he'd emphasized the bizarre word the second time.

"You're *happy* you're paralyzed? You're *happy* your life is ruined?" In contrast, his own speech pattern sounded stupid in his ears; he was enunciating every syllable and putting in lots of emphasis.

"My life—isn't—ruined. My—life is—changed."

"You're fooling yourself," Bill told him. He was so frustrated now that *he* could hardly talk. This was exactly what he'd gone out of his way to avoid, this kind of damn-fool conversation.

"I wouldn't—have asked—to be a—quad," Will said. "But—I'm not—sorry—it happened."

Bill was crazy with fury and revulsion. If he didn't get out of here he would hurt somebody. The kid would be easy to hurt. Fucking helpless freak. When he turned and walked out and slammed the door behind him, neither one of them even tried to call him back.

He backed the XKE out of the driveway practically without looking, laying a little rubber, and took off down the street. The car responded so smoothly that it was like all he had to do was *think* "turn," *think* "faster." Will had been driving Bill's Jeep the night of the accident. Totaled it and totaled himself. Bill had planned on buying him a brand new black XKE for graduation. He'd bought it for himself instead, which was fun, but every time he drove the thing he thought about how Will couldn't. Just another way he'd been cheated.

Thought about the boy's hands, limp as fish on the ends of his thin, limp arms, that couldn't grip anything, couldn't move. Thought about his legs and feet that couldn't step down on the gas, couldn't walk. Thought about his dick, also limp as a fish, more like a goddamn worm. Thought about the bony spot at the base of his spine, right above his ass, that got sores on it.

Thinking about all that, Bill found the car going faster and faster, which was all right with him. No cops around. He took a swig of beer. Suddenly impatient with small town streets, he took the ramp up onto the highway, not much caring which way he was heading, heading west.

The highway cut through farmland between towns, and it would have been hard to believe Denver was so close if it hadn't been for the brown smudge along the southeast horizon. Green-gold cornfields and gold-green wheatfields under blue sky that was wide, high, and low.

A few gold-brown fallow fields sent up dust. Here and there cottonwoods clustered around farmhouses or along streambeds, most of the streams dry this time of year but the trees' roots had found moisture somewhere. Bill had heard there was as much of a tree below the ground as you could see above it, but he didn't think he believed that. He caught sight of Will running along the ditchbank and was grinning before he thought about it.

He laughed bitterly at himself, finished off his beer, and tossed the can out the window, rubbed at his eyes. He didn't *feel* that soused; in fact, he wouldn't have said he felt any effect of the beer at all, other than a mild queasiness that could just as well have been from the heat and the motion of the speeding car. He was deliberately speeding, but nowhere near fast enough.

But it was asinine to think, even for a minute, that the boy he saw running there was Will, so he must be drunker than he'd thought. He pressed on the gas pedal. He still saw the boy, keeping up with the powerful car, which was ridiculous.

The boy was about ten years old, and he was running, strong, young legs bare and gold-brown in the high sun. Athlete's legs. It wasn't Will. Of course it wasn't Will. But Bill fucking *wished* it was.

In grade school and junior high, Will had had a friend who'd lived on a farm out this way. Now that kid was on a basketball scholarship at some school in Kansas or Nebraska. Probably when they were kids, the two of them had run along this road or one like it, cut across the fields like that, blue shirt flapping, light brown hair plastered back. Bill didn't think he'd ever seen them do it so it wasn't exactly a memory, but they'd more than likely done something like that a dozen times.

Strong, young body. Bill felt the age in his own body, and Will's wouldn't do a single goddamn useful thing anymore. It just stayed wherever somebody else put it, and it broke down—the skin, the muscles.

Strong, young voice, this kid whooping over his shoulder in the sheer pleasure at being alive. Will didn't whoop anymore, and Bill knew, though both Brenda and Will insisted otherwise, that the kid couldn't possibly be glad to be alive now.

The boy who looked so much like the boy Bill had lost disappeared between rows of tasseled corn that by rights shouldn't have been tall or thick enough to hide him like that. There was a flicker behind him, as if somebody else was moving there, keeping up with the car. Light and shadow, then nothing. Bill punched the steering wheel, grazing the horn, and the car swerved, but he pulled it back into his lane with no trouble. Now that he'd thought about when Will used to run like that, it was like his own sharp memory of something that had been stolen from him. Angry tears, caustic with beer, backed up his throat into his nose.

Kathy answered on the first ring, obviously waiting for his call. That was gratifying, but it was also way too easy. It didn't take much to persuade her to drop whatever she was doing and meet him at the motel outside of Nederland. He didn't ask what she was doing.

By the time he got there and checked into the room, he was flat sober again. He should have stopped in town for a couple of six-packs. But he didn't want to get up and get dressed, and he was feeling downright sick now, so he just stayed under the sheet on the lumpy mattress watching the CU-CSU matchup on the tiny black-and-white and getting more and more pissed off.

Kathy finally showed up. Bill greeted her with, "Took you long enough."

"Sorry, babe. Had to wait till the bread came out of the oven."

"I don't have a lot of time."

"I don't need a lot of time," and she was already sucking at his cock, which was trying and failing to get hard. Bill kept his attention on the game and was trying to relax when he saw Will bending over Kathy from behind, grabbing her tits, then an old lady with her bony hands on Kathy's slightly sagging belly.

"What the—" Bill sat up, the suddenness of his movement pulling his limp dick out of her mouth with a disgusting little *pop.*

Kathy rolled over onto her back and wiped her mouth with the back of her wrist. A thin stripe of sunlight from under the windowshade cut across her left boob. She was panting. "What's the matter, sweetie? Did I hurt you?" She was practically talking baby talk. Bill hated that. He always suspected she was making fun of him.

There was nobody else in the room. Of course, Will wasn't behind her, wasn't touching her, wasn't standing or kneeling or crouching behind her. And there was no old lady. There better not be.

"Just a cramp," Bill muttered, and forced himself to stretch out again. Now his erection was like a fence post in an open field, and it throbbed. He had to hand it to her, so to speak; she was good.

"You want me to stop?" she teased. She flicked at the head of his dick with her long nail, scratching it, making it sway.

"No."

"You want inside me now?"

"Yeah."

She grinned, sighed, got up on her hands and knees, and lowered herself onto him. Bill came almost the second he felt the warm wet walls of her pussy close around the shaft of his cock, and she pretended she came, too. He was sure it was fake. All that moaning and groaning.

He'd noticed before that she didn't say his name, she just said generic shit like "Honey!" and "Oh, baby!"

Briefly, he wondered what she got out of this. He wondered what *he* was getting out of it. He didn't even like it much. Hell, he didn't even like *her* much. But he knew what he got out of it. Every time he was with her, every time she did something to him that he was supposed to like whether he liked it or not, he was doing it for his son. The thought of Will in bed with this cunt—blowing in her ear, sliding his strong young hands up and down her sweaty body—came and went, the way it always did. Stupid.

CSU scored. Pleased, Bill stretched, patted Kathy's back where she'd collapsed on top of him, and started to move out from under her. "Gotta go," he said.

He heard her giggling into the pillow while he cleaned himself off in the bathroom, using the only towel and washcloth and tossing them onto the floor. "Next batch of dough'll be ready to punch down," she told him, but he didn't know or care what she was talking about.

The XKE roared out of the motel parking lot, spitting gravel against Kathy's pickup's wheels. Bill intended to turn east and go home. But all of a sudden he couldn't. Couldn't stand the thought of it. Brenda, and the kid he couldn't even look at. The highway went west and up the mountain, straight as a ribbon, and he took it. The car didn't even labor as the road climbed.

The tension release from fucking Kathy didn't last long. He'd been noticing that lately, and didn't know if it was her or him. Used to be, screwing her or any other girl would relax him for days at a time. But now sex wasn't working any better than booze.

The only thing he could think about for any length of

time was how his life had been ruined. It wasn't fucking fair. He pressed on the gas.

He could hardly see. His vision was blurred by *tears,* for God's sake. Cursing, he pulled over onto the shoulder of a hairpin turn where there were no guardrails and the mountainside dropped straight off for two hundred feet or more, practically right under the wheels.

Now his vision was blackening. He sprawled across the seat, jerked open the passenger door, and threw up on the ground. Maybe he was having a heart attack. Maybe this was the Big One.

He was raging, retching, hanging halfway out of his idling car in the slime of his own vomit. He was giving in finally to what he'd known was true since the night Will had been taken from him: his life, just barely worth living before, was now no longer worth living.

The car was moving.

Bill managed to rouse himself enough to crawl back inside and shut the door. He pulled himself to a half-sitting position in the passenger seat. The car was picking up speed, taking curves tight, squealing tires, heading off the highway onto narrow unpaved roads that branched into smaller roads, all of them heading straight up the mountain.

The old hag was driving. That didn't make any sense.

Will was driving. That didn't make any sense either, but it was true.

Will. Whole and good-looking and cocky as ever. Strong young hands on the wheel and gearshift. Muscled tanned young legs. Shirt off, muscles rippling across his shoulders the way Bill's never had. The odors of sweat and sun-warmed skin and beer. Whistling a Metallica tune Bill had pretended to like but never had.

Will announced, "Hey, old man, I got somethin'

fuckin' *cool* to show you," and turned the steering
wheel sharply to the right.

As they sailed off the cliff, both father and son yelled.
Red slammed into green; silver splintered into black. Bill
was thrown into his son's arms as the vehicle rolled and
crashed.

8

Make new friends
And keep the old
One is silver
And the other gold.

Every time, Hannelore sang along.

Corinne Ogilvie took a half step forward with her right foot, ignoring the twinge in her knee when she put her weight on it. She extended her outside arm with the elbow just slightly crooked and the palm up, fingers spread. Olivia, beside her, was new, and didn't quite have the move right, which worried Corinne about competition; you were supposed to match your position and timing to whoever stood on either side of you, so that the chorus moved as a unit in the same way that it was supposed to sing with unit sound, which meant that if Olivia was wrong Corinne would have to do the move wrong, too.

She was going to say something but the director beat her to it. Lila had been their director going on five years now, and most of the time Corinne trusted her to know what she was doing. Better than the last one, anyway, the young man who insisted on laughingly referring to them as "my girls" but who hadn't been willing or able to teach them much of anything. Besides that, he'd kept

bringing them music that had originally been arranged
for men's barbershop, adapted to women's range but not
very well, so that the bass part was all over the place.
Once they'd hired him they'd had a terrible time getting
rid of him, because some of the girls didn't want to hurt
his feelings; Corinne and the rest of the board had been
very relieved when his company had transferred him to
Houston.

The one good thing he'd done was to encourage Corinne and her daughters to form the basis of a quartet
which had sung together for six years. One year they
competed. They didn't place, but they were good
enough to be onstage in front of eight hundred Sweet
Adelines from all over the region. That year Judy Franklin
had been their baritone. The year Maura stopped singing, the bari had been Marge Bender, and they'd re-
cruited Edith Morelli for tenor to take Maura's place; Edie
had a nice enough voice but it wasn't very strong and
everybody else had to pull back to balance the sound.

Since then, since Maura had died, Monica had been
talking about starting up the quartet again. "She
wouldn't want us to give up our singing," Monica kept
saying to her mother, as if anybody'd ever known what
Maura wanted since she got sick. Corinne did give it
some thought. Nobody sang tenor as purely and clearly
as Maura had, until the depression got so bad she
couldn't sing at all, couldn't even get out of bed, and the
truth was Monica wasn't an especially strong lead; she
kept letting herself get pulled off her part.

"Once more," the director said, "from the edge."

Corinne concentrated on keeping her soft palate open
as she sang the nice low bass line of the intro to
"Daddy's Little Girl," their ballad for this year. Lila had
proposed it to the music committee last year and the
year before, but Corinne had said no. She thought she

could do it this year, three years since she'd lost Maura, and so far, by keeping her mind on all the things you had to think about this close to competition—lifting on the ends of phrases, getting rid of all your breath before you take the next one, singing tall vowels, keeping your face on, making the choreography moves crisp and definite— she'd been okay. The baris came in over the basses with their downward half-note scale, and it sounded *good.* Women singing bass could knock your socks off when it was right.

During the years Corinne had been section leader, there'd sometimes been as many as six basses. Now there were only three. Vicky stood in the front row, and the vocal coach had just moved Dolores to the far end of the risers. They'd both passed this song without too much trouble, and Corinne could hear now that their notes and words were okay, but somebody was a shade flat on the D. Dolores, probably, who'd been in Sweet Adelines practically as long as Corinne but who still didn't understand what it meant to aim for the top side of a note.

Corinne started stewing about how to tell Dolores, again, at sectional next week, and then she got to thinking about Maura's flawless pitch even on impossibly high notes, and marveling again, as she had so many times, that her own range was so definitely bass, the lower the better, while her daughter's had seemed to get higher every day until the depression took it all away. Thinking about all that, Corinne missed the choreography on "you're the Easter bunny." Annoyed with herself and with Maura for distracting her, with Maura for dying on her, she took some comfort in the fact that the baris missed their interval and the leads were dragging. But the tenors, even without Maura, were perfect. Corinne sighed. Competition was less than a month away. She hoped it wouldn't be a complete disaster.

"Basses, it's higher than you think," urged Lila. "Keep it nice and light. Remember, you make the foundation for the pyramid of the barbershop sound." Her hands traced a pyramid shape in the air.

Out of the corner of her eye, Corinne saw Monica fidget and whisper something to one of the other younger members. That made her mad. Monica really didn't have the commitment you needed to be a Sweet Adeline. Her sister had put forth more effort than she ever did, even fighting depression, until the depression finally won out.

Corinne scowled, then caught herself. She could not afford to think about either of her twins now, the dead one or the live one, or about how mad she was at Maura for being dead and at Monica for still being alive. She put her performance face back on just as the director yelled "Faces!" Monica glanced over her shoulder and tried to catch her mother's eye—she was always doing that—but Corinne looked resolutely past her.

"From the edge," said the director again. Lila was a banana-shaped, cheerful, vaguely foul-mouthed, musically accomplished lady close to Corinne's own age, who had never lost a child. Had never slept on a mattress on the floor of her daughter's room, night after night after night, years of nights, to keep her from killing herself. Had never snapped awake one midnight to find that she'd dozed off, and then, reaching up, to find her daughter's bed empty.

Nobody Corinne knew had lost a child, unless you counted miscarriages, which Corinne didn't. No one else in the chorus had lost a child. That's why they could sing "Daddy's Little Girl." She could sing it, too.

They could have been singing anything. The words

didn't matter, except in how you said them: tall vowels, practically no consonants. Corinne's attention went smoothly to the joy of the music, women's voices in tight a cappella harmony. When they achieved the right sound, it was a seamless, impersonal intimacy that lifted her out of herself and away from Maura. They sang the song all the way through, and it was very nearly perfect. Gooseflesh rose on Corinne's arms as they held the last beautiful chord and then the silence afterward. The overtone came pure and high, the unsung note above a perfectly balanced and matched chord. Corinne held her breath with everybody else in the chorus, and she swore the overtone sounded just like Maura's clarion tenor. But that, of course, wasn't real.

"Yes!" cried the director, her face aglow as though they'd given her a gift, and everybody, Corinne and Monica included, cheered. Lila held her fists in the air for a minute, then relaxed and, slightly out of breath, told the chorus, "That's enough for tonight. Be on the risers at eight o'clock sharp tomorrow morning. We've got a long day ahead of us."

Almost immediately, Monica was beside her. "How ya doin', Mom?"

Corinne eyed her. "Fine. Why?"

"Just thought you might need a hand getting down off the risers," Monica said, extending her forearm. "They're pretty high."

Unwillingly, Corinne thought of both the twins coming to help her down; it seemed she'd almost always been placed on the very top riser and her knees had almost always hurt. They'd come up on either side of her, young women identical in build and coloring though not, by then, in demeanor, and they'd take her hands, and the three of them would improvise some cute little three-part riff as they made their way down. Every now and then somebody'd say there ought to be such a thing as a barbershop *trio* for Corinne and her girls.

"No, thanks," she said now to her surviving daughter, and stepped down off the risers under her own power, although her old knees objected. Monica visibly recoiled and Corinne felt bad, but she could not bear to touch her any more than she absolutely had to, this child who had not died.

Dolores came up beside her and put a sisterly arm around her waist. Happily, Corinne hugged her back. She suspected Dolores of being her Secret Sister again this year; the little gifts and cards had a hint of Dolores's particular thoughtfulness, and were personal—a ceramic pig covered with hearts for Valentine's Day because Corinne collected pigs, a scarf for no special reason in January that just exactly matched the sweater Monica had bought her for Christmas. Corinne hadn't much liked the sweater, to tell you the truth, until she got the scarf to go with it.

"So what do you think, section leader?" Dolores wanted to know. "Are we ready for contest?"

"We'll have a bass sectional sometime tomorrow," Corinne decided. "There are a few things. But mostly I'd say we're ready."

Everybody else had migrated either outside or to the far end of the big room, where chairs and tables had been moved to make room for the risers and snacks which Edie and Judy were setting out. Corinne would like some of the cheese popcorn Suzanne always brought, or more of her own sour-cream-and-onion chips and guacamole dip. But she thought of her blood pressure and triglycerides and instead joined the group outside, trying not to mind that some of them were smoking.

Corinne was impatient with the very notion that

smokers had rights, and sometimes she'd cough more loudly than necessary and back away with exaggerated fuss the instant a stranger lit up, before any smoke had even reached her. For women who were supposed to care about their voices, and in this pristine place, smoking seemed especially ludicrous.

Neither of her girls smoked. Maura hadn't died of lung cancer or emphysema or heart disease. There were so many reasons a body and mind could die that sometimes Corinne couldn't imagine how anybody stayed alive at all. Monica was still alive. So was she.

Looking around at the high, sharp angles of the mountains, trying to breathe the sharp air, Corinne reminded herself that it was beautiful up here. She'd lived in Colorado all her life, but she'd never felt at home in the mountains. Since Walt had left and the girls had grown up, she never came up here except when she had to once a year for the retreat.

Patches of snow were silver blue on the ground and up the slopes on all sides of the lodge. There'd been years when the snow had been several inches deep, and in '89 they'd very nearly been snowed in. Stars glittered in swatches across the black sky from high horizon to horizon. The moon was pink, for some reason, and didn't look at all like a disc or a hole in the sky; its globular shape made Corinne's tongue and palms curl as if to receive it.

Maura hadn't liked the mountains either, especially when she was depressed. Something about the altitude, the change in air pressure.

''Come sit with us, kid,'' Dolores invited, and Corinne smiled and went to join the nonsmokers at the west end of the porch. Her knees pained her when she lowered herself onto the top step, and she knew she'd have trouble getting back to her feet. She leaned companionably against Dolores's knee.

Having the retreat here was a whole lot better than trying to fit fifteen or eighteen or, one year, twenty-two women of various sizes, shapes, ages, and personal habits into somebody's house with, if you were lucky, two bathrooms. Here, though, with all of them in bunks in one cavernous room, it was always hard to sleep. There were snorers, a few of them truly phenomenal. Among the younger ones, there were partiers and talkers. Janice was usually complaining about her husband, recounting to a new member if there were any—or, if not, to somebody who'd heard it all before—stories illustrating how stupid and piggish and boring and insensitive he was. The year Dolores had changed from tenor to bass and had been panicked about having to learn the songs all over again, she'd dozed off listening to her learning tapes, and in the middle of the night her earphones had slipped off, blaring the music out into the room.

Corinne would have thought she'd be used to interrupted sleep. For years she'd spent every night on a mattress on the floor beside Maura's bed, which had been pushed into a corner so that Maura would have to actually step over her mother if she got up in the middle of the night to commit suicide. Which she did, maybe a dozen times during those two years. Corinne would hear her, would sense with a mother's profoundly fallible instinct that her child was in even more danger than usual, and would struggle on painful knees and ankles and hips to find her daughter before she slashed her wrists or took the hoarded pills or hooked up the hose to the exhaust pipe.

Ten or a dozen or twenty times, who knew, and then one time Corinne hadn't gotten up. Simply had not. Simply had said to herself in bleary anger and exhaustion that she couldn't do this anymore, she was too old and tired for this, Maura was a grown woman anyway, thirty-three years old, and it was her life, sooner or later she had to learn to be responsible for herself. Corinne had, though it was hard for her to believe it now, fallen back asleep and, apparently, slept soundly for the first time in two years, as though relieved at no longer having to save her daughter's life.

And had awakened refreshed and alarmed in early morning sunlight to find Maura's bed empty. Had stumbled downstairs to the basement as though she knew where to go and found Maura hanging from a rafter, dead for some time already. The note said, "I know this will hurt you, Mom, but it's my life and I don't want it."

Utterly enraged, Corinne had raised her fists and been about to pummel the motionless suspended body of the daughter who had won, the daughter she had failed, when from upstairs she'd heard Monica's voice and footsteps. Then she'd come to her senses and shrieked her daughter's name. *"Maura!"*

"Isn't it pretty up here?" Monica said.

Corinne hadn't noticed her there on the bottom step. "Same as every year," she heard herself say and, vaguely, wondered why she was being mean. Monica looked up at her, then without saying anything else got up and went back inside the lodge.

Dolores rested a hand on her shoulder and said mildly, "Corinne." But she didn't go on, and Corinne didn't acknowledge the reproach. She'd known Dolores for quite some time, but not well.

When the chorus had first started coming up here for retreats, Corinne and Maura and Monica would sometimes be the only ones inside. They'd sit around the popcorn and giggle together over some Secret Sister gift one of them had given or gotten. They'd work on songs. They'd talk about family problems or plans.

For just a second now, Corinne missed that. But she put it out of her mind. No sense missing somebody who didn't care enough about herself or anybody else not to take her own life.

Instead, though, she found herself thinking about how much the twins had looked alike. When they were born and until they went to school they were very nearly identical. Even when they were teenagers, the differences between them had been easy to hide, although Monica especially sometimes wanted to accentuate them.

Friends, teachers, the pediatrician, even their father had been readily fooled. They answered for each other. They went to each other's classes; Corinne suspected them of taking each other's tests on occasion, even though she'd warned them not to and they'd always denied it. She was a teacher; she could have found out, but she never did. At least once, Monica had gone out with her sister's boyfriend, because Maura was getting tired of him and wasn't ready to tell him so; the boy never knew, but Monica came home saying he was a real creep and she'd told him she didn't want to see him anymore.

They'd switched positions on their soccer team, seats at the dinner table, beds at night. Their adoring daddy would come in and kiss them and say, "Good night, Maura. Good night, Monica," to the wrong girl. They'd learned to suppress their triumphant, slightly mean laughter until after he'd left the room, poor man, and Corinne had thought that Walt never knew he'd been tricked, had never realized that he couldn't tell his beloved little girls apart. Later, though, she'd come to wonder if that wasn't one of the reasons he'd left, for a much younger woman with only one son.

Corinne had felt a little sorry for him and for the rest of the people in her daughters' lives. A little smug, too, because she was sure *she'd* never confused one with the other. As the years saw Maura's depression spread and deepen while Monica remained untouched by it, Corinne had noted with growing panic and outrage how vastly different they were turning out to be.

Suddenly now her heart plummeted and she caught her breath as a wholly new thought surfaced: what if, after all, she had mixed them up? What if it was Monica instead of Maura who had died, and Maura who was still alive? What if for these three years she'd been mourning the wrong child? What kind of difference would that make?

Dolores began massaging Corinne's shoulders. It was a friendly, sisterly gesture and Corinne liked it a lot. That was a nice thing about being part of a group of women: there was a good deal of easy and undemanding affection, touching and thoughtful little gifts and cards in your mailbox when something important had happened in your life. They'd sung at Maura's funeral without her even asking, because she wouldn't have thought to ask— just stood up and sung, tears in their eyes, harmony tight and sweet, and they'd come to the house afterwards with casseroles. Corinne had been surprised how nice it was to have other women cook for you at a time like that.

"The anniversary is coming up, isn't it?" Dolores asked gently.

"Tomorrow," said Corinne.

"Are you okay?"

Corinne never knew how to answer that question. In a way, she was perfectly okay; she'd picked up the pieces of her life, she'd never lost Adelines, and she still had one surviving daughter. In another way, though, she would never be okay again, and that was her daughter's fault. So she just shrugged under Dolores's hands.

The other woman patted her once and let it go. That was as personal as things got around here. She'd known some of these women for seventeen years, and nobody ever pressed for details. It was a funny sort of friendship, she thought, but it was fine by her.

Monica came and sat beside them just as Corinne decided she'd had enough of the great outdoors, especially since it was getting dark and chilly, and was going back inside the lodge. Exasperated, she made herself stay put for a few minutes so her daughter wouldn't think she was leaving because of her. Monica was so touchy these days.

"Mom," said Monica. "I've got something to tell you."

Corinne was instantly fearful. At first she didn't say anything. Then, when Dolores and Monica both just sat there like lumps, she had to say something. "I'm all ears." She hadn't meant it to sound sarcastic. Lately it seemed to her that she was always mad at Monica, and she was almost afraid to have anything to do with her for fear it would show.

Dolores said, "I'll leave you two ladies alone," and moved to the other end of the porch where Lila was telling Olivia what to expect at competition. Trying unsuccessfully to get her knees into a position where they wouldn't hurt so much, Corinne stared at the spherical pink moon and waited helplessly for what her daughter had to say.

"Jay and I are going to have a baby," Monica told her.

"Oh?" Corinne said. "And are you going to bother getting married first?"

Monica shook her head. "We're not ready for that kind of commitment."

Corinne exploded, though she managed to keep herself from yelling. "What do you think having a baby is? Don't you think that's a commitment? A lifelong commitment! Longer than lifelong, even!"

"Husbands leave," Monica pointed out.

"And babies die." Maybe she shouldn't have said that, but it was the truth.

Her daughter gave her a long look. It was much darker in the mountains than it ever got in the city and Corinne couldn't have really seen her face even if she'd been looking at her, but she could feel her staring and it bothered her. Behind them, Lila was recounting for Olivia's benefit the story of the time at International when somebody from Canyonlands Chorus had meant to take off her overskirt at the stomp in the uptune and somehow had gotten hold of the underskirt, too, so there she was standing up in front of three thousand people in her pantyhose, but she'd finished the song because the show must go on and her chorus had placed third. Corinne was laughing to herself, remembering, when Monica said quietly, "Look, Mom, I know you think the wrong twin died, but I'm glad I'm alive and I'm going to have a good life whether you want me to or not." Then she turned and walked off down the gravel road away from the lodge.

She came back, though. Corinne saw her come back just a few minutes later, saw her sit down on the floor with the ones who were singing songs from the sixties, heard her join in. After a while she heard the others shriek and coo, and knew that Monica had told them her news. Corinne gathered herself together and went to bed.

She was the first one downstairs, and she chose a bunk in the far corner and opened her suitcase on the bunk above her so at least nobody would take that one. It took her a while to get herself ready; she'd been to a lot of retreats by now and she'd learned what she needed to be comfortable—foam mattress pad, electric blanket, a cool nightshirt under a heavy flannel gown so she could add or remove layers when somebody turned the heat up or down. She settled herself in her bunk with the portable reading lamp visored around her head, read a chapter in the newest Koontz novel, which in her opinion wasn't as good as some of the others, and fell asleep. As she was drifting off, thoughts of Maura and Monica threatened to seep in, but she was able to keep them in the background by rehearsing over and over in her mind the bass for both contest songs.

She woke up when Lila and Janice came in, noisily whispering, and again because she got cold and had to turn the electric blanket up. Both times her first thought, before she was even fully conscious, was that Maura wasn't in her bed above her, Maura was gone, Maura was going to kill herself, she had to save Maura, and by the time her mind had organized and understood the real reason she was awake, her heart was rattling in her chest and her palms were clammy and she could hardly breathe. But both times she went back to sleep without too much trouble.

She woke up again. The big room echoed with snores, Lila's whistle, Dolores's rumble and wheeze. *Maura's going to die I have to save*—Maura was crouching on the floor beside her bed, not saying anything, not touching her, just watching her and waiting for her to wake up and know she was there. It couldn't be Maura. She'd already let Maura die.

Maura.

Corinne didn't think she'd said her daughter's name out loud, which was a good thing because it wasn't Maura, of course. It was Monica. The one who'd died was Maura. Monica was the one left alive.

The enormous, terrible, deceptive relief Corinne had felt when she'd fleetingly thought she was seeing Maura had been replaced now by rage. Even as the rage swelled and exploded inside her, knocking her back on the bed, she recognized that it was out of all proportion to anything Monica had done. Except survive. Except be spared the suffering and death of her twin sister.

"What *is* it?" She wanted to holler, but she did her best to speak quietly, mindful that the room was crowded with her Sweet Adelines sisters trying to get some sleep.

"Mom, I need you," her daughter said in an undertone just above a whisper.

Stiff and awkward on the narrow mattress that bowed in the middle, Corinne rolled over and pulled the covers up around her ears. "Whatever it is can surely wait till morning."

She heard no movement, felt no approach. But now there was an insistent touch through the blankets at the nape of her neck, the small of her back. Though she didn't feel breath across her cheek, the voice came full in her ear—the timbre and speech rhythms the girls had shared, with Maura's latterday flatness of effect, weak support, many fewer words. "No. Now. Please come."

The treacherous thought came to Corinne that there might be something she could do for her daughter. The last time she'd allowed herself to think that, she'd failed and Maura had died. She shook her head and burrowed under the covers.

The voice and touch followed her. "Mom. Please."

With effort, Corinne rolled back to face her daughter and propped herself on her elbow. She was shaking and sick at her stomach from the shock and deprivation of interrupted sleep, and from enormous reluctance ever to feel that way again. Two years was enough. She'd sacrificed enough for these children. "What do you *want*?"

"I need you."

"No, you don't need me. You're a grown woman. You've got your own life, and so do I."

"No, you don't."

In exasperation, Corinne closed her eyes, rubbed them. When she opened them again, not knowing what she was going to say, nobody was there. Good. Monica had given up and gone back to bed. Corinne even heard the gentle whistling of her daughter's breath from the next bed, as rhythmic as if her sleep hadn't been disturbed. Corinne had listened for just that sound for a lot of frantic nights; it repulsed her to find herself listening for it again.

Her bladder was full. Wide awake now and testy, she stared at the crisscrossed springs on the underside of the top bunk, which caught some stray light here and there, and carried on with herself an unpleasant little debate, the discomfort of lying there with a distended bladder versus the discomfort of clambering across the cold floor on aching legs. It was pointless, because now that she was awake, she'd have to get up.

Trying to wince silently when the pain shot through her knees, Corinne managed to extract herself from the covers, sit up, and find her slippers. Some of the girls brought thongs, but she didn't like the way they rubbed between her toes, didn't like the feel of rubber soles at all, so she had to be careful in these old soft cloth things not to step in puddles and not to slip. Hanging on to the heavy metal frames of the bunk beds, she made her way past Monica, who still looked sound asleep, past Lila and Janice, to the gentlemen's bathroom, which was closer to this end of the sleeping room than the ladies'. With only women here it didn't matter which she used, except that the stalls in the men's were open, without even the flimsy and too-short curtains that hung crookedly in the ladies'.

Feeling conspicuous, Corinne sat there for a while and tried not to think of anything but music. Her hands rested with sad affection over her bare swollen knees.

In the last years of Maura's life, she'd been so afraid of leaving her alone at night and it had been so hard to get up off the mattress on the floor that she'd lie there for hours in misery, pretending it wasn't misery, and had given herself chronic bladder infections. When at last she really had no choice, she'd hoist herself to her feet—or, terrified of waking Maura who might well kill herself if she was awake, she'd crawl. She'd try her best to hurry, leaving the doors open, stopping the stream of urine more than once to listen for her daughter, thinking how she'd never have believed it if someone had told her she'd be spending her nights like this. She'd leave the toilet unflushed until morning, afraid she wouldn't hear Maura over its noise.

Most of the time Maura was still asleep, or at least still alive, when Corinne got back to the room. Sometimes she'd whisper, "Hi, Mom. I love you, Mom," whispering as though there were somebody else in the room that they didn't want to wake up. Corinne would kiss her good night and assure her softly that she loved her, too, which she did, and her heart would break again for this unhappy child. Sometimes Maura wouldn't say anything and Corinne would bend over her to make sure she was still breathing, would look down at her and wonder what either of them had done to deserve this.

Once there was blood. When she hurried back into the bedroom she smelled something, heard something, saw something glisten, and she turned on the light and cried out at almost the same instant because there was blood all over the room. How could there be so much blood in such a short time? Had she fallen asleep on the toilet and been gone longer than she knew? Had Maura hidden the razor blade and been cutting on herself while Corinne was right there on the floor beside her? She called the ambulance. She cleaned up the blood. Maura didn't die that time.

She heard something now. She'd been standing up, readjusting her clothes, testing her knees to see if they'd get her back to her bunk, and she stopped short and held her breath. The sound came again. A rustle. An irregular series of faint thumps. The hint of a climbing tenor harmony, its melody lost.

And Maura's voice, felt in her bones rather than heard. "Hi, Mom. I love you."

Corinne blurted, "Leave me alone," and instantly felt stupid. You couldn't get much stupider than talking to somebody who wasn't there.

"Mom. Mom. I *need* you."

"No." Now Corinne was feeling really terrible. But it was the start of something she'd wanted to say for a long time, and even if she was just talking to herself she went on in a fierce whisper. "I never was a good enough mother for you."

She saw something glisten, felt a tug at her sleeve. "Come with me."

"Where?"

"Outside."

"If you think I'm going outside in the mountains in the middle of the night, you're crazy. With snow still on the ground? With these knees?"

The glistening, the music, the tugging on her sleeve vanished, and Corinne felt tears gather behind her eyes. Damn. Hadn't she cried enough over this child? And why would she be having dreams like this now, three years after Maura's death?

She went back to her bunk and stood there, ruminating on the inescapable fact that she was wide awake now. It was almost four-thirty in the morning and she'd have to be up at six anyway. If she got herself down onto the bunk she'd have to get herself back up. She sighed. Wincing at the noise the clasps of her bag made as she eased it open, she managed to pull out flannel shirt, sweatpants, and underwear, but couldn't find socks or a clean bra. They could wait.

Being the only one up meant she had the shower room to herself. She'd taken baths for so long, because they were quieter than showers, that by now she didn't much like how the jets of water beat at her, splashed and rattled against the tile, and it was hard to stand that long.

She combed out her wet hair without looking in the mirror. She'd let it dry flat and might curl it later, though here she didn't much care what it looked like. For competition she'd have Janice fix it high and curly, a silly style to go with the silly stage makeup and high heels. Secretly, Corinne had always enjoyed the way she looked all gussied up. Maura had worn her long hair in all kinds of fancy twists for competition; Monica had cut hers short the summer after Maura died so now, Corinne supposed irritably, she didn't have to think about it at all.

She went upstairs to see if she could find the coffee and figure out how to operate the big coffeemaker, but for some reason the kitchen was locked. A veteran of many an early morning at retreat, she'd brought her little portable pot, and she considered going back downstairs to get it. But the mere prospect of navigating all those steps made her knees hurt, and she really dreaded waking anyone else up, wanted to be by herself as long as she could.

When she went to let herself out the sliding glass doors she almost tripped over somebody bundled in a sleeping bag on the floor. Corinne chuckled to herself; the snorers must have really been sawing wood. She shut the door quickly and quietly, caught her breath at how cold it was, coughed because she couldn't catch enough breath in the oxygen-thin air. The sun wasn't even up yet.

She made her way carefully down the steps and around the end of the lodge, where she backed up against the wall and began warm-ups. "Eh-eh-eh-eh-eh-aw-aw-aw-aw-aw-aw." Her voice seemed to boom, especially as she went lower and lower, taking care to push the sound out through a tunnel of air and not to swallow it.

Still vocalizing, Corinne limped away from the lodge. There wasn't any path, but the ground was fairly smooth. You had to be careful, though, because there could be drop-offs where you least expected them, sheer cliffs with no warning. The ground here did seem to be slanting upward; she could feel the pull in the muscles on the tops of her thighs. "Fla fla ne na ne na ne na ne," she sang, steadying her chin with her knuckles and making the tip of her tongue do the work. She let her voice out to its natural, easy volume, what Lila liked to call a 3, with lots of good breath support.

Paying more attention to her vocal exercises than to where she was going, Corinne found herself entering a small grove of trees. It could be called a grove only because half a dozen pines and scaly-barked aspen happened to be growing in the same general area; there was nothing dense about it. Among the cold branches were stars and Venus, she thought, while the pink moon looked ready to set.

She stood straight, rested her hands under her ribs, set

her mind on her breathing, and began the warm-up with the ascending scale, all four parts together, and then the chord fanning out downward as each part held its note on the descending scale. The basses, of course, had the last, lowest note, so Corinne imagined the other three, imagined the beautiful balanced chord that could make the hair stand up on the back of your neck if they sang it just right. "Loo loo loo loo loo loo loo loo," she sang, again and again, and suddenly there was the high tenor note being held with perfect pitch and breath support, and there was Maura singing it, long hair a little disheveled as though she'd just been awakened, too, eyes locked on her mother's so they moved up and down the scales precisely together.

Stubbornly, Corinne kept on singing. Whatever this was—a vision, a waking dream, the first sign of a nervous breakdown, a trick by Monica wearing a wig and straining the upper limits of her range—she would *not* have her life taken over again by either one of her daughters. She'd more than done her duty by them.

Fleetingly, there was just the suggestion of a cracked, ancient voice lifted in song, too, but it was gone almost before it could be noticed. The two of them, the high note and the low, created an overtone that shimmered in the mountain air like the song of angels, like the music of the universe. When it finally faded, Corinne breathed "My God," and Maura whispered "Mom."

Maura or Monica started singing again as she moved away, and Corinne, following her, sang with her, precisely with her. Not a recognizable tune, but scales and intervals, halftones and vowels, phrases extended beyond normal breath capacity so that she was light-headed by the time they stopped. Corinne kept her attention intently on her daughter, following her as she moved through dark woods and across open spaces, upward, following her as she sang. The music they were making together was very nearly perfect, and Corinne would not be left behind.

Her feet went out from under her. Her knees buckled. She fell.

Her daughter was still singing, high and pure, impossibly high. Maura, still upright and still singing, went down the cliff with her, and Corinne didn't even try to stop herself from falling. Red green blue brown silver brown white, blinding white, the bass tone resonating in her head, the clarion tenor pulling her forward, and she decided it really was Maura as she lost consciousness in the anguished, heavenly chord.

9

She teased. She licked his balls. She flicked the head of Bill's dick with her long silver nail, scratching it and making it sway. She rubbed her twat against him. He didn't even like this. But it made him think of Will.

"I love you, Gabriel Carmichael," whispered the mother who wasn't really his mother because his real mom was coming to get him someday. Carmichael wasn't his real last name. Probably he didn't have a last name. Gabriel was his real first name, though. "Gabriel, can you tell me your dream?"

It was *not* a dream. It was real. It made him mad to think it was a dream. He didn't mean to tell her anything, but he heard himself saying, "My mom came to get me. She was right over there." He kind of pointed at the peaks of the mountains that were the same color as the sky now—dark blue, almost black—but didn't have stars on them. He didn't really know if that's where she'd been, because he saw her and heard her and felt her everywhere, not just in one single place.

The mother patted his cheek, moved her hand softly up and down his back like he was a cat and she was petting him. Or like he was a little baby. It felt nice. Gabriel squirmed because it felt nice. Her hand quit moving but stayed on him. He wished she wouldn't do that. He was afraid she'd stop. It was real warm where her hand was on his back under the pajama top, and that one spot didn't hurt. Gabe didn't know that the rest of him hurt so bad until one place didn't like that, so it was her fault that the rest of him hurt so bad.

"What would you say to your birthmom if you saw her again?"

"I dunno," he said, as fast as he could.

"Come on, Gabe. Let's pretend."

"No." He shook his head hard.

But she wouldn't stop. "You're looking up at that mountain, way up there where the trees stop growing and maybe there's still a little snow on the ground, and you're thinking how pretty it is and maybe you'd like to climb up there, and all of a sudden there she is, your birthmom. On that mountaintop, too far away for you to touch. But you can see her clearly. What does she look like?"

Dark dark hair, like his. Dark dark eyes, with long eyelashes like his, that ladies were always saying were wasted on him because he was a boy, and he didn't know what they meant except he had something he didn't deserve. Skin his color.

Gabriel turned his face into this other mother's shoulder and mumbled, "Like me."

"She looks like you. So she's beautiful."

Before he could stop himself, Gabriel grinned. Even though it was a secret grin it made him mad, like she'd won something and he'd lost something. He turned himself away from her as much as he could in the sleeping bag and pretended he went back to sleep.

The mother stayed quiet for a little while, but then she said to him, "What do you think you would say to her, Gabe?"

He didn't say anything, because he was pretending he was asleep.

"What would you say to her if she appeared in front of you right now, right this very minute?"

Gabriel squeezed his eyes shut real tight and whispered, "I don't *know.*"

"Let's pretend, though. What's in your heart that you'd say to your birthmom if she really did come back for you the way you dream? Would you say, 'hi'?"

That was stupid. Gabriel didn't say anything.

"Would you say, 'How come you left me like that?' "

" 'In the garbage can.' "

The mother's arms got tighter around him and her voice sounded funny when she said, " 'How come you left me like that, in the garbage can, when I'm such a wonderful boy?' "

"Yeah," Gabriel admitted in his quietest voice, and then wished he hadn't.

"Good. And what else, Gabe? Would you say, 'I love you'? Would you say, 'Take me with you'?"

Gabriel put his hands over his ears and pretended some more that he was asleep.

"I love you, Mom," was what he said right away when he opened his eyes and there she was, he couldn't tell how close but for sure closer than ever before in his whole entire life, except before he was born and the first few hours after he was born when he must have been *really* close to her but he couldn't remember that time at all.

Dark dark hair with moonlight on it. Gabriel couldn't find her eyes because there was a shadow over her face, and her skin looked kind of bluish because of the moonlight, too. But he could tell that she was beautiful and that she looked like him.

"Mom," he said to her, all in a rush. "I been waiting for you. Where *were* you?" He tried to grab hold of her, but his hands went right through her and then she wasn't there anymore, just like every time before.

Gabe was crying. He didn't even know it until the other mother, the fake one, wiped his tears away and kissed his cheek. "I love you, Gabe. Dad and I will always love you," she said to him out loud. "And we're really really glad you're our son."

Gabe must have gone to sleep for reals then, because he woke up. The mom and dad were already up, doing stuff around the campsite. Dad was singing. Birds were singing, too, a whole lot of them. Gabe lay still in the sleeping bag and listened to his dad and the birds singing together. Then he realized he liked it, and that made him sit up and yell like Tarzan to make the singing stop. He yelled again.

"Gabe's awake," the dad said, grinning from the other side of the clearing. "Morning, son. Are you hungry?"

Gabe didn't know if he was hungry or not, but he said, "No," like always.

The dad looked at him for a minute, then shook his head and said, "Well, breakfast is ready anyway. Up and at 'em."

Breakfast was pancakes. One of the foster families used to make pancakes. He didn't remember their name or anything, just the smell of pancakes in the morning. Sometimes they'd have pancakes for dinner, too, which was pretty weird. The foster kids had to sit at a separate table from the real kids. Sometimes he was the only foster kid, so he ate by himself. He didn't live there very long. He'd been just a stupid little kid, so he'd thought he was going to stay, but he didn't. That was before he'd understood that Mom wasn't going to let him stay anywhere because he belonged to her even though she'd left him in a garbage can when he was just born.

Gabe ate six pancakes. After breakfast he and his dad

went for a walk. Gabe raced up the trail and down the trail, into the woods and down to the very edge of the river, even into it. His dad kept saying, "Gabe, slow down, son. Don't do that. Stay where I can see you," but Gabriel didn't. The dad wanted Gabe and the rest of the world to think he said stuff like that and acted like that because he cared about Gabe, but that was fake. He just got off on bossing Gabe around, and Gabe wouldn't let him. Wouldn't let anybody. If he couldn't count on any grown-up to take care of him, which he couldn't, then no grown-up was going to tell him what to do.

Except his mother.

Besides, when he was running, climbing, splashing, throwing stuff, digging, doing stuff that could hurt him but he never got hurt, when he filled up his mind and his body with *action,* then nothing else much could get in. Except his mother. She always got in, no matter what he did.

He found a giant pinecone, big as his fist, and not a single one of those little tonguelike things broken or even loose. He was looking at it and looking at it when the dad caught up with him and squatted down beside him, out of breath. "Look at that. A perfect pinecone," he said before Gabe could hide it from him. "That's neat, Gabe. Do you want to take it home?" He started to touch it.

Gabriel snatched it away and threw it against a boulder as hard as he could to smash it, but it didn't break. He saw the side of his mother's foot behind that boulder, but she didn't say anything to him or show the rest of herself to him. He scrambled to his feet and ran over to the big rock and looked behind it and underneath it where the dirt was all loose and all around it and all over it, and Mom wasn't there anymore. She never was there when he got up close.

Gabriel pretended he was hunting for the big giant pinecone, and he couldn't find it, either. Probably it wasn't perfect anymore. Probably it never had been perfect in the first place. He was just a dumb kid who thought stuff was perfect when it wasn't.

A really old lady reached out from behind the rock and tried to grab him. She looked like a witch. He jumped back out of her reach. He knew she could get him if she wanted to.

He got up off his hands and knees and ran. The dad yelled after him, but he didn't stop. He ran into the woods.

The dad chased him. Gabe could run pretty fast for a nine-year-old kid, but the dad was bigger and he caught him and picked him up. Gabriel thought he was going to get hit and he started to scream and fight. He wouldn't be able to protect himself or get away or hurt the people who hurt him or find his real mother, but he screamed and fought anyway.

But the dad just put his big arms around him so he couldn't get loose and he couldn't hurt himself or anybody else. The dad kept saying, "Gabriel, Gabriel, I love you." He carried him back to the campsite where his mother was waiting, only she was not his mother.

They had fun then for a while, and he didn't think about his real mother. They threw rocks in the stream. Gabe got one of his to skip two times after the dad showed him what kind of stone to use, flat and not very thick and just big enough to fit in your palm when you bent your hand over. Dad held his hand and helped him throw it at just the right angle, too. The stone skipped one big time and one little time. One of the mother's skipped six whole times and went all the way across the stream to the other bank. Dad said if Gabe practiced he could learn to do that, too, but Gabe didn't want to practice so he didn't.

Gabe and the mother walked back and forth across the stream on rocks. Some of the rocks were real slippery or teetery and you really had to concentrate to keep your balance. One time she slipped and sat down in the water and got the seat of her pants all wet, and she laughed and laughed and so Gabe did, too.

They had cheese sandwiches and apples and brownies for lunch. Gabe loved brownies and this time they let him have however many he wanted. He was a little disappointed that he could only eat three, and he didn't like the thought of somebody else getting the ones he couldn't eat, so he thought about burying them somewhere but the mother put the lid on the margarine container she'd brought them in and put them back in the cooler. That kind of made him mad. For dinner they were going to roast hot dogs and marshmallows over the campfire. Gabe could hardly wait. All three of them went looking for sticks to roast stuff on, thick enough so they wouldn't break but not so thick they wouldn't poke through a marshmallow or a hot dog. Gabe found one that was forked so you could roast two things at a time, and both the parents said it was the neatest one of all.

They taught each other songs and sang them real loud and real soft. The dad knew "Puff the Magic Dragon." The mom taught them all the verses to "I Know an Old Lady Who Swallowed a Fly," and then they made up some, which got sillier and sillier until they were all giggling.

Then Gabe taught them the only song he could remember much of, which was "BINGO," where you left out one and then two and then three and then four and then all of the letters, and you clapped your hands and stomped your feet instead. They clapped their hands when he told them to and stomped their feet and hooted and hollered, and everybody laughed at Gabe's funny song.

He didn't remember where he'd learned "BINGO." Maybe kindergarten. He'd been in two or three foster homes while he was in kindergarten, and none of them liked him enough to keep him. None of them could handle him. Even when he was that little, he could make anybody send him away. Sooner or later he'd make Vaughn and Liz give him up, too, even though they said no, they said this was forever. He could make *anybody* get rid of him, except his real mother. That's how he knew she was his real mother. She might have left him in a Dumpster when he was just born, but she never gave him up, she never got rid of him, no matter what he did.

She wasn't the one who'd taught him "BINGO," though. He'd been just a baby so he couldn't really remember anything about her, he had to make all of it up. He could do that, easy. He could make stuff up and it was as real as if it had really happened, which maybe it had. But he didn't think she'd ever taught him anything. At least, she hadn't meant to.

The weird thing was—and this made Gabriel stop in the middle of the song, stop in the middle of staring at a big hole in a tree trunk and thinking what all might live in there—the weird thing was, he *did* remember something about her. Not a whole memory, not like a whole entire story or anything, but a flash, like: the blanket she'd wrapped him in to put him in the garbage, soft, yellow, kind of fuzzy. She must have loved him some if she'd bothered to wrap him in a fuzzy yellow blanket. Gabe wondered whatever happened to that blanket, and all of a sudden he was furious at whoever had found him and at all the social workers and foster parents and these parents because nobody'd kept that blanket for him.

Gabe yelled, "And Bingo was his name-O!" real loud, and everybody laughed.

So by the time they were sitting around the campfire eating marshmallows and hot dogs—they said he should do hot dogs first so he didn't, he ate three gooey marshmallows before he even started on a hot dog—by that time it had been hours since he'd thought about his real mother, and when she showed herself to him, right at the edge of the firelight circle, he at first didn't know who she was. Didn't know what she was, even.

He kind of jumped onto his hands and knees and on purpose stuck his hand into the hot coals. He yelled. The other mother who wasn't his real mother yelled, too, and pulled him back, and so the burn wasn't very big or very deep, and his real mother had disappeared again.

After they found out he wasn't really hurt, the dad said, "Story time."

"I don't want no story," Gabe said.

"I do," the mom said. "Dad's going to read out loud to us."

"Stories are dumb." Making as much noise as he could, Gabriel stomped inside the tent and started jumping up and down and making the poles wobble and ramming his fist, the one that he'd burned a little, into the side of the tent so it swayed and bowed. After a while, when nobody tried to stop him, he got bored and he lay down on the floor on his stomach, pried up a flap on the back of the tent, and kind of stuck his head out.

He could hear the dad's voice, reading, but only a couple of words, "hobble," he thought, or something like that, and "rings." It made him mad that they'd gone ahead and read a story without him.

He was looking up at the woods. It was like being a real little kid in a roomful of grown-ups, looking at their legs. He stuck his hand out and could touch a tree right from here, could touch a prickly bush. He thought he saw eyes, but they closed or moved or something and he didn't see them anymore and didn't know what animal they belonged to. Raccoon, maybe. He'd like to have a raccoon for a pet. Or bear. He'd say he saw a bear.

"Mom! Dad!" he'd yell. He'd go crawling and running out of the tent, kind of crying and kind of laughing, and he'd yell, "Mom! Dad!" because if he called them that they'd listen, they'd probably believe him. "I saw a bear! There's a bear behind our tent!" Then they'd come running, and they'd try to protect him, and maybe they'd have a gun and they'd shoot something. That'd be cool, to shoot something. By the time they saw there wasn't a bear it would be too late, and they'd think he'd scared it away and even if they secretly believed he'd been making it up they'd never be able to prove it and by then neither would he.

Gabriel stopped breathing for a long moment. He remembered a gunshot. A loud noise, anyway, and now, thinking about shooting the bear outside the tent, he called it a gunshot. Once a long time ago he'd heard a gunshot, and he couldn't see anything to go with it. Could he have been still inside his mother's stomach? Did you hear stuff when you were in there? Thinking about being inside his mother's stomach made Gabe feel weird, like she'd eaten him and then puked him up, but safe, too, like it would be neat to go back in there.

Bear. There was a bear. Somebody needed to kill it. Vaughn was still reading. Liz was still listening. They wouldn't know there was a bear until Gabriel told them.

Maybe he wouldn't tell them. Maybe he'd just hide and let it get them. Then he'd be alone in the mountains without anybody to tell him what to do.

Thinking about bears and gunshots and Vaughn's voice and Liz's kiss when she found him on the floor of the tent and said she loved him and took off his shoes and tucked him into his sleeping bag for the night, Gabriel fell asleep. He never did tell them about the bear, because when he woke up they were both sound asleep and the bear wasn't there anymore. Mom was.

It was really really dark. No streetlights or anything, no light inside the tent at all. His other mother and father were breathing in their sleep, and no matter how hard Gabe tried not to match his breathing to theirs he couldn't help it. Maybe he was tied to them somehow. The darkness was like a wall of flesh. It was like being inside somebody else's body. Maybe he was going to die. Maybe he was going to be born.

Mom was there. This time he didn't see her or hear her or feel her, exactly. He smelled her. It was weird, but he tasted her. Even weirder, he knew she was calling him to her.

He didn't want to go. He didn't *want* to go. "Mom," he pleaded out loud, and the other mother moved in her sleep and said something he didn't understand, maybe his name, and he shut his mouth. He wanted her to wake up and save him, but he didn't want to wake her up.

Gabe put his head inside the sleeping bag. Then he crawled all the way down into the bottom of the sleeping bag and curled up tight. Mom followed him. Her smell and her taste followed him. She didn't smell or taste like anything else he'd ever smelled or tasted. She could go anywhere. She was inside him. Or he was inside her. Or something.

All of a sudden the sleeping bag turned into a tunnel and the walls of it started moving. Gabriel tried to yell but nobody could hear him because the stuffing of the sleeping bag was in his mouth and his head was all covered over.

The tunnel smelled funny. Like blood, kind of. Gabriel's belly hurt. In the walls of the tunnel were stripey things that got tighter and looser and tighter and pushed him toward the opening at the end where his head was going to come out somewhere, he didn't know where. He tried to hold on to the walls, but they were moving, and they were slick, like with blood.

The stripey things, like rubber bands, were squeezing him really hard. Then they got loose for a minute. Gabe was breathing hard and crying. Then they got tight again, kind of wound up around him, pushed him along. He tried to fight. He tried to hang on to something to stay where he was, but the only thing he had to hang on to was the walls themselves. The tunnel was taking him down, down somewhere. He was falling. He was being pushed.

His mother was in his nose and his mouth and his throat. His mother wanted him. He'd always known this would happen someday, she'd come for him someday, but now he was scared, he didn't want to go, it would hurt, he would die, he wanted to stay where he was with his parents.

Gabe remembered something like this before. He didn't want to remember, but he did. Something like this happening to him before, being pushed along like this even though he tried to hang on, being pushed out the end of a warm slippery tunnel into cold air, everything hurting, everything scaring, something being cut, and then he was all alone and he never saw his mother again.

But there she was. *Here* she was. It had happened again but different. He'd come out of the tunnel and *she* was the tunnel, only now the tunnel was closed up and he couldn't go back and here she was, she hadn't left him, there weren't any maggots, he tasted her and smelled her and now he saw and heard and felt her, too, her hands on him, her voice in his chest where his heart hurt all the time, the smell of her hair with cold moon-light on it, something fuzzy and yellow where she held him in her arms a baby just born.

"Gabriel."

He felt his name everywhere in his body, because it was his real name.

He was screaming. He was so scared. Already he didn't remember where he'd been before or who, but there was this awful feeling of having left someplace safe and been pushed into someplace dangerous.

There was also the feeling that finally he was where he was supposed to be.

"Gabriel," his mother said.

10

Welcome to Revenant.

Revenant holds layers of grief deeper and more complex than anyone can comprehend. Even me, I think; I have come to suspect that this place has grown beyond me, that even my story is only a piece of all that happens here.

I cannot possibly relate all the tales in Revenant, nor would I have the patience. One loss is like another, unless it is my own. But I will tell you some of the stories in some of their iterations. And I will tell my own.

You stand now at what has been the center of town, the square formed by the intersection of Revenant's four streets. During the years spanning the turn of the twentieth century, seventeen men and two women died very near the spot where you are standing, combatants and bystanders in the bloody mine labor wars.

Sam McKinney was beaten to death here in April of 1899. He was twenty-one years old. An adventurous and ambitious young man, he had come to Revenant from his parents' farm outside Hayes, Kansas, fully intending to make his fortune in the gold mines, and he very nearly managed it. He had just staked a claim somewhere in the hills west of Revenant, which he had already christened the Mary Catherine Mine in honor of the girl he would marry someday, someday. Sam had come down into town to celebrate, guarding his secret, planning his life as a rich man, already wondering if Mary Catherine was the wife a rich man needed. Crossing Rattlesnake Avenue on his way to the Paydirt Saloon, he was jumped by men who might have been union organizers—Sam disdained the union, which was a dangerous position to take—or might have been thugs hired by the big mine owners—Sam had been openly and with equal recklessness unimpressed by the companies' determination to keep out independents. He put up a good fight, but there were five of them, and he died there, just off Rattlesnake Avenue where the edge of it faded into hard red ground, before that April night fell. There, where your foot is, smudged red.

Mary Catherine Norris followed him here, thirty-three years later. She had never married. She had never moved out of her parents' home. Nearly at the end of her life by then, Mary Catherine never missed an opportunity to declare, "I am Sam McKinney's fiancée. When he makes his fortune out West, he's going to send for me."

Send for her he did, in the form of recurring dreams, and Mary Catherine came to Revenant to rejoin the man who most likely would never have sent for her at all if he had lived. She was an old woman, over fifty years old, and not well. The trip had been taxing. The thin air of Revenant did not fill her lungs. I heard Sam tell her, flat out, that he had not waited for her; I heard him name the girls he had been with, some of whom were real and some of whom he made up on the spot. Mary Catherine would not believe that, would not believe he was dead, would not believe that the mine with her name on it never had panned out.

She was mine, then, and so was Sam, and their energy kept me nourished for an appreciable time. But they were next to nothing. Their grief did not compare to mine; no one's ever does. Their story was meager, their loss only one thin strand.

Revenant's white frame schoolhouse—the pride and joy of some members of the community, though not all —stood in the middle of the last long block of Pine Street. It was destroyed and rebuilt three times. Now there is virtually no sign of it; the ground is not smoothed by small restless feet, and there are not even any splintered boards. I can show you, though, exactly where the schoolhouse stood; I will pace it off for you— here to here, between the two of you, then this way and back that way behind where you, sir, are standing.

In the spring of 1902, a flash flood swept the schoolhouse away. The streets and buildings of Revenant all were flooded, but only the schoolhouse was destroyed, and with it nearly all of the town's children.

Arabella Montez was the teacher that year. She could swim; she was tall and could reach the ground; she was strong and could hang on. She survived. She left town and went to teach in Denver, but before she was thirty she had come back, led here as if by the hand by several of the children she could not let go, especially now that she herself was pregnant.

From the ridge where I sometimes sit like an enormous tear-shaped rock, I saw them coming. It was a clumsy and touching procession: Arabella redolent and terrified with child, Margaret and Arthur and the Bowlen twins tugging at her skirts. "Teacher! Teacher!" I heard them cry, like distant birds, children forever unable to think of her other than in relation to themselves.

And she them: they were the children she had not taken care of, the children she had not saved. They had, with their drowning, changed from Margaret Haas and Arthur Lorry and the Bowlen twins, specifically, into Arabella's personal symbols for the danger of the world from which she could not protect her own coming child.

Coming from where? From the place we will go after we die.

Going where? To the place we were before we were born.

The Bowlen girl dropped Arabella's hem and scampered down a slope after a pale yellow butterfly. Arabella caught her and pulled her back, held her close. "Let me go! You're hurting!" shrieked the child. "I don't wanna stay here!" But Arabella held on tight, not to lose her again.

Watching them, listening to them, drawing them to me in a sustained frenzy of never-satiated grief, I thought they were mine, and I reveled in my skill and power, my good fortune in the midst of profound and unending misfortune. A woman with child, sure to transmit her guilt and fear, sorrow and bitterness to the child in her womb, would keep me going for some time, and the child would come out of her straight into my arms.

But Arabella Montez was no match for her little ghosts. Arthur, Margaret, the twins, and all the other children in her charge who had drowned in the schoolhouse flood persuaded her to release them. They tore themselves away from her and scattered, to become part of the wind and the red rocks and the blue-green-gray fog. Arabella and her child went home.

I went hungry. I weakened as my grief weakened. But not for long.

Johnny Johnson was hurt in a mine cave-in in the summer of 1911. Both his legs were crushed. Howling, dragging himself on his hands along dusty Aspen Street, he made his way to the Paydirt Saloon and never left it again. The ghost of Johnny Johnson walks Aspen Street yet, whole, tall on two good legs, or plays a hand of solitaire at the back table of the Paydirt. But it's restless, tormented, never having been released, and does not know the true nature of grief. Neither do you. In all the world, in all the history of all the world, only I know that.

On the eastern edge of town are half-walls and the bottom of a window opening in what was once the Double Rainbow Hotel. Kitty Pardee did business for decades out of room number 3, and fell in love with one of her regular customers, a married businessman from Denver. The lover rode off one snowy winter evening; she knew he was going down the mountain to his wife and family, but she thought he would return. He never did. Sometimes of a winter evening, Kitty Pardee still lights a candle in the window of room number 3, but if her lover came back now she wouldn't know him, and she would send him on his way unreceived.

Kitty Pardee knows nothing. Her grief is scarcely worthy of the name. Her ghost fades, shimmers, is transparent, is not real.

Revenant is a ghost town, and it is full of ghosts. There, in the post office where only part of a chimney remains and the blackened ground around it, letters that cannot be delivered. Here, where your children play on the broken tracks by the old train depot, where someone is always being carried away from someone else. And the doctor's office, which occupied the now-collapsed second story of the pharmacy on the corner of Rattlesnake Avenue and Pine Street, where people have died and people have been born so different from what their parents had dreamed them to be that they are never claimed. And the general store—lately repaired and refurbished, open during the summers although not many tourists come here, where you can buy treasures that turn out to be fool's gold.

* * *

Years earlier, when these mountains truly were wilderness. Before settlements. Before roads, buildings, streets. But not before grief. In all of human history, there has never been a time before grief. My story:

"You will come back to us," my mother promised me, "a woman, and closer to God." Tears made her eyes glisten. I was sixteen years old.

The wind is rising. •

I was sixteen years old, and determined not to believe my parents about anything, although I did, fervently, believe in God and in doing God's Will. My mother was still taller than I was though I had probably reached my full growth, and much more beautiful, though I dared not see it then. Gray eyes set off by lacy wrinkles. Hands strengthened and roughened by years of work and service, years of service to God, sixteen years of taking care of me.

My hands will never look like my mother's. My eyes will never be that clear, steady gray. My mother was the most beautiful woman there will ever be, but I didn't know it then. I didn't know. I will never love God the way she did, for she was betrayed. We were all betrayed.

The wind is rising. Dust devils rise and fall on thin shelves up and down the canyon walls. The river bubbles and leaps, subsides, little geysers only barely breaking the already riffled surface. My heart rises and leaps, subsides, a whirlpool edged with jagged lace.

My father was not a large man, as tall as my mother but not tall for a man; I constantly took his measure. A preacher; a philosopher. Obsessively eager for me to understand God and myself and the world, he explained everything, in every possible way, until there were no meanings left for me to discover for myself. "We are the chosen people. God has chosen our tiny band to live the contemplative life of service, and in return He grants us favor. This is the Way of the Lord."

I yearned for him to stop talking. What I remember most incessantly about my father is his voice. I swear, I remember his voice, exactly the way it was.

"Now is your time to go Into the Mountains," he said, proudly, somewhat nervously. I remember thinking, as guard against my own awe, what a nonsensical way that was for him to put it since we already were and always had been as far as I was concerned, all my life, in the mountains. Then he reviewed for me, as if otherwise I would not have known—and perhaps I would not: "You will go away from us for three days and three nights, as far Into the Mountains as you can, and you will open yourself to God in every possible way. You know the ways. You will pray. You will fast. You will find a place to sit without moving and stare into the sun. When you return, you will be changed. We will be the same here, waiting for you, but you, you will be changed. And you will bring us all closer to God."

The wind, oh, the wind is rising. Aspen leaves twist on their long stems, exposing pale undersides like the inner surfaces of torn hearts. Pine needles clatter softly, spiral around their branches, and make rapid hissing arcs to the ground.

I never said to my mother: "I'm not as beautiful or as wise or as competent as you are, and that's not fair." I have said it countless times since, arranging and polishing the words just right, said it and said it and said it, till my words have become essential parts of the story and I must use them every time in order to tell it right.

Sixteen, I had just begun to experience flashes of comprehension—unwelcome and useless to me then— of what it must have meant for a beautiful, wise, and competent young woman like the woman who became

my mother to forsake the worldly life for eternal high
and hidden retreat. She never spoke at all of her former
life, so in truth I had no idea what it might have meant to
her. But I was just beginning to peer through the adolescent membrane of utter self-absorption, quite unwillingly, and, fleetingly, to wonder. What I wanted to say to
her was, "Thank you," and "How could you?"

How could you, Ma?

To my father: "Stop telling me what to do! Stop telling
me what to believe! I'm almost a woman! When I come
back you won't be able to tell me what to think anymore! I will know God myself!" And: "Please, Pa, please,
tell me what things mean. Tell me what is real."

Tell me, Pa, what my life means now.

Black clouds roil in the bright blue streak of sky, between peaks which are made to sway and spin as shadows of the clouds race across them. Clouds are insubstantial, but the shadows they cast are dense and wild.
Sunshine takes on a metallic sheen, and tilts. The valley
is nearly dark. The creek runs black, with whorls of
white.

Frederika was my friend. Remembering her, I have
said to myself and proclaimed aloud, again and again,
that she was my only friend. She was my only friend. I
lost my only friend.

Nineteen months and twelve days older than I—in the
obsessive ways of children and teenagers, we counted
and measured; in the obsessive way of mourners, I repeat the phrase and it adds detail and texture to my anguish—Frederika had returned from her sojourn Into the
Mountains not much changed, it had seemed to me.
Dirty, hungry, a bit more thoughtful, a little less impetu-
ous—but all these effects were transitory, washed or
worn away before she'd been home a day. I thought she
was no closer to womanhood than she had been before

she'd gone, no closer than I was. And in no way visible to me any closer to God.

But then she married Andrew, whom I loved and she did not.

Andrew, my love. The love of my life by default, because I was to lose all others, the hope of all others. Andrew, who would sit in a sheltered spot he'd found or created between two red boulders on the slope across the river and stare at—what? The mountains? The sky? God? The gathering swirling clouds and swirling river? Perhaps I saw him sit there no more than three or four times, but grief ascribes heavy import to final things—final words, final scenes—which otherwise they would lack, and which, in turn, nurtures grief. So that particular sheltered spot between two red boulders became Andrew's Place. Years later, years ago, when one rock slid quietly into the river leaving the other solitary and unsheltering the spot, uncreating the spot altogether, I howled with fresh bereavement.

The spun strands of the waterfall plait and plait again, tangle in the stream above and the stream below. Rocks, which themselves are more or less stationary, bend the flow of the rushing current, loop it over and over on itself. Rocks in the streambed create funnels. Wind rushes through the canyon, picks up water and rock and branch and sound and echo, sets rapids gyrating. I lie on the surface of the rotating earth, held to it by a force only barely more powerful than the force that would fling me into spiraling freefall. I weep. I weep.

There were not many of us. We strove to be good. We labored to understand the Will of God and to do as we were bidden. We loved one another. We were, our little community, the world.

And we had begun to multiply: Frederika and Andrew had a son, sooner than nine months after their marriage though no one but me seemed to count; I harbored a secret conceit that perhaps their baby David was really the Son of God. And the night before I began my sojourn, which we knew would change my life but the true nature and magnitude of which none of us could have imagined, Ma told me she was with child.

Would there ever have been anyone for me? Would I have married? Would I have borne children? If the wind had not risen and the rain had not torrented from heaven and the valley had not filled with swirling water and my world had not been swept away, tell me, Pa, what would my life have been? If I had not gone away, run away, sojourned Into the Mountains to find God who was at home all the time waiting for me to leave, if I had drowned, too, tell me, tell me, Pa, what would my death have meant?

Multicolored pinwheels of lightning, balls of lightning, zigzags of lightning ravel red into gold, blue into green into violet. Thunder rolls. I twist my hair around clawing fingers, twist, tear it out.

Frederika, you were my best friend. Frederika, you were my only friend. I will never have another friend, I promise.

Andrew, I love you. I would have wished you well, I would.

How could you, Ma?

When I went Into the Mountains on my sojourn to become a holy woman, I might also have been running away. I was sixteen years old and afraid that life would never start for me. I might have been running away. But I came back. I did. And they were all gone. God was gone, too. The town had vanished. I was alone.

I left them in a fine morning mist, motionless and silver-gray. It could not yet be called dawn in the valley, though I knew from the cast of nascent light and spreading shadow that the sun had risen not far away. The others saw me off: Ma radiant, her duty as a mother and a servant of God fulfilled in me; Pa, saying nothing but, "I love you, Daughter. God loves you," in the final moments between us, though I waited longer than I meant to for him to say more. Frederika and Andrew, holding hands. David, asleep on Andrew's shoulder; he smiled in his sleep when I kissed his cheek. The baby, asleep in our mother's womb, believing itself to be safe. And God. God saw me off, too, though He made no promises.

The sky never cleared. The sun did not seem to me ever to rise. The fine, still, silver gray mist, instead of burning away, turned to rain—swirling, streaked with vivid color and texture. I became lost almost immediately. I found shelter of sorts in the bow of a felled tree, under an imperfect canopy of brush that dripped and sagged. I was terrified, almost at once; I kept telling myself there was nothing to be afraid of, which was, of course, untrue.

I never knew whether I stayed out the prescribed three days and three nights. Huddled against my tree, which was no more mine than any of the others around me, I slept and woke without much boundary between the two states. I tried to pray, but there was little difference between praying and not praying. I tried to think where I would go when the rain stopped—home? Some distant, worldly place? Farther, farther than expected, in my search for God? But I did not believe the rain would ever stop.

I had no visions. I heard nothing from God. It rained. Wind bent trees double, twisted rock into unbearable shapes. Violent funnels of wind and water sped across the mountains. Lightning crashed; I heard near and distant terrible sounds of trees being cleaved down the middle, trees being torn up by their roots, boulders being shattered and thrown, and the air smelled of fire and brimstone, water and fear.

It may have been three days and three nights. I may have done it right. But I heard nothing from God until finally I crawled out from my shelter, which really had been no shelter at all, and went home. The storm continued fierce and everywhere. My hair whipped across my eyes, hurting, bringing more tears. My clothes were rent, exposing skin and flesh, but clothing was a pitiable attempt at protection and concealment anyway. My breath was torn from me again and again, and my voice, shrieking into the wind, and my tears.

I had not gone far. I stumbled, crawled, slid down-slope, not far, and there was my valley. There was the place I had lived all my life. There was my world, and it was filled nearly to the brim with raging, spinning water that left no room for anything else.

Later I would find their bodies, every one of them: Andrew, my love, with David still in his arms. Frederika, my only friend, eyes and mouth wide open as though to take in as much of the water as possible. Pa, torso eviscerated by then but face still intact; I would sit by his side for a long time and try different forms of lamentation—howling, tearing my hair, pounding the already-dried earth with my fists and forehead—waiting for him to tell me which was right. Ma, no longer beautiful, bloated, hair uncoiled in dirty loose plaits across the red rocks. I would see that the baby had died, too, drowned in the womb that never had been safe.

I prostrated myself between the water whorling up from the ground and the water spiraling down from the sky, and I waited for God to take me. He did not. But He spoke to me. He called me with dreadful loss. He called me with grief past bearing. He called.

And I said to Him, have said all my life, will say for all eternity: "No."

Revenant is a ghost town, and it is full of ghosts. Yours, too. The love of your life who left you, sir, whose memory keeps you from loving anyone else. The beauty you were in your youth, my dear, whose reflection blurs the reflection of your real self in every mirror. The dead wife, young widower; child, the mother who abandoned you at birth. The husband, the son, the child-lover who are not what they once were, what you yearn for them to be still. The lost children.

Let them go. If you let them go, I will have no hold on you.

Or hold on to them, insist by the power of your grieving that they haunt you. Bind them to me, and stay with me. Don't heal. Don't leave Revenant. Don't leave me.

11

"Get away from me, you little butt-head!" the teenage girl shrieked at Gabriel. "You are *revolting*!"

Gabe had had a lot of fights with a lot of kids, so if this girl wanted to fight he was ready. Some of them had been out in the open and those got over pretty fast. Some had been secret. Some had gone on for a long time, as long as he'd lived in any one place, longer.

He'd discovered a valuable strategy: a boy could almost always beat a girl, even if she was bigger and stronger and older, if he got something disgusting on her from his own body. Snot and spit would work. Puke was good; he'd learned how to make himself throw up at just the right time. Once he'd managed to get some poop out of the toilet, and a couple of times he'd hit himself in the nose on purpose and then made sure the blood dripped on her. He'd never met a girl, no matter how tough she thought she was, who wouldn't freak out and back off and let him do whatever he wanted after he did something like that, which didn't gross him out at all because he was a boy.

Whatever this stuff was that was all over him now *was* pretty revolting, though, even to him. It smelled funny, like the inside of something live that wasn't him. It was thicker and darker than nose blood, and there was something kind of milky mixed up in it. It made his hair stiff, like mousse. It was streaked all over his clothes and all over the yellow blanket he was sitting on, turning the fuzz into gooey little peaks and balls. Gabe wrinkled his nose.

"Who are you, anyhow?" the girl demanded.

"Gabriel." On purpose he didn't say Carmichael, because that wasn't really his name. "Gabe."

"I'm Annie Miller."

"So?" Gabe stuck out his tongue at her and then wished he hadn't because the truth was he didn't feel so good.

Annie relented a little. "Are you lost, too?"

Gabe shook his head. "Nah. My mom brought me. She knows where we are."

"Your mom did?" Annie made a show of looking around. "So where is your mom?"

Gabe pointed. "Right over there, stupid."

"Don't call me stupid," Annie protested, sort of half-heartedly.

A woman in white was standing by some trees with white bark and greenish yellow leaves that glittered like heart-shaped earrings. Annie got the impression that she was about Paula's age, maybe a little older, and sort of pretty, and then the woman started walking toward them and Annie saw the baby in her arms. "Hey!" she called, and stood up from the pile of stones and broken concrete she'd been sitting on, where she was sure she'd seen her baby all curled up. "That's *my* baby!"

The woman in white smiled and shook her head, but it was an old lady coming along the crooked wooden sidewalk, arm in arm with an old man who was walking really straight while she leaned on him, who spoke to Annie. "Oh, for heaven's sake, dear, what are you talking about?"

Annie had never seen this old lady before in her life.
For that matter, she'd never seen the disgustingly dirty
kid before, either. The only person in this weird scene
that she'd ever seen before was her baby, which the
other woman was carrying as if it belonged to her. If
she'd known any of them, she probably would never
have said, "I had an abortion. That's my baby. Right
there." She pointed at the woman and the baby, too.

Elinor took her arm out of Warren's. She grunted with
the pain of her bruised leg, but stood upright on her
own for the time it took to put her hands on her hips and
fix Annie with an impatient glare. "You're not making a
speck of sense. If you did that, then that can't be your
baby, now can it?"

Elinor would never in a million years say the word
"abortion," although such things had been far from un-
heard of in her day. Under ordinary circumstances she
might not have said anything at all to this girl; she might
have just let it go, pressed her lips together and tried to
get away as soon as she could without being downright
rude, and then later she'd have carried on to Warren,
whether he could follow what she was saying or not,
about how the girl wasn't *all there*, you know what I
mean? Why, it was terrible the way young people today
would just talk about anything to anybody.

But these weren't ordinary circumstances. For one
thing, she'd been jarred, first by having Warren cured
when she'd just started to get used to him the other way,
and then, as if that wasn't enough, by the nasty fall he'd
caused. For another thing, she did *not* appreciate having
her time wasted by a teenage girl who'd gotten herself in
trouble and her little brother who badly needed a bath,
when what she needed to do was figure out how to get
back to the cabin, where Katie would be worried to
death.

"What's your name?" she demanded of them both. Warren started to say something and she shushed him. If she'd had time to think about it much, she'd have been surprised by how much fun it was to just take charge.

Annie told her her name. Gabriel didn't.

Elinor leaned toward the boy and almost lost her balance. Warren caught her elbow. She insisted, "What is your name?"

"None of your fuckin' beeswax," he said, as rudely as he could, and went running off toward the aspen grove.

Even Annie was shocked. Warren glowered, and Elinor exclaimed, "Well, I never! Didn't that child's parents teach him any manners?"

"That's his mother," Annie said. "At least, he *says* that's his mother."

"My name is Elinor Dietrich," Elinor said, continuing her unaccustomed boldness. "This is my husband Warren. He found this town here. What's it called again, Warren?" She winked at Annie and confided, "It's kind of a funny name."

"Revenant," supplied Warren, unamused. "It means 'one who returns.'"

"Well, for heaven's sake, why don't you just say that instead of coming up with words nobody's ever heard of?" Elinor's laugh managed to put down both herself for not knowing big words and her husband for using them.

"It's another term for 'ghost,'" Warren said, either defending himself or rubbing it in or both.

Elinor actually threw up her hands. Annie had read descriptions of that in books but she didn't think she'd ever seen anybody do it before. "Oh, land, nobody in their right mind believes in ghosts!" She laughed again, in that way that said, "Don't take any of this seriously," and Warren frowned.

Annie thought about the little ways that people

who've lived together a long time have with each other. Probably this old lady had been acting coy and this old man had been irritated by it for fifty years or something. Mom and Dad had stuff like that, habits of talking to each other and acting with each other that they probably weren't even aware of anymore but that everybody else saw and sometimes it was nice and sometimes it drove you crazy. Parents and kids did that, too. She and her dad joked around a lot, even when they were trying to discuss something serious. She and her mom snapped at each other even when they weren't mad.

Annie missed her parents. Here she was, with complete strangers in the middle of nowhere, in this weird town with the weird name, following the ghost of her aborted baby even though she didn't believe in ghosts, either. It wasn't like she was a little kid or anything, but she needed her parents to tell her what was real. She couldn't tell what was real. And she wasn't ready to never see her parents again.

She wasn't ready to never see her baby again, either. Which was bizarre because she'd actually never *seen* it in the first place. It was just there, and then it wasn't.

Annie fought back tears and thought about how she and her baby had little ways of being with each other, too, little habits, even though they'd only been part of each other's lives for such a short time. It was those little habits you missed so much when the person was gone.

"My husband brought me here," Elinor told her confidentially, although her husband was standing right there. "Who knows why."

"I'm not your husband," declared the old man.

Elinor huffed. "Warren Roy Dietrich, you stop that right now! You've been my husband for forty-three years and you're not getting out of it now!" She was still making faces at Annie, to make her an accomplice to the joke, or to signal that he wasn't in his right mind and the two of them knew something he didn't know. But Annie thought she also looked scared or hurt or something.

"You are not married to me anymore," he insisted. "You are married to *him*."

Annie looked around, thinking, *Who*? But Elinor knew. She was not going to cry in front of this girl or in front of Warren, for that matter; especially not in front of Warren. Grimly she said, "The Warren Dietrich I married can take care of himself. He doesn't ask the same questions over and over, and he doesn't get lost every time he sets foot out of the house, and he doesn't forget who I am, either. Maybe he says hateful things to me sometimes, but he knows who he's saying them to. You know what I'm talking about, Warren. You're doing this on purpose."

"Divorce me," he said. "Marry him."

"Never in a million years," Elinor retorted. "Oh, that'd just make you happy, wouldn't it?" She was crying now, though she wouldn't have admitted it. Her voice broke. She stamped her foot, which was a foolish thing to do because pain shot up her leg and made her sick to her stomach. She grunted and grabbed on to a tree. Annie thought maybe she ought to go help her but she didn't know how and she didn't want to. She didn't want to think about what was going on between this old lady and this old man who might or might not be her husband. Maybe they were both senile. It didn't have anything to do with her. All Annie wanted to think about was her baby.

And getting out of here. She had to concentrate on getting herself out of here and back to her sister's. She couldn't afford to think about somebody else's problems right now. She also couldn't afford to panic. Once this was all over, she could fall apart. Not yet.

Deliberately, Annie walked away from the others, even away from where she'd last seen the baby, telling herself she hadn't really seen it, it was all in her head. Maybe this was altitude sickness. She'd heard you could hallucinate from altitude, like tripping or something. Which was not a comforting thought, because she'd also heard you could die from it. Nervously, she reminded herself that the baby had been appearing to her at home, too, where there wasn't any altitude.

Reluctantly she looked over her shoulder. The way this weird, thin, slanty light came between pine branches and those heart-shaped yellow-green leaves sparkled, she couldn't tell if she was seeing the baby and the lady in the white dress or not.

Annie followed first a railroad track, then a street, and then a sidewalk farther into the town. For some reason, she felt safer going toward the center of town rather than away, even though she knew that sooner or later she'd have to go away if she was ever going to get home again.

Following these old pathways took guesswork. At most, there were just pieces and hints. Broken boards for the sidewalk—Annie wondered if there was some other name for this thing, because a sidewalk ought to be cement. Metal and wooden bars for the railroad tracks, bolted together here and there but not making a track anymore that anything could travel on, and so skinny that she could walk along it with one foot on each side, so how could a train ever fit? For sure there was another word for these streets; the street signs, which were weathered and splintered but still legible, called them street, avenue, boulevard, but they were really trails. Annie remembered hearing about trails in history class, but she hadn't been paying a lot of attention because that was when she'd been pregnant. Pregnant, meaning that the baby had been alive then.

She passed by a piece of a church with a piece of a cross on it, but because she was fifteen she didn't think about whose weddings and funerals and christenings might have taken place there, who might have prayed there, who despaired. She stepped right over the remains of the Paydirt Saloon where it had scattered across Aspen Street, but she didn't know and didn't care what it was.

Something hit her in the side of the leg. It didn't hurt but it startled her, and she cried out and turned. There was that kid, Gabe, standing way up on top of a wall taller than she was, throwing stuff at her.

"Knock it off, creep!"

He didn't say anything back. He also didn't knock it off. He tossed something else, a lump of red dirt that missed her, landed on the red dirt of the trail in front of her, and broke apart into a whole bunch of smaller clumps that she could have picked up and thrown back at him if she'd wanted but she was too old for anything that childish.

"Dammit, *stop* it!"

"Make me," he sneered. "What are you gonna do, tell my *mother*?"

"Where is your mother?"

Now he was walking along the wall, which was uneven and crumbly and way too high. He was going to fall and break his bratty little neck. "Says she ain't my mother."

Annie could barely hear him. She didn't want to hear him. She didn't *care*. But she went closer to the wall anyway, stepped over prickly bushes that snagged her socks and scratched her legs, and stood there looking up at him, ready to catch him if he fell, listening.

"Says go away and leave her alone. Says she's still too busy. Says she's got her own life and I've got mine."

Annie had no clue what she was supposed to say. Finally she asked, "What did you say to her?"

Gabriel whooped, "Fuck you!" and leaped off the highest part of the wall before Annie could get to him to stop him or catch him or anything. Then he might as well have disappeared off the face of the earth—which, she said to herself furiously, would be fine with her. He was quiet. The wall hid him from her.

Annie was seriously pissed. It was not up to her to take care of this dumb kid. It didn't make any sense that he'd be here alone—but then it didn't make much sense that she'd be here alone, either, and here she was. Maybe those old people that had been talking to her before, Elinor and Warren or Ward or whatever, maybe those were his grandparents. Even though she remembered that Elinor had asked him what his name was, which a grandmother wouldn't, Annie still looked hopefully around for them, but nobody else was in sight. Annie realized that insects in the tall grass were making a lot of noise, buzzing and clicking, and the instant she thought of that her legs started to itch as if bugs were crawling on them, which they probably were. She started to walk fast, then to run, just to shake the bugs off.

When she stumbled around the end of the wall she was shocked by a really spectacular view, layers of different-colored mountain ranges from a gauzy purple way far away up through different shades of blue till right here, practically right at her feet, they were blue at the top with snow on them, dark green and dark purple in the middle, and a brilliant yellowy green at the base where they spread out into this valley, this meadow. She was so stunned by the beauty of it, maybe the first pure and unself-conscious beauty she'd ever been a part of, that for a few moments she forgot to look for Gabriel or for her baby, forgot about being lost, and just stood there, taking it in.

Then it occurred to her that if anybody else was looking she'd be part of their view, and that thought pulled her back into herself, made her run her curved fingers up under her hair to make it fuller, made her look around to see if anybody was watching her. Nobody was, but there was Gabriel, apparently not hurt but talking to a really really old lady, a lot older than Elinor.

Annie didn't think he ought to be talking to strangers. Now that was a stupid thought, she told herself, since she had no way of knowing who were strangers to each other around here and who weren't—for all she knew, *this* was his grandmother. Or great-grandmother, more like it.

But something wasn't right. The kid was in some kind of danger from that old lady. Annie didn't stop to think how she knew that, whether it was the look on his face or something in the way their joined silhouettes looked against the shaft of sunlight that suddenly shot through a pass, or some fine-tuning in herself now that made her sense danger, or some connection between herself and Gabriel. She did stop to think that she didn't want to do this, it wasn't her job, she had other things to do. But not for long.

She hurried toward them, yelling, "Hey!"

The old lady looked up and smiled, not at all surprised. Keeping one hand on the boy's shoulder, she held out her other arm to Annie.

12

Bill couldn't move.

Wait. He seemed to be able to move his eyes, because one minute he was staring up at one part of the cracked gray ceiling and the next minute he was staring up at a different part of it with different cracks and the gray a slightly different color. Or maybe the ceiling was moving. Or maybe it wasn't a ceiling.

Also he could move his mouth, apparently, because he heard himself groan and then whisper, "Shit." At least he thought it was himself doing that. How would he know?

"Hey, old man." Will was standing beside him. Standing.

What the hell is going on? Bill didn't think he'd said it aloud. Will—it couldn't be Will, Will wouldn't be standing there like that and wouldn't be talking loud—didn't answer, but thinking the question triggered an answer in Bill's own mind. He remembered: *car crash. Over the cliff. Hitting. Blacking out. Kid driving. The XKE totaled.*

That last thought made him sick to his stomach. He turned his head, which was possible but not easy, and spat up, and saw that he was flat on his back on some kind of table, splintered wood right up close to his eye.

The table felt like it was tilted back and to the right, but Bill didn't know if it really was or not because he was also dizzy.

Spitting up didn't help a whole helluva lot. What he needed to do was puke his guts out, but he couldn't. His guts, along with most of the rest of him, appeared to be paralyzed.

Kathy came into his mind. The thought of her consisted of the remembered feel of her mouth on his dick, his dick in her cunt, just the feel of certain parts of her body, not much else. Bitch wouldn't want anything to do with him if he was paralyzed. Not that he blamed her. Bitch.

"Where—am I?" He did say that more or less out loud. He found out the only way he could talk at all was to force air out with words on it, which made his speech halting and breathy and put lots of spaces in between words. He had to say it twice before the kid heard him at all, a third time before he understood. Bill knew he was just being an asshole, making him beg. "Where—am— I?"

"Revenant Infirmary."

"What?"

"You know. Hospital, clinic, whatever."

I know what "infirmary" means, shithead. What's the other word? He couldn't say all that without completely tiring himself out. "Where's—the doctor?" No answer. *Asshole.* "Where—the—goddamn—doctor?" He wished he hadn't wasted energy and breath on swearing. He had a feeling he'd just become a man of few words. Wonderful. That would help to sell cars.

The boy laughed. *Laughed.* Bill longed to slug him, but his arms wouldn't move. He couldn't even feel his arms, and he couldn't look down to see if they were there. "There's no doctor in this town, Pops. Doctor's been gone a long time. Not much need for one, y'know?"

Bill was seriously in need of a drink. There was a practically full bottle of whiskey under the front seat of the car. Which he had no way of getting to. Which was gone, totaled with the car. "Shit." How would he drink whiskey even if he had some? Could he swallow? He swallowed tentatively, thought he swallowed. Was he going to starve to death now? Just one of the many ways you could croak after some asshole drove your car with you in it off a cliff. Most likely he'd die of thirst.

The kid who looked like Will used to look was pouring whiskey out of a practically full brown bottle into a glass. Bill could hear it and smell it, and out of the corner of his eye he could see it. There was nothing he could do but wait. He *hated* waiting. It took a helluva lot longer than it should have. The kid was just rubbing his nose in it.

Then the kid came over to him and roughly raised his head and shoulders. It didn't hurt. It wasn't even uncomfortable. He couldn't feel a thing. But it pissed him off to be manhandled like that. Not that he could do a thing about it.

Now he could make out a gray wall down there past the peaks of what had to be his feet, and a crooked door. Something was poking at his lips. Irritated, he opened them. Something, a bent straw, was shoved too far into his mouth, and he was able to suck and swallow greedily but without a lot of strength. Whiskey burned going down but it only burned partway and then he didn't feel it anymore.

He sucked too fast, then not fast enough, and then the straw and the glass were pulled away. There was more whiskey, he was sure there was more, and he felt like bawling. Maybe he was bawling, maybe there were tears on his cheeks but his cheeks didn't feel wet. His head and shoulders thumped back down onto the table and the kid moved to someplace where Bill couldn't see him. *Don't leave me alone* was what he was tempted to say, but all he could get out was, "Who—are—you?"

"What?"

"Who—are—you?" *Not Will.*

The kid laughed again, threw his head back and laughed, too loud and long. Bill couldn't stand it. "Who do I look like?"

"Like—my son." *Like my son used to look,* but that was too many words to say.

"Well?"

"Will's a—crip."

"You're the one who said the crip wasn't your son."

Confused and infuriated, Bill thought his mouth might still be hanging open, like he had more to say. He concentrated on shutting it and thought it did, but he couldn't tell for sure. Bad enough to be paralyzed, for Chrissake, he didn't want to be flat on his back with his mouth stuck open like a goddamn idiot. Whoever the fuck this smart-ass kid was and whatever was going on here, he was obviously not going to get a straight answer.

So he tried to think straight, couldn't tell if he was or not. The kid must have broken into the car and been hiding in the back seat when Bill came out of the motel. But why? What was the point? Obviously not the car, since he'd promptly driven it over a cliff. Sickness made Bill kind of pass out or something.

Then he heard noise. He guessed it was from outside the room, but that didn't mean much since he had no idea what the dimensions of this room were. Young people's voices, carrying on. Looking for trouble or causing their own. Getting louder, coming closer. Then getting quieter, going away.

Helpless, both sober and paralyzed, Bill had to admit he was scared of these kids who were so much younger, stronger, surer of themselves than he was. Though he'd never been in this particular circumstance before, the fear was familiar, and he'd done a lot of shit in his life to avoid it. Now he couldn't.

He thought of Brenda. She ought to be here to take care of him. Where was she? Bitch.

The crooked door in the gray wall swung open.

"Danny, for God's sake, you are such a *prick*. You can't carry her by yourself. Look at her. She must have gained a hundred pounds since we died. She's a *pig*."

"She's my mother. She's your mother, too, in case you forgot."

"Only in theory. Only because she's nuts. You know as well as I do she's not anybody's mother anymore."

They wedged themselves in through the opening that had once been the door to the infirmary—Danny first, carrying the enormous and unconscious body of Hannelore, with Debbie behind, vociferously and profanely objecting. There were no cots anymore, and the broken-down table was occupied, so Danny stood there for a moment, undecided, and then knelt—carefully, grunting —and laid his mother on the floor in the corner. She took up a great deal of space, her hips and shoulders spreading across the rotted floor and clay hardpack it no longer covered, her belly and breasts mounding almost knee-high.

"She's not dead, is she?" Debbie demanded, squinting down at her. She guffawed as a thought occurred to her. "Jesus, now *that* would be confusing, wouldn't it?"

Danny sat back on his haunches and sighed. "No. She's not dead. But she'll wish she was."

"Might as well be," Debbie sniffed with an adolescent's heavy scorn. "She hasn't had a life in fourteen years. Didn't have much of a life before that, if you ask me."

Danny stood up. Fondly, worriedly, he looked down at Hannelore, his reddish hair falling over his face. To his sister he said mildly, "Yeah, well, nobody asked you, did they, Deb?"

"Fuck you."

"This is a serious situation," said Warren sternly. "Don't you young people these days treat anything with respect and dignity?"

This was a voice Bill hadn't heard before, from somebody he hadn't known was there. Now that he was pinned flat on his back like this, there were going to be a lot of times when he didn't know people were there. He strained mightily to raise his head just enough to look around, but as far as he could tell no part of his body responded at all; it was just his mind straining, which did a helluva lot of good. He imagined flopping back onto the table in frustration, though nothing moved then, either, and his thought, *This is going to be a real pain in the ass* didn't even come close.

But he was also feeling proud, like he'd finally done something for his kid that nobody else could have done. Like now Will would think the old man was worth something.

Warren and Elinor had been strolling arm-in-arm along Pine Street. No, that wasn't true; although Elinor liked the sound of the word "strolling," and would use it if she wanted to, it was more that Warren was taking her somewhere and she ought to make him tell her where but she didn't. She had aches and pains all over her body, but she allowed as how she actually felt pretty good for a seventy-six-year-old lady who'd been through what she'd been through these past years and who'd just taken a nasty spill. Her mind would be all confused, too, if she'd allow it. She would not allow it.

She set herself to thinking about Warren, how steady and sure of himself he was now, how he drew himself up to confront this disrespectful crowd of young people, how it was perfectly possible that he hadn't had Alzheimer's after all because you couldn't diagnose it for sure until there was an autopsy and Lord knows doctors had been known to make mistakes a time or two. Maybe he'd had some other thing wrong with him which had cleared up by itself. Such things happened.

One way or another, if she was going to get out of here and back to Katie and eventually back home, where she and Warren could live out their golden years in peace, she had to depend on him. On the face of it she didn't like that much. But, seeing as she didn't have any choice, she had to admit it was a relief.

Elinor took a step forward to be right next to her husband again and allowed herself a quick peek into the dim space made by three cracked and leaning walls and a partial roof. She gasped and put her hand to her mouth. On a table was a man who looked to have been in an accident. He had bruises and bandages, and there was something funny about the way he was positioned. In the back corner she saw, even though she didn't want to, a big woman on the floor just now struggling to sit up, and she heard her cry out.

All of which embarrassed Elinor more than anything else. She never had known what to do about other people's troubles, so she used them to feel better about her own. When she and Warren used to walk down by the lake and they'd see that blind girl with her dog, she'd say to Warren when they were barely out of earshot and to Katie later, "I feel so *sorry* for that girl!" When her stepmother had died, she and Warren had gone back for the funeral, but otherwise she'd let her sister handle it; even though it had been three hundred miles, she could have gone back more than once a year after that to see her father, or she could have called. When Katie'd started having trouble in her marriage, the only thing Warren had ever said was they'd loan her money for the divorce, and Elinor hadn't said anything at all. She'd always kept her distance from other people's troubles, and she was not about to get involved with the problems of these complete strangers. Let somebody else handle it.

Pressing Warren's arm, she murmured, "Let's go." He came with her. Hurriedly they turned the corner onto a street called Rattlesnake Avenue. With every step Elinor watched her feet anxiously, laughing a little at herself but perfectly serious about not wanting to come anywhere near a snake.

"Ma," Danny urged. He was kneeling beside Hannelore, one hand supporting her back and the other wrapped partway around her waist, trying to pull her up. Her girth made sitting up almost impossible, because her bending body had virtually no fulcrum. He couldn't hold her weight and she collapsed back onto the floor with a loud thump and a little wail.

"Oh, for Christ's sake!" Debbie exclaimed in exaggerated disgust. "This is not going to work." She stalked out. Hannelore called pitifully after her.

She was answered by another voice neither she nor Bill had heard before, from somebody else they hadn't known was there. An ancient woman, crouching beside the fallen mother on the floor that was as much bare earth as laid wood, spreading her variegated cloak so that it covered both mother and son. Bill managed to get his head turned enough to catch her form and motion out of the corner of his eye.

"She will come back," the old woman assured Hannelore. "Or you will find a way to go after her. I promise you, neither of your children will ever leave you again, if you want them enough."

Hannelore could barely talk, but she could move. Her body felt more substantial to her now than it had been in fourteen years, more her own. She heaved herself upright and pulled Danny to her.

He felt small, of course, because she was so big. But that didn't take anything away from the physical reality of him, at last, after all those years of being only a figment of her imagination. Since very shortly after her children's deaths, Hannelore had known that they existed only in her imagination, her heart, her memory, and she'd made that be enough. But now it made perfect and wonderful sense to her that Danny should really be here in her arms—his breath on her hair, the young-man smell of him—and that Debbie would be here, too, if she wanted it enough. Of course she wanted it enough. She had no life but her children, and wanted none. "Oh, yes," she managed to say.

The old woman smiled and nodded. In the shadow of her cowl, her eyes burned. There was a concentrated sickly-sweet odor, from her breath or from the orifices of her body, which were more numerous and deeper than normal because her body folded and cupped and bent back upon itself in odd ways. Hannelore didn't turn her head away, and the crone promised, "You and your children will stay here in Revenant with me. None of you will ever leave."

Dizzy with pain and frantic joy, Hannelore was astounded to hear her son plead, "No, Ma, let us go."

At the same time, Bill, from his fixed supine position on the table above them, breathed, "Hey—what the— fuck—about me?"

The old woman's laugh made a vortex, and the air in the room thinned so dramatically that Bill and Hannelore suddenly couldn't breathe, thought they were suffocating, fought the dying which they'd have said they welcomed if offered it before. But now their children had been restored to them: Danny Ambrose all grown up and in his mother's arms, Debbie Ambrose able to be brought back, Will Cleary whole and handsome and everything his father couldn't be. Both bereaved parents managed to catch their breath.

The swirling of the cloak set up multicolored wind and light and spun the old woman up from the floor to the table, where she hovered over Bill. She was *in his face.* Old biddies usually didn't do that, and Bill didn't much like it. Her breath had the meaty smell that women's breath got when they were on the rag, though he'd have thought she was long past that. Her eyes were filmy, like maybe she had cataracts or something, but Bill was sure she could see him. She clutched the sides of his neck; he didn't feel anything. She dug at his heart; he didn't feel anything. She shook him, and he saw the blurry room go back and forth, the cracks and gaps in the ceiling spread, the door swing open and shut on broken hinges. But he didn't feel anything. "What do you want?" she demanded.

"I don't—know."

"Can't hear you!" She was shrieking in his ear like wind through a living canyon. "What do you want?"

"I—don't—*know.*"

He saw Will behind her, the way he'd sneaked behind Kathy in the motel bed, and at first Bill thought with incredulous pride that his son was even more of a stud than he'd thought, trying to fuck this old cunt. But Will was struggling to pull her off. He was young and strong, but no match for her. She shook her head and arched her back, and Will, if that's who he was, was thrown off the end of the table out of Bill's line of sight.

"Don't listen to her!" Will yelled. "It's a trap! You only get one life! You can't have mine!"

The old woman pressed her mouth over Bill's before he could gather his breath to answer. "Stay," she was telling him as he passed out. "Stay here," and he was trying to say, "I—don't—know."

13

 Eyeing Juliet suspiciously, Gabriel put himself between her and his mother. He didn't like other kids. He never had friends and didn't want any.

For his ninth birthday the mom and dad had told him he could have a sleepover and go to WaterWorld and he didn't know who to invite, there wasn't anybody he liked any better than anybody else, so he just kind of told it to the whole entire class. Thirteen boys came—he *really* didn't like girls. At WaterWorld none of them played with him so he splashed water in their faces and kicked them and they got mad. In the middle of the night Marcus and Brian had a peeing contest on the rug behind the couch and they got sent home. Actually, Gabriel had won. If the parents had known that, they'd have sent him away, too.

He didn't have brothers and sisters, either. Didn't want any. When the social workers had asked him, like he cared, what kind of a forever family they should look for him, he'd told them two things even though it didn't really matter because it wouldn't be his forever family no matter what, his mother was his forever family *forever*: "People who don't hit," he'd said, thinking maybe he was saying too much, and "no brothers or sisters."

Both things he'd asked for he'd got. That made him mad when he thought about it. Liz and Vaughn never hit, even though he knew sometimes they wanted to, and he was their only child. But they weren't going to be his parents. One mother was enough.

He wasn't going to think about Liz and Vaughn. His real mother had come to get him, just like he'd always known she would. She was right there. But she might like that girl better than him, so he made sure he kept himself between the two of them. She was with some guy. Her father. Gabe wondered if it was her real father. He didn't have a father. Didn't need one.

"Hey, you her father?"

On guard as always when there were other people around, Patrick said, "No. Why?"

"Just wondered." Gabriel grinned and shrugged.

"I'm her brother." He waited. The kid didn't say anything more and Patrick tried to relax, but the kid kept watching them. *Go away,* Patrick wanted to say. *Leave us alone.* He'd wanted to say that to a lot of people, to the whole world that would judge their love and try to turn it into something dirty, but he never had dared.

He'd prided himself on being very discreet. It was only after Juliet had made him stop, when she was twelve, that Patrick's self-control had slipped; he had been so desperate, from the terrible day she first said no until the day she ran away—desperate for her to love him again, desperate that she might tell—that he knew he was looking at her, talking to her, refraining from looking at her, in a manner that could easily have aroused suspicion. No one had ever noticed.

On principle, that bothered him. How did people know that Juliet was safe with him? What if he'd been some pervert, intent on doing her harm? It worried Patrick how vulnerable children were in this world. He was honored to have been able to protect and defend his little sister as long as he had. Once they grew up, there was so much less you could do.

This little girl should not be wandering around in the mountains alone. Maybe she was lost; quickly Patrick imagined her parents' frantic gratitude when they found their daughter safe with him. Then he would be like one of the family, invited to their house for birthdays and holidays once they discovered he was alone. They'd ask him to babysit. They'd be glad to let him take her places. After all, he would have saved her life.

An even more gratifying fantasy, though, was that she'd been abandoned up here and her parents would never be located. He'd be appointed her guardian, because the court would agree that it was in the best interests of the child. Then neither one of them would be alone anymore.

Patrick shook his head to clear it. He understood why he was thinking these things, however premature they might be, and he didn't fault himself for it; both his need and the little girl's were great and demanded immediate attention. But they would have to wait. At the moment, he was in a situation he did not understand, and it was crucial that he be extremely cautious.

This could not possibly be his little sister Juliet. Juliet was twenty years old, and this child was no more than six or seven. It was simply an association, because she looked so much the way Juliet had looked at that perfect age, and she had told him her name was Juliet, which was not a common name—he'd assumed she'd said ''Julie,'' but she'd insisted Juli*et*. She'd come right up to him and said his name. How did she know his name?

He had had other little lovers before her—his cousin, the summer she was two and he was fourteen; the daughter of his best friend—but no one like Juliet. No one as lovely and loving as Juliet. There had been no one since. Her ugly accusations had broken his heart. He'd been afraid of getting caught and, more, of getting hurt again. He could not stand to get hurt like that again.

But now, holding in his lap this little girl who swore she was his Juliet, he allowed himself to think about the possibility of falling in love with her, whoever she was. It was almost too much, too sweet to bear. When things were at their best with Juliet, he had felt that way a lot—high on the sheer joy of their relationship, which would shock the world with its beauty if anyone ever found out. He buried his face in her hair, which smelled exactly the way Juliet's hair used to smell, one of his most vivid memories of her—slightly oily, slightly sweet. He felt himself trembling and didn't try to stop. He had been so lonely without her, and so afraid.

Patrick doubted the boy was old enough to be aware of anything, but he was still staring at them and Patrick didn't like it. There was a woman with the boy, and Patrick was wary of her. He had always been wary of grown women, and with good reason. Surreptitiously he looked her over. She had shoulder-length light brown hair through which sun rays shone as if it were glass, as if it were not there at all. Her ankle-length, wrist-length dress was made of a white material that should have been see-through when light was behind her, but he couldn't catch even a glimpse of even the outline of her legs or breasts. He didn't dare stare at her openly, but he got the impression she was beautiful, which made him even more anxious; beautiful women were the worst.

She gave no sign of having even noticed him. That was typical, a relief and an insult. He held the girl in his lap, reveling as he had so many times so long ago in the feel of her little bare legs and bottom on the tops of his thighs, fantasizing about taking his pants off. Her little bare arms were sweet and tight around his neck.

(Wasn't she cold? The brisk wind seemed to be blowing from all directions at once, or to change direction so fast that it made whirlwinds and dervishes. Juliet's blown hair tangled across his face. He tightened his embrace, but she wasn't shivering. He was. No body heat radiated from her. He wondered about that. He clutched her, thinking he would force her to warm him, expecting her to squirm or cry out or cuddle obediently against him. She didn't.)

There were subtle differences between this child and the child Juliet. This one was quite a bit more forward, and she had less of the neediness he'd found so appealing in his little sister. The prospect of forming a new relationship with another little girl filled Patrick with a kind of reverence, both dread and excitement. He'd told himself it would never happen again.

He put his hand under her soft baby chin and tilted her face up toward him. "Who are you really?" he asked her gently. "What's your real name?"

She leaned back away from him so she could stare into his eyes. Her eyes looked like Juliet's, big and liquid brown. The expression on her thin face said he was crazy, or he was playing a trick on her, starting some new game that she was supposed to figure out. She frowned and stuck out her lower lip in a classic pout that almost made Patrick laugh.

She looked so adorable when she did that that he longed to carry her off somewhere right now and make love to her. He glanced around, but none of the buildings he could see was intact enough to provide privacy and he didn't know the area well enough to venture off into the woods and canyons, especially not when he was responsible for a child. Reluctantly he gave up on the idea, for now.

"I'm Juliet," she said, watching him. "C'mon, Pat, *you* know."

Losing patience, Patrick tickled her ribs and she squealed. "No, you are not. You're not my little sister Juliet. You tell me. Who are you?"

The real seven-year-old Juliet would have been crying by now. It never had taken much. This one grabbed his hands to stop the tickling and insisted, "I'm Juliet. I'm Juliet. Stop it, Patrick."

He gave up. To regain his composure while he tried to understand what was going on, he went back to watching the wind whipping down the blue-and-green valley, the scudding clouds, the flickering sunlight, and the woman and boy. From observation and overheard snatches of conversation, Patrick had gathered that this woman was the boy's mother and that, like himself and Juliet, they hadn't seen each other in a long time.

"Mama," said Gabriel. "I always knew you'd come back." The words were happy, but he looked furious, as though he had only the one expression.

"You made me come back," she told him, and shook her head.

"Didn't you want to?"

"Oh, Gabriel, I don't belong here."

"Yes you do! Yes you *do!*" He flung himself into a full-fledged temper tantrum. His yells echoed. The rocks he threw into the stream splashed mightily; the rocks he threw against trees thumped. He jumped up and down. He fell down, beat his fists on the ground, kicked. He shrieked every obscenity he knew and some he made up, and he sobbed as violently as he could.

Juliet, who had always been given more to whimpering than to rage, shrank against Patrick and put two fingers in her mouth like a much younger child. She always had seemed younger than her years, until all of a sudden she was grown up. His heart went out to her. He didn't want her to be scared. Smoothing her hair, he murmured, "It's okay, honey. Patrick's got you."

Gabriel's mother, unhurried, went and sat beside the boy in the tall brown grass. She settled herself, then pulled the hysterical child onto her lap. He arched his back and fought her. She held his wrists in one hand and his legs with the other arm, bent her head, and spoke to him in a soothing singsong that at first he did everything not to hear but that eventually brought him down against his will, wore him down.

The noise of Gabriel's solitary struggle traveled farther than it might have elsewhere, because of the thin air and the converging canyon walls. It blended with the rush of the waterfall and the whine of the rising wind. Birds stopped cawing and twittering while it was going on. Woodchucks and deer froze in place to listen, then hurried away.

It did not come close, though, to drowning out the clarion tune being sung in the church at the corner of Aspen Street and Rattlesnake Avenue in Revenant. The high tones, a melody that seemed simple until it repeated and repeated itself, were underlaid by a deep bass line, also a female voice.

After a while, Gabriel finally quit yelling and thrashing. Mostly, he got tired. He didn't know why he'd been fighting his mother anyway. She was holding him and bending over him. He'd never been closer to her in his life, except before he was born.

But when he got quieter, she leaned back. Her grip on his wrists loosened and she let go of his legs. Gabriel understood that if he stopped crying and calmed down, his mother would go away. He held his breath and balled his fists and gathered up all his energy to start another tantrum, but he couldn't. He collapsed against her and just cried. She rocked him. She didn't leave yet, but she would.

An old lady lowered herself onto the ground beside them. She was the same one Gabriel had seen behind the big rock at the campsite. But he was too tired to be afraid of her now, until she stuck out her arms and said, "I'll take him."

His mother didn't hand him over. He hadn't really thought she would. "Not yet," she told the old lady. "Give us some time."

The old lady just laughed, which was not a very nice sound. Gabe's mind felt swollen, and he was trying to use it to figure out what his mother had meant by "not yet"—was this old lady supposed to be his next foster mother or something? He was *not* going anywhere with her—when he realized she wasn't there anymore.

"Let's play," his mother invited. Gabe was glad; he'd just been thinking he couldn't stay still in her lap much longer even if he wanted to.

He squirmed to his knees, then stood on one foot and then the other in front of her. "What do you wanna play?" he asked, being polite.

"How about hide-and-seek?" She poked his shoulder. "You're It!"

"No!" he yelled, but already she was hiding from him somewhere and he hadn't even shut his eyes and counted backward from ten. No fair.

The first time it didn't take him long to find her. She was just standing in the middle of a bunch of white trees, probably trying to look like a tree herself, but she didn't fool him. Then he hid—not in a hard place, either, just kind of behind a big rock—and she didn't come and she didn't come. When he got bored and peeked out from behind the rock, he didn't see her, and he went running down the hill calling her. But she hadn't left him. She was just standing by the creek, not even trying to find him. "How come you didn't hunt for me?"

"*You* found *me*," she said. That didn't answer the question. It occurred to Gabe that she looked sad, but he didn't want to know about that. It was her turn to hide.

Patrick was finding it quite pleasant to sit in the warm mountain sunshine with the cute, affectionate little girl in his lap, watching the mother and son cavorting in the meadow. He cautioned himself against relaxing too much until he knew more about what was going on here, but the sun and the wind were soporific, and he was tired. He stroked her hair, ran his fingers up under it to get out the knots, and drowsily watched the domestic tableau.

He began to notice something peculiar. When the mother was with her son—ruffling his hair, holding his face in her hands, bending to talk to him—she looked as substantial and three-dimensional as the boy did. As substantial as this Juliet. Every bit as substantial as Patrick himself. But when she was alone—before the boy found her hiding place, or when she was waiting for him to reveal himself to her, or when he, tired of hide-and-seek, darted off in search of some treasure for her, a bristlecone or a perfect skipping rock—Patrick could actually see glistening water and the snow on the next mountain range, right through her.

This odd optical illusion unnerved him. He wondered whether the woman would see the same kind of thing when she looked back across the meadow at him (though he never once saw her even glance in his direction). Patrick eased one hand under the little girl's dress and let it rest on her soft tummy, to assure himself that she was real and so was he.

He'd always found it laughable that people did things like that to prove to themselves that they weren't dreaming. Sensory impressions were often stronger in dreams than in waking life. Experimentally, Patrick tipped his little girl forward. When he felt her tense, his erection stiffened in response. He ran the tip of his forefinger down the crease in her bottom. Both of them shuddered in anticipation. This proved nothing.

Patrick had been under such terrible strain for such a long period of time, because of what Juliet had done to him, that it wouldn't surprise him if he was imagining all this. From personal experience he knew that the human mind was capable of playing all sorts of bizarre tricks on its host. Until Juliet betrayed him, he'd always been careful to keep his mind healthy and active—writing poetry, which Juliet had loved to hear him recite, especially those love poems that they and no one else knew were written to her; taking college-level psychology courses. But these years without her had dangerously eroded his mental discipline, and he would like to think that extreme love and extreme loneliness could bring on an elaborate hallucination like this.

The bench on which he was sitting with the pretty child (maybe he should just give in to the fantasy and pretend, along with her, that she was Juliet), had apparently once been flanked by a raised wooden platform; a few of the pilings were still visible, marking now-useless corners. The platform had abutted a train depot, he guessed from the spur of narrow-gauge track that ended virtually at his feet. Nothing was left of the depot itself.

From this vantage point he could sight along a straight dirt street, erratically lined on both sides with remnants of abandoned buildings. On the right was a short, squat tower—a steeple, he realized—and on the left, a blackened and tumbled chimney with no structure left around it. The buildings looked burned, he thought, or watersoaked; probably at some point in the history of this town they'd been both. He'd taken several Revolutionary and Civil War history courses, too, but no Western history, and he really didn't know what he was looking at.

In the small meadow to his right, between the town and the stream, there were other people. Maybe this child's parents were among them. Patrick knew he should set her on the bench beside him, so no one would think he'd been entertaining improper thoughts, but he couldn't bear to lose touch with her until he absolutely had to. Someone was singing, a female voice very high and pure, with no words that he could make out. The windblown sunshine created haloes and doubles around the figures, and Patrick squinted. He did rearrange his and the child's hands and legs into more decorous positions, so that to these additional potential witnesses he would look like nothing more than a doting big brother, an older man concerned for the welfare of an innocent young girl. Which he was, but he could be so much more if she would have him. With that thought Patrick knew that the die had been cast; he was hopelessly in love with this Juliet. Once the surrender had been made, he was very glad.

In the crook of the river, where the current thickened to white water and then flattened out over a narrow slick of mud which became a little alpine wetland on the edges of the meadow, one of the figures Patrick watched was Tom Krieg, who sat on his haunches and watched his dead wife on the other side of the river. Emily made her characteristically careful way, testing the ground before she put weight on it to find where it would be least likely to hold the imprint of her footstep. She never picked a weed. She never put a pinecone or a bird's feather in her pocket. She tried her best not to disturb any object, animate or inanimate.

Tom had always loved this about her, at the same time

that he considered it a modern version of the Pathetic Fallacy, both pathetic and fallacious. He did not believe that human beings could usefully be conceptualized apart from nature. The house, the garden, the superhighway, or shopping mall designed and built by human beings were no less a part of the natural environment than the beaver dam, the structuring of alpine tundra by wind-driven snow, the "gopher gardens" of soil brought to the surface when pocket gophers destroyed plants by devouring their roots and other plants took their place, the convection currents in the earth's mantle which caused land masses to drift into each other, creating, for instance, these Rocky Mountains which then broke the weather patterns across the North American continent. Every time Emily had come out of the wilderness she'd brought something of it with her—its scent, its essence, the dust on her shoes and the light in her eye. And she'd left something of herself there. All of which had seemed to Tom precisely as it should be.

When the canoe had capsized, water had filled her lungs. Her fractured skull had, in return, let blood and brain matter seep into the rocks and water. Bits of her skin had scraped off onto branches and into mud, to be eaten by aquatic fauna; pieces of her hair had been scavenged by birds to plait into their nests, which altered the design of their host trees. The ultimate exchange. The fundamental blending of one life form into others.

Which was not as it should be. Because this was Emily, Emily in specific, Emily whom he loved.

The apparition of Emily faded into the gold and brown weeds on the other side of the river. Tom took passing note of his own lack of reaction. Every event since Emily's death had been on an emotional level with every other event. He cared no less about a morsel of food in his mouth than about his life's work, no more about the pain of a scalded forearm than about who won the Super Bowl. This flatness seemed utterly appropriate. But he was dimly surprised that it would extend to both the appearance of Emily's ghost and its subsequent disappearance. He did not care. He accepted this phenomenon with as little interest as he accepted the rising of the sun every morning and its setting every night. It had nothing to do with him. He could not have said whether he believed in ghosts. He didn't care.

What mattered, only, was Emily's absence. Around Emily's absence he had organized his life. He drew up his knees, buried his head between them, and crossed his hands at the back of his neck, thus creating a recess out of his own body for protecting the fact of her absence from any assault. It was all he had. He would not give it up.

14

Corinne Ogilvie was one of that rare breed, a native Coloradan, a status in which she took considerable pride. Everybody else in the chorus, except her twin daughters, had come here from somewhere else, so when they did their travel package one year, singing songs like "San Francisco Bay Blues," "(Do You Know What It Means to Miss) New Orleans," and "New York New York," and in the intro they all called out what cities they were from, she was the only one who could claim "Denver!"

But the Rocky Mountains were as foreign to her as if they'd been the Alps. She had no idea where she was, even though by now it was completely light. She didn't regard the scenery with the pleasure of a nature lover or the enthusiasm of a hiker or a skier; a long time ago she'd let the girls talk her into going skiing, once, and after one interminable trip down the bunny run, she'd spent the rest of the day in the lodge, which was drier and more level than the slopes but barely warmer.

She knew next to nothing and cared less about the probable history of this place in which she found herself. She was not impressed by the fact that this building had obviously once been a church, although she was a churchgoing woman, or, though she'd been a teacher, by the old schoolhouse she'd glimpsed in the next block west. If she'd known about the melodramas that for several summers had been staged in the ornate playhouse across the river, or about the unsuccessful attempt to make Revenant a Chautauqua site, she would not have cared, although music had been part of her life since she'd been a Sweet Adeline, which was a longer continuous period of time than she'd been anything else except a mother.

Her daughter said urgently, "Mom, I've got to talk to you."

"It'll have to wait till we get out of here." She checked her watch. She'd been looking at her watch practically every five minutes since she'd been here, as if knowing what time it was would help her figure out where she was, which she only wanted to know so she could get out. As she looked at it now, the digital display changed from 9:11 to 9:12 A.M., making her feel even more anxious and rushed.

Her daughter took hold of her with hands that were icy through Corinne's flannel shirt, and Corinne had already been cold. She shivered and pulled away just as her daughter was pleading, "You have to listen to me."

"I *don't* have to listen! Don't tell me what I have to do, young lady!"

Saying that reminded Corinne of how Monica and even Walt used to tell her what to do when Maura was so sick. "She needs to be hospitalized, Mom. You're not doing her or yourself any good." "Corinne, for God's sake, what are you trying to prove?" Remembering that made her really mad, and she tried to get up from the pew but couldn't quite. She'd pushed herself too hard, walked too far when her legs had already been hurt. She tried to get comfortable with both legs stretched out along the seat of the old pew, then eased her left foot down, which wasn't comfortable either.

"I brought you here so we could talk this out."

"Well, that was stupid. Wasn't it? That was really stu-pid. Look what you've done to my knees." She pulled up the legs of her sweatpants, one after the other, to expose her badly swollen and discolored knees. The right one, especially, was almost purple and the size of a grapefruit, and she couldn't bend it at all.

The girl reached down to touch it. Corinne flinched, though the touch didn't really hurt. It was, in fact, sooth-ing, the cold fingertips on the inflamed flesh. "I'm sorry. I didn't mean to hurt you. I never meant to hurt you. But you weren't paying attention to me."

"I pay attention to you girls all the time."

"Not enough."

"It's never enough! I could eat with you and sleep with you and go to the *bathroom* with you, and it *still* wouldn't be enough! You're a grown woman! You're go-ing to have a *baby*!" Corinne heard the sneer in her voice when she said that and made no attempt to soften or hide it. "You should not be needing attention from your mother anymore."

"I'm not Monica," her daughter said, with a straight face. "I'm Maura."

Corinne was not going to sit still for this. She strug-gled to pull herself up, but her right knee wouldn't sup-port her, so for a few long seconds she had her left leg under her, knee flexed and then extended and then flexed sort of haphazardly but holding, with her right leg twisting all over the place and hurting like hell. Finally she sat back down with a thump, which also hurt. When she had caught her breath enough to talk, she scolded her daughter. "Monica Lynn Ogilvie, this is not the least bit funny. You think it's funny that you're alive and your sister is dead?"

Her daughter moved closer. Corinne slid as far away

as she could. The pew tipped, which surprised her considering it was granite. She felt under it with her feet and realized that it had only two legs, one in the front left corner and one in the back right, so it had to be balanced just so in order not to fall over onto its side. Through her growing annoyance she did not marvel that it hadn't fallen over before now, or wonder how many years it had stood there in precarious, perfect alignment, how many more years it would stand.

When they'd righted the pew and themselves again and distributed their weight so the pew was as steady as it was going to be, the girl grabbed both her hands. Corinne was reluctant to make as much of a scene as it would take to break her grip for fear of tipping the pew over again. "Come on, Mom, you know who I am. You were the one person we could never fool. You could always tell us apart. *Look* at me."

Corinne knew what her daughters looked like, how they were alike and how they were different. She'd hardly looked at Monica since Maura had died, and she hadn't viewed Maura in the casket. She knew perfectly well which daughter this was. She was their *mother,* whether she deserved to be or not. She knew which one she'd let die and which one she'd let live.

She turned her head in the opposite direction and, for lack of anything better, focused on the part of the church that must have once been an altar. There was a raised platform—also stone, also cracked—and part of a wide-mouthed stone bowl that had probably been a baptismal font. She'd read a newspaper story once about a toddler who'd wandered away from his family at a church dinner and drowned in the baptismal font. Corinne had felt terribly sorry for the parents, whose stunned or distraught faces had been all over the papers for a few days, often enough for her to come to recognize them but briefly enough for her to forget them quickly once they were no longer news. Secretly she'd also felt a little smug; parents had to have done something really wrong, incompetent or immoral or both, in order for their child to die. The twins had been about eleven then, with no sign yet of Maura's illness.

Fixing her gaze stubbornly on the ruined altar while her daughter kept entreating, Corinne thought the word, "sacrifice," followed instantly by, "Ha!" She'd sacrificed. She hadn't let Maura out of her sight for two years. She'd slept on the floor beside her bed for two years; never mind what that did to her knees and back. She'd given up her own life to save her daughter's. But her sacrifice, the best she had to give, hadn't been enough.

Rage murmured at the very edge of Corinne's consciousness. She'd sensed it there before, like an overtone that would hurt her eardrums and break her heart if she ever actually heard it. In order to keep it quiet, she started to hum. "Hmm, hmm, hmm, hmm, hmm."

"Mom, don't."

Corinne wrested a hand free of her daughter's grasp and pinched her own cheeks with thumb and forefinger to keep a space between her back molars and force her soft palate up. Opening up the tone, she went lower and lower, "Ah ah ah ah ah. Ah ah ah ah ah. Ah ah ah ah ah."

All this time Annie Miller had been wandering around looking for a phone. There weren't any, and now she guessed it had been kind of dumb to think there might be in a place like this.

This must be what in movies and books and stuff they called a ghost town. Nobody had lived here for a long time, which was creepy. There weren't any whole buildings. The streets were just bare spots across the grass, sometimes with these really deep ruts or pieces of broken pavement, and the names on the splintered and dirty old street signs didn't even sound real, like Rattlesnake Avenue. Alongside the streets were broken slats of wood and built-up metal things; she didn't know what they were because she'd never heard of wooden sidewalks and iron cookstoves would never have crossed her mind.

She looked around for telephone poles, pretending in case any of these weird other people were watching—like that old couple holding hands, which was kind of disgusting, or the snotty kid—that she wasn't looking, because that was dumb, too. Some of the trees were straight and tall enough to be telephone poles, pine trees without any branches for a long way up, but of course there weren't any actual poles. She squinted and looked up for phone lines, knowing there wouldn't be any, and saw gray and black clouds gathering over the mountains all the way around her, filling in the patch of bright blue sky over her head. She'd never known before that a storm could come from all directions at once.

She was cold, her arms and legs rough and tingly with goose bumps, and she didn't have any warmer clothes. If it rained she'd get soaked. Already there was a mist, and the air felt charged, as if anything could materialize out of it at any minute.

Thanks a lot, Sean, she thought, and laughed at herself for blaming him, although it wasn't funny. She tried being mad at the baby—*Thanks a lot*—but it was even more ridiculous to blame somebody who didn't exist. She'd gotten herself into this mess; now it was up to her to get herself out.

So Annie started walking. She had no idea where she was going, but she reasoned that if she walked far enough in any direction, sooner or later she was bound to come to civilization, a town or a gas station or a trading post, someplace that had a phone.

There was the danger of going in circles. She fixed her

gaze on a mountain peak over there that was silver-purple and shaped kind of like horns, and headed for it. But even as she watched it, it changed shape and color and she wasn't sure it was the same mountain peak anymore. The baby was floating ahead of her, almost close enough to touch. Annie started to put out her hand.

It was *not.* The baby was dead.

As it happened, Annie was making her way north along the east edge of town, though she didn't know which direction anything was and it wouldn't have helped her if she had. On her right was the mountain that has sometimes been called Columbine Peak because of the profusion of Colorado's official state flowers at its base, and sometimes Shadow Mountain because of the startlingly cool dimness it casts over the valley when the sun is not high in the sky. It forced an eastern limit to the town, although now and then miners' shacks or trappers' cabins have straggled across its slope.

Annie didn't know either of the mountains' names, but she was aware of it. In a way it was a relief, like the wall you can run the back of your hand along when you walk through a dark and unfamiliar room. It was also a little spooky: pockets of shadow and light kept rearranging themselves; trails led nowhere across its red-gray rocks and green, brown, and white woods; it muffled and thickened sounds so that wind, thunder, birdsong sounded different in her right ear, against the mountain, than in her left, away from it. The peak was, in fact, higher and closer than the others surrounding Revenant, but it didn't look that way to Annie because it was foreshortened now by stormclouds and distanced by quickening streaks of rain.

Annie had noticed the street sign and was wondering uneasily if there really were rattlesnakes around here, if they really would rattle before they bit you, if they really could kill you. Her white fake-leather sandals didn't provide much protection, and their soles were hard and slippery, not much good for walking shoes. Her feet hurt already. So did her belly button, a weird interior kind of hurt; she rested her hand over it and felt her internal organs shift as she walked. This was going to be a long walk. She should have worn sneakers. Right, she told herself, like she'd known she was going to end up lost in some stupid ghost town. She wondered if a rattlesnake would come out of a hole in the ground, like that one, or if you'd just stumble over it like a pile of old boards. She wondered what color rattlesnakes were—brown like that broken-down gate? Gray like that long skinny thing that made her jump back but turned out to be just a piece of rubber or leather with a knot in one end?

At another time and place in her life, Annie might have been interested in the story of Molly Holliday, fifteen years old like Annie when, a century ago, she'd been struck on the ankle by a rattler here at this very spot. She'd been walking with her summer beau, whom she might have married and might not because Molly, though not especially pretty by the standards of the day, had had many beaus. They'd stopped to steal a kiss behind Molly's parasol right here in front of the Double Rainbow Hotel, which in those days had been at the height of its elegance and was one of the reasons Molly's father had brought his family out to the Wild West for the summer. The hotel had still been decades away from its subsequent incarnation as an equally high-toned and renowned house of ill-repute, and even more decades away from its current condition so dilapidated that Annie, passing by it, couldn't have deciphered even if she'd tried what kind of building it had been.

Molly died alone on the porch of the Double Rainbow while her beau was frantically searching for the doctor,

who'd gone down the street to the General Store to re-
plenish his supply of pipe tobacco. Her family would
have taken her back home for burial if the trip hadn't
required many long, hot days. Instead, they buried her in
the little cemetery west of town where her grave, like
most of the others, is by now unmarked and her body
has certainly decomposed. Her young man, heartbroken,
had never married and never left town.

Because of Molly, the name of the street was changed
from Main Street to Rattlesnake Avenue. Some towns-
people objected on grounds of tradition. Others insisted
that it should have been Molly Holliday Avenue to be
more in her honor than the snake's.

When Annie came to the place where Rattlesnake Avenue made a fuzzy intersection with Pine Street, she hesitated. She didn't know which way to go. She didn't
know how to decide which way to go. Something tugged
at her waist and when she put both cold hands under
her shirt she felt her belly button sticking out, a string-
like thing hanging on the end of it, which was so awful
that she flung her hands behind her back and clasped
them together hard and just *walked*. The cold, charged
wind made her nipples stand up against her shirt, and
the left one hurt as if it was being sucked. Instinctively
Annie cupped her left hand over her breast, then hastily
took it away in case anybody was watching.

Which somebody was. A man and a little girl were
hurrying down Rattlesnake Avenue toward her, and the
man had looked right at her while she was touching herself and then looked away but not fast enough. Seeing
how tenderly he held the girl's hand, how he picked her
up when she started to cry from the cold, Annie missed
her own dad, who would help her out of this mess if he
could, but he didn't even know she was in trouble let
alone how to help her. Dad thought she'd gotten over

both Sean and the baby months ago. In fact, Annie suspected he was a little worried that it hadn't affected her more.

To avoid the man and child, not because she thought there was any difference in going one way or the other, Annie turned left onto Pine Street. Catty-corner across the intersection was the doctor's office and infirmary where Bill and Hannelore lay, but Annie didn't know it had been a doctor's office and didn't know anybody was inside.

The sky was now entirely filled in with three-dimensional black clouds. Metallic yellow sunlight shot underneath them. Lightning zigzagged from one mountain range to another like secret sky-writing that Annie couldn't read. The baby called to her.

Annie had had it. She stopped and screamed, "What do you *want*?" No answer. Maybe she didn't wait long enough. Maybe she interrupted. Her mom was always complaining that Annie interrupted, and Annie complained back that people shouldn't stop talking if they weren't done. She missed her mother. She flipped off the world with both hands, one after the other, and shrieked, "Leave me alone! What did I ever do to you?" Which was a stupid question, because she knew what she'd done. She'd killed it. She'd killed her baby, and now it was coming to get her.

The baby came and filled her arms. She wasn't ready and she had to bend her elbows and fold her arms in to her chest in order not to drop it. It was soft and warm. Its warmth seeped into her when she bent over it to protect it from the wind. Its triangular, oversized head filled the crook of her arm. Its little hands pawed at the front of her shirt, and Annie guessed it must be hunting her breast.

She blushed and whispered against the side of its head

where its ear would have been, "I don't have anything for you. I don't have any milk. I'm sorry."

At that moment, Warren and Elinor Dietrich were turning onto Aspen Street at the other end of Rattlesnake Avenue. Elinor was limping badly. She'd been worrying about the approaching storm, and when she first heard the deep moaning she thought it was the wind or an avalanche. It came again, from inside the tumbledown church on the corner, and was obviously music. Testily, she asked Warren, "Now what is that?"

"That's someone who's seeing a ghost," he answered without missing a beat.

Elinor stopped in her tracks, put her hands on her hips, and stamped her foot. "You stop this right now, Warren Roy Dietrich. Ghosts my foot. Such foolishness."

Now a very high, clear tenor joined the low voice, matching the descending scales of the bass with ascending scales of its own. "Loo loo loo loo loo loo loo loo."

"And that," Warren announced, with the stubbornness she'd never thought she'd miss until the Alzheimer's had turned his mind to mush, "is the ghost."

15

Around the turn of the last century, Revenant
boasted an amusement park that was the talk of
the whole region. Somewhat coyly called Peak
Park, it was constructed on the thirty acres of
grassy alpine meadow south of town and on a few hundred square yards of cleared woodland on the other side
of Broken Mirror Creek.

Considered in the context of the entire ongoing history of Revenant, Peak Park didn't last long. It opened in
May of 1900, with much fanfare playing off the significance of the year—which, as in so many other instances
where people impute intrinsic meaning, was actually
presumed and ascribed. Its last season, 1911, was cut
even shorter than usual by a blizzard the last week in
August. No one made a decision to close the park; it just
didn't open again in 1912.

But during those few years, Peak Park was gloriously
popular and chic. People from the District (which included all the little mining towns on this side of the Divide), from Denver and Colorado Springs, from Kansas
and Wyoming, even from back East came up here on
holiday train specials and paid the ten-cent admission
that allowed them to play in the mountains as long as
they liked. That first Labor Day weekend, almost ten
thousand visitors came.

The trains came into the depot in the southwest corner of town, looping around between the jail and the school. A footbridge with a high graceful arch spanned the tracks and the creek, leading from one side of Peak Park to the other. The lacy design of the bridge was echoed in three spacious dance pavilions with bandstands, in the archway over the entrance to the Peak Park Zoo, and in the scalloped doorways and windows of the half dozen restaurants serving spirits and a variety of foods, even Chinese.

Inside one of the cavelike openings in the partial walls that remained of the zoo, Gabriel Carmichael's mother was sitting on the ground rocking and crooning to Annie Miller's baby. These had been the bear pits and they had never had roofs, their purpose having been to protect the public from the bears and not to protect the bears from the elements. Now wheatgrass, fescue, and purple wild aster grew raggedly among the ragged planes and angles, and rain, snow, hail, hot and drying sunshine fell into them unimpeded. But the structure served this mother and baby perfectly well, for they were ghosts and had need not of shelter but of boundaries.

Gabriel's mother had no name other than an abandoned child's various versions of "Mother." Annie's baby, the ultimate abandoned child, had never been given a name. Both were identified solely in relation to their mourners: Gabriel's mother, Annie's baby.

Gabriel's actual mother, the woman who nine years and three months ago had in fact left him in a garbage bin—not to be found, not because she loved him so much she wanted him to have a better life than she could provide, but to die, to get out of her life and leave her alone—was a forty-six-year-old sometime prostitute. She'd had five or six other kids, none of whom she'd kept past a couple of days, but none of whom she'd tried to kill, either. She had a sour, sallow face that nobody had reason to look into.

She had Gabriel under the Twenty-third Street Viaduct, cursing him with every pain, and cut the cord with the penknife she carried in case a trick got funny or some asshole on the street tried to take what was hers. It happened. She wrapped him in the tattered, smelly yellow blanket because she didn't want to touch him with her bare hands. She didn't bother to name him. She never knew anybody had found him. Over the years she had never thought about how old he was or what he looked like or what he was doing now. She'd never owned a filmy off-white dress with sleeves like wings in her life.

But the mother Gabriel knew was beautiful, of course, a little boy's idea of an angel. She had brown skin like his, dark brown hair like his, long, curly eyelashes that weren't wasted on her because she was a lady.

She had on a dress that was white, or maybe more like the color of eggshells. It had sleeves like wings, and it came down around her where she sat on the ground, but it never got dirty. There was glittery stuff in her hair like stars or like snow on top of mountains or like the tiny little specks of mica in the rock that Gabriel had found in the middle of Pine Street while he was running after her.

He'd escaped from that mean old lady who looked exactly like the witch in "Hansel and Gretel," and he was like Hansel following breadcrumbs home. Only there weren't any breadcrumbs; he had to figure it out for himself every step of the way. Gabriel already knew that, though: you couldn't count on anybody but yourself. And he could count on his mother. Wherever she was was home.

It took him a long time to get to her, even though she didn't seem all that far away. All of a sudden he got shy, and he stopped and looked down at his feet, and right there between the scuffed toes of his tennis shoes was this neat sparkly rock. Gabe squatted and picked it up. He liked how it looked, how solid and heavy it was in his hands. When he got brave enough to look up at his mother again, sure she wouldn't still be there but she was, he saw sparkly stuff like mica all through her hair and across her one shoulder and down her back.

She was carrying a yellow blanket, his yellow blanket, the one he remembered. He could tell from here that it was soft, and his nose itched and twitched just thinking about the fuzz the blanket had on it. It had his name pinned to it, black writing on a white piece of paper. GABRIEL, it said.

"Gabriel," she said. He heard her.

So now she wanted him. She'd come back for him just like he'd always known she would. Gabe was so glad.

He was also really mad. What took her so long? His whole life. Did she think he didn't have anything better to do than wait for her his whole entire life?

She said, "Let me go, son," and started to back away from him.

She'd called him "son." She was trying to leave him again. He'd been just a tiny baby when she'd left him the first time, just born, and people said there wasn't anything he could have done about it. Gabe knew better. There had to be something, he didn't know what. If he'd just been a better baby, his mother wouldn't have left him in the garbage. How could she? Now he was a big kid, nine years old, and he was not going to let her leave him again.

As slowly as he could stand it, he got to his feet and started walking after her, really carefully like when you don't want to spook a wild animal. He said the only name she had: "Mom." He held out his hand to her, offering her his rock. She didn't come any closer, but she didn't disappear either.

Maybe if he told her about the rock. He started talking really fast, because he knew a lot. He was a real smart kid. The parents said he was really smart. So if he showed her how smart he was, maybe she'd stay.

"See, Mom, this rock has been in the ground for like a million years and then it pushed itself up to the top and I found it. It's granite. You want it? Here, you can have it."

She didn't take it. He kept talking and kept holding it out to her because maybe it was his voice and his going after her that made her not disappear forever. He wanted her to stay with him because she wanted to, but most of all he wanted her to *stay*, period, no matter why.

"See, that sparkly stuff in there is called mica. My dad says—"

Gabe caught his breath and glanced sharply at his mother's face to see if he'd made her mad. He couldn't tell. Good thing he hadn't called Liz "my mom"—that would have driven his real mom away for sure.

To show her he didn't care about the dad or about anything except her, Gabe threw the rock as hard as he could. He didn't exactly mean to throw it *at* her, but it hit the railroad track right by her with a loud ping and rolled under her skirt. She didn't look down and jump or anything, so maybe she didn't even notice. He wanted her to notice.

"Gabriel," she said and her voice was ugly and he didn't want to hear what she said with it but she said, "get out of my life and leave me alone."

He didn't know what to say. He remembered that voice. He had to say something. "You're my *mother*," was what he came up with.

"So what?" She was frowning. He'd done something

to make her mad at him. He knew what it was: he'd been born. "You've got parents now. You don't need me."

So it was Liz and Vaughn's fault. Gabe had known this would happen. Rage at them made him kick at a rock in his way. The rock didn't move or break but his foot hurt. "Yes, I do! I do so need you!" he tried to say, but his mother talked right over him. It wasn't polite to interrupt.

"You've got other things to do and so do I. Same as back then."

Gabe had never quit following her all the time they'd been saying that stuff to each other and now he decided she was close enough to jump on so he did. He missed. He landed flat on his face and skidded in the dirt halfway into the cave. For a minute he couldn't breathe. His face hurt a lot and he could feel it bleeding. His hands hurt, too. He didn't cry.

If Gabe had known this was a pit where bears used to be trapped so people could gawk at them and sometimes throw stones at them, he'd have thought it was cool and maybe he'd have felt sorry for the bears. If he'd known that a girl not much older than he was had been mauled by one of those bears the last season Peak Park was open, blinded, and eventually sent to an orphanage because her parents couldn't stand the sight of her so changed from the child they'd planned on raising, he might have been a little more careful but maybe not.

But Gabe never would know any of that. What he knew, in a nine-year-old's way, was that he'd staked everything on finding his mother, his image of his mother, and now if she had her way he was going to lose it all.

"We're part of each other's past," she was telling him. He was trying not to listen. "We don't have anything to do with each other now."

* * *

Annie had stumbled accidentally off Pine Street when rain started coming down in sheets—no warning sprinkles, just a downpour that didn't go on very long but was blinding and deafening while it lasted. Now, drenched and shivering, hair dripping into her eyes, she found herself standing in the middle of a muddy field. Her toes were caked with mud and one of her sandal straps was broken. Wet weeds stuck to her bare legs and itched. Some lady in an off-white dress that didn't even look damp was sitting on the ground by a cave, nursing a baby. Annie blinked and wiped her eyes. The woman and baby didn't go away with the drops of water; if anything, they were even more clear.

The baby didn't look normal. Maybe it hadn't been ready to be born. For a minute, Annie was convinced this was her baby. But when she tried to come up with a logical explanation of why it should be, she couldn't. She told herself she was thinking crazy thoughts because she was cold and scared. She *was* scared.

It wasn't even really a baby. It was a fetus. Actually, it was a collection of cells. But it was perfect and beautiful because a perfect and beautiful baby was what Annie had lost.

She hugged herself in an attempt to get warm and to hide her raised nipples, which you could clearly see through the soaked T-shirt. She stared across the meadow at the woman and baby. Sun broke through the clouds and shone on them while everything else was still in damp shadow, then spread and shone on everything else, including her. They looked a lot closer now. Annie didn't understand how either they or she could have moved without her knowing it.

The baby had a heart-shaped head with a cleft down the middle and frizzes of chestnut hair. She'd seen that head a hundred times. Its thin pink scalp stretched over the opening in its skull like a paper seal over the top of a bottle, and Annie realized she was seeing its brain, like a tangle of pale pink yarn.

Seeing its thoughts, little clouds. Seeing its ghost dreams.

The baby's heartbeat was making the whole valley tremble. Annie felt its heartbeat in the palms of her hands, all the way up her arms into her own heart.

It *was* her own heart. It had to be. She pressed her fists over her heart and found it beating wildly, which she'd expected because she could feel it in her throat and in her temples and it was making the whole valley throb. When you were pregnant, the place you carried your baby was under your heart.

Gabe's mother was standing right there, close enough for him to grab on to her skirt, which he did, but it was silky stuff and it slipped right out of his hands. She didn't do anything to help him. She was talking to him about the past and all this stuff he didn't care about, and she didn't say, "Oh, Gabriel," or "Are you all right?" Gabe just lay there, not bleeding very much even though he wanted to be, crying even though he didn't want to.

He missed his mom and dad.

That scared him.

Being scared made him furious. Missing fake parents made him even more furious, when he was right here with his real mother, the only mother he was ever allowed to have.

That girl came and knelt beside him and said, "Are you all right?" That teenager. That ugly baby was hers, he thought. She ought to take her stupid baby and get out of here, get out of his way. Gabriel hated babies. A long time ago he'd been one himself.

Annie touched the scrape on his cheek. It hurt. He hit

her hand away and bellowed, "Leave me alone!" He struggled to a sitting position and threw his arms around his mother's legs, like a two-year-old making sure she was still there. When Gabe actually had been two, she *hadn't* been there, and he hadn't hugged anybody's legs.

She just walked away from him. She didn't push him or jerk away or anything, and she didn't dissolve. Through her silky cream-colored dress, Gabe felt the muscles in her legs move to take her away, and he hugged her as tight as he could, but it wasn't tight enough. She didn't go far, just over there by that long pile of rocks and wood and stuff that looked like it used to be a wall going all the way around this part of the field. "Mama," he pleaded.

Annie said softly, "You and I have got our whole lives ahead of us, you know?"

Gabe yelled at her, "Shut up!" and punched her in the arm. He tried to stand up to run to his mother but he was dizzy and he stumbled back into Annie, who caught him, but they both landed on their backs on the ground.

Annie was thinking too hard to really be mad, even though this kid was a creep. "I guess we have to let them go. I don't think they want us to keep on feeling bad forever."

Gabriel's mother, just out of his reach, turned so she was facing him and unbuttoned her dress all the way down the front. He couldn't believe she did that. Mortified, he stared and blushed, but he didn't look away.

Annie looked, too. She noted with disapproval that the lady wasn't wearing a bra or a slip or anything. Her breast caught a shaft of sunshine that, Annie was sure, made it look bigger and more beautiful than it actually was. The nipple was the color of dark chocolate and the skin around it was a little bit lighter than her other skin but still a deep brown. You could also see her belly button. Maybe she wasn't wearing any underwear, either.

Now Gabriel's mother was nursing Annie's baby again. Neither Annie nor Gabe had seen her put the baby down or pick it back up, but for a while she hadn't had it and now she did again. The baby opened its rosebud mouth, which had looked really tiny and now was enormous, a monster mouth, and took her nipple with a very loud sucking noise.

It wasn't *fair*. This was *Gabriel's* mother and he'd been waiting for her his whole life. He cried, "Mama!" but she said, "No, Gabe," and the baby that didn't exactly look like a baby stared at him with muddy blue eyes. It didn't have any eyelashes yet. It never would.

It wasn't fair. This was *Annie's* baby, and *she'd* never had a chance to nurse it. Annie's nipples and belly button hurt. The perfect baby stared at her with clear blue, long-lashed eyes.

She walked right over to it. With every step she thought she'd be able to tell that this wasn't real, because it couldn't be real; she kept thinking about what Paula would say if she told her, which she never would. But the baby didn't disappear or even waver, and neither did the lady with her breast exposed, the color of a brown eggshell in the opening of the white-eggshell-colored dress.

Behind her, Gabriel was sitting cross-legged on the ground like a little kid, crying. Annie thought she ought to do something for him, but right now she had to do something for herself.

Cautiously she put out her hand, expecting it to pass right through the two figures (and wondering what that would prove anyway—that these were "real" ghosts?). Instead, she encountered solid flesh.

Her hand had recoiled of its own accord before she

could feel any details. Nobody moved except something that ran through the weeds by her foot, but right now she didn't even care what it was. Nobody said anything; high up in a pine tree a black bird cawed. The sun was too hot now on her back, and her shirt was drying stiff and itchy. The sandal strap that wasn't broken was cutting into her ankles.

She sat down on the ground again and took off her shoes. Quickly then, before she had time to think about it, she leaned forward over her crossed legs and took the baby out of the other woman's arms. Nobody resisted. The baby came willingly, a warm and solid little bundle. The woman buttoned her dress, folded her hands in her lap, and gazed off into the distance as if she wasn't even interested anymore in Annie and her baby. She wasn't watching her son, either.

Annie took a deep breath and looked down at the baby, which was looking up at her. Its huge eyes were a blue paler than any eyes she'd ever seen. They weren't quite focused; she couldn't be sure they were actually seeing her at all. But when she brushed her fingernail under the eyelids, the eyes blinked.

The baby's breath had the faintly sour, faintly sweet smell of all babies. Annie wrinkled her nose. When she buried her face in the folds of its neck, its skin smelled exactly like a baby's skin.

What impressed her most, though, was that she could *feel* the baby. It was three-dimensional; it had bulk, weight, texture. Of all her senses, touch was for some reason the one she trusted most. It had seemed plausible that she might be hallucinating sight, sound, and smell—crazy, but plausible. But she couldn't imagine a tactile hallucination this convincing.

So she proceeded to touch the baby all over. She cupped her palms around its plump cheeks. She slid her forefinger into its tiny palm, activating its grip reflex like those Chinese party favors you stuck your finger into and they wouldn't let go. She unwrapped the fuzzy yellow blanket it was swaddled in and kissed its tummy where the umbilical cord was still attached like the string on a pull-toy. Her own navel stung again in that weird interior way, tugging way deep inside.

"See." The baby spoke to her wordlessly while she was bent so close over it that it was practically inside her again. "I'm real. I always was real."

Bracing herself for what was coming, Annie started to cry.

The baby said, "And I'm dead."

"Oh," sobbed Annie, "I'm sorry."

"You can stop being sorry now," the baby told her. "But you have to say what's true. Then you can let me go. Then you can go home."

Gabriel had picked up the yellow blanket and swaddled himself in it. Taking baby steps because the blanket was tight around his ankles, he hobbled over to his mother and fell into her lap. He didn't need to touch her to know she was real. She'd always been more real to him than anything else. She didn't go away from him this time. She stroked his hair. He liked that so much it hurt. She murmured, "Oh, Gabriel."

Gabriel believed in ghosts. He also believed in dragons and monsters. He wasn't sure about aliens. He was too old for Santa Claus and the Easter bunny and the tooth fairy, but he didn't exactly not believe in them anymore, either, and the mother and father Liz and Vaughn said he didn't have to give them up yet if he didn't want to.

But his mother wasn't a ghost or an alien. She was real. This was where he belonged. He snuggled against her, found her arm and tried to pull it around him, but she wouldn't let him. "No," she said to him. "Leave me alone, Gabriel."

"How come you left me alone in the garbage when I'm such a beautiful boy?" Gabe demanded of her at last, and burst into tears.

There were so many tears, the weeping might have seemed endless, although it needn't be. Annie cried. Gabriel cried. The Revenant Valley, though, was bathed in clear new sunshine, which was not in any reaction at all to the tears of the mourners.

At the southernmost edge of the meadow, along the bank of Broken Mirror Creek, which had filled in eighteen inches or so since the summers of Peak Park, an ancient woman danced by herself. She often came here to dance with the mourners. This was where the smallest and most intimate pavilion had been, the bands with the sweetest music, the dancers most in love and with the most to lose.

She hugged herself. She scored her own flesh with sharp broken nails. She danced and sang to the harmony of Corinne and Maura Ogilvie, which neither Gabriel nor Annie could hear, and to Gabriel and Annie's keening.

She danced and sang to the echoes of the dance music from the hot July evening in 1906 when Elias Burns, engaged to be married to Nell Maguire, had instead danced with, fallen in love with, and that very night run off to Laramie with Lucinda Wahl. The band was still playing when Nell climbed up Shadow Mountain, trailing the ghost of the man she'd planned to marry. No one who knew her ever saw her again.

Annie, of course, had never heard of Nell Maguire. She was hurting deep inside. This was exactly what she'd been trying not to feel since the baby had died. Though the baby was outside her, solid in her arms, it was also inside, attached to her, touching her from the inside out because it hadn't ever touched her any other way. Its little hands patted the inside of her uterus and vagina, the inside of her heart. Its fingers closed in a tiny reflexive fist around its end of the shriveled umbilical cord, and, horrified, Annie felt the cord reattach to the inside of her belly button.

She was going to die. The pain was going to turn her inside out. She screamed as if she were giving birth, giving something up.

The dancing old woman raised her arms, crooked as the branches of mountain mahogany wind-buffeted at timberline, and shrieked.

Gabriel's mother got to her feet, spilling him onto the ground. He yelled in protest and clutched at the yellow blanket, but his mother tugged it loose, rolling him facedown in the weeds and dirt and tiny blue columbines.

Annie realized that she was curled around an empty space; her baby wasn't there anymore. Through tear-filmed and swollen eyes she squinted into the glare of the bright sky and bright golden meadow. The baby's tugging at the umbilical cord sent searing pain through Annie's intestines and down into her groin. She was going to die for sure.

Gabriel's mother was wrapping Annie's baby, still attached to Annie, in the fuzzy yellow blanket again. She started to walk away with it. Across the meadow of columbine and fescue. Toward the blue and green scalloped mountains.

Gabe had raised himself onto his hands and knees. He cried, "Mom!" and thrust out his hands, trying to reach her, trying at least to get his blanket back. He couldn't reach. Frantic, he stretched his lanky little body as long as it would go, but he still couldn't reach, and he couldn't seem to get to his feet to chase her. He wailed.

Something like a long worm wriggled out of Gabriel's mother's dress, farther down than where she'd unbuttoned it to let that other baby nurse. *Gabriel* wanted it. He wanted everything from her, her milk, her nipple in his mouth, the slimy cord filled with stuff from her body that he had to have in order to survive.

The cord stretched out. Gabe thought it looked like one of those maggots in the Dumpster, only a lot longer. It squirmed, then all of a sudden threw itself around his neck. Too tight, too tight. He choked.

Still sobbing, Annie saw that the kid was choking and she understood that she had to do something. She didn't want to. She wanted to stay curled up on the ground around her grief and never do anything else. But she forced herself to scramble to her feet.

The woman in the white dress had stopped walking and turned away. The baby in her arms was attached to Annie by a firm pink umbilical cord that had somehow regenerated or never been cut at all, and another cord just like it had wrapped around Gabriel's neck and snaked up to wrap around his mother's. He was choking. His mother was choking. It seemed to Annie that she was the only one who could help any of them.

She grabbed the cord in both hands, hoping to loosen or break it. It quivered and tautened. It was tearing her apart. And it was pulling so hard, cutting so deep, that it was dismembering her baby. A little arm came off. Annie twisted. The woman in white turned around as if she were dancing, or as if she were trying to get free. A little leg broke. Annie heard the snap of bone and the ripping of flesh, but the baby didn't make any sound. She was making enough noise for both of them.

Then Annie's baby and Gabriel's mother both yelled, "Let me *go*!" and Annie and Gabriel both screamed. Gabriel screamed, "No way!" Annie didn't use words. She didn't need to. The baby would know what she meant.

Annie clutched the cord in both hands and braced her feet against the rubble of the long-ago semicircular enclosure. She made herself stop following the baby. The baby, though, kept going, out of the other woman's arms. It burst out of the yellow blanket, hit the opposite wall of the bear pit, and exploded. Parts of it flew back and splattered Annie's face.

She wiped blood and tears and fetal brain matter out of her eyes and ran for Gabriel. The little boy was curled up on the ground with the maggotlike umbilical cord wrapped around and around him, under his orange Broncos shirt, over and under his high tops like a fancy shoestring. His brown eyes bulged and his face was mottled. He gagged. He was croaking, "Mama," but the lady in the bone-colored dress was pulling as hard as she could on the other end of the cord, obviously trying to get away from him again.

Annie crouched beside the strangling child and desperately clawed at the cord noosed around his neck. It was slimy, like a piece of spaghetti, and she couldn't get hold of it. Every time she managed to work a fingertip under it, Gabriel squirmed and fought her and tightened the cord again.

When he squeaked "Ma!" again, for a crazy second Annie thought he was talking to her. But he wasn't. He wasn't her child and she wasn't his mother.

She was with him, though, when he died of his grief, which had a will to live more stubborn than his. She had her hand on his sturdy chest when his strong little heart stopped beating. At the moment his warm breath abruptly ceased, her cheek was against his lips.

The cord connecting Gabriel to his mother lived longer than they did, long enough to reel them violently together. Annie scrambled to her feet and flung herself out of the way as mother and son were finally joined in a jumble of flesh and bone, memory and spirit, and the old woman widened her dance of ecstatic anguish to suck them both in.

Then Annie fled for her life.

16

"Dance with me, Patrick?" A sprightly waltz was being played on a tinkly keyboard that Patrick thought was probably a harpsichord. In the background piped the syncopated lilt of a carousel tune, and in the middle distance two women were singing. Though the proximity of other people did make it impossible for him to relax completely, the music had already set his body swaying and his feet in motion, and high in his arms was Juliet, seven years old.

She was naked except for the pretty heart-shaped locket he'd given her so hopefully. He fingered it, read the inscription: "To Juliet from Pat With Love." He wished now he'd had it say more, been bolder in declaring his love, but back then he hadn't had the courage. He would now, he promised.

The fine chain glinted like the cut of a very thin blade around her neck under the tangled hair, and the pendant rested in the delicate hollow of her clavicle. The locket was open, and he saw, with a rush of pleasure that brought grateful tears to his eyes, that she had after all put his picture in there. His own miniature visage stared back at him, stylized because of the clipped pose and the unnatural curves of the frame, perfectly set off by the background of Juliet's pale flesh and smooth bone.

She was humming in her tuneless, wordless way. Her

arms were around his neck, and her legs around his waist were spread to reveal her seedlike clitoris in the pink petal-like bed of her vulva. Her fragrance wafted freely up to him: baby powder, fear, child's sweat, not even a hint of musk.

He didn't understand what had happened to him to bring him here with her, but he was willing to accept anything to dance with this beloved little girl who had grown up and left him so many years ago.

"Pat, don't."

He didn't know what she was telling him not to do. Everything he did was because he adored her. He tightened his embrace, hearing the way she caught her breath against his shoulder. Over her head he took stock of their immediate environment, as he used to do by second-nature.

They were dancing under a wide wooden-lathed canopy. The floor was made of narrow planks fitted snugly together, sanded smooth, polished. The outer walls of the structure were gracefully, lacily arched so that cerise aspen leaves and their white bark could flicker romantically through the lattices. There was no one else in the pavilion.

The singing women, one very high and one very low, must be somewhere else, or were not real at all. When he listened directly for them, their voices blended with the lovely natural sounds that contributed to this perfect setting for him and Juliet, birdsong and the gurgle of running water and brisk wind high in the treetops. Only when he listened with his peripheral hearing, the equivalent of looking out of the corner of his eye, did he actually hear them.

There were no dancers but himself and Juliet. There were no musicians, although the harpsichord still played somewhere. The carousel was turning by itself. There were no observers.

Still swaying and stepping to the sensuous, romantic melody, Patrick shifted Juliet's minuscule weight so that she was lying backward across his arm. She sniffled and whined. Tenderly he insisted, knowing from long and inventive experience that she would like what he had in mind once she became accustomed to it.

He tickled her vaginal opening (*pussy,* he thought in the well-rehearsed but long-unused litany that helped arouse him, then wondered with a secret chuckle whether it was accurate to call the female genitalia "pussy" before there was any fur). She moaned and squirmed. He held her close as they moved around the floor, gratified that she still enjoyed their little games and that his own pleasure, so long denied, was rising so rapidly. He pushed his index finger into her vagina. The harpsichord gave a pretty little riff. Juliet cried out.

Patrick was so certain it would be a cry of ecstasy that he didn't hear what she had said until she said it again. "Stop!"

"Oh, no, sweetheart, not yet," he murmured, twirling and dipping her to the steady rhythm of the music. "We've only just begun." This last he sang, more and more pleased with himself and her.

"Let me *go!*"

But he didn't let her go, he would again never let her go, because he knew she didn't really mean it and she knew he knew. He spread her thin thighs and labia with his finger and thumb, tipped her to raise her pelvis, and brushed his lips and tongue across her vagina.

The music stopped. In the sudden silence Juliet was whimpering, "I don't wanna *do* this anymore, Pat!"

Breathing hard, he asked her as he had asked before, only once or twice because that was all the reminding she'd needed. "Don't you want me to love you any-more?"

In a small, choked voice, she said, "I want you to *love* me but I don't want you to touch me in my private place. It's not right, Pat. It's not."

Before he could prevent it, she had twisted out of his grasp. Hearing her hit the wooden floor of the pavilion, he was terrified that he had hurt her. He wouldn't hurt her for the world.

But she scrambled to her hands and knees. The rounds of her bottom were like marble in the leaf- and cloud-filtered twilight. Patrick reached proprietarily to stroke and slap her bottom but Juliet was on her feet and running away from him, wailing, "Let me go! Let me go!"

Now he could not, of course, ever let her go. Things had gone too far between them. Almost grimly, he followed her through an archway, down three wide bowed steps, and into the long-deserted street, but now he didn't see where she had gone. Hiding from him had always been part of their sweet little ritual. When he found her, he would play his part, the role she expected of him.

Patrick didn't dare take time to stop and try to get his bearings, but he made himself acutely observant as he hurried to follow Juliet. Apparently, they'd wandered into some kind of mountain ghost town. He could tell that the path he was walking on had once been a street; in fact, he came to an intersection marked by a wooden sign that had probably originally been designed to look weathered and now really was: ASPEN STREET in the direction he was heading, RATTLESNAKE AVENUE perpendicular to it.

The sign didn't give him much useful information. Because of the peculiar narrowed slant of the light and the fact that this was a high valley ringed on all sides with mountains, he had no way of knowing which compass direction was which. The disorientation was just frightening enough to be titillating. Excitement and the altitude were making him light-headed.

Lining the streets sporadically were buildings in various states of disrepair. Most had deteriorated into only partial structures, a collapsed wall, a jagged bit of roof, and Patrick worried that it wasn't safe for his little sister to be playing here. Some, though empty and obviously unused for decades, appeared more or less intact, and it was possible to guess what they'd been—this church, for instance, with its square steeple only slightly higher than his head. When he came to the next corner, where Aspen Street crossed Silver Alley, he turned left past the General Store, which actually looked to be still in operation; uneasily, he speculated about the existence of a tourist trade.

The elegant pavilion where he'd danced with Juliet had vanished. It seemed to him that he'd walked three sides of a square and so the pavilion ought to be ahead of him now, but there was no sign of it, and he heard no music anymore, only the echoing of thunder among the peaks and a chorus of birds reacting to the coming storm, whether in alarm or in anticipation Patrick couldn't discern.

There was Juliet, well away from him. Her skin took on an even more dramatic pallor in the odd interplay of lightning and low sunshine that now was illuminating the valley. A chilly wind had come up again, and the first fat raindrops of this system fell now. Even from this distance, which he was closing rapidly, he could see that Juliet was shivering. But she didn't hug herself, as though it hadn't occurred to her that she might keep herself warm; her little arms hung stiffly at her sides.

Patrick didn't want her to be cold, or to get sick from

standing naked in the rain. He also couldn't bear the image of her taking care of herself. He must be the one to warm and protect her. He yearned to have her depend on him again for her very survival.

He took another step toward her and held out his arms. That was their signal; she was supposed to come running. But she backed up an equal distance, which required two or three of her skittering child's steps, and sobbed, "You let me go, Pat, or I'm telling!"

It had never failed to hurt and frighten Patrick when Juliet threatened to disclose the nature of their love to the plebeian world, but he had several ways of handling it. Sometimes he'd convinced her, without much effort, that nobody would believe her. This time he said, "If you tell, they'll put me in jail and then I really won't love you anymore."

Juliet's little face contorted, and she ran away from him again. Understanding that this was a game and she wanted him to chase her, Patrick did. He was finding it difficult to run because of his erection, which was so bulbous that it caused him discomfort when it rubbed against the inside of his fly.

This time she was easy to follow. Although the valley was now in deep, shifting shadow from the thick clouds and the declining sun, lightning flashed in sheets from peak to peak and he could see where she was going. Her body was almost bright as she stumbled through the ghost town.

Throughout his relationship with Juliet, there had been numerous points, like knots on a string, at which Patrick could have challenged his own accumulating sense of reality. He could have allowed himself to realize that it wasn't love for him that made her submit to his sex games and even to take the initiative, but a desperate child's corrupted instinct for self-preservation. More than once it would even have been possible for him to understand that it was sick need and not love for her that obsessed him. But every time he'd been presented with the opportunity to examine what he'd convinced himself was real, he had turned it down.

Now it happened again, for the last time. All his senses, distorted from years of systematic misuse, informed him that his idolized little sister-lover, Juliet at seven years old, had not only been restored to him but was leading him somewhere he yearned to go. The tiny intact parts of both his conscience and his consciousness, warning that none of this was real, were silenced, and Patrick made a final, fatal, nearly deliberate decision to believe and to act upon a reality that ought to have made no sense, but for which he had been thoroughly prepared.

She took him from one end of town to the other, which was not very far. They went past the post office and the school, both of which might have been recognizable if Patrick had known what to look for or been interested in looking. They crossed a rickety bridge over a creek which looked to be fairly low and slow-moving now but which, Patrick guessed, would swell over its banks if this storm delivered the downpour it was promising. Lightning lit up the sky, the creek, and a building on the opposite bank, an apparently whole structure into which he saw the child Juliet disappear, white skin and glistening tears into darkness.

"Let me go!" she yelled over a string of thunderclaps.

Patrick took it as a challenge. It was just part of the seduction game this seven-year-old girl played with such finesse. He wasn't really supposed to let her go; she would be heartbroken if he did and think he didn't love her anymore. When the truth was, he loved her more than sanity, more than life itself.

He scrambled up the short, steep creekbank and into the long-abandoned building. Juliet shouldn't be playing in here; it could be dangerous. He had the obligation to rescue her, and then to punish her so that she would never do this again.

This was the most intact of all the buildings he'd seen here. Once inside the four close walls, complete except for a hole here and there, under the roof that stretched almost unbroken from corner to corner, he felt totally enclosed, claustrophobic. A small window at the top of one wall was crisscrossed by bars which, from his perspective, looked like solid and unrusted iron. Lightning lit them like the bones in a child's spread hand.

Just such an elfin hand nudged into his back pocket. The flesh of his hip crawled, with pleasure and with anticipated pleasure. He kept himself very still to see what she would do. Lightning flashed and, without time for any count at all, thunder crashed. The lightning illuminating for a long, eerie moment the heavy walls, dirt floor so packed there was scarcely any dust, and barred windows and door.

This was Revenant's jailhouse. People had died here and been mourned, but Patrick had no interest in any of them. The hand in his pocket tugged him downward and, obediently, he sat. She shoved at his right shoulder and, playing along, he allowed himself to tip over onto his left side. With both hands encircling his wrists, his left and then his right, she bent his arms up behind his back. "Juliet, sweetheart," he said with a laugh, delighted, "what are you doing?"

She didn't answer. Behind his back he heard her humming that ubiquitous, nervous little hum he had long associated with her. Something hard and cold snapped around his wrists. Handcuffs, he realized, with the first faint thrill of fear.

"What are you doing?" He tried to free his hands but couldn't. "Is this something new?" The terrible thought struck him that she had been with someone else. She was too young to have a boyfriend. "Juliet, who taught you this?"

"We did," answered a chorus of female voices.

Between lightning flashes it was very dark in the jailhouse, and from his awkward position on his side on the hardpack floor Patrick could make out only shapes, the suggestion of a cheek here, a breast there, a dark pubic triangle between ashen thighs, the sparkling of an eye. "Who—" he started to say, and tried to struggle to his knees but was immediately pushed back down, this time with his face in the dirt.

Hands were all over him then, strong women's hands. He was surrounded by women. He was afraid of them, for they were grown women, and naked. He was afraid of their bodies with all their secret orifices. He was afraid of all the things they would want him to do. He had always been afraid.

Women's hands rolled him over onto his back and bound his ankles together, too tightly, cutting into the flesh. Women's hands forced a gag into his mouth, sawing at his clenched teeth and tight lips until he had no choice but to let the cloth in and it was tied hard behind his head. Leaning very close to him, her teeth only inches from his, was Juliet, grown up as she really was and therefore despising him, as all women did once they were grown. "There, big brother," the adult Juliet spat, "*now* let's hear you say how much you love me."

Patrick's eyes ached with the effort to see with reasonable clarity in the gloom of the cell. He could see the women, at least. There must be at least a dozen of them, all naked, all mature with full breasts and thick pubic hair and rounded limbs and bellies. They milled around him. They caressed and pummeled him with their women's hands and said his name in their women's shouts and whispers. He had no chance.

One of them crouched in front of him. Her musk, wafting from between her spread thighs, turned his stomach. He felt her hard fingers as she tore his shirt and pressed the heel of her hand against his ribcage. He was convinced that she intended to break it, and then his heart underneath.

Another woman roughly unzipped his pants and pulled them down just far enough to bind his knees. She reached in and took out his penis. He thought he saw something glint in her hand, and terror made him black out for what seemed only an instant. When his vision cleared again she wasn't holding anything but his penis, which she rolled back and forth, back and forth between her palms while it thickened and elongated exactly the way she wanted it to. As usual, he had no choice.

She bent her head and took his penis in her mouth. Her short hair was feathery against his belly, and she skittered the fingers of her free hand across the exquisitely sensitive underside of his scrotum. His body was responding to her. The others were laughing softly and making soft cooing sounds which were vaguely encouraging and definitely mocking. Patrick hated women's laughter.

Squatting beside him now was the oldest woman Patrick had ever seen. He'd long regarded old women as much like little girls, with their sweet vulnerability and willingness to trust him to be in charge. Though he'd never actually made love to a woman this old, he'd fantasized about it enough that he'd come to accept its fundamental innocence and rightness.

This old lady put out her hands to him in a way that could be nothing other than seductive, and Patrick would have taken the chance of pulling her to him if he hadn't been bound and gagged. As it was, he watched her while the other woman brought him skillfully to the brink of orgasm.

Then spat him out, sat back on her heels, and wiped her mouth. The ancient woman cackled. Patrick tried to say something to her but couldn't.

They left him like that. Engorged and humiliated and desperate with desire, bound and gagged, exposed, he was left alone on the floor of the jail. Even his little sister and child-lover Juliet left him; not the last to leave, she stood in the doorway for a moment and regarded him. She was a child again, and he loved her so much. "I *told* you to let me go," she said with petulant triumph, and was hustled away by the others.

Everything was abruptly very quiet. The air shimmered with electricity; Patrick saw sparks, felt it stir his body hair, smelled it in the recesses of his nostrils.

He managed to work his way toward the door, which was shut now and closely barred. He wondered if it could be locked. If it was, he didn't know how he would unlock it, or what he would do once he had escaped.

Thunder shook the old building and made the bars rattle in their frames. Lightning struck the splintery roof, which went up in flames one piece after another so fast it was all one stream of fire, a waterfall of fire, white fire like white water. Beams burned through in a matter of split seconds and collapsed onto Patrick. They piled up around him like a glowing fort, which pretended to be protecting him while it hungered for his destruction. His shirt caught fire, then the frayed edges of his jeans pockets, and his zipper grew so hot it glowed around the base of his penis.

The pain was real.

The storm settled over the valley for most of the

night. By midnight rain was falling in earnest, a cloud-
burst that carried the creek over its banks and finally,
after decades of exposure and use, destroyed the bridge.
Before morning the rain had extinguished the fire in the
jailhouse, but by then Patrick's captive body and the cap-
tivated energy of his grief had become one more of the
many strata which underlie the ghost town Revenant.

17

Hannelore had never liked taking sides in her children's disputes, but it had bothered her that Debbie always won. More verbal than Danny, she'd also become bigger and stronger and faster just before they died—one of the things that might have changed if they'd had a chance to grow up—so she could beat him at a shouting match, a battle of wits, or a physical fight. Hannelore had thought it so unfair that she'd stepped in often—too often, she knew—to defend her son against her daughter. She regretted that, for both their sakes.

It was still going on. Danny was still the nice one, and Debbie was still prickly, bossy, determined to get her own way no matter what the cost to anybody else. It made Hannelore feel bad to think ill of the dead.

Even now they were squabbling. Danny was standing in the doorway of the infirmary with his back to her and she couldn't hear what he was saying, only the whine he so often used with his sister. Debbie was outside in the street shouting, and every word she said came through loud and clear.

In fact, the whole town could probably hear her. The two other people in the room, the man who was hurt and his son, were having their own argument, but Hannelore was sure they were also listening.

During Debbie's short lifetime she'd embarrassed her parents more times than Hannelore could remember. Temper tantrums in the grocery store. Going to school in clothes that were dirty or torn or didn't fit, when she had a dresser and a closet full of perfectly nice things to wear. More phone calls from the teacher her first month of kindergarten than during Danny's whole two years of school.

Hearing Debbie haranguing Danny again now and trying to decide what if anything she should do, Hannelore actually felt a certain affectionate nostalgia. At the same time, she fretted about the future of this obstinate child, a worry which was no less real and disturbing for having lost all relevance to anyone but Hannelore fourteen years ago.

"You're too damn *nice,* Dan!" Debbie was complaining loudly to her brother. "I keep telling you, she's not going to listen just because you want her to. We've gotta *make* her listen."

Danny murmured something. The tone of his voice was conciliatory, apologetic.

Debbie was having none of it, as usual. "Oh, for Chrissake, you are such a mama's boy!"

Hannelore's head was aching, but she wasn't dizzy anymore and she thought she could stand up if she had to. She readied herself. It was like the old days when the children were small, listening in the hallway to see if she would have to intervene, almost always deciding sooner or later that she did.

"You make me *sick*!" Debbie's voice had risen. She sounded enraged.

Hannelore should have learned a long time ago not to take that too seriously—Debbie could become enraged over the least little thing—but it still made her nervous because it was often a prelude to her flying at Danny and actually hurting him. Hannelore tried to hoist herself up, but she couldn't get her feet under the weight of her body and she fell back onto the floor. Her knee landed in a puddle of rainwater, and she squinted up to see a hole in the roof almost directly over her head.

Debbie was still yelling. "We'll be stuck in this hell-hole forever, and it'll be your fault!"

It upset her so much when they fought. She'd always hoped they'd outgrow it. "Brothers and sisters ought to be friends," she'd tried to tell them. "You don't know how lucky you are to have each other. Some people don't have any family." She'd be thinking of her parents when she said that, ashamed of how unreal, how like a fable, the camps seemed to her, only a single generation removed. The truth was she hadn't known anything about loss then, either, until she'd lost her own children, in a way so different from the tragedy of her ancestors but with the same end. There was no end to the ways you could lose someone you loved. Everyone who'd ever lived on this earth had done it, one way or another. Hannelore didn't think that was fair, either.

Danny said something, and Debbie hollered back, "Time? How much fucking time do you think we've *got,* bro?"

He shrugged, spread his hands. Debbie's sharp voice came closer, and Hannelore had the alarming impression that she grabbed her brother, his shoulders or the front of his shirt, because his body jerked and bent awkwardly forward. Hannelore made another great effort to get up and managed it this time, hanging on to a jagged and damp section of the wall, which threatened to collapse under her weight.

"Fine," Debbie said through audibly clenched teeth. "You've got *one chance,* you hear me? Give it your best shot, Danny-boy, because then it's my turn."

She was gone then. Wondering how many times in a normal lifespan Debbie would have stormed off like that when people didn't do what she wanted, Hannelore felt fresh loss and, to her shame, fresh relief. The relief made her more fervent than ever when she cried, "Debbie, please come back!" Although that didn't bring her daughter back to her, it did make her son turn and hurry across the small room to her.

"Sweet chick," observed the young man who'd been standing on the other side of the table in the middle of the room. His laugh was sarcastic, and Hannelore took the offense that had been intended. The older man on the table made a series of breathy puffs that must have been his laughter.

The nasty conversation between them earlier, from which Hannelore had picked up the information that this was an infirmary with no doctor, had also informed her that these two were father and son. She didn't like either one of them. She didn't trust them anywhere near her children; she had a feeling the son would be a bad influence on Debbie especially.

She met Danny halfway and put her arms around him again. She started to say something—how much she loved him, how glad she was she'd kept him and his sister alive all these years when everybody including their own father and grandmother had told her she was wrong to do it.

But Danny spoke first. His face was against her shoulder so his voice was muffled and she could feel his warm breath against her neck. The sensation thrilled her. "Ma," he told her, "we don't want to be here."

Hannelore patted his back and stroked his thick curly hair. "I know, honey. Let's just go home."

She felt him shake his head against her and, even though she tightened her embrace the way she'd learned to do over the years, he extricated himself enough to pull back and look at her. "No. Ma," he said gently. "What I mean is, we don't want to be here with you."

How children could hurt their parents! Wounded, Hannelore stared at her son and saw him blur suddenly as tears sprang to her eyes. It had been a long time since she'd cried. Quickly she looked down, and the tears rolled down her cheeks and off her chin to pool, sticky, in the cowl of her sweater.

Danny wouldn't stop. It wasn't like him to be so persistent or so unkind. "I'm sorry, Ma, but it's the truth. This is important. We don't belong to you anymore."

"Daniel Philip Ambrose, why are you saying such terrible things to me? I've given you everything! Are you telling me now that I did wrong? That you and your sister don't want to stay alive in my heart?"

"Yes," he said. "That's what I'm telling you. That's why we brought you here." His hands were on her shoulders, firm through the sweater's weave. The thought occurred to Hannelore that Phil had bought her this sweater the Christmas before the children were killed; it was all stretched out now and still way too tight, and its bright blue had faded splotchily. Maybe her children would realize, seeing her look like this, just how much she'd sacrificed for them.

"Let us go, Ma," her son was saying. He could not possibly know what he was asking. "Give us up."

"Are you listening good, Pops?" demanded the snotty young man by the table, and his father breathed something unintelligible.

Talking over both of them, for this was not their conversation, Hannelore declared to her son, "I could never do that. I'll never give you up. You and Debbie are all I have."

Danny stood there for a moment and Hannelore

thought maybe she'd won. Maybe he would so admire her unwavering grief that he would let himself continue to be animated by it. Maybe he would stop talking such cruel nonsense. He sighed, shook his head, and turned away. "I give up. Let's go find Deb."

Hannelore didn't entirely want to do that. Her son had always been easier to be around and much easier to parent than her daughter. She'd felt bad about that while they were alive and even worse after they'd died, but it had seemed important—in the way that precise repetition of correct syllables would be important for other kinds of magic—to stay rigorously true to their memories.

So she admitted to herself that she was a little afraid of Debbie, even as she allowed Danny to lead her out of the infirmary into the street. Timorously she nodded in the general direction of the man and boy as she squeezed past the table. The boy said, "Have fun," unquestionably smart aleck.

Even though parts of the infirmary building's walls were missing, it was still dimmer inside than out, and Hannelore's eyes filmed when the brilliant sunshine hit them. A rainstorm must have just passed, though she didn't remember having heard thunder; that must have been why the floor and walls were wet. Out here, everything sparkled and shimmered—beads of water on waist-high bearded grass, sheened clusters of needles like fans on the ends of drooping pine boughs, tumbledown buildings and piles of rubble turned from gray to silver and from brown to amber.

The ground rolled, and her ears rang. Dizzy again, she was also sick to her stomach. She clutched Danny's hand. Maybe she'd just gotten up too fast, or maybe she'd had a concussion from the fall that had brought her here. Phil would tell her to see a doctor. She hadn't had medical attention since her children had died; after the first night she'd stopped taking the sedatives Phil had brought her from a doctor friend of his. Phil would never know about this. Over these past fourteen years her living husband had become so much less real to her than her dead children that she found it perfectly reasonable to think she would never see him again. She was going to stay with them here—wherever "here" was. She was going to stay forever—whatever "forever" could mean to her now.

Something was burning. There was, or had been, smoke in the air, which contributed to the stinging and blurring of her eyes. She glanced around and didn't see any flames. Beyond that, it was easy for her to put it out of her mind.

Danny took her as far north as Rattlesnake Avenue went, then west on Aspen Street—away from the burned-out jail and on the opposite edge of town from the amusement park. Hannelore could have observed what was happening to the others, but years of self-referent and self-absorbed mourning had developed her into a solipsist, and she just didn't notice.

Still inside the infirmary, Will abruptly became impatient. "Get up," he ordered his father.

Bill couldn't believe it. "I—can't," he breathed, but even as he said it he felt something in the fingers of both hands.

"Get *up,* you fucking asshole! I'm not giving up without a fight!" Will came at his father. Bill thought about defending himself, was convinced that he couldn't, then found he had raised both forearms across his face to take his son's blow. Will's fist came up under and struck his jaw, a glancing punch but enough to jerk his head to the side and propel him off the table onto the floor.

At the corner of Aspen Street and Silver Alley, the

General Store had been Revenant's first actual building, so it was older than either of the churches or the saloon, much older than the hotel or the school. But through the years it had been restored numerous times and so was not nearly so dilapidated. Several of its windows still had panes. Its walls were constructed of layer after layer of various materials, wooden shingles over tarpaper over round-cut logs.

The building was only a single story tall in front along the street, but in back there was a garret upstairs where the proprietor had sometimes lived. None of the floors was horizontal anymore and none of the walls vertical, and there were no true angles left, because the ground under this part of town had shifted, strata realigning themselves and hollow spaces forming between them.

At times a real or made-up name had been painted on the store sign—MAGUIRE'S GENERAL STORE, BOWLEN'S, JUMPIN' JACK'S. Most often, and most recently, it simply announced, GENERAL STORE. Sometimes the sign had been nailed flat to the front wall, leaving on one facade after another weathered rectangles or nail holes in perpendicular rows. The current sign was suspended from a black iron post; it had come loose on one end and hung crooked now, but was still readable. Danny turned in there, leading his mother by the hand.

By the time they'd climbed the three steps, whose risers were an awkward height and whose treads were too shallow, Hannelore was gasping painfully for air, and the first thing she noticed as they crossed the threshold was the smell. Musty, dusty, with faint but inescapable underlying odors of decay and excrement. The doorway was so narrow that she had to turn herself slightly sideways to fit through. Thick spiderwebs adhered like gauzy curtains to her face and hands.

In the dim interior of the store, the glaring lopsided

square of light framed by the window in the back wall made it even harder to see. Though Hannelore could make out only murky shapes, she had the vivid impression of crowdedness, of countless objects jumbled together in both space and time.

Somehow she'd lost her son's hand. "Danny?" she asked fearfully. "Debbie?"

She took a few hesitant steps and stumbled against something. A rocking chair, unpadded except by thick gray dust. Someone was sitting in it, rocking, rocking. Ancient, despairing eyes glittered. Hannelore peered, assured herself that it wasn't either of her children, and lost interest.

Floor to ceiling on every wall were overladen shelves, some just long unadorned pine boards, others made into display cases by partitions and latticed or cutout doors. Hannelore glimpsed handles, corners, knobs, edges, contained spaces, exposed surfaces, colors, shapes, textures. But she paid only enough attention to avoid coming into contact with any of it as she passed through.

Accumulated here were countless mementoes, some of whose significance would never have been accessible to Hannelore. But others she could have identified if she'd looked at them, listened to them, held them in her hands awhile. Four composition books Arabella Montez had used for her older students, one with writing in it. A set of squat whiskey glasses, one missing, on a chipped red enamel tray with "Paydirt Saloon" scrolled in silver around the edge. The lace bedspread from room number 3 of the Double Rainbow Hotel, once white, sepia-colored now. A hymnal, water-stained and warped. Part of a yellow blanket. An empty locket.

Her shin hit something, and she flinched and looked down. Among barrels that had once held pickles and crackers and flour, later geodes and souvenir pinecones, sat a long-open trunk. It wasn't very big; Hannelore thought sadly that it was about the size her children's caskets had been. The trunk was overflowing. If anyone had tried to shut its lid now, something would have surely been damaged.

The trunk was full of clothes. Baby clothes, bonnets and jumpers and booties. Fancy dresses for parties and dances; a bridal gown. A man's flannel lumberjack shirt. Pairs and pairs of shoes.

Hannelore had no interest in other people's artifacts. She had no interest, either, in the commotion out in the street behind her, beyond the unwelcome thought that Phil might have come to rescue her. But even if that was true, and certainly if there was some other explanation for the noise, it had nothing to do with her, and so she ignored it.

In the shadows at the back of the room, she was sure she saw her children, looking like ghosts in the radiating glare from the window. She didn't know why they had to be shadows and ghosts now, after all this time of being so real, and panic made her try to move faster than she actually could through the crowded store. She knocked over a crate of tin advertising boxes, which made an extended rattling crash as they hit the wooden floor. "Sorry," she breathed, but out loud she called again, "Danny? Debbie?"

"Can't catch me!" Debbie yelled, but in her young-adult voice it didn't sound playful at all.

"Honey, don't," Hannelore pleaded, but the girl had already slipped into the next room. Danny went, too, and Hannelore believed without question that she had no choice but to follow them.

The smaller back room was almost completely taken up with stacks and bales of newspapers, some of them bound with fraying twine, many loose. The room reeked of the pulpy, powdery odor of old paper and the sharper liquid-chemical smell of ink.

A stairway along the right-hand wall led steeply upward. Hannelore's children were scaling it, Debbie so roughly and rapidly that the railings swayed, Danny more carefully and with many backward looks at his mother.

Hannelore stopped, panting, hand to her heaving bosom. She could not possibly climb those stairs. It was too much to ask. The exertion would give her a heart attack for sure, and the rickety structure would never support her weight.

She made her way across the room as fast as she could, making aisles where there were none by heaving or toppling newspapers. Headlines caught her unwilling eye: FIRE DESTROYS SCHOOLHOUSE. DOZENS KILLED AND INJURED IN UNION BRAWL. PEAK PARK OPENS! When she got to the foot of the stairs, Danny's sneakered feet were just disappearing upward, and footsteps crossed the ceiling. Frightened, she implored, "Don't hide from your mother!"

Debbie's face was hovering in the squarish opening at the top of the stairs, disembodied and very pale. "Ma, we're dead!" she insisted. "Go away!"

This was the impetus Hannelore needed. She put one foot on the lowest step and steadied her grip on the splintery railing. "I'm your *mother*! I can't leave you here." She pulled herself up.

"God*damn*it!" Debbie shrieked. "Haven't you done enough? You'll ruin everything!" The face vanished.

Hannelore had to look down to position her hands and feet and hoist herself up the next step. But she lifted her gaze again right away, determined not to lose sight of her daughter ever again. She could see her son, too, behind Debbie, their images scalloped like mountain ranges fading into the distance. "I'm coming!" Hannelore cried weakly. "Don't go away, I'm coming!" The steps bowed under her weight.

Straining, she was just able to hook her fingers over the rough edge of the upstairs landing. There was a sickening ache in her shoulder and pelvic muscles. Her legs and arms were trembling violently, and she was dizzy. If she looked down, she'd fall. She had no reason to look down.

Preparing herself for another terrible effort, Hannelore tried to take a deep breath, looked up and saw her daughter's descending fist just before it landed on her fingertips and dislodged them. She fell backward, off the steps and through the rotted floorboards into the cavity that for decades had gaped in the foundation of the structure. She didn't have enough breath to scream.

Her head struck a jut of the red rock which, though soft by geologic standards, was hard enough to cause serious trauma to her brain. She lost consciousness too abruptly for dreams or visions; one instant she was falling backward, trying to scream and thinking of her children, and the next instant she was dead.

Piece by piece, the General Store collapsed on top of her. The back section and its contents came first, the newspapers waterlogged and heavy with ancient and ongoing headlines of disaster, the stairway still intact but wrenched loose from top and bottom, the uninhabited upstairs room and her children whom she'd trapped up there.

But the hollow in and under the foundation was cavernous, and not nearly filled. The rest of the store, which had stood longer than any other building in the town, slowly sank into it. Shelves of iron pots and pans, rusty black among the iron-red rock, were layered over by the trunk full of clothes that nobody would ever wear again, rags from Gabriel's yellow blanket jumbled among them.

The globe of a kerosene lamp shattered, and its pieces embedded themselves in a tangle of leather wagon straps like mica in granite. Furniture was dismembered—a deacon's bench, a cradle, the rocking chair from the corner by the door—and flung with firewood and sections of the building itself into the hole.

Once started, the destruction of the General Store didn't take long. When the noise had stopped and the dust had settled, there was a new pile of rubble at the corner of Aspen Street and Silver Alley that looked old, and the ground around the edges of the hole was not much disturbed. It could have been there forever.

Hannelore and both her children were buried there. Their trapped spirits layered into the spirit of Revenant. Their lives and deaths fed the consciousness of Mother Grief, who would use them up.

18

Will didn't seem fazed by the collapse of the building behind him. He didn't even look over his shoulder. Bill kind of admired that. He himself had no idea anybody had been inside, and he wouldn't have much cared if he had known. But the fact that there'd been a building there, probably for years, and now there wasn't—the sight of it being swallowed up, the sound of it, the dust and debris of it—did shake him up a little.

He was on his face in the dirt. Will had picked him up off the infirmary table like a pile of empty clothes and carried him down the street and dumped him here. Bill didn't know why and didn't see what he could do about it. It surprised him that he wasn't madder than he was.

He turned his head. Brown and gold stretched out almost flat, with here and there, at root level, a dark green or dark brown shrub. Flat on his face like this, he had no feeling of being in a valley. Because he couldn't see the tops of the mountains they didn't look high or close.

Will was standing with one foot on each side of Bill's head. His black high tops, his white tube socks with maroon stripes, his rolled jeans were all familiar, but for some reason now looked threatening. Will snarled down at Bill a ridiculous challenge: "Come on, old man. Let's see you take me now."

Bill raised himself on his elbows. He got ready for the wussy, breathy way he'd been having to talk, an echo of the way Will used to talk but didn't anymore, but when he demanded, "What the fuck you talking about?" it came out strong and not choppy. He tried some more. "What happened, you get a miracle cure or something?"

"You ain't gonna get away with this," Will insisted. Bill didn't think that was an answer to the question he'd asked. Always a smart-ass. Just like his old man. "You ain't gonna keep me like some kind of animal in your own goddamn private zoo."

"What are you *talking* about? Get away with what?"

"Man, I'm *outta* here."

"You little fucker!" Even half paralyzed, even twenty-five years older, this time Bill was quicker than his son. He threw his arms around the boy's leg and pulled him down. "You ain't going *nowhere* till I say you can."

It wasn't the first time they'd rolled around in the dirt, hitting and cursing each other, each struggling for a headlock or a knockout punch. When Will was growing up, a lot of times a good swift backhand had been the only thing that would get his attention. By the time he was thirteen he'd been fighting back. Pissed Bill off, but he was also glad to see it. Kept both of them from getting soft.

Since the kid got hurt, they couldn't settle things that way anymore. Couldn't settle things, period. Jesus, how Bill had been tempted to smash that blank face, that idiot mouth, to dump him out of his fucking wheelchair just to get some kind of reaction! But you couldn't hit a crip.

So Bill had ended up feeling permanently bested. At the same time, he was now a helluva lot more of a man than his kid would ever be, sorry excuse for a man though he was.

Will's face was right up close, so Bill could smell the booze and smoke on his breath. No longer deformed and scarred from the wreck, his face was contorted with rage. The same kind of rage his father had felt all his life but not, Bill guessed, the same kind of shame.

The kid grabbed his head, one hand flat on each temple like a violent lover, and threw him onto his side. Bill's legs were bent uselessly under him and he didn't have anywhere near normal strength in his upper body, but he managed to bring his forearm up hard between the boy's legs. He felt the hard-on just before his arm slammed into it, and the kid groaned.

In the ruined church near the other end of Aspen Street, Corinne sang, and without realizing it drowned out all this noise. There wasn't much left of the church— a few pieces of pews that had been only plain benches in the first place, the suggestion of an altar. There never had been stained glass windows because of the difficulty of bringing them over the pass. Some mountain communities of the era, though, had had stained glass; the Lutheran Church at Pinnacle, for instance, had boasted a "Last Supper," small and not very detailed but stained glass nonetheless. For a time, this caused considerable competitive consternation among some of the citizens of Revenant. But Pinnacle was abandoned years ago, when its single mine played out, and the Lutheran Church with its famous window is long gone.

Corinne sang. In order not to have to pay attention to either of her daughters, the one who was with her or the one who was not, Corinne closed her eyes, raised her cheeks, opened her mouth, and sang.

You weren't supposed to close your eyes. Even if you were just singing in the shower, you should have your face on. But Corinne didn't want to risk eye contact with anybody.

Sooner or later she'd have to stop this. If nothing else, her voice would give out. But for now, it seemed to her that she'd never do anything but sing, and singing would take care of everything. She'd learned how to concentrate fiercely. When you were doing it right, you became a conduit ("Think of a tunnel," the director would say; "think of a stream"). Nothing else came out of your mouth but the music, and nothing but the music could get into your head.

She focused her attention on vocal production. The resonators were open at the base of her skull, the top of her head, the bridge of her nose. Her tongue stayed down. Her ribcage expanded. Her stomach went out when she breathed in, in when she breathed out. She knew how to do this. But something was wrong.

She could tell that she was singing better than she ever had before. Maybe there was something about the acoustics in here, or about the mountain air. She didn't dare think about it too much. She just sang, and it was practically perfect, but something was getting in the way.

Without planning it, Corinne had moved into an extended warm-up riff. It had no actual words—just sibilants and glottals and other very quick consonants, all in the service of tall vowels and diphthongs turned as late as possible. The purpose of the exercise was to make you as open as humanly possible to the music. It went round and round and round, and she couldn't get off.

Somebody was singing with her in tight barbershop harmony, attacks and releases perfect, vowels matched. Corinne frowned. The other voice was distracting. Maura's pure, sure clarion taking on the color of any other voice so that it sounded like a single voice no matter whom she sang with, or Monica's lead, both more tentative and more distinct—whichever, she didn't want either of her daughters to sing with her.

The other, higher voice finished its phrase and cleanly started the next one. Corinne was getting mad. Not to be left behind, not to be the one responsible for ruining the song, she took a quick, practiced breath to be able to come in on the downbeat when the bass line came around again, once again went past the place where she could naturally have stopped, and started over from the edge.

Something wasn't right. Something was blocking her singing. Certain it was the other voice, she managed to hiss between phrases, "Shut up!"

The other voice stopped immediately, allowing Corinne to finish the song alone. Every part in barbershop felt like the melody when it was yours; the other parts harmonized with you, and when you sang alone it made perfect melodic sense to your ears. Corinne held the final bass note, at the bottom of her low range, that would have laid the foundation for the last pyramidal chord if anybody else had been singing, and then stopped.

There wasn't any overtone. The space inside the church was small and only partly enclosed, so there wasn't any echo, either. Once Corinne stopped singing, the silence was complete.

But something was gathering, just beyond the range of what she could hear, beyond the range of anything she'd ever sung. Her knees wouldn't allow her to stand up yet, so she sat as straight as she could on the edge of the pew, rounded as many resonating spaces as she could think of in her head and body cavity, breathed, and opened her mouth to whatever would come out.

What came out was a roar so startling that Corinne tried, too late, to shut it off. The full, deep, profound rumble started from an empty space in which her heart and brain were suspended unattached to anything, so that they vibrated and twirled, changing position relative to each other, relative to the rest of her. Corinne couldn't imagine herself making such a noise, but it came through her again and again, building, interrupted only by her rhythmic need to take a quick breath, undiffused by any other voice.

Bill roared, too. He'd done that many times in his life; roaring, in fact, had long been his standard way of getting somebody's attention, especially his son's, and now that he could do it again he did. He grabbed the front of the kid's shirt and pulled the pain-dazed but still sneering young face close to his own. "What's your *problem,* you little fucker? What more do you *want* from me?"

Will could move his legs and Bill couldn't. That was Bill's point. The kid didn't get it. Hands cupped over his crotch, he kicked at his father's knees. Bill didn't feel a thing, and didn't let go. "I want you to leave me the fuck *alone!* I want *outta* this shithole once and for all!"

"Listen here, sonny boy." Bill was losing his breath, which made it harder to roar. "You ain't going *nowhere* till I say you can. You're my son."

"I am not your son! *He's* your son!"

He was getting loose. Bill tightened his grip, but the boy was up on his knees, then his feet, and Bill couldn't do that. "I am *not* going to lose my son again!"

"You asshole!" Will bellowed, half in his father's frantic arms and half out. "You lost one son but you've got another one! You're gonna end up losing him, too!"

"He's a goddamn fucking *crip!*" Bill thundered, and risked taking his hands off Will's shirt long enough to get the kid's head in a lock, one hand on each temple. From that position he could have pulled him close to kiss him or to look into his eyes. Instead, he gave a savage twist that wrenched the boy over on top of him. Voice muffled now by the heavy young body, Bill was having trouble catching his breath. "He—can't feed—himself! He can't —walk, he can't fuck, he—can't even wipe—his own— ass. I can't—stand to—look at him. He can't be—my son, Will! *You've*—gotta—be—my—son!"

The boy lay still on top of Bill with his head at an unnatural angle, as if his neck had been broken again. Winded, pinned on his back, Bill struggled not to pass out while he waited helplessly for the kid to say or do something, to make the next move. He prayed the boy wasn't hurt bad (but then he'd prayed the night of the accident, too, for all the good it had done him or his son), and at the same time he kept telling himself that the kid deserved to get his ass whipped, trying to run out on his old man like that.

Bill was sliding toward unconsciousness but there wasn't much of a difference in the way things felt. He swore he could hear wind whistling and throwing up dust, but he didn't feel either wind or dust. From far away and then too close he heard women's voices, one high and piercing, the other one so low he'd have thought it was a man's except it had a definite female quality to it. Maybe it was some lesbo or something. Too high and too low, and he was in an empty space in between holding on to his son and nothing else, and another thin voice was singing, too, an old lady's voice. The last thing Bill knew was that he was afraid.

The power of Corinne's rage, the production and conduction of the sound itself, had propelled her to her feet. Sometimes when music burst free of the minds and bodies that had been working so hard to create it, it was like this—you simply could not stay sitting down for it.

Pain stabbed through her knees. She wasn't surprised. There ought to be pain. Her right knee buckled. She held on to the split corner of the pew, then on to nothing as thin air engulfed her, then on to Maura's hands.

How many times had she held Maura's hand to give her comfort and support, and in the end she'd failed? Now Corinne wouldn't take any support from her daughter, from either of her daughters, living or dead. They'd both let her down.

She shook her hands hard and twisted them to get free, but Maura hung on tight. The strong young hands kept Corinne from falling and urged her to move forward. She resisted. She was having enough trouble just staying on her feet in one place.

She concentrated on her breathing. She brought as much of the thin air into her body as would come, then used every last atom of it for the sound that passed out of her again and again and again, getting rid of it, pushing it all out so there'd be room for more. Her mouth, held so wide for so long, ached. The back of her tongue curled against being forced down. Her lifted cheeks trembled and strained, and she knew her face was contorted way past what would look animated to an audience, but that wasn't the point anymore.

Now she was standing before the rubble of the altar, drawn there by Maura even though she'd tried her best not to move. Only someone who already knew what it was would have recognized it as an altar, and Corinne didn't. She braced her hands, with her daughter's hands still gripping them, on the chipped granite slab, leaned all her weight on them, and gave full voice to the fury that resonated and swelled.

Maura was singing again. Her clarion tenor matched Corinne's bass precisely, as if they were one voice.

Corinne couldn't say anything without interrupting

the furious music. She managed to take one hand off the altar and gestured, flat-palmed "Stop!" Maura didn't stop. The high climbing harmony made Corinne's plummeting tone deeper, made the raging song resonate till she thought the back of her skull would fly off or her vibrating throat would explode to give it the room it needed.

Maura sang, "Look at me."

Corinne's eyes flew open, though she hadn't wanted them to. She saw Maura, long blond hair up in performance style, away from her forehead and sprayed stiff, stage makeup gaudy on her death's-head face. It was Maura and not Monica. It always had been. Corinne tried to close her eyes again against the image, but now the music was streaming out of her eye sockets, too. They buzzed and bulged, and still there weren't enough open passages to let it out of her.

As Corinne stared—still singing, pushing the limits of her range deeper and deeper—Maura, still singing high, swung herself up onto the altar. Bits of mica embedded in the granite caught some stray light otherwise invisible to the human eye and briefly sparked. Unwillingly, Corinne noticed them and was moved by their brilliance, which had been obscured from her before and would be again.

Maura stood up on the altar and raised her arms. Her voice lifted out of the clarion range and soared off on its own until it was a scream, then a pure sweet wail.

Corinne allowed herself to open still deeper and wider. She worked at projecting the resonating tones instead of swallowing them. She supported them, sent breath under them. She locked her gaze with Maura's as she went deeper than she'd ever dreamed she could and her daughter went higher. They were perfectly matched, a unit sound stretched wider and wider, until at last they both flew free. Maura soared up through the hole where the steeple once had been, and Corinne—letting her go though she'd thought she'd stay furious with her forever —moved to sing profound melody by herself.

19

An early evening was falling over the Revenant Valley when Tom Krieg came upon his wife Emily, who was dead. Shadow Mountain was sliding its flattened shadow eastward as the sun set behind it. The white of aspen bark and of the rapids in Broken Mirror Creek, the greens of ponderosa and lodgepole pine and Engelmann spruce, the browns of mountain mahogany and bared earth all were taking on a glimmering metallic sheen. Long streaked clouds were burnished yellow, burnished gray, and the sky was a glowing white with a bluish patina against which all the surrounding ranges, Shadow Mountain's included, were dark scallops with dense presence but virtually no detail.

Emily would doubtless have preferred to call it Columbine Peak, fascinated as she'd always been by local flora and their ecosystems. Tom knew nothing about the mountain's two names, but for some time he had understood how the way one chooses to think about an object, what one calls it to oneself, expresses and alters both the object's nature and one's own.

When he caught sight of his wife kneeling in the meadow—fringed by tall fronds of needle-and-thread grass which in different light would have looked like yellowed antique lace, surrounded by tiny blue and white columbine barely visible in the twilight—he didn't go to her right away. He stood and watched her, knowing she was dead, reluctant to intrude on her in her world.

Emily's world had always been more found than built, and his the opposite. It wasn't that he wanted things neat and predictable, although there was undeniable pleasure when they were, but that he'd loved creative juxtaposition and the organization of surprise. Often, for instance, he had worked across genres, sending one axis of a formal Japanese garden, say, through an urban plaza, or coaxing epiphytic orchids to grow in the crotch of a spruce tree in an alpine courtyard. He'd sometimes built bridges to span waterways that could have been stepped across in half an easy stride. Once he'd designed a complex topiary garden in which privet hedges had been fashioned to look like unicorns—a simile for a simile— and junipers trained into freeform sculptures which, if they'd really been free, would not have been sculpted at all.

He couldn't escape it. Declaring life meaningless without Emily, he'd thereby imposed a meaning. And here she was, an apparition taken form out of the formidable creative impulse of his grief. Tom was familiar with the process.

Emily, on the other hand, had been happiest when she could adapt her designs to the environment with which she'd been presented. She seldom would put flowers in beds, for instance, preferring to scatter them singly and in small clumps and then see how they would adapt in each miniature ecosystem. She'd leave fallen branches and broken bricks where they were, working to their forms. She stopped using the phrase "noxious weeds," a staple of the landscaper's jargon, and had convinced more than one client of the inherent beauty of the glossy mat made by bindweed's runners and round leaves dotted in late summer with fingertip-sized white blossoms, the brilliant buttons of dandelions, the velvety gray-green cabbage-shaped packages of rabbit ears, even the pulpy spiky stems and purple flowers of Canadian thistle that bees loved and homeowners struggled to cut out. It was impossible to root them out; the root systems of Canadian thistle could travel and tangle underground for miles. Emily had loved that.

Now, kneeling quietly among the grasses and wild-flowers at the base of the shadowing mountain, she was absorbing the ambience of the place, the found reality of what had happened to her. Tom understood that he was to do the same.

Standing behind her, looking over her shoulder, was a slightly built elderly man whom Tom at first thought was his father. Of course it wasn't; his father had already been here and had already returned. Tom thought: *Cecelia, my father's first love, could have been my mother. Who would I be then?* Then he thought: *If my father hadn't left Cecelia in this place, I would never have been born.*

Flickering across the dusky meadow was another shadow, featureless but still recognizable as an ancient woman, thin hair flying, thin arms crooked. Tom thought, *Cecelia,* but it wasn't Cecelia, of course. Cecelia was gone.

The elderly man—clean-shaven and nearly bald, dapper in a navy blazer and maroon-and-navy slacks—was a stranger to Tom. Emily, though, seemed to know him. She tilted her head in a familiar way to look up at him. She smiled at him in that favor-bestowing way of hers. She spoke to him animatedly, as though of things that mattered, and the two of them appeared to be on rather intimate terms.

Tom took a step toward them, then stopped. Jealousy was unreasonable under these circumstances. This man was old enough to be her father, and with him was an elderly lady who was presumably his wife. And, in any event, Emily was dead. But something about the tableau implied the threat of new loss, which he thought he ought to refuse if he could, and he started carefully down into the bowl of the meadow.

Elinor was with Warren, standing in the meadow getting her shoes dirty. She hadn't let him out of her sight since he'd been himself again, and she didn't like it one bit that he was paying so much attention to this girl. It wasn't *that* kind of jealousy—the very thought made her blush, which made her mad—for heaven's sake, the girl was younger than Katie. But she was jealous. She had reason to be. She'd almost lost her husband. She'd come *this close* to resigning herself to having to live with the Alzheimer's Warren for the rest of her life. Good thing she hadn't, because now he was back to his old self and she'd have had to adjust to *that*.

So she wasn't about to just stand there like a shrinking violet. "Warren," she said, but he didn't answer. "Warren," she said more firmly. "It's time for us to go home."

He gestured toward her, shushing her or waving her away. He used to do that when he was watching some discussion show on television or reading a book she'd never have wasted her time on. It used to make her mad then, but then when he took to following her around and staring at her all the time she'd wished he *would* tell her to leave him alone. Now it made her mad again. Who did he think he was?

She folded her arms and glared at him. The last of the day's sunshine, slanting like a butter knife through a dip in the edge of the dark purple mountains, shimmered behind him like a halo. She snorted. Warren Dietrich was anything but an angel.

The girl he was talking to was down on her knees in

the tall grass. She had auburn hair tied up on top of her head—not very neatly, Elinor noted, fuzzy strands coming loose all along her neckline. Elinor wished for bobby pins. The girl was wearing a sleeveless thin blue blouse that she'd unbuttoned partway up and then tied around her waist, and those frayed shorts young people made by cutting off their jeans unevenly and not bothering to hem them.

She didn't like it one bit that Warren was talking to a scantily clad girl like that, and somebody she didn't know. How could he know people she didn't know? Since he'd retired they'd spent twenty-four hours a day, seven days a week in each other's company.

She also didn't like it, come to think of it, that she was standing right beside Warren and couldn't make out what they were saying to each other. What were they doing, whispering? Or talking in some secret code? Elinor did not like secrets. She raised her voice and snapped "War-*ren!*" just as a young man she also didn't know, coming across the meadow, said "Emily." At first she thought he said "Elinor," and, flustered, tried to think if she did know him from somewhere. But then she realized he'd said "Emily," which must be the name of the girl.

Emily and Warren smiled at each other. Elinor saw that and was really put out. Tom saw it, too, and thought dolefully that, of course, Emily would now be full of secrets. She was, after all, dead, a fundamental mystery which he could not possibly comprehend.

Warren turned and put his hand under Elinor's elbow. It was true that she needed him to do that—she'd hurt her hip when she fell, and at her age a broken hip was as likely as not the beginning of the end—but she jerked away from him. It was the principle of the thing. She almost fell, and Warren caught her with both hands on both her elbows, and over his shoulder said, "This is my wife Elinor."

Elinor did not want to be introduced to anybody. She wasn't dressed for company, her hair surely looked a fright, and she couldn't trust her hip. But the girl was looking up at her, smiling and nodding. The polite thing to do would be to stand up. Not to shake hands, though; ladies didn't shake hands. The girl stayed where she was kneeling on the ground. Young people these days had no manners whatsoever.

Seething, Elinor shot Warren her best withering glance. Then she put on her polite smile for the rude girl.

Tom thought again, endlessly, how much he loved his wife as she looked fondly at the delicate purple Compositae, still attached to its stem, that she was isolating between her fingertips. He knew its name because of her; he'd never been especially interested in flora per se. She let it go without disturbing it, as was her way. When she stood up, the long muscles in her thighs rippled, and Tom's hands flexed in sudden intense desire to lay themselves there.

"Tommy," she said, "there's somebody I'd like you to meet." Her hand was on his arm. He saw the characteristic dirt under her nails.

Tom had no interest in meeting anyone. He did not want to socialize, make small talk, be polite, put forth a public demeanor, extend himself to another living human being in any way. He had not done so since Emily had died.

But she said, "This is my husband Tom. Thomas Krieg, Jr."

At her wordless urging, Tom shook hands with her elderly companion. The old man's grip was stronger than

Tom intended his own to be. "I am very pleased to meet you," the man said gravely.

Suddenly the oddity of the situation broke through the pall of Tom's depression, and his first clear thought since Emily had died was: *Something strange is going on here.*

"I will take care of your wife," declared the old man.

"We'll take care of each other," Emily said promptly. Even in the form of an apparition, she did not take kindly to being patronized.

Tom found himself entering into this improbable debate. "I doubt my wife needs care, and if she does I am the one to give it." His voice was hoarse. It had been a long time since he'd said so many words at once.

"No, sir," insisted the old man, "you cannot. Your wife is dead."

He knew that, but from habit he began to say "No."

Emily had, without his noticing it, moved so she could put her arms around him from behind and lean her head between his shoulder blades, the way she used to do. "It's the truth, Tommy. You know it is. Say it."

So Tom took a deep breath and said aloud, "Emily is dead." The words were not nearly so difficult to say as he had imagined all this time they would be, the juxtaposition of his beloved's name with the word "dead" not so painful. He said again, "Emily is dead," and to his amazement the sentence was quite possible to declaim—quite possible, in fact, to live with. "Emily is dead," he said again.

He felt Emily's head nod, and she hugged him, then took her arms away. Where she had pressed against him, his back ached with the cold of her absence, which he was fully feeling for the first time, but he could stand the cold until the slanting sun and eventually his own body heat would warm it again. He hadn't thought he could.

Emily said to Elinor, "Mrs. Dietrich, you are welcome to leave your former husband here with me."

Startled, still trying to be polite, Elinor threw up her hands. "Oh, land, no, I wouldn't hear of it, dear. He's my husband. I have a duty."

Both Warren and Emily shook their heads, Warren frowning and looking severe. "No, ma'am," said Emily, "your duty is to the husband you have now."

There was a pause. Then Elinor said stiffly, "I have to do everything, you know. I know I'm not always as patient as I should be, but it's such a burden and I think about how things used to be and how they are now." To her horror, her voice broke and she found herself in danger of crying. She held her breath and tensed her whole body to turn the sadness into anger, and from lifelong practice she managed it.

Emily positioned herself in front of Elinor and took her by the shoulders. Elinor was aghast. If her hip gave out it would be the fault of this forward young woman. "Listen to me," Emily told her. Elinor didn't have to listen to anybody. She started to interrupt, but the girl talked right over her. "You have lost this husband. He's not coming back. Things are not the way they used to be. They're the way they *are*."

"You're talking nonsense," Elinor fumed.

"And you're losing the husband you have now because you won't see *him*. You won't accept *him*. You won't love *him*."

Elinor had had it up to here. She grabbed Emily's hands but didn't try to push them away. "How can I accept? How can I love?" she cried. "He's not the man he used to be."

"That's true," Warren agreed crisply.

"He's not the man I married."

"That's right."

Elinor glared past Emily at Warren. "You come back home with me where you belong, Warren Roy Dietrich!" she commanded fiercely. "I want you back!" She stomped her foot, and the pain in her hip flared. That was a foolish thing to do, but she didn't care anymore.

"No," he said, calm and self-assured as he used to be. "I loved you, Elinor, and we had a good life together. But I'm gone for good. It's up to you what you do with the Warren you have now, but don't waste your time waiting up for me."

Suddenly Elinor couldn't stop herself from thinking about the Warren she must have left behind to chase this Warren here. She thought of his childish pleasure when she played his Mozart tape for him, again and again and again till it like to drove her crazy and she could practically hum it herself even if it was classical music. She thought of his fear, which sometimes she could calm by just staying where he could see her and sometimes she couldn't. She thought of him sitting with Rocky at his feet, both of them staring at her for hours on end as if she was the most important thing in the universe. And—tentatively, fearfully—she wanted to go home to him.

The sun had sunk below the ridge now, and the sky was almost dark. Tom put his arm around Elinor's shoulders. After a moment, she raised her arm around his waist, and they leaned into each other. "I want to say good-bye," Tom said. His voice broke, and he waited awhile. Then he said, his voice still breaking, "Good-bye, Emily. I love you," and Elinor nodded.

Together, they watched their loved ones leave them. Warren and Emily seemed not exactly to touch but to glide in and out of each other, their outlines blurring. It was hard to tell with any certainty, but another figure seemed to join them, another young woman with long light hair. The essences of them—that which had made them, in particular, Emily Wilson Krieg, Maura Ogilvie, and Warren Dietrich—scattered across the meadow and the mountain, drifted up to join the clouds and down through root systems to subsoil, bedrock, core.

Then Tom and Elinor found one of the roads leading out of Revenant, up out of the valley and down the mountain. They went slowly because Elinor couldn't walk very fast, but Tom was in no hurry, either, and before they had gone far Corinne had joined them. As dark was falling in earnest, Tom's father met them with the car and drove them the rest of the way home.

20

 It's twilight now, but it will be midnight again, and morning and noon. *A boy runs through a cornfield, his legs the color of silk.* It's autumn, and will be deep winter, then spring and hot high summer. *The gold of the locket has tarnished, and it has settled like a nugget not worth panning at the bottom of the stream. Silt covers it, then shifts again and leaves it bare. The spring current tumbles it a little way downstream, in the summer it lies exposed on the bank, and sometimes by early autumn it has frozen into the ice. Inside there is no picture, no lock of hair.*

Another storm is gathering in the valley. This one has snow in it, or cold rain. *Birthday parties marked the passage of years that weren't passing. Fossils in older strata were bent upward so that to the careless eye they looked to be more recently laid. Crepe paper and party favors, brand new cars and animal-shaped balloons, a tick's body swollen with some other creature's stolen blood—all trapped in the transition from one form of matter to another, so that their outlines are left if not their substance.* Deer, elk, bighorn sheep, back-country hikers, and snowmobilers are forging new trails across the four streets of Revenant and the numerous roads that lead in and out, which will themselves be covered over and heaved through and turned into approximations and artifacts.

Maggots take a long time to do their work, here where it is so dry and cool. A tatter of a yellow blanket lasts a long time, the hem of an off-white dress, a little boy's fat pinecone picked up for show-and-tell—all looking like one thing and then another, suggesting, reminding.

Those who were desperate to stay in this place have been consumed and are now part of me. Those who would leave have left. I am not satisfied—I am not ever satisfied—but I am, for the moment, sustained.

I am alone again, but not for long. Never for long. In the swirling white darkness I see another eddy of them coming up my valley. In the ferocious quiet of the snow I hear their lamentations.

In this world there will always be loss. There will always be mourners and their ghosts, ghosts and their bereaved.

Here they come. I ready myself. I am Mother Grief, and I say to them:

Welcome to Revenant.

You thought you knew everything there was to know about him...
You were dead wrong.